Come Back

The District Line #3

Best Wishes
C.F. White
xxx

C F White

Author Note & Dedication

To Rebecca, editor extraordinaire. Thank you, for believing me, for boosting me, for teaching me how not to roll my eyes.

And for James, wherever you are now. It saddens me that you weren't able to read this before you had to go, or that I didn't have the chance to tell you how much of an influence you had over this story. Thank you, for listening to my whining and for giving me the strength to finish this. Rest in peace x

And to Rob, who James left behind. I hope you find some comfort knowing that James lives on within these pages. It was his love for Jay and Seb that gave me to courage to complete their story.

"Sport has the power to bring us together.
Every player, every athlete, every team is stronger
when sport welcomes and supports everyone.
When we all play our part, we can make
sport everyone's game."
  —Rainbow Laces Campaign, Stonewall

All I am, all I ever was, is here in your perfect eyes.
They're all I can see.

  —Snow Patrol, Chasing Cars.

OUT!

Premier League footballer comes out as GAY!

West Ham United's Jay Ruttman has announced that he is gay and in a relationship with another man.

After the East End football star was snapped at a West London nightclub cavorting with a mystery man, the widespread speculation about the Premier League player's sexuality has been put to rest at a press conference.

The twenty-three-year-old from Plaistow, East London, was joined by Hammer's manager, Sergio Amodoro.

Amodoro said, "We wholeheartedly support Jay's decision to come out and hope that by being open and honest, the focus will now be on his football rather than his love life."

Ruttman joined the Hammers last year on a free transfer and has since played twenty-six games as their main centre forward and was fast becoming a fan favourite.

The left-footed striker said, "This wasn't an easy decision to come out. But I don't want to hide anymore and the fantastic support I have received from the club has been beyond my expectations. I am gay. I am in a relationship. But that's all I'd like to say on the matter."

Ruttman refused to answer questions about who his partner is, stating the pair would like privacy.

Fingers do point to Sebastian Saunders, front man of the Drops, a new indie rock band to hit the UK Charts this year and were the opening act for West Ham's international friendly against the Red Bulls in New York during their summer tour.

Time will tell if Ruttman's coming out will have an effect on his football career and many within the sporting industry claim that the decision was bold, yet foolish.

One source said, "This will most certainly affect him, on and off the pitch. Ruttman's a great footballer. But playing at a top level isn't just about the physical skill of a player. It's about their mental aptitude. We've seen how even the mere speculation of footballer's sexuality can cause catastrophic reactions — look at Fashanu, Campbell. Ruttman better have a thick skin."

CHAPTER ONE
Movers & Shakers

January 2007

"Y'know they just make you look more conspicuous down here, dun't ya?"

Seb curled a finger around the arm of his shades and slipped them to the end of his nose, his chocolate-brown doe eyes focusing on Jay. "Conspicuous?"

Jay raised his eyebrows to the point they were hidden underneath the peak of his baseball cap. He stepped in closer to Seb, avoiding another influx of commuters to the Underground platform. The musty smell of a day's office work wafted from the nearest suited male, masking the dust and cast-iron scent, and the echoing tap of kitten heels ricocheted off the curved walls.

Tutting, Seb slipped the glasses back up. "That's four syllables, Champ." Bashed by another oversized handbag passing him, Seb grimaced. "Careful, you'll quash the stereotypical notion that footballers are all as thick as shit."

Jay snorted and glanced up to the digital timetable display. "Two minutes."

"Fuck's sake, why did you have to trade in our tangerine machine? We could have used that car right now."

"I had to, to get the upgraded motor. Least the BMW will be more subtle. With blacked-out windas, an' all."

"Damn right. But we could have taken a cab."

"And fork out a fuck ton to pay some geezer to sit us in midday traffic? No, ta."

"Isn't now a little prudent to be counting the pennies? If that last contract you signed at West Ham for a cool half a mil is anything to go by." Seb tsked. "*New* money."

"I'll always count my kilkennies," Jay retaliated. "No matter what I earn now. Just like you'll always be an entitled rich kid who throws away his mash the moment it touches his sky rocket."

"I won't even attempt to decipher what you just said." Seb twirled a crunchy tip of dark brown hair between his fingers. "And I swear you do it to confuse the fuck out of me."

"Nah. I just know you like it."

"Ha." Seb ran his tongue along his front teeth. "That I do. Say more."

Jay chuckled. A group of rowdy lads bundled down the underground steps to the platform, each one wearing a replica Tottenham football shirt, and the remnants of their drinking session hit Jay in the face. Jay cursed under his breath. Why he'd agreed to do this on the same day as a London derby was due to kick off, he'd never know. Edging closer to the yellow line, he impatiently awaited the next train, hoping to avoid any undue attention.

It had been getting harder to venture out in public, but he couldn't remain inside with Seb forever. Not that it was a particularly bad thing when they did get to close the doors to their poky flat and shut out the world for a while.

"Ah, bollocks." Seb shoved Jay on the arm and squirmed through a crowd of commuters. "Who the fuck invented a fucking camera on a fucking phone? How is that ever going to be fucking useful?"

Stumbling to the end of the platform, Jay peered over Seb's shoulder. The flash of a mobile camera illuminated the tunnel, and all the other passengers scrambled to see who or what had been the target of the non-consensual snap. Him? Seb? Both of them. *Together.* Bowing his head, Jay gripped the peak of his cap to conceal as much of his face as possible into the shadows.

This was also taking some getting used to — the attention, the random cameras being shoved in his face, the recognition on the street that his status as one of the top goal scorers of last season had brought him. Seb seemed to take the attention in his stride. But he'd always been destined for celebrity status, and revelled in the public's scrutiny. Like a moth to a flame, Seb was drawn to the bright lights of the media circus they'd inadvertently created for themselves. Jay wouldn't have him any other way, of course. *Well... Maybe sometimes.*

"The specs ain't working."

"Nor is the cap." Seb slapped the peak of Jay's hat and it fell to obscure his vision.

"Piss off." Ripping it from his head, Jay huffed and slicked back his floppy blond hair. His hooded sweatshirt rose to reveal his stomach, but he slapped it down, double lively, on seeing Seb's roaming gaze. "And you can put your tongue back in."

He almost wiped the corner of Seb's mouth with his thumb. But that would have caused even more of a stir, and they'd made their pact not to fuel the speculation in the press about them. Jay may have outed himself last year, but he refused to speak of his love life—of Seb. Keeping that firmly in the shadows aided his survival on the pitch, the training ground, the changing rooms, even if he claimed it was so Seb could find his own path without the links to him. And he was.

"You show those abs," Seb licked his lips, "and I'm going to drool. Sue me. I got a lawyer."

"Speakin' of cash..."

The tube train shunted into the station and the doors bleeped open, stifling the conversation that Jay had been meaning to have for a while. Well, since this had all got a bit more serious. Steering Seb onto the carriage, Jay pointed toward two vacated seats and Seb grabbed the copy of the *Metro* newspaper left on the multicoloured cushion.

"Hmm?" Seb sat and flicked through the pages, eyes hidden behind his dark glasses, but Jay knew they'd be darting across the printed words and no longer focused on him. *Priorities*. Not for the latest news in the capital: probably more for the entertainment section. The hottest in music releases, more specifically.

"We need to get the finances sorted."

"Like how?"

"The club are setting up a meetin' with an agent, so I gotta know what we got between us."

"An agent? Why do you need one of those money-grabbing sleazes?" Seb slapped the paper to his lap. "You have *me* to swipe your hard-earned cash off your hands."

"Ain't that the truth. But the club recommended it. Could be a good move. Getting someone to, y'know, deal with all the shit. Especially with what we're about to go do right now."

Seb chewed his lip. "How much?"

"They'll take ten percent."

"Of your *wages*?"

"No, off my boot laces." Jay tutted.

"That'll make it hard to kick a ball."

The train pulled out of the station and Jay rocked against the window pane. The raucous banter from the group of lads all squashed into the vestibule drowned out the squeal of the metal wheels on the track. Jay tensed, wriggling in the seat and adjusted his trackie bottoms down his legs. This train couldn't go quick enough.

"And what do these people do for the sweat off your back?" Seb returned his interest to the *Metro*.

"Sort my life out."

"They'll tell you to stay in the closet."

"Bit hard that now, innit?"

Seb smiled. "Whatever you want, Champ." He trailed his gaze back to the printed text on the newspaper. "But you are aware of my own background in business? I can sort your finances out into various investments that'll mean you won't be destitute by the time you're thirty."

"You mean, put *my* hard-earned dough into *your* band?"

"No sell-by date on rock and roll. Look at Bowie." Seb grinned. "No, you don't need an agent. You just need some sweet talker to answer all those *OK!* and *Hello* requests. What about your dad? Surely the man wants to give the decorating stint up at his age? I would pay good money to read John Ruttman's response to a photo shoot, *'Fuck off, sweet'art, my son ain't no piece of meat to sell your*

11

shit rag, so you can stop gettin' your knickers in a flap over 'im. And you at the Mail, *you homophobic twat with a microphone, you can go fuck yourself.'"*

Jay glared. Hard. "And that's the reason, right there, why *you* ain't allowed to talk to the press."

Seb chuckled.

"And my old man don't speak like that."

"Pretty much word for word what he said when the journo's knocked on his door after your press conference. Absolute legend. The man's going down in history. Love him."

"I meant the accent. It was shit."

"Knees up, Mother Brown." Seb over-pronounced every blasted syllable.

Drumming his fingers on his knee, Jay settled back in the seat. Seb had been right, they should have got a cab. But Jay's habit of saving money was so deep-rooted that he hadn't been able to shed it even after a year of earning a professional footballer's wage. Now on a packed tube train at the busiest time of the day, with a bunch of football supporters heckling through the latest scores, Jay's instinctive fear was getting the better of him. Splashing out on a little indulgence, like Seb might say, would have been better all round.

One of the blokes slammed up against the pane beside Jay's seat, rattling the glass and Jay's nerves. The geezer shoved his mate out of the way and started up with a play fight inappropriate for a packed tube ride. *New Year in the city and people go mad.*

"What a fucking load of wank." Seb slammed the paper shut.

"What is?"

"My latest album is *not* a pitiful self-indulgent ramble from a group of private school boys trying to

12

proclaim the working-class hero subculture as their own."
Pouting, he shoved the *Metro* between his and Jay's seats.

"What was it then?"

Seb crossed his arms, jiggling his leg so the designer rip on his black drainpipe jeans tore farther across his knee. "Firstly, Kensington Boys is a state school."

"Yeah, but you were at private school before that."

"Unnecessary details." Seb waved a hand. "Secondly, the album was a deep and meaningful glance into the angst of discovering who you are and where you really belong." He grinned. "And a brief fuck-you to the bourgeois hypocrisy."

Jay nodded. "Yeah. Your usual stuff."

"Don't humour me."

"I ain't. It was good." Jay shrugged. "What do you care what a tosser from the *Metro* thinks, anyway? Don't ever read the rags. That's what I've learned. Ain't worth the agg. What does some journo who sits on the side lines know about it? He ain't out on the pitch, doing it."

"Good point."

"You got to number one. So, fuck 'em." Jay smiled. "Can be our New Year motto if you like?"

Seb bounced his knee, but his arms did unfurl from their stiffness. For all Seb's confidence and the fuck-you to the world he composed on a daily basis through his rocking guitar-riff songs, he could be seriously affected by a local rag review. No matter, Jay would relieve that for him later. After they'd done the grown-up stuff, that was.

"Next stop." Jay nodded to the sign and flinched when another loud burst of laughter exploded from the group beside them.

The train screeched into the next station and Jay shot up from his seat. He had to squeeze through the lads, accidentally stepping on someone's toes. "Sorry, mate." He tapped the man's arm in apology.

"Watch it." The bloke spat lager breath onto Jay's face, then stopped, gawked and pointed. "Fuckin' 'ell. Lads, it's Rutters. From West Ham."

"What, the queer?" another one blurted out, scrambling through the mob to get a proper look. "You should be on the girls' team, mate!"

Head down, Jay jumped off the train with his heart pounding and his gut wrenched in knots. Another thing he should be used to by now — the casual homophobia of fickle football fans. It never made it any easier to cope with, no matter how many times he heard the usual rants. And certainly not when on a packed train and having to witness his boyfriend swivelling his middle finger in the air whilst bounding off the carriage behind him.

The lads all bundled forward, and Jay had to grab Seb's arm to yank him away. Luckily, the doors dinged shut, preventing the group from clambering off and no doubt pummelling Seb, and him, to the concrete. Instead, they all offered the wank sign through the glass and Seb had delight in keeping his skull and crossbones tattoo erected high until the train had left the station.

Jay shook his head, inhaling a fierce breath.

"What?" Seb slapped his arm down to his side.

"You remember our deal, right?"

Seb smiled. Then shrugged. "Fuck 'em?"

"Keep everything on the low-key. Don't make a scene, don't engage, don't—"

"Retaliate. I know, I know." Seb angled his head and they both made their way to exit the station via the twist of steps and emerged outside where the freezing mid-evening temperature smacked Jay in the mouth.

He yanked his hood over his cap and rubbed his hands together, shaking his head at Seb's inappropriate slim-fit leather jacket barely being any protector of the thin T-shirt beneath.

"Right, this way." Jay tugged on Seb's fingers, but he didn't entwine his with them. He couldn't. Not here. Not after what had just happened on the train. *Will I ever be able to?*

Seb hurried alongside him, through the bustling high street, passing the gastro pubs and the trinket gift shops selling Harry Potter memorabilia and university branded hoodies. They ambled through the busy market place wafting an array of international spicy street foods, and dodged the after-work crowd bundling into the nearest boozer with an open fire.

A stone-brick church stood on the corner, prominent along the cobbled streets, and gazed down on the area as its master and protector. Jay chucked a left, leading Seb over the road and snaked through the bumper-to-bumper cars until they hit the first residential street. Everything calmed to the point that the tweet of birds was noticeable over the burst of exhaust fumes.

"This one." Jay stopped, squinting as he lifted the shield of his cap.

Seb's mouth fell open.

"You like it?"

"Shit, Jay. It's—"

"Ain't as big as your Kensington gaff, I know, but it's five bed. Music room already sound-proofed. Kitchen-diner. Conservatory and two reception rooms. Ain't got a clue why you need two—"

"One for guests."

"Well, yeah. 'Spose we could shove Martin, Noah and Ann in one room and we fuck off in the other."

"That's a recipe for disaster, and a headline waiting to happen."

Jay chuckled, then tilted his head toward the house. "It's also got all the latest security features. Take it you wanna go in?"

Seb grinned, then leaned closer to whisper in Jay's ear. "Try and stop me, Champ."

That warm soft breath danced down Jay's spine, but he shook it off to allow Seb to walk through the open gates first.

It didn't take much convincing on Jay's part. Not that he thought it would. He knew Seb needed more room with their Limehouse loft flat now filled to the brim with Seb's music gear. The stunning light-brick detached house situated in one of the more affluent areas of Greenwich, east London, had already been refurbished and decked out to pristine standards. Even without Seb's knowledge of property development, Jay knew this was the right place for them. And after one brief look around with the vendors, Jay signed on the dotted line with Seb's signature scrawled beside his. Their house. Their first joint home. Seb might be crap with money, but Jay had managed to get him to save enough of his royalties over the past year of touring the indie music scene to afford the hefty mortgage on the place. Things were looking up. *Ain't nothing, not even the slurs from those wankers who think there ain't room in football for a gay player, can ruin this.*

"Come on." Jay nudged Seb with his elbow as they emerged back out to the street. "Got one more thing to check out."

"What?"

"Let's run."

Seb blinked. "What?" He shot a frantic look over his shoulder. "Why? Which paps are chasing us now?"

"None. Thank, fuck. But we're right by the park. Run with me. To the top and back. Promise the view is worth it."

"Baby, I love you. I do. And you know I'll do anything for love." Seb breathed in, glancing up the street to Greenwich Park and its huge slanted hill. "But I won't do that." He grinned. "Meatloaf, FYI."

Jay tutted. "I know. See you up there, then."

He bounded across the road, setting a pace to pound the pavement until he reached the black gates to enter the park. It was generally a clear run, but he could imagine how the place would get crowded in the summer months with it being the optimal place for kite flying and other family sporting endeavours. This season, though, it was mainly a few couples snuggled together on the benches dotted beside the greenery, and dog walkers sipping from take-out coffee cups. Jay smiled, inhaling the scent of fresh, cold air that he drew into his lungs to sprint faster up the steep rise. Off-season, he'd still need to maintain his fitness and this hill work-out would be perfect for morning runs, and dusk ones if he could ever convince Seb to come with him.

The January wind chill slapped against his cheeks, that ever-present reminder of his early morning runs from his old gaff in Plaistow to the university in Beckton. Where he'd met Seb. That industrial working-class East End he'd grown up in now swapped for the affluent and leafy Greenwich with his live-in boyfriend. *Pretty amazing how much life changes within a couple of years.* Reaching the top, he swerved in front of the bronze statue of General Wolfe and, hands on hips, breathed in the glorious view. The crisp, clear sky allowed for the winter sun to shine over the city. *His* London. Although, now, it felt bigger.

The Royal Museums of London and the University of Greenwich spread out before him like a panoramic picture-postcard. Beyond that curved the River Thames, and farther still new London appeared in Canary Wharf's gleaming silver skyscrapers that reflected the sun's rays, as did the iconic rods poking out of the 02's dome like structure. The view brought a whole new level of beauty to a city that Jay had grown up in. That he'd never leave. He'd just made it to the top. And he planned to stay there. Even if that meant having to live as far away from the flurry to keep his life as much in the shadows as he could.

"Hey." Emerging from the pedestrian walkway a short time after, Seb sipped through the hole in a plastic top of a cardboard cup and offered over one to Jay. "No sugar. No syrup. No milk. No taste."

"Cheers." Jay took the cup and ignored the jibe. *Water*. He smiled as he took a sip. Seb had learned that nothing was allowed to slip through the net of Jay's strict diet now it was controlled by the club's nutritionist, not even for him.

"I was not in any way prepared for running." Seb held out his arms to display his tight ripped jeans, fitted shirt and leather jacket. "Next time. I promise."

"Sure."

They slid down to sit on the grassy bank, taking in the view that now belonged to them. Seb slurped away on his no-doubt sugary sweet coffee, not saying a word. Not even singing, or humming.

"You're unusually quiet," Jay remarked, voice low.

Seb waved a hand, indicating the view.

"I know, right." Jay leaned back on one arm. "It's somethin' else, innit?"

"Yes. Yes, it is." Seb gripped the cup between his legs and inhaled, his chest rising. "This'll do, Champ. This'll do. So *us*."

Jay swallowed. It was. It was *so* them. Away from everything and up in the clouds. Things were different down there, amongst the hustle and bustle. Least he could stay here for a while.

Until football beckoned.

CHAPTER TWO
Back to Reality

A few weeks into the move and boxes still cluttered most of the house. With the football season in full swing, Jay's training and away matches took precedence, leaving Seb waking up alone most mornings. The desire to unpack by himself hadn't been a particularly great motivator. So he'd done what he could, which was next to nothing, and cursed on tripping over yet another load of piled-up crap in cardboard that hindered his late-morning scramble to the kitchen for a coffee to mask his mild hangover. Late-night gigs, and Seb always had to indulge in the odd beverage or two.

After a quick glimpse inside the top box revealed a perfectly folded set of Jay's old football kits, he shoved it aside and headed into the kitchen to switch on the cafetière. He'd learned many a thing since moving in with Jay, the most important being how to make a decent cup of coffee for himself. Jay hadn't allowed him to slink back into his old lifestyle of having everyone do everything for him. Cooking wasn't his strong point, but he'd managed it enough to make toast of a morning when Jay wasn't there to reprimand him for his jam-slash-sugar intake. So he shoved two slices of bread into the toaster and awaited the machine to spurt out his coffee fix.

He rubbed his eyes, sitting at the breakfast bar to eat and sip his coffee in front of his laptop. Such was the norm. Biting off a chunk of toast and jam, he was unable to chew it all without half choking. And that, there, was a metaphor for his fucking life at the moment. Not only was he a front man, the face, main composer and lyricist, he was also his band's overall manager, creating the Drops' image, deciding on which of their singles to release and which to upload for free, utilising social media channels. He also handled most of the financial accounts himself — his degree coming into good use after all. *Thanks, Dad.* Signing with a relatively small independent label had given him the ultimate creative control, but it had also taken him away from the part he loved the most — writing music.

Discarding the remaining quarter of toast, jam-down, onto the marble surface, he rubbed his hands together and tapped out a few lyrics onto a Word doc, the tune buzzing around in his head. *Now? Now, I get my creative juices flowing and want to write a new song? Surrounded by boxes with a fuck-ton of marketing and promoting to get through? Fucking typical.*

His mobile buzzing on the surface snapped him from having to make the difficult choice of what job to tackle first. He knew what it would have been, but liked to fuck with himself that it was a tough one to choose. "Wei."

"Right, I know you said day off, but you'll wanna hear this."

"Good morning to you too, Martin. I haven't seen you in, like, eight hours. What, pray tell, could have happened in that amount of time?"

"I got laid."

"Lucky you." Seb sipped from his coffee. "I got batted off at four a.m. this morning with a declaration that I stink of alcohol."

"Dude, you did. You downed a dirty pint on stage."

"Rock and roll."

"Bet Jay wasn't pleased at having to get up at stupid o'clock after that."

"He says that now we have a spare room, I should sleep in that if I come in later than midnight." Seb pouted. "Anyway, go."

"Oh, right. So, Attax pulled out of V Fest."

Seb nearly spluttered out the coffee over his laptop. "Where did you hear that?" Tapping on his keyboard, he tried to find the latest confirmations for the top festival on the live music calendar.

"I got laid, remember?"

"Of course." Seb nodded. "Leah."

"Yeah. She's more than just a beautiful face."

Seb emulated throwing up. Martin had turned into a right sap since meeting Leah during one of their festival gigs. Live event manager, Leah had insider knowledge, clout and kudos. All that had been in the band's favour when Leah had hooked up with Martin on a more regular basis. She'd, by default, become a superfan and managed to get them on the bill, and a couple of main stages, at the last few late summer gigs. That had aided the Drops to rocket up the charts. *My father was right, business is about who you know and who you can charm to get the right deal.*

"Why'd they pull out?"

"Think one of them's having a baby or some shit."

"That's a bit difficult. They're all men. Trust me, I've tried it all ways and I'm still not up the duff."

"Ha bleeding ha."

Seb chuckled and slurped from his mug.

"How is married life? All joint mortgage now, is it? It's like you've grown up. What's your next song going to be about? Who's turn to pay the council tax?"

"There's a *council* tax?" Seb elevated his voice in sheer horror.

"Who do you think you pay for the blokes to take your bins away?"

"I have absolutely no idea."

"So Jay pays it then."

"Or his new agent."

"He get one, did he?"

"Fuck knows. I'm not privy to that life." Seb pouted. "Anyway, digressing, Martin."

"So, V Fest are looking for another main stager. And guess the fuck what, my friend?"

"Arctic Monkeys?"

"Nope."

"Muse?"

"Already on the bill."

"If this is heading where I suspect, then can you just give me a sec."

"Sure."

Seb slammed the phone on the surface without hanging up, scrambled out of his stool and leapt into the air, punching his fist and jumping around like a complete loon. Or more accurately, like he would during one of his more energetic gig performances. Straightening out his ruffled T-shirt over his boxers, he cleared his throat,

23

stroked through the tufts of his fuzzy hair and picked the phone back up.

"Feel better?" Martin asked.

"Tell me you weren't joking."

"Technically, I haven't said anything yet."

"So fucking say it."

"We're on the bill. The Drops. Headlining. Our name, Seb, up there among the greats. Over a hundred thousand people. By this August, we'll have just played one of the biggest festivals in the fucking world."

"Shit."

"Yep. So get the contracts all signed. Earn your position in the band. I done my part."

"And what a chore it must have been for you." Seb could hear the returning grin without any spoken confirmation.

"We celebrating this?"

"Of course."

"Tonight? Combined house warming?"

"Ah." Seb winced. "Tonight's out, I'm afraid. I have the in-laws for tea."

Martin's cackle down the phone stung Seb's ear. "Look at you, man! Refusing a night on the drink for a family roast. You've changed."

"For the better?"

"Sure. Sure. Just don't let the press know. They kinda like the idea you're a proper rock star, y'know?"

"Luckily I made a pact with Jay to keep our relationship out of the press," Seb grumbled. Bone of contention. Whilst Seb could only increase his visibility by talking about his relationship with the first out-gay professional footballer, he knew it wasn't quite the same for Jay on the pitch.

"Smart move. The bloke knows you well enough now to know you get verbal diarrhoea, eh?"

"Exactly. I'll chat to you later, I have to make this house presentable."

"Good luck with that. Zai chen."

Seb hung up, threw the phone on the counter and slipped back onto the stool. A few more minutes of band work, then he'd do some unpacking for sure.

* * * *

All wrapped up in zip-up waterproofs, base layers and trackie bottoms over their shorts, the lads all tried to stave off the fierce downpour while completing the man-to-man drills. Football training doesn't stop even in the freezing February temperatures, nor, evidently, a waterlogged pitch—you can't practice high-intensity tactics in a covered gym. So Jay and the other twenty-one men were forced outside at their Chadwell Heath training complex to pace through the possession-intensive game on one of the three main full-sized training pitches. They all earned a mint for it, even the new signings, so it wasn't like they could complain about looking like drowned rats when the coach drew the session to a close.

Bruno, West Ham's captain, had been partnered with Jay throughout the session, both of them having to stick to each other wherever they went in order to drill home the defence and clearing the opposition tactics. On the whistle, he slapped Jay on the back. "Good session, Rutts."

"Yeah. That kid Davies is looking pretty sweet." February meant an influx of fresh signings and Academy boys moving up to train with the Firsts, meaning Jay wasn't the new kid on the block anymore.

Bruno arched an eyebrow. "Let's not start hitting on the team, eh?"

"Fuck off." Jay wiped the sweat from his top lip with the sleeve of his base layer, smearing mud across his mouth. At least the banter had started up again. A year of playing and being openly gay had caused most of the team to develop tight lips and a petulance toward PC. Slowly but surely, they were all drifting back to their more stereotypical brutish ways. Jay could deal with that. It meant he'd been accepted.

"Ruttman!" Sergio, the manager, stood at the side lines under an umbrella held up by the First Team coach, zipped up in an oversized rain jacket that prevented him from soaking through to the bone like Jay was.

"Yes, Gaffer." Jay blew away the sodden hair slapped across his forehead.

"My office." The man of many words stormed off and entered the main building at the edge of the complex.

"Trouble?" Bruno asked.

"Think it's the agent talk."

"You not got one yet?"

"Nah. My dad's been keeping me afloat. Don't see why I need anyone else."

"You'd be surprised, Rutts. A good agent is worth their weight in gold, diamonds and open-top Ferraris."

"Yeah, and that's what all of 'em will cost."

They bundled into the first team changing room, the stale musky scent of damp and sweat wafting down the corridors along with the lad's riotous laughter. Jay headed to his section of the wooden bench where he'd left his kit bag and swigged from his bottle of water, zoning out of all the discussions that always seemed too forced, too trivial. He got on with his team. Most of them. He respected the majority. All the ones that had accepted him, anyway. The ones who hadn't had been sold to other clubs during the recent transfer window — Sergio having kept to his word. His gaffer had supported Jay every step of the way, and that had meant casting off the dead weights who had been a little too vocal about Jay coming out.

"How'd the move go? You all settled in?" Bruno ripped off his jumper and base layer.

"Still mostly in boxes, but hoping it'll be unpacked by the time I get home."

Bruno nodded. "It's serious, then?"

Jay didn't respond. It was obvious it had always been serious. For him anyway. Seb had taken some moulding, but had fallen into the role of dutiful long-term boyfriend with an enthusiasm that had knocked Jay for six. And a footballer doesn't declare his sexuality to the entire world for a passing fling.

"Paps found you, yet?" Bruno picked out his shower gel from his bag.

"We're keeping low. Head down and all that. Like I've been told."

"It's for the best."

Jay nodded. He'd heard the same spiel so many times over the past year, from Bruno, from his dad, from Sergio, that he'd gotten the apathetic nod down to a tee. They'd all been behind him one-hundred percent on coming out; now it seemed like they wanted to bury it. They certainly wanted to bury Seb. *Deep.*

Half an hour later, refreshed and restored, Jay sauntered through the building toward the back offices, where the door to the manager's room was shut. He knocked and awaited the reply from his gaffer. Players

27

didn't often find themselves in these parts of the club, except during the transfer window when signing the contracts, or if there were any problems — press leaks, bad behaviour, family issues — anything that would affect a player's game. Jay, however, had found himself there quite a lot. Against his will, most of the time.

The door was opened by Samantha Jones, the club's secretary and the vital cog in the well-oiled machinery that was West Ham United. That startled Jay. He'd been expecting the usual frustrated bellow from his gaffer to get himself inside. Her presence meant that a financial transaction could be required. And she wasn't the only one in there either.

"Come in, come in." Sergio beckoned with his overdramatic hand. "Sit. Sit. I need to introduce you."

Jay eyed the backs of the two men sitting opposite Sergio's desk. One was quite a bit older, possibly his dad's age, with greying flecks scattered throughout dark hair and a bald spot on the back. The other bloke had a healthy mound of light-brown hair swept to the side and held firmly in place by a gel that would rival Seb's choice. They were both kitted out in perfectly tailored suits, power suits. For powerful men. *Agents*.

"Jay, meet Jeremy Booker and Riley Burton." Sergio waved between the two men.

They twisted in their seats, offering Jay dashing smiles as he took up the only place left to park his arse — the armrest of the over cluttered leather sofa pushed to the side wall.

"They are here to discuss the possibility of representing you." Sergio scurried through the papers scattered on his desk rather than offer the men, or Jay, any real attention. Clearly preoccupied, the manager obviously wanted a quick sign from him in order for any more 'nonsense' business to be conducted through a different channel other than Jay himself. Or his dad.

"Representing me for what?" Jay knew, but he thought he might as well play the dumb-arse footballer.

"Allow me." The older gent—Jeremy—twisted in his chair, blocking out the younger bloke completely.

Sergio gesticulated with his hand in a circular motion, skimming through the back pages of a tabloid. Hand gestures were Sergio's main source of communication. Being Italian, his English was good, but he liked to pretend it wasn't to feign confusion rather than a clear lack of interest. Especially to the media.

"I'm a sports agent." Jeremy held down his tie as he lifted up from the chair and offered his hand to Jay.

Jay shook it, then settled back on his uncomfortable perch. There was a reason R and R came directly after intensity training. His muscle fatigue was setting in from the gruelling session and not having had time to get the recovery massage in from the club therapists. *Maybe Seb'll be up for it later? His long piano-playing fingers are perfect for a deep tissue massage.*

"We represent the interests of our sporting clients. Not just footballers, although they seem to fill our books mostly. So we have a wealth of experience of managing professional athletes like yourself. Riley, here, joined us recently and we'd like you to consider having us represent you. On and off the pitch. We're not just about the contracts or getting you the best deal with your club—"

A harrumphed sniff came from Sergio, but he didn't look up from his reading. Jeremy smiled it off and returned his attention to the charm offensive Jay knew he was getting.

"We're also about making every other aspect of your life easier for you. Because if things are sorted off the pitch, then that makes you a better player on it. Which is why the club have called us in."

Jay lifted his gaze to Samantha at the door, then Sergio who gave the faintest of eye contact back.

"You think I ain't dealing?" Jay challenged.

Jeremy held up a finger, cutting off whatever Sergio might have found to say. "No one has indicated that there is a problem. You've played well. You've dealt with things most players would have cowered under. You've held it together by yourself for one season. And whilst the hope was that the spotlight on you would soon fade, it seems it's only getting brighter. The press are waiting for your fallout. We can do everything within our power to prevent that happening."

"How?" Genuinely intrigued, Jay sat forward.

"We'll be a team. I can work the press, getting them to steer away from your personal life and focus on your football. I can work with the club to do that. Riley can work your image." Jeremy sat back, allowing the younger bloke to have an in on the scene.

Jay met with brown eyes that for some reason threw him off guard. The bloke looked familiar, *too* familiar. Like Jay should most definitely know who he was.

"Jay." Riley smiled, eyes softening. "It's been a while."

So Jay should know. He straightened on the armrest, racking his brains. Sergio peered up, renewed interest flickering across his dishevelled features, and even Jeremy whipped his head from one to the other. At least that meant Jay wasn't the only one in the dark here.

"Do you know each other?" Jeremy asked.

"Sort of." Riley shrugged with one shoulder.

Suddenly, it hit him and Jay's chest rose at the realisation. *What sort of fresh horse shit is this?* He stood. "Look, I ain't—"

"Jay," Riley cut him off, joining him in the stand. "It's all good, mate. Water under Stamford Bridge. I've grown up a lot. So have you. I'd really appreciate it if you could hear me, us, out. I think we can work something good here. For you."

Jay could hear the bloke talking, and pick up on the confusion spreading from his gaffer and the other agent in the room, but all Jay could see was his fists pounding into the face of a seventeen-year-old boy who lay on the soggy grass of a football pitch—in front of the spectators, in front of the West Ham Academy crew, in front of his dad.

"Gaffer?" Jay faced Sergio, doing his utmost to keep his voice from cracking. "This ain't a good idea. Cheers for thinking about me, but I'm good. I don't need anyone running my life for me."

With that, he lunged for the door, where Samantha pushed to the side to allow him to pass.

Jeremy stood. "I'm sorry, is there a problem?"

"No problem." Jay yanked open the door. "Sorry for the wasted trip, fellas." He bounded out into the corridor, head down. He had to get away. From in there, from the memories, from everything.

"Jay, wait, hold up."

He got as far as the reception area when that voice halted him in his tracks.

"What the fuck are you doing here?" Jay couldn't help the fierce attack in his voice, but it was warranted under the circumstances.

"I know, I know, it's weird." Riley approached him, palms open.

"A head fuck, more like."

Riley laughed. "I know. But hear me out. I been working as an agent for a couple of years, since I got back from Australia where I was doing similar out there. When my boss recommended this to me, he had no idea I knew you. Or our past."

"And, what, you thought, hell yeah, you'll represent me? Why? To ruin me? Get back at me for what I did?"

"Christ, no. No, Jay, I was a kid. So were you. I deserved it. Every hit."

Jay exhaled a fierce breath. Riley looked genuine. *But ain't that what these agents are meant to be like? Smarmy wankers?*

"I've grown up a lot since then. I never made it pro. Chelsea released me over what happened back then and I buggered off to Australia rather than do what you did. That's where I grew up. What you've done is fucking brave, man. I admire it. I do. And I'm here to help. 'Cause if anyone is gonna know what you deal with, it's a bloke who put you through it, right?"

Jay shook his head. "No offence, mate, but I don't think you even have the first fucking clue."

"Beg to differ. But that's not the point. The point is, we can help you."

"How?"

"By controlling what gets out, what goes in the press, your image."

"Why me? There's a fuck ton of Academy boys who need their lifestyle controlling. I can assure you, I don't."

"On the contrary, Jay. Who's the one in the limelight right now?"

Jay hung his head, his nostrils flaring. Didn't he bloody well know that? He'd thought by coming out, there wouldn't be any more interest in him. That he could get back to just playing football and stay off the press's radar. He could deal with anything the fans and the other players threw at him. He'd had years of practice at that. But the media? That wasn't something he had experience with.

"You want it off you? Off your personal life?" Riley probed. "Then I can do that. We focus on your football, on charity work, re-establishing you as the every-man and not single you out as one exception to a hundred-year rule."

It was almost tempting to say yes. But to Riley? Jay couldn't.

"All right, just think about it." Riley flicked open his blazer and fished a business card from his pocket. "Here. Take it. Jeremy can talk the finances with the club, how much he thinks we can be of worth to you and them. Me? I just want to do good. Make up for being a prick in my early career."

Jay took the card out of ingrained politeness. But he pocketed it double lively, twisted and flew out into the parking lot. Head down, Jay headed over to his car just as a few of the other players emerged from the changing room.

"The geezer didn't even know who I was!" Davies, the new signing, walked beside Pablo Santiago who had been giving the kid a lift to the training complex since he'd come up through the ranks.

Santiago nodded, his bouncy curly hair billowing wildly in the wind as they approached his silver Merc parked up a few spaces from Jay's BMW.

"I told him, watch the game on Sat, then you'll be sorry you didn't let me in without ID." Davies tutted and slapped Santiago on the arm. "Faces, man. I couldn't even get into fucking Faces. What's the point of playing for the firsts if you don't get recognised?"

Santiago yanked open his car door. "Be careful kid. That place is full of brass and gold-diggers. Sometimes they're both."

"I don't know what you gotta do around here for some attention." Davies lifted the handle on the passenger side. "Fuck a man?"

Jay straightened, shooting a narrowed glare over his car bonnet. He caught Santiago's eye and at least he offered a wince. Davies caught onto the three-way stare.

"Shit, Jay, I didn't mean—"

"Forget it." Slip of the tongue from the newbie. Whatever. Jay wasn't one to go telling on his teammates. *That's a sure-fire way to be shunned from the team and find yourself on the scrap heap at transfer deadline day.* So he bundled into his own car and, in the solitude of his blacked-out BMW, smacked his fist on the steering wheel.

He had no idea why.

CHAPTER THREE
Team Tactics

"Have you only just got up?"

Seb peered over his laptop. "Huh?" He had no idea how long he'd been sitting there at the island working on band stuff, but by the look on Jay's face Seb assumed it must have been quite some time.

"It's three in the afternoon, Seb!" Jay waved at all the boxes still obstructing the archway from the hallway to the kitchen. "And you ain't moved nothin'!"

"Oh. Right. Shit." Seb slapped the counter and stood. "Don't go all nuts on me again."

"Seb, you promised you'd clear it."

"To be honest with you, baby, it's mostly yours."

"Yeah, so I see. Your music room got kitted out first day we moved in. You even have pictures hanging on the wall!"

"The nails were already there."

Jay made a face that pretty much summed up that Seb was in the dog house. "I'm meant to be on rest right now."

"Wait, hang on." Seb furrowed his brow, checking the clock on the laptop screen "It's three already? You're a bit late for nap time."

"Yeah. I had to meet with that agent they trying to palm off on me. Gaffer's orders. I would've called —"

"Agent? And?"

Jay chewed his bottom lip. "Pointless."

"Told you." Seb drifted his gaze to the laptop screen. "You want someone to look over contracts, I'm your man." He smiled. "I'm your man for most things. Generally, I'm just your man."

Jay breathed through a smile, relaxing from his stiffened stance. "Let's unpack. I can get in the sleep later before tonight."

"Sure, but I also have some news that might help all this disappear." Seb grinned, waggling his fingers in the air as if he could rid the boxes by magic.

"We ain't getting a housekeeper. We don't need one."

"What? No —" Although, yes, they did. But Seb's phone buzzed on the counter, striking the conversation to an end there. "I won't answer it." Slipping out from behind the island counter, he shrugged. "It'll only be the mother."

"Yours or mine?"

"Mine. American number. The longer I keep this address a secret from her, the longer it is until I have to deal with her demands to see me."

"She's trying, Seb." Jay's features softened.

That sympathetic look from Jay meant all was now forgiven, so Seb seized the opportunity with both hands by wrapping them around Jay's neck and yanking him forward for a sloppy kiss. It took a while, but Jay soon slipped his hands around Seb's waist and tugged him closer, indulging him by deepening the kiss.

Jay pulled away. "Oi, hold up. That's your dirty kiss."

"Is it?" Seb hummed, and smiled, pecking down Jay's neck to taste the salty residue and breathe in the customary scent of football. Even if Jay had showered, the remnants of a hard session were always noticeable. "They need to bottle you."

"That means somethin' else where I'm from."

Seb chuckled, his lips tingling against Jay's stubble. He scrambled to lift Jay's top up and Jay lifted his arms for Seb to rip it over his head. Throwing it on the nearest box, and shrugging at his boyfriend's disgruntled eye roll, Seb put a stop to any more arguments by sliding his tongue inside Jay's mouth and lapping up sugar-free mint chewing gum. *Dirty kiss, indeed.*

"Seeing as you started this…" Jay gripped Seb's arse, almost hoisting him clean off the ground. "Wanna go upstairs for a bit? I could do with a deep massage."

"When you said deep, I had other ideas."

Jay smiled, trickling sweet breath onto Seb's cheek. "That an all, then."

Seb grinned and moaned a delicious purr from the pit of his stomach.

"Yoo-hoo, only us, loves." Barbara encroached on the moment by entering their kitchen. Jay's mid-fifties mother stopped, blinked, and probably would have covered her eyes if she weren't carrying a heavy casserole dish in both arms. "Oh, sorry."

Jay's dad also joined in on the intrusion and almost bashed into his wife at the doorway. With his hands unoccupied, he did cover his eyes. "Fuckin' 'ell, lads."

"Mum, Dad." Jay let go of Seb and shot his exasperated glare on his parents. "You're a bit early. And the key was for emergencies."

"Sorry, love." Barbara stepped over the boxes and set the dish on the counter. "But I made this and it needs to go in your oven."

Seb peered into the meal-on-wheels and sniffed. Lasagne. Mum's special. Jay's mum's, not his. Sylvia had barely cooked before her estrangement and she hadn't gotten any better since their reunion a year ago. Or so Seb assumed. They only spoke long-distance and irregularly at that, with her living in New York. Still, it was more than he conversed with the man who lived on the other end of the District Line, had brought him up from the age of nine, then cut him off completely twelve years later. *Good times.*

"I said I'd cook." Jay flicked out his hair, his cheeks a delightful pinky tinge.

Seb had a sudden urge to tell the in-laws to bugger off and slam Jay up against their American-style fridge freezer and lick him all over. He resisted though. That was apparently called progress.

"But I like it. Keeps me busy since I left the garage." Barbara smiled.

She'd given up her job at the local Tesco garage, which meant she now had an abundance of time on her hands. She claimed the early retirement was due to her not needing the money now both her boys had moved out, but Seb had a sneaking suspicion it was to do with not wanting to read the front pages of the tabloids that had borne her son's face more than once over the past few months.

"And your dad said he'd have a look about, see if anythin' needs fixing?"

"Cheers." Jay swiped an arm along his forehead, beads of moisture trailing the fair hairs of his arms.

Seb dug deep into his resolve, hefting out a disgruntled sigh. Why did his boyfriend have to be so goddamn fuckable?

"That plasma screen could do with puttin' up in the gym room." Jay nodded to his dad.

"Done." John scurried off, tool box in hand.

Seb bit his bottom lip, masking the chuckle. Jay's dad was a legend and wholly accepting of their relationship, but Seb guessed he didn't want it rammed down his throat by walking in on the two of them snogging half-naked in the kitchen. Cock-blocking aside, though, there was some good to having the in-laws close by. Food and free home help. Kissing Barbara's cheek, Seb leaned toward the box and grabbed Jay's T-shirt. He supposed he should cover up, considering he was standing there in just his boxers.

Barbara yanked out an antibacterial wipe from the packet on the side and cleaned the crumbs and jam stuck to the surface around Seb. "I spoke to Ann's mum the other day. Such a shame about Ann and Lucas."

Seb caught Jay's look of confusion, swiftly followed by guilt, as he poked his head through the T-shirt. Jay hadn't had much time with his bestie from school since their move, and he'd obviously realised he wasn't up with the latest gossip in Ann Baker's love life.

"He can do that, Mum." Jay pointed to the now gleaming marble counter top.

Seb stuck the two appropriate fingers up behind Barbara's back. Yeah, he was a loudmouth punk rocker, but he still had some respect for his surrogate mother. He'd start having to write songs sans swear words soon.

"I don't mind, love. Now, where d'you want me to start?" Barbara glanced around, hands on her hips. "Where's Seb's lot?"

"That's all been done." Jay headed over to the nearest box and lifted the flaps.

"Oh." Barbara's tucked a lock of greying blonde hair behind her ear. "Did you not get any stuff from your old house?"

"Which one?" Seb drummed his fingers on the counter.

"The one out west?"

Seb snorted. "No."

Jay straightened and Seb braced for what he knew was coming next. Many a conversation had over the past year about why Seb had refused to try and retrieve the things still left at his father's house usually had Seb reaching for his guitar and a closed-off room.

"You should." Jay's gruff voice had an air of threat and authority that Seb usually shivered on hearing. This time, it just made him clam up.

"We've talked about this, Champ."

"You can't give up everything you ever owned. Surely there's stuff there you want to get back? Something you need. Want? That's rightfully yours."

Seb sighed and slapped his laptop shut. Scrubbing a hand down his face, he didn't respond. Not even when Barbara turned her own set of blue eyes on him. Obviously sensing the unrest, she hurried out of the room, hopefully to find some unpacking to do somewhere else.

"Seb—"

"Jay, leave it."

"I'll go with you. Your old man's being a stubborn git. He's had time to get over it. He's just saving face, feeling a bit guilty and waiting for you to make the first move."

"Guilty?" Seb furrowed his brow. "One, that's an emotion my father does not possess and two, what the fuck would he be guilty about? I walked out on *him*, his business."

"For good fucking reason." Jay clenched his jaw, his features hardening. "He's gotta know that now, right?"

Ah. Seb hung his head. "Go sleep. I'll unpack with your mum and see if your dad needs any help."

Jay arched an unconvinced eyebrow.

"As in hold the tool box, make the tea, that sorta thang."

Jay snorted. "Don't cook, don't clean, DIY non-existent. What do you do?"

"When I look this fucking good, I don't need any other skills." Seb grinned, then scooted around the island and kissed Jay. "Get some rest before the Ruttmans take over this house completely."

He tapped Jay's cheek then bounded off to find which box Barbara had her nose buried in. It also allowed him to exit himself from the awkward conversation of having to deal with all that birthright nonsense. Jay banged on about it more often than Seb appreciated. He never wanted anything to do with any of it. *Ever.* He'd given all that up, for this. And he couldn't be happier about it. Nothing would get him contacting his father again. Not even the hidden box in his wardrobe in Kensington that he often pondered over whether to get

Yulia to sneak it out for him. But even that wasn't worth the fight.

Fuck 'em. The new motto was working out pretty damn good so far.

* * * *

It took the best part of the rest of the day, but with his parents' help the unpacking had been done by the time Jay awoke from his pre-planned shut-eye. For all the rigid schedules the club put on him—from training, gym work, watching repeated matches for opposition tactics, nutrition and physio—the monitored sleep was the hardest to stick to. Especially when his boyfriend was a night owl, and Jay was up with the lark with a timetabled no-disturb nap in the late afternoon—which was the only real time they seemed to get with each other. Apparently, according to the Sports Science guys, sleep and recovery was more important than muscle work. A tired body wouldn't be able to achieve optimum results on the pitch.

When he entered the kitchen, dressed appropriately this time, the place was packed out. His mum hovered by the counter, preparing the salad to go with the lasagne bubbling in the oven. His dad was mid-chuck of two-year-old Lily, her blonde curls bouncing around her cherub-like cheeks. She giggled and it was so infectious that Jay had to laugh along with her. Bryan, Jay's older brother, clean-shaven for a change, but clutching his usual can of Stella, had an arm draped over fiancée Cheryl's shoulders and she had her manicured fingers wrapped around a wine glass.

One person was noticeably missing. "Where's Seb?"

Barbara sprinkled the bacon bits into the bowl. This was an all-out accompaniment to the meal, then. "He said he had some stuff to do."

"Play music!" Lily declared after being tossed in the air.

Course he would be. Jay did the rounds, shaking the men's hands and kissing the women's cheeks. When he got to Lily, she tapped a finger to her lips and Jay honoured her with a kiss there instead. She snickered uncontrollably after.

"I'm here, I'm here." Seb rushed in, running his fingers through his hair to spike it up in the right places. "Sorry, very important business to take care of." He kissed Jay, then yanked open the fridge. "You want?" He waggled a half-empty bottle of Pinot.

"Nah. There should be some lemon water in there?"

"Lemon water? At a dinner party? Champ, you need to loosen up."

Bryan snorted a laugh and Jay flipped him off.

"James Arnold Ruttman!" No matter how old, or how successful Jay got, his mother would never miss an opportunity to reprimand him.

Seb chuckled and poured the wine to the brim of his glass, then topped up Cheryl's and Barbara's, chucking the now empty bottle into their recycling unit. He settled in close to Jay and his familiar spicy aftershave oozed off his smooth skin. It smelled better than the bubbling cheese coming from their pristine and pretty much unused farmhouse oven.

Jay got himself a water. "What important business anyway?"

"Well, you're gonna flip your shit when you hear."

"Sebastian! We have a minor present." Barbara brandished the wooden salad tongs at Lily.

"You just got full named, fella." Bryan held up his can in cheers. "Official welcome to the family."

"I'm actually honoured." Seb raised his glass to the room. "And the middle name's Michael, just for next time, and we all know there will be one."

Barbara tutted and went back to tossing the salad.

"And might I say, Babs, that necklace really suits you. New, is it?" Seb pointed to the pendant draped around Barbara's neck.

Smiling, she stroked a finger over the silver heart. "Why, yes, it is. John bought it for me. A Tiffany, no less."

"A Tiffany?" Seb raised his eyebrows, impressed. "Nice one, John."

John set the panting Lily to sit on the island counter. "Cheers. Got it Romford market. Right bargain, an' all."

"The market?" Seb sipped from his glass, masking an amused smile.

"Yep." John cracked open a beer can and slurped from the bubbles protruding from the hole. "Came with a box, so I know it's legit."

Seb plucked the jewellery from Barbara's chest between his fingers and swiped his thumb across the smooth pendant. Jay exchanged confused glances with his brother as Seb settled the pendant back and picked up his wine.

"Beautiful, Babs."

"Thank you, Seb. I've been wanting one for ages."

"Me too." Cheryl elbowed Bryan beside her. "But this one 'ere's a right tight arse."

The Ruttman chitchat started up again, with Lily demanding more throwing about and Cheryl and Barbara now locked into a conversation about the latest in costume jewellery.

Seb leaned in to whisper in Jay's ear. "Fake."

"Really?"

"You can't get a real Tiffany from Romford market, I'm afraid."

"Shit." Jay glanced over to his smiling mother. "Don't tell her, she looks so happy about it."

"I won't. Where is Romford anyway?"

"Up near where I train."

"Right, right." Seb nodded and took another swig of wine. "And I know exactly where that is."

Jay sighed. "One day, you might even learn the offside rule."

"Oh, Christ, no. Please don't make me sit through that again. There isn't enough time in my life, nor condiments to act as players."

Chuckling, Jay caught onto the sparkle in Seb's eye that reminded him why Seb might be acting so antsy. "Well?" He bumped his shoulder to Seb's. "What's the news?"

"Oh, yes." Seb held out his arms in display of himself. "You are all looking at the main stager and headline act at this year's V Festival." He added in a boastful bow.

The Ruttmans, and the honorary one, all offered their own congratulatory cheers, clinking cans or glasses. Jay slipped a hand up Seb's back and pulled him in to plant a kiss on his ear. "Congrats." He meant it, even though a sudden twinge settled within his chest. That was going to elevate Seb's celebrity status sky high.

"Right, it's ready." Barbara ushered everyone into the back dining room, plonked the still bubbling dish into the centre of the oak table and slipped off the oven gloves.

45

Everyone else brought the various extras to go with it and set them down on the table, taking up their chairs with Lily placed in the booster seat at the end. Seb sat next to her and sneaked over a biscuit. He winked, she giggled and Jay tucked in beside Seb with an odd feeling of mush in his stomach. He was hungry. That was all.

"How's the new signings?" John helped himself to a plate of grub and sat to eat immediately after. "That Davies is quick footed."

"Yeah." Jay avoided the eye contact and served up a plate, which he handed to Seb. "He's good."

"There been any...banter?" John shovelled in a mouthful of lasagne.

Jay eyed the occupants around the table, each one giving some look of sympathy or concern. They had his best interests at heart. They worried about him and about what he'd dealt with since coming out. And they all, in their own way, had sacrificed so much for him to get where he was. Which was why he had to give them what they wanted to hear.

"There's always banter, Dad." Jay stared at his plate, rifling through the salad contents. "Ain't nothing I can't handle."

"Good." John waggled his fork. "'Cause that's all it is, son. You know that, right? That's what changing rooms are for."

Jay heard the heavy intake of breath beside him and knew Seb was doing his best not to cut in and retaliate. Least he was learning the ways of the Ruttmans.

"No point callin' out every twat in there," his dad rattled on, stabbing through the leaves and dipping them in copious amounts of salad cream. "'Cause you know what snitches get, dun't ya?"

Jay nodded. "Yeah, Dad, I know. Cheers."

Seb bounced his knee beside him, so Jay rested his hand on it beneath the surface and gave it a squeeze.

"Nah, what you need to learn is great fucking comebacks." Bryan wriggled forward in his seat. "Y'know, when some tosser on the stands yells at ya, you just tell 'em to shut their pie-eatin' cake hole and that you might be bent but at least your teeth are straight."

Jay pinched the bridge of his nose as silence descended over the Ruttman table, except for Seb, who burst out a laugh.

"Holy shit. I take it back." Seb wiped the snorted wine under his nostrils. "Him. He needs to be your agent."

Bryan winked and Cheryl slapped him on the arm.

"I fear for your child, Bryan." Barbara shook her head in disapproval.

"Don't panic, Ma. You know what her first word was."

Barbara tutted. Lily giggled and Seb offered her another biscuit from a stash that Jay had no idea where he was getting them from. It couldn't be his pockets because his jeans were far too tight. Jay decided he didn't want to know where he was producing the chocolate chips from and just allowed his niece to be bribed.

"You gettin' an agent, son?" John swiped garlic bread through the Bolognese sauce.

"Nah." Jay shifted in his seat. "No point." That was all the explanation that needed. He had no desire to bring up the reminder of Riley Burton and how the bloke had set Jay's life on a completely different path to the one he'd been destined for from the age of eight.

"Why don't we talk about something other than football?" Barbara suggested. "I saw that Manor place has a wedding show on this weekend. Thinking of going?"

47

"Ma, they've only been together a year." Bryan waved his beer can between Jay and Seb. "Marriage is a bit far off."

"Nor is it legal." Seb pouted.

Jay flinched. Marriage had not been something that they had discussed. Because they couldn't. But that pout from Seb suggested that he might want to, if they could. *Would he?* Jay met his boyfriend's doe eyes and checked for any signs of the man's usual sarcasm. Seb shrugged.

"I meant you two, you prat." Barbara sipped her wine. "You're the ones engaged. Thought you could set an actual date soon."

"Indeed." Seb nodded. "How long is it one must wait from hooking up, getting engaged, then producing offspring before actually setting a date to make it all official?"

"We don't all have cash to splash. You know how much a wedding costs these days? Especially when she wants a bleedin' Vera Wank."

"Wang, you tosser." Cheryl whacked him on his arm again.

"Would you stop that, woman!" Bryan rubbed his biceps. "I keep spillin' me beer!"

Seb chuckled, bouncing Lily's hand up and down. Jay mouthed the words *'I'm sorry.'* It didn't matter how many family dinners he made Seb attend, Jay was still more than a little embarrassed by how they turned out. He doubted Seb's family gatherings back at his Kensington mansion would have played out like this. It would have been all black tie, classical music playing and talking through the latest in the stockmarkets.

Seb mouthed *'I love you'* back. Jay smiled, his cheeks warming.

"You should check down Romford market." Seb curled a lock of blonde hair around Lily's ear. "You might find a cheap knock-off there."

John clanged down his cutlery and Barbara cleared her throat, hand trailing to the pendant around her neck. Jay nudged Seb's knee with his own in warning.

"Or, you know, a legit going for a decent price." Seb bit his lip.

"Do they do wedding dresses there, John?" Cheryl asked, her blue eyes sparking in genuine interest.

"Not sure, love." John scraped the last of his dinner into his mouth. "I'll check next time I'm there. Got a block of flats to repaint for the council."

"I don't think she should get her dress from a market." Barbara wrinkled her nose. "We can definitely help chip in, can't we, John?"

"Shouldn't it be the bride's family who foot the bill?"

"Well, yes, in the eighties. We're all equal opportunities now, aren't we, love." Barbara smiled across at Jay and Seb.

"What'll be your first dance?" Seb cut in.

Jay knew he did that to steer the conversation away from the awkward subject of money. He kinda loved him for that. Jay had been planning to offer his brother some cash for his big day, but as a date hadn't been set, the subject hadn't come up and he didn't want to announce it to the table. That could come across like he was gloating. What a way to emasculate your dad and older brother.

"James Blunt." Cheryl smiled, flicking her plait over her shoulder. "*You're Beautiful*."

Bryan gave a look that suggested he hadn't been on board with the agreement of that one. Jay doubted the bloke had much say in any of it at all. He chuckled.

49

"I keep tellin' her she can't have that. Not when we use the geezer's name as the ultimate insult."

Barbara narrowed her eyes in confusion.

"Cu—"

"You can't have that song," Seb broke Bryan off before he could finish. "It's about *not* getting the woman of your dreams. She's with someone else."

"Is it?" Cheryl balked, her button nose wrinkling.

"Listen to the lyrics, people. But I guess that's understandable as his voice sounds like a cat's being strangled to put up with it until the end."

"No it does not!" Cheryl folded her arms.

"You want a beautiful love song? I'll write you one."

Cheryl glanced around the room. "Don't you, like, swear, in all your songs?"

Seb managed to disentangle his hand from Lily and twisted in his seat. "My older tracks were of that ilk, yes. And I am more prone to a heavy guitar rock-out, but, recently, my muse has changed from the anger fuelled and angst-ridden punk into a more… fluffier sound." Seb gave a lopsided smile. "I can produce an acoustic love song better than Blunt. In fact, I've been working on one recently. But I don't think it really goes on any of our albums without a fight with those at the label. So…" He waved his hand. "It's yours, if you want it."

Cheryl clapped her hands. "Really?"

"Sure. But you need to set a date by the end of the night." He winked across the table at Barbara.

Jay draped his arm over the back of Seb's chair and tangled his fingers through the hair on the nape of Seb's neck. Seb could work his charm to the best of his ability. Cheryl and Barbara were putty in his hands right then. But, then, so was he, so who was he to complain about it?

50

"I'll need to hear this shit first." Bryan sat back in his chair.

"All right." Seb leapt up and bundled out of the dining room.

Jay's arm suddenly felt the cold in Seb's absence, and he watched with anticipation as Seb returned with his acoustic guitar in hand. He settled back down in his seat and Jay itched to caress Seb's skin whilst Seb twisted the pegs and tuned the strings, like he sometimes did when Seb did this when they were alone and Seb was sans clothing.

There was something about him when he played acoustic. He didn't have his usual brash persona that he wore when on stage in front of the crowds that swarmed to see him play. Still confident, but as Seb's fingertips drifted over the strings, plunking and thrumming through the repeated chords, he appeared vulnerable somehow, like the real Sebastian had been stripped bare. Jay often watched him composing a new song, oddly fascinated by the process. Stop, start, stop, continue, and repeat. When the words eventually fell from humming lips, it was like witnessing Seb become himself, shedding the layers of thickened skin and crumbling those walls he'd built around his heart. He was set free by his music.

So was Jay.

Slipping into a rhythm, Seb shuffled on the seat and cleared his throat. "Lyrics aren't exact," he spoke, then gently hummed a sweet melody, words following a short time after.

The heartfelt love song sent shivers along Jay's spine, and the others stared in awe. Seb didn't get far into it before the doorbell interrupted his flow. He flattened his palm over the strings. "I swear I did not invite Martin or Noah."

51

"Ann, then." Jay bounded up from the table and jogged through the house. His mouth instinctively fell open on opening the door.

"Hey, big guy."

"Tom!" Jay wanted to smile, but something caught in his throat. The guilt. The memories that had flooded him on seeing Riley after all those years. *Should I tell him?*

"I got your card. With the new address. Thanks. And congratulations." Tom flicked his quiff up higher and peered over Jay's shoulder. "I won't stay, I know you're probably busy with Seb. I was just in the area. Kinda." He shrugged, his retro tan satchel falling from his shoulder. "I'm off to the airport."

"Where you going?"

"Back home. For a while."

"Yeah?" Jay gripped the door, shuffling his feet, undecided whether to invite the guy in. Seb and Tom hadn't exactly made friends, and he suspected neither of them believed there was no love lost between them. "Is everything all right with that now?"

"My parents? I don't know. We'll see." Tom glanced down to the floor.

"Come in." Jay waved a hand. "There's a bunch of us here."

"No, no. Thanks. I wouldn't want to intrude."

"You ain't."

"Thanks, but Julio's waiting." Tom angled his head toward the running taxi at the end of Jay's drive. "I just came to say goodbye. It's been great hanging out with you and, y'know, seeing you come out of your shell. It suits you, y'know."

"What does?"

"Contentment."

Jay bowed his head. Was he contented? He wasn't sure. Recently he'd been getting the Jekyll and Hyde vibe.

Tom flipped open the flap to his bag and pulled out a brown paper wrapped gift. "I also wanted to give you this. House warming, goodbye gift. Whatever."

"What is it?"

"Open it." Tom smiled, fastening the buckles on his bag.

Holding the door open with his back, Jay untied the rough rope that held the paper together and slipped out an elegantly framed photograph. He screwed the paper in his hand and stared at the images behind the glass. Two photos, side by side, both similar shots. The first one, a captured action shot taken at one of his latest football matches. Jay had seen the same photograph in papers, online, up for sale in certain memorabilia shops and he'd scrawled his name on many a replica postcard outside the stadium. It was a perfectly captured image of one of his blasts at goal, his blond hair sticking out from the effort and determination plastered on his face as his boot made contact with the ball at hip height. Next to it, separated by a white border, was a similar image. This time a much younger Jay, seventeen to be exact, studs in the air and tapping a toe to the ball and the same look etched on his youthful features. Except his eyes didn't shine as bright. Jay knew they'd been over clouded by fear back then.

"Tom," Jay breathed. "Where did you get this?"

"The first one, from an online seller. It's not the original, I'm afraid." Tom tapped the frame, wiping away some of the frays from the rope. "That one," he pointed at the photo of Jay from his youth team days, "I took."

"You?"

53

"I hung on to it. Sorry." Tom adjusted the bag on his shoulder. "I never told you, but I came to a few games and hid in the shadows more than just that one time."

Jay sucked in a breath and opened his mouth to speak, but nothing came out. Things were best left in the past.

"You've come a long way, big guy. A real long way. Let that remind you of how far." Stepping into the doorway, Tom kissed Jay's cheek. "Keep showing the world they should be more tolerant, eh? Be a hero. You've always been mine."

With one last stroke of Jay's cheek, Tom stepped away and rushed across the drive into the waiting taxi. Jay closed the door. *Blast from the fucking past today, or what?*

"The home delivery guy's pretty friendly." Seb's voice startled Jay and he tucked his hands into his jeans pocket.

"Tom." Jay passed over the framed picture. "Looks like I got my own stuff to hang on the walls now."

He kissed Seb on the lips, then sauntered passed him. He wouldn't indulge the bloke in his jealousy. There was nothing to be jealous about. Tom was past. Like that second image was. Jay was living the other one now.

Whether it was how he'd imagined, or not.

V FEST Welcomes the Drops!

New indie punk-rock band, the Drops, to headline V Festival 2007.

London-based trio are taking over from Attax, who pulled out of the second largest summer festival in the UK, citing personal reasons.

Signed by indie label Armstrong Records, Seb Saunders, Martin Chang and Noah Fitz have climbed the UK download charts in record time since their first release of rock-ballad *Bitter Love* in November last year.

The Drops began their career online, building up a fanbase using My Space and holding private gigs only open to their subscribers. But with their unique and brave style of crossing music genres from emo-anthem rants to power-pop with a post-punk revival nostalgia, the Drops have fast become the modern-day success story for the independent label.

Some in the music industry have condemned the decision to have the relatively unknown three-piece as the headline act, blaming the hysteria built up around the Drops' front man rather than for the band's musical talent.

Twenty-four-year-old Seb Saunders from West London has been tied to West Ham footballer, Jay Ruttman, since the player's public coming out last year. Seb has been open about his sexuality since the early days of the band's career, yet has not confirmed or denied the rumours that he is in a relationship with the east Londoner.

Festival manager, Jake Pickford, said, "We're thrilled to have the Drops at V Fest. Having such a new band as the headlining act is refreshing, and shows that the festival moves with the times and consistently produces a programme catering to different tastes."

CHAPTER FOUR
Offside Trap

Seb shoved up the sleeves on his leather jacket, revealing the Chinese number nine symbol tattooed on the underside of his wrist. It always helped in these situations, giving him that gentle nudging reminder. Adjusting the chair on wheels closer to the large microphone dangling in front of him, he slipped one side of the studio-wear headphones away from his ear.

It had been a month since the announcement that the Drops' were headlining V Fest and the press interviews and media appearances had thrust the band, and mainly Seb, further into the limelight. Not that he begrudged any part of it. Far from it. He loved the chance to talk about his music: if only the journalists would stick to the pre-vetted questions, that was. And most of them did. The usual suspects that wrote for magazines or online articles had come to learn that as soon as anything off-topic, mainly a certain front man's relationship status, was brought up, Seb drew the session to a close. Luckily, no one had pushed the mark. And the exposure was certainly aiding their latest album to rocket the download chart, putting the Drops firmly on course for a UK top ten album before the end of the year.

He glanced up at the sign above the door, the words ON AIR emblazoned and highlighted. Clearing his throat, he nodded to the radio presenter on the other side of the table masked by the tons of equipment that did who knew what, to declare he was ready. Which was lucky, as the last few lyrics and guitar pelting solo of the Drops' latest single blared out of the speakers to the million or so listeners of the most popular weekend radio show.

This was their first live interview. Their record label had managed to bag the best slot on UK radio due to the increased sales of their latest album that had more of a mainstream appeal than even Seb had prepared for. He'd believed the Drops' to be a more minority band, a niche, the outcasts in a music industry that seemed awash with macho posturing and male bravado. The Drops' certainly didn't offer that, with their image having been crafted by the Marmite affect—people either loved or hated them. Him, mainly. Not that he was knocking the unexpected popularity, nor the pound signs that came with it, but live on air at nine o'clock wasn't exactly a Drops' friendly slot, especially when most of their songs couldn't be considered as pre-watershed material. And Seb couldn't be bleeped out when live on air. Thankfully he had Martin and Noah on either side of him to cut in when he tended to go trigger-happy on the cussing.

"And that was the latest single from the Drops' new album, *Breaking Through.*" Christian O'Leary's infamous gravel tone, perfect for radio, grated through Seb's earphones and into homes of his millions of avid listeners. "And we are so excited at the studios here today, as we have the Drops with us. Welcome, guys."

"Thanks for having us." Seb offered a limp smile and the other two band members nodded their nonchalance—the fashioned image of morose rockers honed to a tee. Seb knew inside they were either bricking it or jigging to the Snoopy dance.

This was the top. This music station only brought on the best, as indicated by the signed records hanging in frames on the walls. Bands scrambled for a chance to chat with Christian, not just for the sheer number of loyal subscribers to his show, but because he knew his shit, and if they got on his good side, he'd play their song to death and they'd reap the royalties and the free promotion that came with it.

"It's a great record. You guys seem to have come out of nowhere. Just over a year ago, no-one had even heard of the Drops. Now you're almost a household name. How have you taken to the fame?"

"Like a pig in—"

Martin's first nudge made Seb's elbow fall off the swivel seat's arm rest. *Breakfast show, live. No swearing. Right.* Seb straightened out.

"We're well and truly embracing our unexpected success and have taken to the rock and roll lifestyle with tremendous enthusiasm." Seb grinned.

Christian laughed, his breath blowing through the microphone. "I'll bet. So reading between the lines, you're all living it up large?"

"Not exactly," Seb replied, taking the regret out of his delivery. "If we had the time, we would, I'm sure. We've worked hard to get where we are. I know it looks to everyone else as if we exploded on the scene with no real effort. But it's quite the contrary. We've had a hard

59

slog getting here. We've gigged the dives. We've had the rejections. We almost quit. We're the epitome of the saying if at first you don't succeed, stick two fingers up to the haters and carry on regardless."

"And your latest single really reflects that." Christian nodded in encouragement, giving a thumbs-up as an indicator all could be heard okay. "But you've made your mark by singing candidly about how you feel about the current landscape. Would you say current affairs affect your music?"

"Definitely." Seb licked his drying lips, then made a cup sign with his hand to the girl under the highlighted sign clutching a clipboard to her chest. She scurried off and Seb sat forward. "Unless you walk around with your eyes closed, as a creative, it's hard not to be affected by what's happening in the world. We're living in decadent times, and that fuels my song writing. *Breaking Through* focuses on how a luxurious and self-indulged state of living can eventually implode, and forces us to take a look at what we really need, can live with and what should be important. I can't write a song without meaning behind it. I have to say something. State something. And usually it's a pretty big something."

"I see." Christian tapped the end of his pen to his chin. "So did your background influence your choice of songs on the album? Having listened to it, I could really feel the theme of leaving the past behind, about living a truth."

"That's exactly what it's about. Becoming who you really are. Over the past year, we became who we really were, having just played around with it before then." Seb mouthed a thanks to the returning girl who handed him a glass of water and he took a sip, moistening his drying throat. "We've shed some layers and shown ourselves, confronting the prudish attitudes of the bourgeois."

"But in doing so, you've been accused of trying to claim something that isn't really yours — the ethics of the working-class hero. What do you say to that?" Christian raised dark eyebrows across the threshold, urging Seb on. He was walking a fine line. That wasn't a vetted question. But Seb could deal.

"I say that's bullsh—" Another nudge and Seb heaved an annoyed breath. "We know who we are. I know who I am. We know where we came from. We don't claim to be anything we're not. We're being open and honest about having not fit into the round holes that we were born into. And by speaking out about those issues, we're inadvertently appealing to the masses, without us really having expected to." Seb shrugged one shoulder.

Christian nodded. "Can you see, though, how some might regard this album, and your succinct style in particular, as punk rock? Something that has its roots in the working class?"

"Punk is a way of life, not a sound. The Drops' embrace that lifestyle wholeheartedly. We say be different, be who you are, go against the grain. Speak out for what you believe in. That isn't something that can be adopted by only one social group."

"But can you, three lads from affluent backgrounds, one of you having attended the most prestigious boarding school in the country — "

"And subsequently expelled at aged fourteen for not conforming to their rigid conditioning." Seb leaned into the microphone and grinned for the delivery of that statement. *Rock 'n' roll the shit out of that.*

"Get you." Christian pointed the tip of his pen across the desk. "But you still had a privileged upbringing. All three of you. You weren't exactly pounding the street with you placards and revolting against your jobs being slashed with the fear of losing your livelihood."

"Rebellion is about resisting authority and control. And that's something I *can* relate to. Just because I had money in my pocket growing up doesn't mean we weren't oppressed just as much as those considered destitute. We're a band that attempts to unify the subjugated, regardless of where you were born, who you are and what you fight against. Listen to my music, you'll hear what's important to me and if listeners find something in there they can relate to, then that's fu—awesome."

"And there's no mistaking your motives with this album. Challenge the norm. Rise against the machine. That fair to say?"

"For sure. There's so much division in music, or anything, really. Society puts us all in little boxes. Emos, punks, teeny-boppers, the jocks, the geeks, gay, straight, trans. We're told not to draw outside the lines. We say, try it. Step over that line, and hold your middle finger high when you do it."

"Would you be referring to anything in particular there, Seb?"

"I'm always referring to something in particular. It's up to the listeners to decide what that is."

"I think many will form their own opinions based on what they already know about you."

Seb met with the twinkle in Christian's eye, and held it. Not biting. Chuckling silently so the households receiving his radio link wouldn't hear, Christian skimmed his finger down the script in front of him.

"'Breaking through the mould', 'reforming myself'. Great lyrics for, say, someone making huge changes in their life?"

"Yeah. We did. We all did." Seb turned to Martin and Noah individually, hoping to bring them into the firing line. "We went from being reliant on other people to going it alone. It's been...interesting."

"But you in particular." The glint in Christian's eye had Seb's Spidey senses tingling. "Your name pops up more often than most."

"Yeah, that's been a...I'm dealing with it."

"There's a lot of speculation out there that the interest surrounding you has all been a publicity stunt, made up by you. That none of it is real."

Seb actually belly-laughed, then composed himself to speak into the microphone. "Perhaps that's what a certain establishment would like to think. Cast me aside. Don't ruffle the feathers of a hundred-year history." That had perhaps been too far. Maybe he did harbour a little unsavoury feeling to those that kept him separated from his lover's life. But he wasn't meant to be talking about that. Certainly not live on air. And Christian smirked for the privilege of being the one to have goaded that much out of him.

Right, back on track. Seb wriggled in his seat, cracking his neck from side to side.

"But considering you don't talk about it, that no-one's allowed to talk about it, how can anyone know what's real and what's all part of this act that you create?"

Seb held Christian's gaze. The man was getting too close to the mark for Seb to feel comfortable. The show's producer had been warned, and Seb wasn't averse to walking out of the studio if necessary. It might actually add to his credibility in the rock arenas. But at the same time, he itched to prove what had been wrongly speculated about. He'd just made a big song and dance about standing up for what was right. He couldn't back down now.

"If we're on the same wavelength, Christian," Seb held his gaze, "then I'm afraid my private life is exactly that, private. I'm not sure what my relationship status has got to do with me selling records." That should put a firm full stop on the questions, whilst actually still proving he wasn't making anything up.

"So, do we take that as confirmation that you *are* the live-in boyfriend of recently declared gay and West Ham footballer Jay Ruttman?"

Seb froze. Okay, so technically, everyone knew that. But the pact was never to talk about it. To keep it out of the mainstream, mainly for Jay's survival on the football pitch. Seb was well aware that the fans, and players, didn't need his loved-up status with another man being discussed in public. That just added fuel to the fire and Jay already had to deal with the unrest each Saturday on the pitch.

"I'm not sure what that's got to do with this album." Seb picked up his glass and took a firm swig, feeling Martin's bouncing knee beside his. "That's what we're here for. Not to talk about who we sleep with."

"Sure, sure, of course." Christian smiled, holding up a hand in defence. "Although, we'll take that to mean that you do actually sleep with him."

"Regularly." Seb was so annoyed that the snap fell from his tongue before he had a chance to stop it, and it carried through the microphone, converted into radio waves and pelted out the speakers to cause the bated breath of millions of listeners.

Fuck.

* * * *

Sliding his BMW into the reserved spot at the Boleyn Ground stadium, Jay shunted the car into complete silence. He shut his eyes, gripping the steering wheel. He didn't often listen to Seb's interviews, mostly because Seb played a different character in the media and Jay had a hard time connecting the rocker with the man he slept with, but right then he'd just heard *his* Seb declaring their regular sex life to everyone who tuned in to the most popular radio show on air. And his chest tightened with the unease of having to set foot into his home ground a few hours before playing one of the toughest teams in the league, who would also be arriving with the most vocal of crowds.

His phone buzzed from inside his sports bag and he considered ignoring it. It was amazing how journalists manage to get hold of his private number, but that wasn't the regular ring-ring of an unvetted number. That tone was set up against those he trusted. So he rummaged through the shit he brought to matches and fished out his mobile.

"Yeah." He didn't even hide his clipped tone.

"Right, that means you heard."

"The fucking country heard, Seb!"

"Calm your shit. I didn't say anything too damaging."

"Really? Taken out of context this time, was it?"

"Ha, fucking, ha. He goaded me, baby. He pushed my buttons like I was his fucking radio whatsit."

"Then you just say no comment, like we get taught in media training."

"*You* get taught. I don't have the luxury of a massive club full of experts behind me, do I? Besides, I pretty much did."

"No. You said we fuck. Regularly."

"Which actually is an untruth, so more fool them, right? I mean, it's irregular at that."

"Don't try and smart your way out of this. I'm about to go play football."

Seb's breath blew down the phone. "I'm sorry. But it's nothing people don't already know."

"That's not the point, Seb! The point is, we agreed. Keep us, our relationship, out of the press."

"Right."

"And don't do that."

"Do what?"

"Sulk."

"Champ, when have you ever known me to sulk? Some of us just like to, you know, speak. *Talk.* Say what's on our fucking minds. And you know what? Maybe I'm tired of all this. Keeping my mouth shut is hard. I love you, baby. And I don't give a fuck if the whole world knows. I thought you didn't either."

That stung. Jay had come out last year for a reason, so as not to have to hide who he was. It didn't mean he wanted it talked about live on air for the whole country to discuss. That was shoving it down people's throats. And what was said about him in the media didn't just affect Jay. It affected his whole damn team. The squad had to put up with the taunts, the jeers, the fucking awful shit that was written about them, or laughed openly about on late-night comedy shows or online forums. Yeah, tolerance in the football establishment was making an impact. Racism, sexism, homophobia: all those things had been challenged by the Kick It Out campaign and for the most part it was working. But Jay wanted to keep his private life to himself and not inadvertently fuel any adverse reaction to it. Just like the lads on the pitch who'd managed to get suppression orders when their private lives were splashed all over the papers, Jay just wanted the focus on his football. Not on his sex life.

"Jay?"

"I can't talk about this right now."

A sharp knock to his side window jolted Jay in his seat. Bruno, team captain, lowered his unshaven face to the glass and angled his head toward the entrance to the stadium.

"I gotta chip." Jay held up a finger from around his mobile to Bruno.

"Take it you want me to stay home? Not come to the match?"

"There's always a seat here if you want it." Jay meant it. But Seb hadn't taken him up on the offer yet, fearing that if he did he would ruffle the feathers of the elite WAGS who ruled the VIP seats on match days.

"Good luck, Champ." Seb hung up.

Jay tucked the phone into his bag, grabbed the straps and shouldered open the door. The bleep from electric locking blasted through the car park and Jay caught up to Bruno leaning against the boot of his BMW.

"Rutters."

"All right, Skip?"

"Yeah. You?" Bruno's flippant question had a multitude of meaning between the lines. "Shut it off. We need to win this game. But that bloke of yours…" He whistled, shaking his head with a chuckle. "Maybe you need a gagging order on him and not the press."

Jay didn't say anything. He knew what Bruno was getting at. Trouble was, Jay had fallen in love with Seb for his outspoken, candid nature and wouldn't want him any other way. He just hadn't realised quite how much Seb's mouth liked to run away with him when in front of a camera, or a radio mic. He hoped that there would be no fallout to the public declaration that would come back to bite him, or his team, on the arse on the football pitch. He cracked his neck from side to side. *Mind back on football and the game ahead.*

They were the last to arrive in the dressing room, with match day rituals in full swing. All the lads were wearing their training gear until the moment it came to change into the full playing kit. Jay headed for his bench and stripped off his tracksuit into the shorts and training top, then went straight to the gym section to the exercise bikes. Engaging in fifteen minutes of low energy cycles eased his muscles and enabled him to get his mind in gear for the game ahead, shedding the thoughts of what had just happened outside in the real world. At least in here, he was Rutters—private life unspoken. Resting his forearms on the handlebars and head down, Jay set the slow pace and started to visualise the game ahead. He thought about his positioning, where he needed to be in the box to receive a cross ball, his shots at goal and flicked through the videos he'd watched of Chelsea's goalkeeper to remember where the bloke tended to favour his dives.

Once the fifteen minutes were up, Jay leapt off the bike and stood in front of the full-length mirror for his three key muscle group stretches — quads, hamstrings and groin. Davies stood beside him, one earphone in, and bopped away to some R'n'B rap. Each lad on the team had his own way of preparing for a game. Some preferred solitude until the hour on the pitch before kick-off, helping to keep focused. Others listened to music or played computer games in small groups, switching their nerves off that way. Jay focussed on his body, loosening it up and preparing it for the ninety minutes of rigorous exercise. Many of the team were so superstitious they kept to the exact same routine for every game, Jay included. Davies had yet to decide what worked for him, and each match day he tried something different.

"Get the recommended eight hours this time, Davies?" Jay asked, smirking at his reflection.

Davies flicked the bud out of his ear and grinned. "I went to bed at midnight." He lifted his leg behind him, tucking his heel into his backside and stretching out his quads. "Ain't saying I slept though."

"You want a rep, dun't ya?" Jay crossed one leg over the other and bent at the hips to stretch his hamstrings.

"I don't think it matters what I do round 'ere." Davies shoved the bud back into his ear and bopped his shoulders. "It's you who gets all the interest."

"Yeah." Jay stood, swiping his hair back from his face. "Tell me about it."

* * * *

Bounding out of the radio studio and into the bustling streets of London's Soho, Seb slipped on his sunglasses. Overcast grey cloud above, but the shades weren't used for their UV protection. Noah threw a Marlboro Red into his mouth, offering the pack out to Seb. He shook his head. Then backtracked and slid one out, allowing Noah to light it for him. It'd been a while since he had to carry a lighter.

"Perhaps we don't do live interviews?" Martin suggested, tucking his hands into his jacket pockets.

Seb blew out a lungful of smoke into the air and glanced down at the floor. He'd fucked up, he knew that. Not just by proving to the journalists that Seb was a gobby posh boy who could easily be riled up, but because of Jay. He'd made that perfectly clear during the phone call.

Seb opened his mouth to respond, but his buzzing phone prevented the reply. He fished it out of his jeans and closed his eyes on seeing the display.

"Hi." Seb answered, cigarette waggling between his lips. He picked it out with his fingers, exhaled the smoke and awaited the inevitable.

"Seb, it's Ted. From Armstrong Records. We just heard."

"Wonderful." Seb inhaled another lungful of finest Marlboro and the vein in his neck popped out through his clenched jaw.

Martin and Noah hovered beside him, checking their own phones, half listening to Seb's one-sided conversation, half responding to whatever messages bleeped their way after they'd had to switch off correspondence for the two hours in the studio.

Ted chuckled. "You are a whirlwind. Thing is, we're having a ton of interest here about you."

"The band, or just me?"

"They go hand in hand, Seb. You want publicity? You want promotion? You just got it."

Seb pinched the bridge of his nose, almost searing his hair with the tip of his cigarette. He wasn't meant to get attention due to his relationship. It had meant to be for his talent. The band's talent. He wasn't one to seek fame and fortune by bedding a footballer and spilling the beans of their sex life in every tabloid. Seb was a musician. A fucking great musician! He'd now just realised why he should have kept his fucking mouth shut.

"We got offers from pretty much everywhere." Ted's amused voice drilled a hole through Seb's banging temple. Of course Ted would be pleased. Being the main promotion and publicity manager at the independent record label that the Drops had signed to meant they'd all be thrust into the spotlight and the *ka-ching* of pound signs would be evident in the man's eyes.

"Tell me, Ted, are they from reputable music magazines? *NME*? *Kerrang*? Or are we talking the *Sun*, *Take a Break*, The fucking *MailOnline*?"

Ted chuckled.

"Call me when Jools Holland wants to talk to me, not *Loose* fucking *Women*, all right?"

"You offer to talk about your boyfriend, you'll get Phil and Fern."

"Goodbye, Ted." Seb hung up and slipped the phone into his back pocket, his blood boiling.

"You all right?" Martin asked. The concern in his voice tempered Seb marginally.

"What do we want, guys?" Seb inhaled the remaining of his cigarette, flicked the butt to the floor and stamped on it with his All-Stars. "Do we want to be known as musicians, or celebrities?"

"Musicians."

"Celebrities."

Seb narrowed his eyes, working out who had said what. Noah shrugged and Seb got his answer. Noah's track record for picking up groupies and girl band members had also produced a variant of headlines.

"What we want is the biggest audience." Noah flicked off his own fag into the road, smoke wafting from his lips and into Seb's face. "It's all about sales."

"No, it's about being *reputable*." Seb spat back. "We'd rather awards than sales."

"You can say that." Noah pointed a finger. "You've got a rich boyfriend. The rest of us rely on royalties and gig ticket prices."

"We're doing all right." Seb said that like he was trying to convince himself. They were. Money wasn't a huge issue. Seb shared the royalties on a three-way split with the other two, even though he was the main songwriter. But they were a band. It was a group effort, and Seb had never been about chasing the money. As long as he could make a living from his music and never have to run back to Daddy or work in an office again, then he was fine. But Noah was right. Jay was the overall main breadwinner in their relationship and perhaps Seb needed to think about a way to separate that.

"We need to discuss what we want to do next. We're getting traction, interest, and I think the label is going to make us go in a direction I'm not happy about."

"You mean mainstream?" Martin asked.

"Yeah."

Martin and Noah both nodded, like the lapdogs they were, waiting for Seb to make the decisions for them. He sighed. "Come back to mine. We'll watch Jay's match, do a little jamming and figure this shit out."

Martin winced. "Leah."

Seb tutted. "Sure." He turned to Noah, who tapped thumbs across his mobile keypad. "Fancy it?"

"Would have, but I just got a booty call I can't turn down." Noah waggled his mobile. "Dirty Martini's do that special cocktail night from seven, right?"

"Yeah." Defeated, Seb held out a hand to hail an oncoming black cab. "You book a private booth, they chuck in olives and dips."

"So rock and roll." Noah slammed his thumb down on the phone, held it to his ear and walked off. "Private booth for two tonight?"

Martin tapped Seb on the back. "Don't panic. They say no publicity is bad publicity, right?"

"Tell that to Jay." Seb yanked open the black cab's car door and Martin closed it behind him and offered an awkward wave as the cabbie pulled out into the road. On meeting with the driver's bemused gaze in the rear-view mirror, Seb's chest rose.

"'Ere you're that bloke, ain't ya?"

Nodding, Seb glanced out of the window.

"Can I get an autograph?"

"Sure." Seb held out his hand. "You got a pen?"

"Oh, no, I meant from your fella. Massive Hammers fan here."

CHAPTER FIVE
Seeing Red

As soon as his studs sank into the mud, Jay remembered why he did this. Why he took all the shit. If football came without the media attention, that would suit him fine. Playing the game was what he lived for and, even at this moment—centre circle, holding the ball with the toe of his boot—Jay felt at home. And it gave him his purpose.

The stadium, filled to the brim with home and away supporters, burst out the accompanying home-game song from the twenty thousand season ticket holders in the stands. *I'm Forever Blowing Bubbles* always gave Jay the tingles, as well as the motivation he needed. But as he awaited the kick-off, Jay did what he'd learned never to do. He listened to the away side.

The gyrating boom of *Irons* faded to allow the visiting fans to make their mark on the game. Jay hung his head, and desperately willed the whistle to blow so he could drown out the chants along with rhythmic clapping from the minority blues fans. The words Rutters, Rear and Regular just about making themselves heard. Out the corner of his eye, Jay noted the fluorescent-jacket-wearing security trailing over to the away side stands. They obviously expected trouble to break out. The home fans weren't going to take the attempt to get their team's striker off his game lightly.

The match hadn't even started and the unrest in the thirty-five-thousand seater stadium was palpable. *Could this really be all because of me*? The whistle shrilled and, switching his swirling thoughts off, Jay tapped the ball over to Bruno. Chelsea were unrelenting, as they always were. Their attacking game play trumped West Ham's lacking defence system. Keeping the ball away from their half was the main state of West Ham's play. And whilst not a particularly great game to watch, it kept them from conceding and tumbling down the league at this point in the second half of the season.

Twenty minutes in, and Jay got his chance. A sloppy pass from Chelsea's central midfielder at the halfway line landed right at Jay's feet. Dribbling the ball, he pelted away and sprinted, eyes on the prize ahead. He had a clear run, what with all the Chelsea players on the attack the other end of the pitch. Jay pounded the grass, and the fire in his heart fuelled the skill of his studs as he expertly guided the ball toward goal. With one peek up at the keeper, who had drifted out of the box to close him off, Jay stuttered on his boots to swerve around him rather than take the shot from there. As he dropped his left shoulder, faking the direction, he was ready to leap to his right and tap the ball with the outside of his foot, but a hard shunt to his back sent him flying. He landed on all fours at the penalty line, white powder spraying into his face as he skimmed the wet grass and collapsed onto his chest. Having used all his body weight to barge into Jay's back, elbow first, Chelsea's defender hurdled over him, his studs missing Jay's head by mere inches.

The crowd roared and the cheers from the minority away fans did their best to be heard over the disgruntled heckles at the illegal tackle from the home crowd. A brief peek to his right, and Jay met with Alejandro Romero, the blue's giant killer fallback, bending down beside him.

"You wanna play a man's game, you take the hits like a man." Alejandro spat on the grass beside Jay's ear. "Poof." He then straightened and offered out a hand with a smile plastered on for the referee who hurtled toward them, blasting his whistle that out-shrilled the most vocal of fans.

Having forced his mind to close off, Jay had evidently lost his ability to rationalise, and he ignored the hand to twist onto his back, then rammed his studs into Alejandro's shin. Lucky for him, the bloke had his pads on. Unlucky for Jay, Alejandro fell to the floor, clutching his leg and declared foul play. Jay sprang up and loomed over Alejandro, utterly incensed.

"Get up!" His face burned with the force of the words. "You want me to show you who's a fucking man? Get the fuck up!"

The referee finally approached and tapped Jay's chest, urging him away. Bruno bounded over, shoving Jay farther while the referee and the first aiders rushed over to tend to Alejandro.

"Ain't nothin' wrong with him!" Jay yelled, waving a frustrated hand and caring less that all the cameras in the stadium would be on him. Live game, broadcast on Sky Sports One. Jay didn't care. "Get the fuck up!" He forced to get past Bruno, but his captain pushed him away, keeping Jay grounded to the spot.

"Calm it, Jay."

"That was an intentional attack, Skip!" Jay scraped away his sweating hair, trying to get a hold on the anger that seeped from his every orifice. Not only had that been a deliberate foul, it was premeditated, and from behind with no attempt at closing in on the ball. It had been about Jay. And from the man's words, Jay now knew why he'd been the target of such a calculated bad tackle. He shook with the rage that boiled through him.

"Yeah, and the ref'll square it. But you just kicked him, Rutts, when the bloke was helping you up." Bruno wiped his mouth as he spoke in an attempt for any closing-in cameras not to pick up his words.

Jay turned away, unable to look upon the scene of first aiders and the opposition players all rallying around Alejandro on the floor. With one tap to his shoulder, Bruno set off to have a word with the ref. Jay couldn't even face the stands with their continued whistling and chants ringing in his ears. He'd lost it. *Again*. His temper had overruled his couple of years of calm and now threatened his clean record. Hanging his head, he peeked over to the sideline. Sergio, hands on hips, glared back from the edge of the manager's box, the other coaches either side speaking double into his ear, no doubt replanning the next few games.

Jay edged away, wanting the match to restart but the screech of the referee's whistle and demanding wave of the man's hand forced Jay back to the scene. Aided by the physios, Alejandro stood and shook himself out. *What a fucking performance!* Jay clenched his hands into tight balls, fingernails digging into his palms. The ref ushered them both over and away from the other players.

No words spoken, the referee reached into his pocket. Out came the yellow card and he held it in the air

77

in front of Alejandro—booked for the tackle. The defender didn't respond and just spat on the floor. Then came the other card. The ref held it high, his whistle clutched between his lips, and Jay glanced up to his first ever red card.

The stadium erupted. Boos bellowed from the home fans and rivalled the roars of delight from the away crowd. If there had been unrest among the rivals before this, it had just tripled and Jay felt it all the way to his sinking gut. Jay twisted from the ref and walked slowly off the pitch, willing his jelly legs to get him to the safety of the tunnel. The continued chants from the crowd banged through his temple and as he stepped over the pitch line, he met with Sergio's gaze. Sergio marched back to his seat and sat, whispering into the ear of the second head coach, Alonzo, seated beside him. He made no additional eye contact and Jay marched through the tunnel back into the dressing room.

He stripped off his shirt and slapped it to the floor, then with a sudden burst of rage he could no longer contain, rammed his fist into the separating wooden border.

"Oi, oi, none a' that."

Jay twisted, shaking out his hand. Coach Alonzo stood in front of him, clutching a bottle of water that he passed over to Jay. Sitting, Jay swigged and poured the rest over his head, allowing the droplets to slide through his hair and slap to the floor.

"We'll ask for it to be looked at." Jim placed a hand on Jay's shoulder.

"Don't bother."

Jim stood, narrowing his eyes. "You sayin' you weren't provoked?"

Jay looked up, the water sliding down his face and he licked the droplets from his top lip. "Don't matter. I did it."

"Three match ban."

Jay ripped the knots from his bootlaces.

"Gaffer says you wait it out here until the crowds gone. He'll wanna word."

The doors clanged as Jim left. Growling, Jay chucked his boot across the room and the studs ricocheted off the wall to crash down onto the plastic mat below.

* * * *

Seb held his hand over the strings on his guitar and stared up the flat-screen TV mounted to the living room wall. He winced. Setting the light-tan Silvertone Harmony to the floor, he stood to watch the replay. Slow motion, different angle, it still looked painful.

"No doubt about that," the commentator's voice sounded over the roar from the crowds and boomed out of the speakers dotted around the room for optimum listening. "The ref won't let that go without a punishment. Romero was helping him up. No need for that."

Seb scraped two hands through his hair as the television cut from the replay to the live match. Jay's entire face filled the thirty-two inches of flat screen High Definition with his previous displayed anger diminishing to defeat as the ref waved the red card to him. Seb's heart hammered. The camera zoomed in on Jay's face as he walked off the pitch, and Seb witnessed the anguish behind those baby blues he knew so well, usually filled with desire and passion. Unable to listen to the commentary anymore, or watch the Chelsea player's sly wink to his teammate captured by a roaming camera, he switched the screen off and sank down onto the sofa.

This was bad. A year being a footballer's boyfriend and Seb had learned that a loss could affect the mood Jay returned home in. He'd gotten used to how to handle him. Mostly, he gave him space and time. When Jay was ready to move on, probably having relived the match in his head several times, then Jay would seek him out for way to forget the loss and Seb only too happy to oblige. A win and Seb was quids in from the moment Jay walked through the door. Jay hadn't ever been sent off the pitch, nor had Seb ever seen that sheer anger in Jay's face before. Well, once. *New York.*

Tapping his hands on his knees, Seb didn't know what to do. Perhaps him even being at home when Jay returned could be the wrong thing. But then coming in to an empty house could set him off more. After a while of indecisiveness, Seb picked up his mobile and rammed in the dial.

"You saw?" the female voice sighed down the phone.

"Tell me what to do." Seb wasn't too proud to go to Jay's best friend for relationship advice. She'd survived a few years of being a footballer's girlfriend, after all.

"I think this one's out of my jurisdiction."

"Come on, should I piss off for a bit? Or will he want me here? What did you used to do?"

"It's been a long time since I had to deal with all that crap from Jay."

"Please, Ann. Was he ever sent off when you were with him?"

"Yeah, couple of times. For a gentle giant, Jay can sure let rip on the pitch, right?"

Seb bowed his head, scratching his temple. "I've never seen him like that. Well, I have, but not over a football game."

"It's not just a game, Seb. Surely you've learned that much."

"Yeah. I know. So help me."

Ann sighed. "I think the tip is, don't let him wallow too long."

"Right."

"The last red card he had, well, that was the day his life changed. And mine. It's probably a good idea to be mindful of that."

"Shit." Seb bounced his knee, realising he was way out of his depth dealing with this. "Can you come around?"

Ann laughed and it stabbed Seb in the chest. "No, chicken. This one's all yours. Think of it like getting your Scout badge."

"I never made it as a Scout."

"Don't doubt it, mate. Anyway, I gotta go. I'm late."

"Off anywhere nice?"

"Just meeting a friend."

Seb nodded. "Somewhere good?" Perhaps he could turn up with Jay as a distraction method?

"Cocktails at Dirty Martinis."

Seb bit his lip, nodding. "Enjoy, Ann. Be careful."

"It's just a friend."

"Yeah. But still."

"I ain't a fucking damsel in distress, Seb. I can handle my fucking self. You worry about your boyfriend." With that, she hung up.

Seb threw his phone on the cushion beside him and jiggled his legs. After what seemed like ages of silence, he decided to shut off his mind the only way he knew how. He remotely turned on the stereo system and blasted out the multitude of tunes he had stored. Cranking the volume up loud, he got himself a few drinks from the fridge.

After a few tunes to drown out his thumping heart, and downing the leftover wine, an idea hit him. He leapt up from the sofa and skidded on his socks to the cupboard under the stairs. The tool box that Jay's dad had left from his last visit had been pushed to the back, unused. Seb rummaged through and found what he thought — hoped — he needed and bounded up the stairs. The framed photo perched on the chest of drawers in their bedroom was always knocked off every time either of them needed the essentials such as underwear. *Right, time to make a difference.*

He slid his fingers over the images and smiled, then stomped over to Jay's gym and gazed around at the four bare walls, well, except for the pride of place plasma screen that Jay faced when running laps on the treadmill. *Maybe this'll be a better motivator.* He settled the picture frame on the floor against the wall and shrugged.

"Thank you, Dad, for not teaching me essential DIY skills. How the fuck do I do this?" He sighed. He was going into this blind. And he might as well have been as he banged away at the nail and the plaster flaked off in chunks to scatter down to the cream carpet. "Bollocks."

He dropped the nail twice, and bent it, but persevered to hammer the message home. With one last thump, the hammer slipped off the head of the nail and he banged his thumb into the wall instead.

"Shitting, fucking, bollocks!" He jumped in the air, flapping out his hand.

"What ya doin'?"

Seb spun, eyes wide. Jay stood at the doorway, arching an eyebrow beneath his baseball cap.

"Hanging your fucking picture." *So much for making this a romantic gesture.*

Stepping in closer, Jay scraped off his cap and spun it across to land on the treadmill.

"You okay?" Seb kept his voice low. If Jay didn't want to answer, he could pretend he hadn't heard it.

Seb knew the drill for these conversations. Jay never liked talking about his games. He kept his football life separate for a reason. Which suited Seb, as even after a year of pretending to be interested, he hadn't learned the first thing about the rules, especially the offside one. But he was fairly sure that kicking a player in the shin was considered a no-no.

"Fine," was all Jay muttered. The fact he had spoken at all gave Seb an in.

"What did he say to you?"

Jay hung his head. "Ain't important." He crouched and picked up the frame. He looked at it once, sighed, then hung it on the bent hook next to the plasma screen.

"Yes, it is. This is exactly the sort of shit you should be challenging." Seb nodded to the picture. "You need to show those arseholes that they can't get to you, that you don't care."

"Exactly. And I do that by taking the punishment and getting back on the pitch without whining like a bitch about it."

"Baby—"

"I'm too riled to talk."

"Fine." Seb threw the hammer to the floor.

"Why hang it there."

Seb shrugged. "As much as I hate that Yank, what he's done there is genius. You need to remember why you keep going, how far you've come and why you did all this in the first place. Perhaps I shouldn't have got my DIY groove on whilst half cut." He held up his red and swollen thumb.

Jay grabbed Seb's wrist and checked over his thumb. Then, without warning, Jay slid the pounding digit into his warm mouth. Seb inhaled, holding Jay's gaze and his heart hammered, without the use of the discarded tool. Jay could make his heart triple with one look from those piercing baby blues and, as he twirled his tongue around Seb's pounding thumb, Seb's spine prickled and the blood rushed through his trembling body to his sparking groin.

Jay sucked Seb's thumb out from his mouth. "Thank you," he whispered the sentiment.

"You're welcome." Seb tilted his neck, amplifying the wide-eyed puppy-dog look to drastic levels. "Now if you'd like to thank me properly, I believe I may have also banged my dick whilst I was hanging that picture."

Jay snorted a laugh. But behind those dancing blue eyes was something more familiar and Seb tingled with the anticipation. Jay pushed Seb up against the wall, flicking open Seb's button fly and lowered seductively to his knees. Seb let out a deep hum and glided his fingers through the locks of Jay's chair.

"God, I fucking love it when you get on your knees for me." Seb bashed his head against the wall and knocked the picture off from the inadequate nail.

It crashed to the floor, but Seb couldn't have cared less that he'd failed spectacularly at his first DIY stint, because his raging cock was now engulfed in his boyfriend's hot mouth and it was doing things to Seb that he failed to find words for.

And I'm meant to be a lyricist… Oh, God, fuck, yeah!

RUTTMAN SEES RED!

West Ham United's golden boy, Jay Ruttman, receives his first straight red.

Last night's home match against Chelsea saw an aggravated Ruttman launch a vicious kick at Chelsea's Romero after a tackle had brought the Hammer's centre forward down.

Romero was seen to offer his hand to help the east Londoner up when Ruttman retaliated by pelting his studs into Romero's shin.

Referee Graham Attman gave Romero a caution for the elbow to Ruttman's back, but couldn't ignore the blatant attack and dismissed Ruttman for the misconduct, resulting in a three-match ban.

Away fans booed as the Hammer's number nine left the pitch noticeably enraged. Ruttman cursed at the crowd during his march from the game that ended in a two-nil win to Chelsea, making the Hammers tumble farther down the Premier League.

Fans have blamed Ruttman's temper on his recent coming out. Ruttman announced that he was gay and in a relationship with another man at a press conference last year and has since remained closed-off to press engagements and shunned media appearances.

One source has come forward declaring that the angry reaction from Ruttman isn't as out of character as the club have argued. Ruttman had originally been kicked out of West Ham's Youth Academy due to a serious brawl on the pitch with an opposing player when he was seventeen. Our source said, "Ruttman's volatile nature is proving that the pressures of being an out-gay player in the premier league can, and will, affect performance."

The FA have also spoken candidly about the incident, "It now falls upon the club to manage Ruttman's temper and control their striker if he is to continue playing at a top level. We want to see that his behaviour will not be tolerated, and that there is no place for special treatment of any players in the Premier League."

This incident comes as a huge blow to those who believed that Ruttman's coming out was a positive change for the future of professional football.

CHAPTER SIX
Down Play

"Sit." Sergio's stare remained fixed on his clenched hands above the boardroom table-top.

Jay glanced around at the others all waiting for his entrance, from the coaching team, to the PR team, to who knew who else taking up every seat on the large oval table. Monday morning's training session hadn't even begun and Jay had been summoned to the offices. He knew what was coming. He sat as commanded at the opposite end to his manager.

"You understand why I called you here, yes?" Sergio finally laid his dark gaze on Jay.

"Yes, Gaffer."

"Three-match ban."

"Yes, Gaffer."

"And it has been pressured upon us to also fine you. We cannot be seen to be taking this lightly. You understand?"

Jay sucked in his bottom lip, preventing his teeth chattering. This all spelled trouble with a capital Barney. "I understand."

"Three weeks' wages." Sergio nodded to the suited bloke beside him, who wrote a few things down on his papers. That was obviously the finance guy. So many people attached to the club that Jay only knew most by their faces or if they wore a claret lanyard. Perhaps the bloke was PR and going to release how much Jay would be forking out for his indiscretion on the pitch to the press to show that West Ham management were serious about consequences. *Maybe I should have agreed to an agent, after all.*

Jay nodded.

"Is there anything you would like to say?" Sergio raised his dark eyebrows in encouragement.

Jay had already spoken with Sergio straight after the last match. He hadn't told him what Alejandro had said. What would be the point? It would only prove that Jay couldn't handle his emotional fallout when his sexuality was called into question. That would mean he wasn't handling it and he'd snubbed the offer of having support to deal with all this crap. He couldn't afford that. He couldn't let them know that he was an easy target. What would that do to his career? He'd never be off that bench.

"Sorry. It won't happen again."

A hush fell upon the occupants of the table. Sergio remained fixed on Jay. Waiting. Expecting more, perhaps? After an awkward few moments, Sergio scraped his hands off the table and leaned back in the seat.

"I seem to recall you claiming that before."

Jay bit down on his bottom lip, then nodded. "This time, I mean it."

"Uh-huh." Sergio scrubbed a hand over his face. "You see, you have put us in a difficult situation. We put our faith in you. We supported your decision and we backed you all the way. Were we wrong?"

"No."

"If you speak up, we can speak up."

"Ain't nothing to say, Gaffer. He pissed me off, yeah. I should have handled the tackle better. And I will next time."

Sergio threw his pen to the table, his whole demeanour screaming that he wasn't happy about Jay's refusal to pass blame. In the changing room after the send-off, Sergio had asked and asked what had caused Jay's outrage. But what choice did Jay have? All he could do was keep up the pretence that he was like any other man on that pitch who had been stopped at goal line by an illegal move and not that it had anything to do with what Alejandro had uttered into his ear and that still boiled Jay's blood. He was a man. *Am a man. And I belong on that pitch, with all the other fucking men!* But his dad's voice that had been drilled into him since childhood rang in his head – *snitches get stitches.*

"You will have appointments with Candice." Sergio raised his chin at the woman a few chairs away from him.

She smiled, kind grey-blue eyes focusing on Jay.

"For what?" Jay asked.

"She is a sports psychologist. She can talk you through tactics to get your head in the game."

Jay swallowed. "My head is in the game." *It is, ain't it?*

"And not on what people say about you?"

"A lot of people say a lot of shit. About me, about all footballers. Why single me out?"

"Because I cannot have you attacking players when your green monster appears. I need to control it. You need to bury it. Or your career will end before it has begun. This was my fear for you."

Jay folded his arms, bouncing his knee under the table. Two years having studied psychology in sport, he knew what would be coming his way from these sessions. He'd have to talk about how he felt. About Seb. And about why the world couldn't just accept them. *Is it the world? Or is it me?* Sometimes he didn't know. When at home alone, he knew. When football was an issue, he just couldn't see straight. And he was backed into a corner here. He nodded.

"Good. Once a week. After training, I want you here. We will release to the press that you have agreed to anger management and the three week's wages and take full responsibility for your actions. Would you like us to add a quote?"

Jay thought. Long and hard. All he had swirling through his mind seem to come out in Seb's voice—*go fuck yourself.* He shook it free, attempting to find his own words, his own comeback, his own remorse for the situation. Should he apologise? Should he claim it was all his fault? Should he cast aside the years of torment that he, and no doubt the others like him who still remained hidden, had endured on the pitch, in the changing rooms, on the training field? Should he suppress it? *Fuck, I really do need an agent.*

"Just say I regret my actions." Jay stood, and his tense body somehow managed to get him out of the boardroom and out to the training field where he had an even more dispirited session of runs, sprinting drills and tactical playing with the rest of the team for the next four hours.

The lads were clearly pissed off with him for bringing their club into disrepute. Jay threw himself into it, even though he wouldn't be playing a match for at least a month, and attempted to quell the belief from them and the coaching staff that he was a liability. He hadn't spent the best part of his life getting to the top only for one slur from an opposing player, not to mention the jeers from the stands and the vilifying write-ups in the press, to have it all crash down on him. He wasn't. He'd play them all that their game and, come the time to shower and change, Jay couldn't remain silent any longer.

"You all think I shouldn't have done it, dun't ya?" Sitting on the bench, he spoke to the floor, not able to look the remaining members of his team left in the changing room tearing their kit off.

"What? Kick the bastard?" Bruno threw his training top into the laundry bin and rammed his hands on his hips. "No. You shouldn't have."

Jay looked up, realising there were only five others in the room. Davies, the rookie, wiped his hair with a towel and his morbid fascination was evidenced by the chewing on his bottom lip. The other three lads added in their own agreed mumbles to their studs.

"No." Jay stood. "I mean come out."

He waited, sucking in a stifled breath. He knew the answer really, but wanted them to admit it to his face. To get it all in the open and not pussyfoot around why he was getting the cold shoulder from a team who claimed camaraderie was their main asset. It wasn't because he was gay. It wasn't because he preferred men over the hundreds of girls who threw themselves at any given footballer. It wasn't because he was the only one. Because he knew damn well he wasn't. It was that he'd been brave enough to tell the world. *Brave? Or foolish?*

Bruno stood tall, chest rising, and his sharp frustrated exhalation had his nostrils flaring. Davies shuffled awkwardly, probably hoping that his skipper did his job and ended this before it got out of hand. Jay eyed the other three, Halliday, Santiago and Cooper, who all gave varying degrees of pointed looks.

"I told you, Rutters." Bruno's voice wasn't as forceful as his stance. "Football ain't just a sport. It's a livelihood for us. That shirt is a fucking badge of honour and should be treated as such."

"You sayin' I don't treat it like that?"

"What I'm saying is, you gotta be careful. We all get shit thrown at us, we all have to deal with it. But yours, *fuck*, Jay, yours is gonna be slung at all of us from a great height. And if you can't handle that, then, well, maybe you *were* wrong to come out. And wrong not to have someone running your side for you."

That was another slap to his face. "Right." It was the only thing he could muster to say.

"I think you're a great player. A fucking brilliant striker." Bruno waved his hand at the others, forcing their agreement. "We all do. But it ain't just about what you can do with that left foot of yours. It's about what you bring to the team. And at the moment, Rutts, you've brought us headaches. I don't give a fuck who you sleep with. Couldn't care less. I don't want to think about what any of these lads get up to of a night time. But as soon as it affects them on the pitch, it affects the whole goddamn team. You get?"

Jay nodded. "Yeah. But it ain't like I can take it back now, is it?"

"You want to?"

Jay paused. "No." The reply didn't come as quickly as Seb probably would have preferred. But at least he'd said it.

"My advice, and it ain't just for you, it's for all of you." Bruno grabbed a towel from the pile on the bench. "Play football. Play fucking great football. Don't give anyone a reason to think you ain't thinking, dreaming, or even fucking football. That's what you are now. A footballer. There's nothing else to you. As soon as you give them something else, you've given the haters a bullet. Don't provide ammunition. Provide a great show for the football fans. They pay your wages."

With that, Bruno stomped off to the showers and left Jay to change alone with his silent teammates, pondering how much of what Bruno had said he should agree with.

* * * *

Seb listened to the recorded track alongside their label's producer, Harvey, and tapped his foot in time with the beat. He swivelled in the huge leather armchair, wondering whether the new song would fit as their new release or stay as an album filler. It was good. Punchy bass, banging drums, and his guitar solo screeched at all the right moments. His voice was a little off in places and could do with a second go on the lyrics, but all in all it was six hours well spent in the Dalston studio.

Harvey clicked off from the audio mixer and faced the three of them. Noah and Martin stood behind Seb, no doubt waiting for their front man's sign off. Time in the fully kitted-out studio cost a fortune, but they needed a step up from their home efforts now they were hitting the big time. The added pressure of knowing they only had a limited time in the professional suite aided Seb's need to

94

get everything right within a time frame. Notorious for tinkering, Seb couldn't afford to keep trying new angles with snare sounds and microphone set-ups, so he nodded and clapped his hands once, rubbing them together as he stood from his seat.

"We'll go with that." He held out his hand to Harvey.

"You sure? We got time for another go?"

Seb exchanged glances with the others. He was well aware they were hitting their longest spell in a studio to date. But they had a rash of gigs coming up, as well as media appearances to promote the festival circuit that loomed on the horizon. It would be a foolish not to squeeze every second out of their pre-paid recording sessions. And to get it perfect.

Seb checked the clock above the door. Jay would only be getting home from training to go for his pre-scheduled nap time. No point rushing, especially as Jay wasn't exactly in the best of moods. He'd had three weeks of dealing with Jay's dwelling on what had happened, and he wasn't willing to get into another argument about how Jay should be dealing with it.

The weekend had been spent with Jay plodding around the house avoiding any media, including turning the television on, opening a newspaper or firing up anything connected to the internet. Seb had been banned from scrolling the outcries after Jay's match or mentioning the red card at all. It meant that the boredom led to many a bedroom session, which Seb couldn't begrudge, but he was well aware that Jay would be facing it all today. And Seb had no idea what the fallout from that would be.

"Yeah. All right. Let's go another round." Seb nodded to Martin and Noah, then headed through to the

95

performance space and picked up his guitar from the stand.

He stood in front of the vocal microphone and slipped on the headgear that he'd left on top of the stand. Nothing like a bit of music producing to help him forget the woes of being a footballer's boyfriend. Martin and Noah took up their positions, adjusting microphones and equipment. Receiving the nod from Harvey through the glass, the three-piece started up with their latest track. Seb focused on his voice this time, and not on what would be waiting for him at home.

The next hour was spent mixing the track, perfecting the sound, and signing it off as a completed record, and Seb emerged from the studio into the bustle of London with revived energy.

"Check your emails when you get home. The list of gigs from AR will have been sent through and we need to discuss the set lists." Seb tapped his bandmates' clenched fists and shoved on his shades.

"We not getting any time off over summer?" Noah grouched.

"You want fame and fortune? Holidays are a thing of the past, my friend."

"Slave driver." Martin clicked on the fob for his Audi parked up behind Seb's camper van along the street. Thank fuck they'd found a studio that offered visitor parking permits, or they'd be forking out a lot more in parking fines.

"Tell me that after V Fest when the royalties come tumbling in, yeah?" Seb grinned and slid open the door to his VW.

He waved off the others and started the engine, music pelting from the speakers, and sped off into the early evening traffic. Slapping the steering wheel in sync with the drum rolls, he made his steady journey back to Greenwich with a clear head. Even scrunching tyres onto the gravel driveway and seeing their mailbox at the front entrance filled to the brim with unopened mail didn't damper his mood of a successful day. He jogged over to the box and yanked out the post. Flicking through, he shoved all the envelopes he knew were bills to the back and wondered whether the handwritten post was worth even opening. Hate mail often got confused for fan mail.

Letting himself into the house, he listened out for any movement. *Silence.* Jay was most probably still on his R & R time. So Seb slammed the post onto the unit by the door and headed straight for his laptop in the music room to print out the list of gigs and festival tours. Rhythmic pounding from above caught his attention, along with fierce, deep grunts.

"What the…" Scrambling past the drum kit, Seb bounded out and up the stairs.

The door to the gym was open and a deep drone of male voices resonated through the walls. Seb paused at the door frame and watched. Jay, dripping sweat from his entangled hair, and vest and shorts covered in wet blotches, sprinted on the treadmill, eyes focused on the plasma screen. Seb peered around. Sky Sports News presenters talked through the weekend's football results and when Seb flicked his attention back to Jay, the distress was evident over his boyfriend's scorching red face.

"You okay?" Seb called over the drone from the treadmill belt, Jay's pounding feet and the squawking of football pundits on the screen.

"Yeah. You?" Jay's voice warbled along with the rickety belt.

Seb stepped in closer. "Shouldn't you be resting?"

97

"No."

Seb looked at the time on the screen. "Normally it's shut-eye now, right?"

Jay glared at him, upping the pace on his strides.

"All right, whatever." Seb held his hands up in defence. He'd learned when to have an opinion on Jay's schedules. "You want dinner?"

"I'll do somethin' after this."

Seb bit his lip. Something was off. Jay was off. Seb could tell when he wasn't needed, or wanted. He'd had enough of those brush-offs in his life to get the hint. So he went to walk back out when the whirring of the treadmill suddenly stopped. Jay grabbed the remote from the shelf on his monitor screen and cranked up the volume on the TV.

"And what do you think about the three-week fine that West Ham have issued Ruttman for his lash out on Saturday's game?" the dark-haired pundit asked the other three behind the newsroom desk.

Seb winced. "Jay, should you be—"

"Shh!" Jay turned the volume up higher.

"It definitely proves a point," the Liverpool-accented man behind the desk replied. "Ruttman acted like a spoiled brat on that pitch. He's not above the laws of the game. He hasn't matured on the pitch like those come up from the Academy ranks, so maybe this will set him on a career-defining path."

"True, true." The main presenter nodded. "And Romero's talk with us after the game was humble, stating he misjudged the tackle and in no way said anything to warrant the attack. Could this be a case of Ruttman not being ready for professional-level football? Especially considering his recent coming out—"

The screen flipped to black.

Seb sighed. "Champ, remember our motto?"

"Fuck 'em." Jay scraped his sweating hair back from his face. "It's fine. I'm fine."

Everything suggested he wasn't, but Seb left it at that. "Three-week-wages fine?"

"Yeah, coincide with not playing for three games. Plus I get to see a head shrink. It's fine. I'll get through the rest of the season, then summer break can't come quick enough."

Seb smiled. "Atta boy. You can come to all these then." He fished out the paper of his festival gigs and waved it in the air.

"What's that?"

"Every gig the Drops are playing. Be good to have you in the crowd. Like all good boyfriends should be." He winked.

Jay grabbed the towel slung over the arm rests and hopped off the treadmill. "I thought we'd get away. Far away."

"Manchester far enough away?" Seb queried, wincing as he searched his boyfriend's face for a hopeful affirmative.

Jay flung the towel over his shoulder and approached Seb by the door. Knowing that look in Jay's eyes, Seb braced for the impact.

"I don't think it's gonna be wise to come along. In spite of all this shit." At least Jay had the decency to look mildly perturbed by the admittance.

"Right." Seb was less diplomatic. "Not even V Fest? My headline?"

"You know that one lands at the beginning of next season. I won't have the fixtures til summer, so can't guarantee I'll be around."

"That's the only excuse?"

"Don't do it, babe. Please." Jay's shoulders deflated, like he'd been poked with a pin and burst. "I've had a gutful from every fucking angle. I can't take it from you and all. You knew the deal."

"The deal? Enlighten me, Champ, 'cause I thought the deal was we deal with it." Seb folded his arms, desperate not to be taken in by the pitiful blue glaze.

"The deal is we don't go ramming it down people's throats. Don't give them ammunition."

"This is new. What happened to 'fuck em?'"

"It got me a three-match ban, a sixteen-grand fine and anger management training." Jay wiped his face with the towel draped over his shoulder. "It's football, Seb."

"Don't I fucking know it."

"I'm gonna shower. Then I'll make us some dinner."

Seb nodded as Jay brushed past him and into the main bathroom. The shower whirred to life shortly after. Not even the promise of one of Jay's perfectly balanced meals could lift the dull ache left in Seb's chest that he'd yet again be alone at his biggest gig to date. Martin now had Leah, and Noah had whoever was flavour of the month.

Seb, he'd be sharing his hotel rooms with petulant after thoughts.

The Drops Finish Spectacular Tour at V Fest

The festival season comes to an end later this week at V Festival, where the Drops are headlining, bringing an end to their first sell-out UK Tour.

The Drops began their tour at London's Hammersmith Apollo in May and have been playing all the major city venues and festival circuits, showing those who believed their success was a flash in the pan that they deserve the top spot.

The three-piece have thrown themselves into their live performances, proving that giving away tracks for free can aid visibility and create mass hysteria for live show tickets. Each date has been sold out, with many tickets being going on the black market for a price well into the hundreds.

Front man Seb Saunders said of the success, "It's blown us away. It's awesome. We're here. We've made it. We're not going anywhere. Enjoy the show, guys. It's going to be one to remember. I guaran—f***ing—tee it!"

One person was noticeably missing from the gigs. Jay Ruttman, West Ham footballer, has been linked to the lead guitarist and main songwriter of the Drops but his absence from any of the UK wide touring dates has fuelled speculation that their romance isn't in as good a state as the Drops' record sales.

Ruttman was sent off last football season after a fierce attack on an opposing player, sparking rumours that his out-gay status is affecting his career. Ruttman declined to comment on this piece.

CHAPTER SEVEN
Mosh Pitt

August 2007

The crowd went wild. Just the way Seb liked them.

The screams, the whistles, the thunderous applause and, not to mention, the outbreak of a fight below adding to the hedonistic thrill that Seb lapped up like liquor and nicotine. To be fair, a Drops gig was never complete without the security guards working for their money by having to break up a mosh pit brawl or two. Or three, or four. And this lot were currently working pretty damn hard for their hefty contract fee.

Seb stood, front centre stage, and slung his modified custom-designed metallic red-wine Gibson over his neck by its strap and settled it at hip height. His heart thumped in sync with the pounding of Hunter wellington boots stamping in the soggy mud. Martin to his left, jet-black hair spiked up with streaks of deep blue gleaming

103

off the spotlights, tinkered with his Jaguar bass and Noah, his dirty blond hair shaved down to a buzz cut and with a new bolt eyebrow piercing, lifted his sticks in the air at the ready behind his burgundy-red SJC full custom drum kit. The three-piece emulated the live version of their latest album cover—the perfected image of a rock ensemble; the one Seb had spent the best part of six years creating. Except Seb couldn't hold his usual morose expression he plastered on for the press photos. Instead, he grinned. *Widely*. He kinda wished he could take a picture of the moment. On his new iPhone camera. Like the fifty-thousand-strong audience were obviously doing as the flashes flickered before his eyes. Hopefully he'd get a squizz at some of the pictures later. *Thank fuck for social media.*

The spring and summer gigging circuit, with a few small-town festivals thrown in for good measure, could never have prepared him for this. Several hundred people swarmed to the front of the barriers, arms flailing over to reach him but batted off by the dozens of fluorescent-jacketed men. The hammering late-summer rain hadn't scared the fans off, so Seb doubted the beefy guards were going to either. During the years he'd been on the other side of the gates, he hadn't been dissuaded to clamber over and cop a feel of those that he idolised, so he shouldn't let the ones who were testing the boundaries of the best spot on the field—front row at the V Stage— depart home without a lasting memento. Crouching, he swung his guitar behind him and leaned forward to grab a few hands. *This* was fucking aces. *This* was everything he'd dreamed about since the age of sixteen and then some. *This is awesome as fuck.*

Leaving them all to scream, faint and whatever else they did after touching their idol's flesh, he settled back to his starting position, gazed out at the sea of bodies and inhaled a flurried breath. Now for the hard part. Because this was it. They'd made it to V Fest as headliners. All those years' hard slog, and Seb's dream had come true. The screams, the cheers, the throwing of bottle caps through the crowd were all for him. And he fucking loved every second of it.

He kept the fans waiting, though. Shrugging, teasing his fingers over his guitar strings, adjusting the microphone, then finally turned his back on the crowd. *Let them work for it.* Smiling, Seb nodded to the others. Noah struck up with a cymbal crash that elevated the shrieks from the mosh pit and the kick drum thumped through Seb's feet to vibrate the tips of his fingers. Martin plucked his strings, rocking the introductory bass line that rumbled through Seb's entire body, reconfirming why Seb lived for these moments.

Seb swivelled, his lips finding the microphone. He opened his mouth, but the whistles from the crowd drowned him out. Laughing, his breath blew out of the festival sound system as if it were the gale force wind predicted to hit the Essex countryside shortly. He stopped, stepped back and checked his watch. Slapping his arms down to his side, the metal wriggled back over the Chinese symbol tattooed on his wrist.

"Anyone know the score?" Seb's voice boomed around the five hundred acres of field land.

Screams. Whistles. *Catcalls.*

"No?" Seb fished out his phone from his back skinny jeans pocket. A couple of swipes and the brand-new iPhone illuminated his face. This miracle of 3G shit was awesome, and a fucking necessity now he came to think about it. How had he coped before not being able to get the net on his phone? *But, bollocks.* Sighing, he leaned

105

into the microphone. "Nil nil." He lined up his fingers to the tune of Martin's bass line, then strummed the A chord. "Come on, Rutters!"

The crowd roared. And Seb awarded them with the latest tune to have hit number one in the indie rock charts. The response from the waves of fans was as satisfying as his boyfriend's response to that morning's vigorous sex session. A summer mostly apart, and without the pull of football, had rejuvenated their relationship and he didn't even care that he'd broken their cardinal rule by mentioning Jay's name out loud again.

Because Seb was on top. Like he'd also been that morning.

* * * *

Wiping the sweat from his brow, Jay peered up at the crowd from the penalty spot. Home and away supporters heckled their unease as the scorching hot sun blazed down onto the pitch. The earlier rainstorm had caused an oppressing humidity for mid-August in the city, and it was obviously getting to those standing in the terraces, as well as the players on the grass.

The three-match ban from last season meant Jay had had to sit on the bench for the final important fixtures of 2006/7. Nearing the end, there had only been a handful of games for Jay left to play, with West Ham in danger of hitting the relegation zone. It had pained him to have to sit on the sidelines, unable to do anything to add a few points in goals to their overall season record. It wasn't until mid-April that Jay had managed to get his studs back on the grass and, with a little help from the anger management and psyche sessions, he'd finished the season caution free. He'd even scored a few goals, saving

West Ham from relegation to the Championship and remaining in the Premier League. He'd received a victory night out with the team after that. He'd not invited Seb, because, well…*reasons*, and Seb had either been rehearsing or gigging, anyway. That was all it was. *Honest.*

Jay had used the summer down-time to clear his head. Whilst he'd thought he'd get to spend time with Seb away from prying eyes, media attention and football fans, that hadn't been possible with the band on their fleeting tour of the UK. Mostly Jay had stayed at home, reeling in the guilt that he hadn't attended any of Seb's gigs, yet not bringing himself to be the centre of another pap storm. His club-led sessions in mindfulness had seemed bizarre and hippyish to start with, but after he'd practiced his mantra in front of the mirror for two solid months, the difference within himself was noticeable to his team on return and he was a positive driving force for the season's kick off. Last year he would certainly never have allowed Seb's morning wake-up session. Not before a match. But he had, and he didn't regret it. And he'd found a way to filter out the crowd taunts. By playing football.

The afternoon's weather wasn't the only oppression on the field, though. The game itself had stirred unrest in him since receiving the fixture list a few weeks back. This inaugural match wasn't going to be an easy ride. The opposition, last year's Premier League winners, would be out to defend their title. And they weren't going to give West Ham, and especially not him, Jay "Rutters" Ruttman, an easy slide home.

Because this was the first match against Chelsea, reuniting Jay with blues fall-back, Alejandro Romero, on *Romero's* home turf, Stamford Bridge. The blues were top of the league for a reason, and they intended to keep it that way by crushing West Ham's strategy to start the season with an attacking mentality. Especially Romero, who hadn't seemed to have adopted Jay's 'forgive and forget' methods, if his permanent grimace since meeting Jay in the tunnel before kick-off was anything to go by. *Just get through these ninety minutes, head held high.*

Launching away from his defender, Jay called for the ball from Santiago's throw-in at the touchline and the moment his studs hit the leather, Jay swerved and headed toward goal at elevated speed. The thwack from his toe to the ball ricocheted through his leg, emulating the vibrating goalpost as the ball slammed off it.

"Bollocks!" Jay's curse leapt through his chest. But he didn't have time to dwell on the near miss as the rowdy stands overpowered him with their boisterous chants and infantile boos designed to put him off his game.

Bruno clapped his hands together, yelling at the team to keep it up. He nodded to Jay across the field, tapping his head. Jay acknowledged his attempt at steering Jay back to the game and he did when he eyed the oncoming ball. Davies had managed a blinding tackle from a blue shirt, and the West Ham players all pelted forward ready to receive a pass any which way it came. Davies had been given a starting position after his successful stint during the couple of friendlies in July, which had clearly given him the boost he needed. Jay watched, impatiently bouncing on the spot, as Davies dribbled the ball down the left, adding a few unnecessary foot skills just to keep the away fans cheering, then sped out from under a defender's arm. Showboating aside, Davies was good. Short, zappy and if he could get the pass over the heads of the Chelsea defenders, then Jay had a clear shot to the back of the net, making the gaffer's tactic of him remaining near the keeper all that more satisfying.

Davies peered up, tracking the distance to Jay as a decent midfielder should, then booted the ball with the inside of his right foot. *Fuck!* For all of Davies' earlier skill, he'd miscalculated the kick and the ball sailed toward Jay but not high enough for his head to pound it home to goal. Leaping in the air, Jay puffed out his chest, the ball hit him just below his right shoulder and he guided it down to his feet. He still had a chance. Not a perfect shot, not when Chelsea had had the chance to reach him and prevent an effort from the edge of the penalty box by sending in blocks and tackles from all angles. A quick rethink and Jay's boots would have to do the fancy work by edging forward and sliding the ball through the keeper's legs. *Nutmeg it. That'd be good for a morale boost!*

Johnson, Chelsea's new signing and beast of a defender, came from the right and hurtled his bulky six-foot-two body towards him, attempting to get his boots between Jay's legs. Shoving him off with his elbow, Jay sped away. Summer had also seen Jay take on extra gym sessions to toughen his physique and it had worked. With the ball under his control, he went forward for the attack. Flashes of colour, mainly blue, rushed forward, closing in. The back of the net was in his sights, and Jay did one last check on the goalkeeper's whereabouts to ensure a blast at target couldn't be saved. Then he spied the oncoming blue shirt from the corner of his eye. He needed to take the shot, now, before—

The deep *crack* set his teeth on edge, and searing pain shot out from his knee, up to his spine and ambushed any response he could have made. His boot slid on the wet grass and he hurtled into the air, dazed, confused. All he could make out through the throb was

109

the screech of a whistle and the roars from the crowds before his nose made contact with the soggy soil, followed by the crunch of his knee impacting on the ground.

Then everything went black.

* * * *

A two-hour set and Seb's adrenaline seared through his entire body as he raged his fingertips over the strings for the climax of not only the last song, but the Drops' final moment on their biggest stage to date. The atmosphere glorious, the rapturous roars from the crowd a euphoric delight, and Seb couldn't quite believe it was going to be over. He could have stayed up here forever, basking in the attention. He threw himself around the stage, sweat pouring from every inch of his skin, and his heart throbbed in sync with Martin's bass. Banging his head with every thump of Noah's pounding drums, he landed on his knees as the high-pitched squeal of his final chord ricocheted off the speakers and vibrated the stage. This was fucking magnificent.

Wiping his brow, he stood and stared out to the spirited crowd, their continued screeching and applause outdoing his pulsating heart that had tripled in beats. He breathed it all in and held out his arms, guitar dangling from around his neck. Maybe a bit too much showmanship, but *fuck it*. This was what he lived for. This was what he had been working so fucking hard for. *Bollocks to modesty*. They rocked that stage. *He* rocked that stage. And every person screaming his name confirmed it with elevating enthusiasm.

"Thank you!" Seb wrapped his hand around the microphone and saluted to the horde. "We've been the Drops. And you've been fucking awesome! Good night."

With that, he flipped his guitar from around his neck and followed Noah and Martin off to the wings and away from the performance area. Both looked as awestruck as he. Noah kept his drumsticks in the air as he bounced down the ramp to land on the concrete cordoned off from the crowd. Vans, trucks and tents all acted as a barrier to the outside world and staff scurried about to ensure a smooth process. Seb looked around for his event crew, wanting to offload his guitar and get out front to enjoy the rest of the bands that the festival had on offer. He had to soak up that atmosphere for as long as possible. He'd just found a new addiction, and it wasn't an artificial one for once.

"Seb!"

Seb whipped around at the hollering of his name. Leah, pink hair and short dungarees thrown over a Drops' tour T-shirt clutched a clipboard to her chest and adjusted her headset. Seb smiled, but the V-stage crew manager, and Martin's now girlfriend, had a look on her face Seb couldn't place. Nor did he think right then that he wanted to. That look was going to ruin his high. Had they fucked up? Had he said something he shouldn't? Probably. *Bollocks.*

"It's Jay."

Right, so that means a loss. Jay hadn't won. *Which, yeah, is a pretty shit start for Jay. Typical.* Still, nothing could stop Seb's high. He'd call him. Tell him to get his arse in gear and get down here. There were still bands to see, people to meet, fan memorabilia and, probably, skin to sign. Seb's adrenaline-induced high was enough for them both. Getting drunk would sort Jay's moping out. No problem.

He fished his phone out from his back pocket, and several missed calls and texts filled up all the space on his screen. He could vaguely make out Leah was still talking to him while he scrolled through.

"Hmm?" Seb furrowed his brow. *Which text should I reply to first?*

"Jay. I think it's bad." Leah squeezed his shoulder and Seb finally looked up to the worry lines wrinkling her forehead. He glanced back to Martin, panic crossing his perspiring features too. What the fuck had he missed here?

"What?" Seb clutched the phone, a sudden dull ache forming in his chest.

"There was an accident." Leah backed off, standing beside Martin. "On the pitch."

"What kind of accident?"

Something scratched Seb's whole body, as if he were being grated like cheese for the Jacket Spud vans lining up the festival field.

Leah swallowed, licking dry lips and glanced from Martin to Seb. "He collapsed on the pitch. They stretchered him off and took him to hospital. London, I think."

Blood drained from Seb's face, his previous euphoria shifting wildly to panic stations. He was having trouble understanding anything. His ears still rang from the two-hour set, with him not having bothered to wear the headgear that drowned out his muse—the squealing and deafening rumble of his electric guitar and the screams from fifty thousand onlookers.

"But he's all right? Like, just a bang to the head or something?" Seb's voice crackled with the uncertainty.

112

"The news says he needs surgery."

Seb's phone slipped from his hand and his mouth fell open. What had she just said? *Surgery?* Jay was just playing football. *Like he does every fucking day!* He was a fucking expert at it. *That's what professional means, right?* What could have caused him to need surgery, and this fucking quick? Crouching, Seb picked up his phone and wiped the now cracked screen, cutting his finger in the process, and managed to open a couple of messages. His throat caught.

"We'll get you a car." Leah scurried off and Martin helped Seb to his feet.

"You all right, mate?"

"I don't get—" As he clicked on another message, Seb froze.

Shit. Shit. Shit. He didn't wait for Leah's return and shoved everything with Martin, bolting over the gated barriers and toward the VIP car park where his VW Camper Van sat tucked in with the other motor homes. He couldn't be sure he didn't scrape some of them in his haste to get out of the packed field and out onto the road.

Bombing down the A12 rattled the hinges of the van that wasn't built for speed. Right then, he wished he'd come in Jay's sports coupe. Or his father's Audi. Both better prepared for the ninety mph he hit, caring less about the cameras that would snap his illegal limit. But he had hoped to be sleeping under the stars in the van he'd modified for those exact purposes. He gripped the steering wheel, his knuckles fading white, and rammed the foot on accelerator pedal to the floor. His phone rang beside him on the passenger seat and he fumbled to answered it. Tucking the mobile between his chin and shoulder, he held onto the steering wheel. To keep the car steady or him, he wasn't sure.

"Don't panic drive." The sharp east London accent sounded distant, and hoarse. But it still made Seb breathe a sigh of relief.

"Baby."

"I'm all right." Jay coughed, not really backing up his words. "Just a bad tackle."

"Yours or theirs?"

"Theirs. Brought down goal line on a run. Stud to the knee and landed on my face. I passed out."

"Shit." Seb would have closed his eyes if he didn't fear he'd slam straight into the motorway barrier. "Where are you?"

"Royal Brompton. I need an op."

"What? Why?"

"Knee. It's pretty smashed up. So the quicker they get on it the better." Jay sounded distant, and not just from the hundred miles of separation between them. He was slurring.

"Fuck, Jay. You okay? I mean, really?"

"I'm a bit high on meds right now."

Seb snorted, though he didn't really feel it. "And there I was thinking I'd be the one offered drugs today."

Jay's chuckle was strangled. "Sorry, babe. I know you had other plans for tonight."

"Don't be daft." Seb couldn't bear the regret in Jay's voice. It hit him right where it hurt.

"I gotta go." Jay coughed again. "Take it easy, yeah? That van ain't built for speed."

Didn't Seb know it. "I love you."

Silence. Seb threw the phone on the passenger seat to concentrate on getting to London. Thank fuck that for once he'd been the professional and not drunk before his V Fest set.

It took a couple more hours before Seb had abandoned the van in the car park of the Royal Brompton and was pacing the sterile waiting area of the private Orthopaedic wing. His boots clonked and squeaked against the freshly cleaned floor. He couldn't sit down. Too antsy. He drank enough coffee to keep him awake for three weeks, and flipped through every magazine on the stand. Bryan, Barbara and John had been and gone. Some of Jay's club staff had hung around until evening became more middle of the night, but now Seb was left alone with his thoughts.

One of the nurses took pity on him and switched on the television monitor to give him something to do, but probably in an attempt to stop him distracting them from their nightly work. Sitting on the squishy leather chairs, he bounced his knees as the evening news filled the screen.

Ten minutes in and the sports roundup came on, the main story of the day detailed from a morose reporter. Jay Ruttman, West Ham striker, stretchered, unconscious, off the football pitch after a high leg tackle by Alejandro Romero. Seb stood and watched the footage in slow motion, rage shaking his entire body as he witnessed the stud indenting into Jay's knee, sending him flailing into the air and then crashing down, face-first, followed by his knee crunching under him.

Seb hung his head. That tackle was premeditated. And as the TV zoomed in on Alejandro's face demanding for Jay to get up, Seb now knew why. Amazingly, the game didn't end there, regardless of their striker being rushed off by ambulance to a waiting hospital. *Send on a sub and forget about him!*

"Mr. Saunders?" A nurse's voice from behind snapped him to reality. "He's awake. Groggy. In pain. We do only allow immediate family members at this time of night—"

"I am family."

The nurse nodded, understanding and sympathy primed and displayed. She ushered him to follow. He did, unsure what he was going to be walking into. The back wing was private rooms only, separated from the standard shared NHS ward. The club paid for the best in private healthcare and had obviously given the go-ahead for Jay to undergo immediate surgery and get a quick repair of the damage to their asset.

The nurse pushed open the door with her back, allowing Seb to walk in and he sucked in an apprehensive breath. Jay, covered in a white gown and a blue sheet draped to his midsection, lay out on the bed. A huge, bulky padding bandaged his left leg and his face was bruised as if he'd been in a boxing ring rather than on a football pitch. His puffy eyes fluttered open and found Seb's.

Seb focused on that leg, that body in disarray. The one he knew intimately. Shock didn't cover this one. That body was his temple, a work of pure art. And now it lay there damaged. Seb couldn't seem to find any words for how he felt. None that came to mind nor should be uttered in front of Jay. He had to remain calm. This was about Jay and not him.

"Hi." Jay's voice came out twisted. "Ain't you meant to be in Chelmsford?"

"Yeah." Seb stepped farther into the room to stand awkwardly beside Jay's bed. He peered over to the nurse, nodded his thanks and she left them to it, the door falling to a close after. "You should have been too."

"Yeah. Sorry about that."

"Fuck V Fest." Seb meant it. He took Jay's hand, linked their fingers and kissed his knuckles.

After a brief moment of silence, Seb couldn't help but ask, "What does this all mean?"

"It means you might have to learn to cook."

"No panic. I know a ton of really good takeaways." Leaning forward, Seb planted a chaste kiss to Jay's lips so as not to hurt his already bruised face. "But, I mean, for you."

"This op'll fix it. I might be off for half this season. I'll need plenty of physio, but I'll be back."

"I'm so sorry, baby. That fucker did this on purpose."

"It's football, Seb. Leave it where it is."

"Football? That would be a court order on the street."

"It wasn't on the street. It was in a game."

"That makes it all right?" Seb's voice elevated. "You cannot tell me you won't do something about this!"

"Like what?"

"Press charges."

"No, Seb. He'll get a ban. A fine. That's football."

Seb held his breath, and his tongue. This wasn't the place to argue. Not with Jay looking every bit beaten already.

"Promise me you won't do anything, y'know, about it."

"I can't, can I? That would mean breaking our cardinal rule."

"Just leave it to the professionals to sort out." Jay tugged his hand, allowing Seb to lower himself and stroke his forehead to Jay's.

"Shit, Jay, don't fucking scare me like that ever again. You hear me?"

Jay smiled, albeit twisted.

OUT AGAIN!

West Ham striker suffers serious blow to knee during first game of the season.

Jay Ruttman received a horrific injury to his left knee after a high legged tackle from Chelsea's Alejandro Romero.

This first game of the new season saw Ruttman reuniting with Romero who had been involved in Ruttman's controversial sending off last season.

Ruttman was immediately rushed to Royal Brompton Hospital in Chelsea, West London, where it has been confirmed that the Hammer's main centre forward has an extensive rupture to his anterior cruciate ligament. Ruttman will be undergoing essential knee surgery to repair the damage.

Recovery is usually expected within a six to nine-month timeframe, keeping Ruttman out for most, if not all, of the current season which will have a serious impact on West Ham United's ongoing season efforts.

Hammers fans have launched an uproar about the attack, saying that their striker was targeted on the pitch and have called for the FA to investigate.

More controversial fans have argued that Ruttman should never have been allowed to play after last season's controversy, stating, "He proved last season he can't be trusted. We should have sold him in the summer signings. Now we have no striker to take his place, or the money to buy one come the next transfer window. It was blindsided of Amodoro to keep Ruttman in the team."

Since coming out as gay, Ruttman has been the subject of controversy for the football establishment. His decision to come out was backed by his club, but he has since received criticism that his selfish approach has caused his team to suffer the effects alongside him.

CHAPTER EIGHT
Speechless & Redundant

October 2007

"I made breakfast." Seb's voice, although light, had an air of exasperation to it that Jay could hardly blame him for.

"Ain't hungry." Jay's muffled reply was shrouded by the mound of soft pillows that he had his head buried amongst.

The soggy remnants and bitter, stagnant scent of tears smeared into the soft cotton had become an all-too-familiar wakeup call for Jay over the past few months. He'd obviously fallen back to sleep and lived in another reality for a while. One where he wasn't broken. *Damaged.* At the ripe old age of twenty-four. The scratching of metal poles along the curtain rail had snapped him back to reality, and the usual morning throbbing pain caused his outright depressive mood. *Can't snap me outta that, can it?*

"I didn't ask if you were hungry."

Jay didn't move. He couldn't breathe under the pillows. Certainly not for long anyway but he vowed to remain there until he could be alone again. He couldn't face Seb's pissed-off face, or worse his sympathetic, let-me-look-after-you one. Seb, unfortunately, had also become all too familiar with Jay's tactics and was obviously waiting it out until he came up for the essential oxygen.

Eventually, Jay scraped his head to the side and sucked in the cool air. Peeping open one eye, he prepared for whichever Seb waited for him at the end of his bed.

Seb looked like he'd been punctured. "You need to get up. I'll help." He stepped forward.

"I'm fine lying down."

Seb shuffled back and chewed his bottom lip. The usual appearance of a man who was treading on egg shells. Jay had put them there, yet couldn't muster the strength to clear them up.

One operation hadn't immediately fixed the problem on his knee, and the couple of months suggested recovery time had now crept by with no real progress to Jay's damaged anterior cruciate ligament—a rather important part of his knee that enabled for a pain-free walk, let alone sprint running. So they'd gone for full-out physiotherapy and rest, that Jay had taken to mean he shouldn't move. Or that was what his crippled self-confidence was telling him.

"Put some clothes on and come downstairs." Seb slid open the walk-in wardrobe.

"There was a time you wanted the opposite of that." He had no idea why he thought that would be the best thing to say at that moment. Or any moment, for that matter. So he shoved his head firmly back between the pillows to avoid the catastrophic response he knew would spill forth any moment now.

Seb yanked a T-shirt out from the wardrobe so hard that the hanger slipped off the rail and landed on the floor with a clang. "You can face me when you say shit like that."

Jay curled his hands into the sheets, digging his balled fists into the mattress and pushed up. Twisting around, he brought his good leg under him. Searing pain shot through from his left knee up to his spine and he sucked in a breath through gritted teeth. First thing in the morning was always the worst. Then he noted the time on the bedside clock. Okay, so late afternoon was now his first thing. Gone were the six a.m. runs. He grunted, making it into a sitting position to face Seb at the end of the bed. Being out of breath hurt more than his battered knee joint.

"Do you need the pills?"

Jay shook his head.

"I'm trying, Jay. Tell me what you need me to do and I'll do it."

"Haven't you got somewhere you'd rather be?" Jay tried to widen his eyes to make that statement more of a flippant question, but his crusted eyelids prevented him from achieving it.

"Like where?"

Jay shrugged. "Rehearsals? The studios? Wherever else it is you go all the time."

"Fuck's sake, Jay. I asked you. I fucking asked you! You said, go. You said you wanted to deal with this on your own. So I kept gigging. I've got a career too." Seb paused, swallowing, possibly realising he shouldn't have let that tumble out. "Sorry."

"I know you have."

124

"I'm here now. And you need to move. And eat."

"Sorry, when did you get your physio degree? Before or after the other one you didn't complete?" Jay bit his lip, wondering why he hadn't clamped down on his tongue. Pain and frustration had created a monster of him.

Seb stomped over to the chest of drawers, cracked open the bottle of painkillers on the side and shook two out. He held them out open palmed to Jay.

"I ain't takin' them."

"Why not?"

"You know why."

"These aren't your problem." Seb curled his hand into a fist. "Maybe I am." He grabbed Jays jogging bottoms lying on the floor and chucked them at him.

Jay caught them, holding onto the garment as if it would prevent the fallout. It didn't. "Seb—"

"You keep being a prick about this. I can take it." Seb twisted and marched out of the bedroom, his feet stamping down the stairs and into the kitchen shaking the open doors of the wardrobe and Jay's resolve.

Bollocks.

The water from the exploding shower taps splattered onto Seb's jeans. He cursed, twisted the taps off and grabbed a tea towel to wipe himself down. After slapping the cloth on the counter, he curled his hands around the sink and leaned forward to gather some inner peace.

He was completely, fucking, helpless and at a loss what to do next. His options to deal with this morning's encounter ranged from punching Jay in the face to wake him up from his stupor, to throwing him over the kitchen counter and fucking the dejection out of him. Neither of which he knew was the right thing to do and would probably only serve to make him feel better in the short-term rather than dealing with Jay's decline into his heavy depression. Plus, he'd been there and it never worked. He shuddered.

The past couple of months, he'd sympathised, offered support, and had steered clear of complaining at the lack of intimacy that Jay had put down to the pills he'd been taking, yet Jay had never turned to him. Seb had a shoulder for him to cry on, but it was still bone dry. He was losing hope that this was all about the injury and Jay not being able to play football. It was about *him*. And that hurt beyond belief. He didn't know how to counter that.

Inelegant stomps from out in the hallway followed by insufferable grunts of agony snapped Seb to. He cleared his throat and shook himself, washing up the pans in the sink to conceal his frustration at being so inept to deal with this. He'd never been a carer. He'd always been the one to be taken care of—by his father's money, by Yulia, by Stephen. *By Jay.* He was trying to step up, before Jay came to the realisation that Seb was just one more useless limb he didn't need to lug around.

Jay limped into the kitchen and rested against the counter. Seb remained with his back to him, his chest tightening with what was coming next. Why did he fear his boyfriend's presence all of a sudden? Maybe that had been why he'd accepted to be away for so long during Jay's recovery time, because it was easier for him not to have to face it. Guilt surged through Seb. *What a bastard. I can't even help the man I love.* Surely this wasn't how it was meant to be. Not this soon in their relationship?

Grabbing the knot inside him, Seb rammed it right down in his stomach to forget it was there and finally turned around. Jay twisted one of the stools out from

126

under the counter and sat, straightening his leg out and rubbing his knee. Seb swore he did that out of habit than because of any real pain, but he daren't ever say that. Pretending not to notice, Seb pushed over a plate along with cutlery but without accompanying words. Apologies didn't come easy to him, and he wasn't sure he should offload his own guilt on Jay right then. That wasn't fair either. Jay tugged the plate toward him and grabbed the fork, but pushed the overcooked eggs and undercooked bacon carelessly around.

Ignoring it, Seb sat and dived right into his and scrolled through the open laptop next to him.

"I'm sorry." That had been said in a whisper and straight at Jay's plate, but Seb peered up anyway and clung on to the words with renewed hope.

Head bowed, Jay shoved the eggs around the porcelain. He looked defeated and Seb couldn't hold it in any longer. He had to do something, regardless of any rejection that he'd been all too used to the past few months. Willing that ball of rage in the pit of his stomach to dissolve, Seb staggered up from his seat. Sliding his hands onto Jay's shoulders from behind, he rested his chin on his head and inhaled the scent of Jay's unwashed, tousled hair. After a moment, Jay twisted in the stool. He spread out his legs and slipped his hands onto Seb's hips to tug him forward. Staggering, Seb fell between Jay's open legs and wrapped his arms around his neck.

Jay buried his face into Seb's chest, holding him close. He inhaled, as though he was breathing Seb in for the first time. Running his fingers through the base of Jay's hair, Seb tugged at the strands, forcing Jay to look at him. When he did, and those sad blue eyes met with Seb's, Seb kissed his forehead and willed for that kiss to be Jay's kiss of life. Of love. Of everything he needed to get himself out of the dark clouds.

"You've got to stop this, baby. It's killing me." Seb spoke lightly, a conscious effort not to fuel any looming argument. "Us...*you.*"

"I know."

Seb sighed and closed his eyes, content to let Jay cling to him. It was the most body contact they'd had in weeks without Jay pushing him away. His vibrating mobile phone interrupted the moment, but Seb ignored it.

"Ain't you getting that?" Jay slipped his arms away, leaving Seb cold.

"Whoever it is, they aren't as important as you."

Leaning forward, Seb kissed Jay's lips. It was a brief and light, but, fuck, it sent ripples of anticipation through Seb. Especially when Jay kissed him back. It had been too long since he'd felt the connection, the yearning, the familiar touch. If there had been any recent kissing, it had felt cold and distant with Jay's injury and the month of anguish to recover from it. But the warmth emanating from Jay's dry lips compelled Seb to want more. He needed to know that his Jay was still in there and wanted to come back out.

He eased his tongue into Jay's mouth and Jay opened up, physically, and Seb hoped, mentally. He allowed their tongues to curl together for just a moment before Jay hesitated and pulled back out. Slumping forward, Jay rested his forehead against Seb's chest.

Fuck. Disappointment surged through Seb. His rage wasn't for Jay, not really. It was for that fucker who'd slammed his studded foot full force into his lover's knee and in damaging it, seemingly beyond repair, had potentially ended not only Jay's football career, but robbed him of the confidence and self-esteem that Seb had fought so hard to help him win.

Dragging his hands through the back of Jay's hair, Seb hugged him to his chest, hoping to coddle away the torment. He kissed the top of Jay's head before pulling away and reaching for his phone to check the incoming message.

"Shit." Seb shoved in the remaining food on his plate.

"What's up?" Jay popped a piece of toast into his mouth and struggled with swallowing it. Regardless, Seb believed the eating to be a good sign.

"I have to go out again." Seb hated that he had to leave just at the point he might be getting somewhere with Jay. "We've got the go-ahead for that central London location. Y'know, the new video? But we have to scout it now."

Jay nodded and reached over the counter to grab his own phone that he'd ignored for days. Sighing, Seb brushed Jay's shoulder blades as he passed him to walk towards the exit.

"Seb," Jay called, faintly, but enough that Seb picked up the plea in his name. "I love you." His lips curved into a despondent smile and he laughed, shaking his head in some absurd display at mocking those vulnerable words that Seb had been craving.

Seb ached. Those words weren't said in the usual casual, carefree way. They weren't lip service to a relationship that had survived through separation, through class division, through family abandonment and two high-profile careers, amidst all the prejudice. They were a call for help. That was *his* Jay, asking him for help. *Wasn't it?*

Rushing back, Seb cupped Jay's chin in his hand and lowered his head to look him in the eye. "I love you too." He dug his fingers so hard into Jay's skin he could leave bruises. "So. Bloody. Much. You remember that. If nothing else, remember that I love you."

Jay wrapped his arms around Seb and held him close, snuffling into his shirt. Seb clasped his arms around Jay's neck, holding him steady.

"We'll get through this." Seb was trying to convince himself, as well as Jay. He hoped he pulled it off. "We will. You will."

Jay sniffed, swiping a hand under his nose and squaring his shoulders to shrug off the vulnerable display. "Go on. I'm all right. I'll see ya laters."

Seb didn't want to go. But he needed to.

So he did, feeling as though his legs were made of lead.

CHAPTER NINE
Injury Time

After Seb left, Jay limped out of the kitchen feeling every bit the crippled shit he was. He couldn't have sounded more desperate if he'd tried. That call to Seb made his toes curl in embarrassment. He might as well have begged the man to stay with him, to wallow in his self-made pit of despair alongside him. But he couldn't have asked him to do that. Seb still had a life to live. A *career*. And one that currently soared higher into the clouds, leaving Jay buried in a deep hole with the rising fear that he'd never manage to climb out. Not with his gammy knee, that was for fucking certain. That had also been the first time he'd cried in front of Seb, usually sobbing alone so he didn't let out the nancy boy everyone expected him to be.

Exhaling through gritted teeth at every wince of pain, he made it to the living room and collapsed down onto the pure-white leather corner sofa. Rummaging behind the various retro scatter cushions that Seb had been collecting, he tugged out the remote control and switched on the box. He hurled one of the cushions onto the coffee table and lifted his bad leg to stretch it out, plonking it on top of the soft pillow. *There. Day set. Just like every other fucking day.*

Jay hadn't ventured out of the house much, other than for physio sessions the club still laid on for him and the daily walks his therapist insisted he keep up. Ewa, his physio, recommended more outside exercise. Something about fresh air being good for the soul, not just the torn ligaments in his knee. Jay wasn't convinced. Fresh air made him miserable. It only reminded him of being on a football pitch in all weathers and that his team were still training, playing…living. And his life had pretty much come to a grinding halt, just like the tube trains when he'd used to fall asleep on the District Line and end up at Upminster.

Flicking through the channels, he stopped on Sky Sports News and squinted at the headlines running across his screen. He couldn't even bear hearing about the football scores anymore, so he skipped up a few channels and landed on the music stations. Someone was having a good old giggle at him today as the first video to pop up was *Breaking Through* from the Drops' debut album released last year. And there was his boyfriend, filling up his wide-screen TV and strutting the stuff he couldn't ever lose.

The video, Jay remembered, had been a relatively small-scale production, considering back then the Drops had little monetary backing. It had been one location — the swimming pool in the back of Martin's folks' house. At some point, all three band members had discarded their instruments and emerged into the pool, fully clothed, lying on their backs to sing to the stars, or in reality, the camera lens. Seb had come home freezing that night, having nearly developed hypothermia for his art. It had taken a particularly long hot bath and them both wrapping up in their double-down duvet to get his spark back. *Why can't it be that easy for me?*

The chime of the doorbell ding-donged around the house and startled Jay away from staring at the screen. He thought about not answering it. Not only was it going to hurt like fuck to move now he'd just got settled, but no doubt whoever was at the door was delivering a parcel for someone else. He'd gotten to know his neighbours more over the past six months than he had all year, due to the amount of stuff he'd taken in for them. But the chime merged into a frustrated knock and Jay decided to use the walk to the door as a way to tick off his daily exercise regime.

"Hey, squirt." Ann grinned on Jay opening the door with a disgruntled sigh. He left her to make her own way in and follow him back to the living room. "Welcome, Ann, how are you? I'm doing good, Jay, thanks for asking."

"What?" Jay shot a glare over his shoulder. He heard her but couldn't be arsed with the standoff.

"Nothing." Ann fell down on the sofa in Jay's primed spot.

"Jump in me grave, why don't ya." Jay hobbled to the other side and parked his arse there instead. At least he'd have a different view for today. "He called you, then." Jay knew Ann wasn't turning up on her own accord. She'd been vetted, prepared and, no doubt, warned.

"No." Ann had always been shit at lying. "Get dressed. I'm taking you out."

"No, ta."

"You need a shower too." She screwed up her nose. "So either you go do that or I'll throw a bucket of water over you and give you a sponge bath right here."

"I ain't goin' out, Ann. Why does everyone think that if I leave the house, all my problems will be solved? Take a walk, get some fresh air, suddenly my knee ain't crushed to tiny little bits anymore?"

"You know what?" Ann crossed her legs. "I always thought Seb was the drama queen. I'm changing my opinion."

Jay shot her the finger.

"Nice comeback. Get dressed. This ain't for you. It's for me. I need to get off my face legless." She smiled. "Excuse the pun."

And now the jokes were starting. *Great.* Just what he needed. To be made to feel a mockery of to normalise his condition. There wasn't anything normal about it. He could hardly walk a few paces without excruciating pain and his fitness had deteriorated, along with his honed body. It was why he hated showing it to anyone anymore. Especially Seb. He'd said it loud and clear—he loved Jay's body. *Had* loved Jay's body. How it had used to be, before the muscle had wasted away and left in its wake nothing of significance for a rock idol adored by thousands to want.

Fuckin' hell.

And on that thought, he frowned. He really didn't want to leave the house. But as Ann sat there, Jay came to the realisation that there wasn't any better way to drown his sorrows. Hey, it had worked for Seb for a while— falling hard to the bottom of a bottle. Maybe he could try it? Might lift his mood a bit.

"All right." Jay hefted up to a stand. "Where we going?"

"Somewhere full of men."

"Ku?"

"Where they look at me and not you."

Jay nodded. "Boozer down the road then." He staggered to the living room door and prepared to tackle his Everest, the stairs.

"You need a hand?" Ann called out.

"I can manage a shower by myself, cheers."

Ann shrugged. "Nothing I ain't seen before. But whatevs. And I meant choosing clothes. I'm parched and on a time limit."

After a particularly painful and slow shower, followed by finding clothes that still managed to fit with his body having shed a few pounds, Jay honoured Ann with a limp down the road to Greenwich High Street.

They tumbled into the first boozer that wasn't jam-packed with tourists. He didn't frequent the local bars that often, a few times with Seb and when his family visited, but mostly he preferred staying in. It was why he'd spent so much money on the house and garden, for it to be their sanctuary. Seb had ventured to the upmarket wine bars on the main stretch a few times when Martin and Noah were in town. Band-planning they called it, with a bar tab that seemed to hit the top end of Seb's credit limit. Seb sure knew how to spend money. He'd had practice at that all his life. Jay, on the other hand, still saved more than he spent. Which was a bloody lucky thing, considering he might soon lose his wages altogether. Sick pay didn't last forever. Lucky the club had a hefty insurance premium that he, and they, would have coming their way if Jay's knee didn't get sorted and he was forced to retire.

And that thought sent his stomach plummeting on reaching the bar of the Court Yard situated on the corner opposite the church. He didn't want to think about the possibility of giving it all up. Of not being on a pitch again. Of having reached his peak. At least he now had a thirst on. And it seemed Ann was also pretty parched if her instant order of a bottle of crisp Pinot was anything to go by.

"On the Saunders' tab?" the barman asked, eyeing Jay hovering behind Ann's head. So Seb had been here. Quite a few times if he had a tab and the barman recognised Jay in one look.

"I think so." Ann grinned at Jay over her shoulder. "Let him pay for it, yeah? Should have ordered Champers."

"He's nearing his limit." The barman plonked down the wine bottle along with a couple of glasses. "So you might need to pay up after this. I can't hang on to it forever."

"Surprised you let him tally up so much. What's the damage?" Jay fished out his wallet, thumbing his credit card.

"I usually set a grand limit. But he's ordered in a couple of Bollingers. Magnum. I put it on his tab as I don't normally have that stuff lying around, y'know?" The barman draped his arms over the draught taps. "So if this is going on, I need it settled up before you leave."

Jay desperately tried not to let the shock show on hearing Seb had ordered in one of the most luxurious brands of Champers on the market and just handed over his card with a nod.

"What you two celebrating, anyway?" The barman took the card and swiped it.

Jay didn't answer, because he didn't actually have one. Instead, he thanked the bloke and tucked the bottle under his arm, limping off to the nearest discreet table.

137

Two Bollingers? That was some expensive shit. Who the fuck was he planning to drink such luxury with? Someone brought up with as much of a silver spoon in his gob as Seb, no doubt. Rather different to his and Ann's indulgence in the house Pinot. And the rate she poured it into the glasses, she was on a mission to drown both their sorrows, double lively.

"So, this." Jay nodded to his filled glass. "You wanna talk about what's goin' on?"

Ann plonked the bottle down, picked up her glass and slurped from the edge. Classy as ever. "It's over. Done."

"Lucas?"

"No, Brad Pitt and Angelina Jolie." Ann deadpanned.

"Team Jennifer."

"Are you 'avin a giraffe?"

Jay shrugged. "No. Pretty bastard thing to do, ain't it?"

"What is? Moving on? Falling in love with someone else?"

"They fucked around behind Jen's back. Everyone knows."

"When things are over, they're over."

"So that makes it all right, does it?" Jay gulped down a load of wine and shivered, like someone had walked over his grave. "Anyway, what's happened with you?" Better to steer the conversation elsewhere.

She sighed. "I'm just done with the waiting. We're, like, mates, who hang out when we can. It ain't got nothing to do with him always being away for basketball, or even that he wants to wait until we're married to have sex. It's just, well, there's no heat. There's no passion.

There's no...*desire*. That's gone. And we ain't even done it once!"

"You two been together since uni. Relationships go that way."

"Has it gone that way for you and Seb?" Ann's gaze lingered on Jay with genuine interest.

Shifting in his seat, Jay grimaced and rubbed his knee. Least the awkward display could be put down to his gammy leg and not the touchy subject of his and Seb's lack of sexual encounters recently.

"Urgh." Ann grunted, flipping her head back. "Sometimes, don't you just wanna be thrown over a drum kit and taken? Ravished?"

Jay coughed back a bit of wine. "A drum kit?"

"You cannot tell me Seb ain't done that to you? I heard his B-side of the *Hideous* single."

"No comment." Jay glugged from his drink, and yet again cursed Seb for that blasted song. "So, you've ended it for good this time? No bouncing back 'cause the bloke's minted?"

"No." Ann straightened, reaffirming her stance on the matter. "I never cared about his money." She shook her head. "We just ain't compatible. I need to find someone who can shove me against a wall."

"I'm startin' to worry about you."

"I think it's about time I gave up on blokes who don't see me sexually, don't you?"

Jay took that one on the chin.

"But then those that do, don't want a relationship. So bollocks to it. Anyway, talk to me about you." She leaned forward. "What's going on with you?"

Jay cracked out a laugh at the absurd look of concern across Ann's boat race. But for some bizarre reason, it was either that or the wine that made him want to blurt it all out.

"Well, nutshell, mate. My knee's fucked. West Ham'll give it one more go before telling me I ain't worth it. I piss Seb off on the daily for moping, I snap at him. I pretty much hate myself and I'll be retiring before my old man." Jay held up his glass. "Cheers to that one." He knocked back the remainder and slammed it on the table.

"You tried finding your own therapist?" Ann poured out more into his empty glass, adding a little to hers as well.

"What? Like a head shrink? No, ta."

"No. Like an independent physio. Lucas told me that when one of the blokes on his basketball team injured his ankle, the club only wanted to pay out for work done in this country. Cheaper, innit? But apparently in the US, they have loadsa specialists on sports injuries and this bloke flew over there, paid it himself, fixed. Done. Back on the court."

"I ain't sure West Ham'll go for that. I'm theirs, ain't I? They have to vet who looks after my knee. It'd have to come out their insurance premium. And I'll bet that's reaching an end. And it ain't like I've given them a hassle-free couple seasons, is it? Far from it. Surprised the club have kept up this much. Sometimes I think I should've taken their offer to have an agent to deal with all this shit. Might've got me a pay-out."

"It'll look a bit pony on them if they get rid of ya, won't it? Oh, look at us, the first club to sign an out gay player. He gets targeted on the pitch, so let's chuck him away after all. Nah, West Ham won't do that. They'll agree to anything if they think it'll work. Unless, well, unless *you've* given up." Ann's eyes bulged so much they were in danger of popping from their sockets. "Have you?"

"No."

"No-one would blame you if you have. It's been tough on you. Can't be easy taking that shit all the time. This is a nice out, if you wanted it? You could go back to uni, play semi-pro. Get outta the headlines."

"That ain't what I want."

"Sure? 'Cause the way you've been acting lately says different."

"Like how?" Jay gripped his glass, his fingertips turning white from not only the chilled wine but the pressure. Yeah, he knew he'd been acting like a bastard. Especially around Seb. But for fuck's sake, his knee hurt. But that in no way meant he didn't want to get better. *Does it?*

"Like it's all over. And I don't just mean the football."

Jay didn't respond. He couldn't think of a single thing to say, and so bowed his head like some shameful puppy.

"He still loves you, Jay." Ann's voice lightened. "I see it in his face. I read it in his daily text messages. Fuck, I even hear it in his bloody songs! He isn't doing a Brad Pitt. You cannot tell me you think that he is?"

"Maybe not. But for how long?" Jay took a deep breath and his squirming thoughts he'd held in for so long came tumbling out unannounced. "I ain't the same man he left everything for, am I? And if it stays like this, then what can I seriously offer him? Shit, he's one of the most desirable men on the planet, according to every bleedin' magazine on the shelf. He's a gay man's wet dream and a straight woman's epic fantasy. And here I am, a raspberry ripple and a has-been. I can't see him hangin' around for long if he knows this is all I am. He'll find his Brad Pitt quicker than you can down that wine."

The fact that Ann decided to finish her glass at that moment instilled no confidence in Jay that she would be convincing him of the contrary.

"So, what, you push him away to soften the blow?" Ann asked, or more stated. "Okay, look, not that I believe he will ever just up and walk away from you. I mean, yeah, he's been flaky in the past. We know that. We forgave him, right? He's more than made up for it. So I don't think it's fair to tarnish him with the Jolie brush."

Jay opened his mouth to speak but Ann cut him off with a wave of her hand.

"Hear me out. Let's say that this is it." She held up a finger from around her glass. "Wait. I don't *think* that it is. I believe, like, a hundred percent that you are gonna recover and be back on that pitch. But we're working *your* scenario. Let's say you don't get to play football again, professionally anyhow. And Seb, yeah, is Mr. Hot Shot travelling the world with a band that gets all the attention right now. I mean they're three mighty fine dudes, without playing the boy-band cliché. They're talented, driven and write songs that rile up a confused nation."

"*You* sound like an agent."

"Maybe I should be. But what I'm getting at is that you can't just give up. He fell in love with *you*. Out of all of those who would take him to bed, he comes home to you. And that says a lot. Believe me." Ann frowned, swishing the dregs in her glass. "You need to keep giving him a reason to come back. And you don't need football to do that."

"What else do I have?" Jay glanced out of the window.

A group of suited men, no doubt clocking off from their day of office-bound millions making, made their way across the road and stumbled into the pub, sending a draught through Jay's floppy hair. The door slammed and their boisterous chatter continued as they crowded around the bar area looking for service. Jay shifted his attention back to Ann.

"I get what you're sayin'. I do." He scratched his thumbnail along the glass, almost wanting to crack it. "Trouble is, I've spent my whole life working toward football. Then I made it. Thought I was set. I don't know how to do, or be, anything else."

Ann exhaled a benevolent breath, and her features softened. "I know." She smiled that smile Jay knew all too well. It made his eyes sting. "P'raps you could start with waiting tables?"

"What?"

Ann brandished the empty bottle with a sassy grin.

"Thought you'd be first up there." Jay nodded toward the men at the bar. "Tall, good-looking, stylish barnet. All whistle and flutes."

Ann gasped. "Did you just check them out?"

"No."

But Ann did, and she whistled. "That's a Boss an' all. They are bang on at the moment. Anyone who is anyone is wearing those suits."

Jay gave an apathetic nod, then hefted to a stand. "Same as?"

Ann snapped her fingers "Quickly, please."

Jay tried not to hobble over to the bar, but grabbing a few ledges and backs of seats as he went certainly didn't help keep up the pretence that he could walk without limping. He winced, slamming a hand down on the counter to take some of the weight off his leg and perched against the stool. The suits next to him were all handed their pints and remained in their huddle as the barman returned to Jay.

"Same again, please, mate."

Another Pinot plonked down after, and Jay swivelled, catching the roaming eye of one of the office blokes. Jay smiled, his usual polite response to having been recognised, but he wasn't really in the mood to do the glad-handing shit. So he took a deep breath, preparing for the walk back to Ann that he was going to attempt sans limp this time. Like scoring a penalty, he had to see the pain-free return in his mind's eye before attempting it.

"Ruttman?"

Jay closed his eyes, masking his annoyance.

"Jay?"

One of the men edged through the others toward him. *Shit, seriously?* Navy Hugo Boss suit, candy-striped pink and white shirt finished off nicely with a deep pink tie, slim-fit and tailored. Clean-shaven face, green eyes, with light-brown neatly styled hair that had a hint of a spike to give it an edge.

"Fancy bumping into you here." Riley grinned, holding out the hand that wasn't clutched around a full pint.

Jay was in no mood for this, but he was in full view of the public and the other men Riley had emerged from were all looking his way. No need to fuel another headline. So he tucked the bottle under his arm and shook the offered hand.

"How's the knee?" Riley nodded downwards, as if Jay would have forgotten whereabouts on his anatomy said injury had occurred. Like he didn't have a painful reminder daily.

"Getting there." Where, Jay wasn't sure. But that had become the standard reply.

"Least you get to do a bit of midday drinking, though, right?"

"Ha. Yeah. And you."

"Perks of the job, mate. Got a client round the corner. We've been working his social media presence." Riley dipped forward to speak out the side of his mouth. "Trust me, he needs it. Likes to say a lot of things that probably he shouldn't, y'know? Plus I'm hoping to get him an endorsement deal to rejig his public image."

"Nice."

"Amazing what getting your face in the right places, and the right gear, can do for someone's public persona."

The apathetic nod came out to play and Jay glanced over to Ann in the hope he could use her finger snapping as a way to make his excuses and scarper off. She was scrolling through her phone, completely oblivious.

"You with her?" Riley nodded over to Ann, taking a sip from his full pint.

"Yeah."

"She's a right sort. That'll work your rep for you."

Riley might as well have slapped Jay round the face. For both his statements. Straightening, Jay ignored the pain in his knee to broaden his shoulders. "That what you'd advise, is it? Get me seen out boozing with a brass? Go fuck yourself, Riley. I ain't ashamed of who I am. And don't fucking dare speak about her like that either."

Riley's face dropped. "No, mate. Sorry." He shook his head, remorse flickering across his chiselled jawline. "That's not what I meant. I been around these dicks all day." He angled his head, indicating the rowdy suited blokes laughing and fawning over one another. "Part of

145

the job is to merge into whatever works. Sorry, that ain't the real me. Believe me."

"Whatever." Jay went to move away but Riley gripped his arm.

"Seriously, Jay, sorry. All I meant was that she's a looker and if the paps were in here, you know they'd say something about it, regardless of how innocent it is. That's all. The press make up their own stories. As I'm sure you know."

"Yeah." He'd avoided most of the stuff that got printed, but occasionally he stumbled upon the trash that was written about Seb, about how his gigs saw him partying late night with random men. He'd never tell Seb he'd seen them. And he wasn't sure if it was because he didn't want to know the truth. The injury had affected more than just his ability to play football. It had affected his sense of reason. And trust. As he'd just let slip to Ann.

"Let me buy you a pint, old time's sake." Riley held up a hand to the barman.

"I got a drink." Jay tapped the wine bottle warming under his armpit. "And I better get it back before she dies of thirst."

"Sure. Sure. Look, it's been good seeing you again. I know this is weird as fuck."

"You can say that again." Taking a stride forward, Jay attempted to mask the dull ache that climbed up from his leg to his spine. He nearly made it another step before Riley curled his fingers around Jay's biceps.

"Sorry, mate, I just wanted to ask if you ever found representation?"

Here we go. "No. I don't need it."

"All right, listen. How about this, I got a contract with a new leisurewear firm looking for someone to endorse their stuff. They want a relatively known sports personality to lift their brand up, y'know? I was offering to this client of mine, but having second thoughts, it could be better suited to you. Earn a few extra quid. Not that you need it, but, well, it's all good for exposure."

Jay shook his head. "If you want me to wear someone's studs while I play, that's pretty much a no-go right now. And I signed that with Nike."

"Nah, it's not pro-sports. More leisure wear, smart cas', y'know? Really, they want a model. But I'm thinking you fit the bill pretty good." Riley raked his gaze down Jay's body, then smiled. "It could be a great mutual benefit. They get a decent-looking geezer, and you get the chance to show who you are to the nation."

"A model?" Jay quirked an eyebrow. "That ain't really me. That's more Seb's bag."

"Your fella?"

"Yes. Boyfriend, partner. Whatever." The casual, carefree way that fell from Jay's tongue at least went some way to proving how far he'd come in the last few years. But also, most people kinda already knew that. And he wasn't in front of a camera, at least not one he was aware of.

"In the band?"

Jay nodded. "You must've done your homework."

"Yeah, yeah. I knew. Just, ah, nothing." Riley scratched the nape of his neck, his cheeks tinging.

"What?"

"He just don't seem your type, that's all." Riley shrugged.

Jay arched an eyebrow. "My type? What would my type be exactly?"

"Someone a bit, well, less out there. Don't get me wrong, he's a good-looking fella. He's just, like, everywhere right now."

Don't I fucking know it. A crash and thump interrupted and Jay glanced over to Ann. She'd thrown her phone on the table, folded her arms and scowled at Jay, tapping her shoe on the hardwood floor.

"Looks like you better get back." Riley chuckled. "Do you believe in fate, Jay?"

"What?" He never had before. But then there was that time he got a fixture in New York...

"I do. And us, being thrown back to each other, is fate, my man. When I got the chance to pitch to be your agent, honestly, I wanted to turn it down. But then I thought, actually it's a good opportunity to bury the past. Now bumping into you here, it's like the world's telling us we could be a formidable team."

Christ, this bloke thinks he's got the gift of the gab.

Riley fished out a business card from his wallet and handed it to Jay. "In case you lost the last one. Call me. We'll go for a drink and discuss this endorsement deal. Bring your fella if you like."

Jay tucked the card into his back jeans pocket. "I'll think about it."

"Great stuff." Holding out his thumb and pinkie finger, Riley waggled it over his mouth to mimic a phone, then slinked off back to the other suited lads holed up in the corner.

Jay hobbled back to Ann. She snatched the bottle of wine and poured it into the two glasses as Jay slipped into his vacated chair.

"Take it that bloke ain't for me." She nodded over to Riley. "Who was he? Hammers fan, or after your number?"

"That?" Jay picked up his wine and took a glug. "Was Riley Burton. And, no, steer clear. He thinks you're a right sort."

Ann lifted up in the chair and peered over Jay's head. She smiled. "Does he now?"

"Don't go there."

Slumping back down, Ann wrinkled her forehead. "Why does his name ring a bell?"

Jay swallowed a glug of wine. "'Cause that's the fella I beat the shit out of on the pitch at the youth academy. Remember? When I got released. And him, evidently."

Ann whipped her head around. "No, fucking, way!"

"Yeah. And he wants to be my agent and offered me a modelling job." Jay held Ann's wide-eyed gaze.

Then she cracked up. Jay didn't blame her.

* * * *

Seb shook hands with the rest of the crew as he tumbled out of the disused warehouse. Their record label had scouted a pretty decent place to shoot their new video. A dishevelled factory on the Hackney/Newham border that had been scheduled to be torn down to make way for the new Olympic Park being built. The plan was to spray paint the inside with a load of graffiti to reflect an urban landscape, perfect for their new release. And no-one would moan considering the place would probably be a running track in a few months. *Take that those who still think this three-piece are a load of toffs playing at being the working-class hero.*

"How's Jay?" Martin stepped up beside him, hands in his pockets.

Seb sighed, fishing his phone out. He scrolled through various missed calls and messages, but nothing of importance. At least not from Jay, nor Ann. Perhaps she hadn't bothered to do his dirty work of making sure Jay got out of the house. He rammed it back in his pocket.

"Same as."

Martin nodded, biting his lip. Noah joined them on the pavement, Marlboro red already in his mouth.

"This no smoking in pubs lark is seriously damaging everyone's health."

Seb snorted. "I think the idea was to do the opposite." He kinda craved a suck on that stick, but thought better of it than to ask to go twos. He was having another go at quitting, for good this time. For Jay's sake. Although, sometimes, it was probably better for Jay if Seb did partake in a bit of nicotine every now and then, just to make him chill out a little.

"Nah, mate, I mean me being in a pub all night without lighting up makes me cranky." Noah shivered. "So I'm getting this one in before we head to the nearest place to discuss this shit."

"No can do." Seb shook his head. "I have to get back. I left things a bit…shitty at home. Plus, we need a proper sleep for tomorrow night, right?"

He bumped fists with the lads before sauntering over to Jay's BMW parked up outside the gates. Sliding in, he breathed Jay's scent still lingering on the upholstery. Musky sweat never left a leather seat. And Seb was grateful for it. He'd taken to driving Jay's car more often recently, considering Jay couldn't use it and the thing would seize up if left too long, but mostly because he felt connected to the sports coupe. Like it was Jay himself.

Shaking his head, he started up and joined the traffic, tunes blasting from the speakers. An hour pile-up meant he was home later than expected. He ground the tyres onto the gravel driveway, noting all the lights in the house were switched off. He sighed, turned off the ignition and headed in, preparing for what awaited him. Whatever it was, Seb would deal. A hell of a lot better than he had that morning. So he composed himself and entered their home, raining his keys on the sideboard and bounded toward the kitchen.

Switching on the light, he jolted at the sight before him. Jay sat at the island, head slumped. Had he even moved? After a moment, Jay peered up and squinted.

"Hey." Seb stepped closer, noting the tub of ice cream in front of Jay.

"How'd it go?"

Seb slipped a hand on Jay's back and lowered down into the stool beside him, rubbing in circling motions that rocked Jay in his slump. "Good."

Jay nodded, licked off the last on his spoon and slid the tub toward Seb. "Dinner of champions, right?"

Seb snorted, took the spoon from Jay and scooped out the remaining dregs of Haagen Dazs. It was rock solid at the bottom, an indicator of the last time that they'd indulged in the only junk food Jay allowed. Usually though, a spoon wasn't needed as Seb would be lapping it up from melting on Jay's sizzling skin.

"How are you?" Seb swallowed, the cream hitting him where he needed it. He was starving.

"Went to the pub. Ann came over." Jay peeked a look at him through the corner of his eye. "But I guess you already know that."

No comment. "You want some proper dinner?"

"You cooking?"

"I got by with the scrambled eggs, didn't I? I'll bet I could go as far as bunging some beans on toast?"

Jay smiled, but shook his head. "Nah. I'm beat. I'm gonna get me head down. I got an early physio in the morning. Knock yourself out, though." He swivelled out of the chair and grunted over to the archway.

Seb hung his head and noted the business card lying on the surface. He slid it over and read the name. "Who's Riley Burton?"

Jay turned, hand on the wall to steady himself. "Some geezer who thinks people will buy shit if I wear it."

"Huh?"

"Don't panic. I told him no. He might tap you up for it, though."

"He an agent?"

"Yeah and wants me to do a Beckham."

Seb grinned. "Seriously? Fucking aces. You could so do that. I mean, I'd buy anything from you if you take your top off." He winked.

Jay opened his mouth to speak, but Seb's phone blasting out a tune from his back pocket stopped him from clearly going to dispute the fact. Seb fished it out, checked the display, and cut it off.

"Who was it?" Jay nodded to the phone Seb threw on the counter.

"No-one of importance."

"You keep ignoring calls around me and I might get the wrong end of the stick."

Seb snorted. Because that line was best left ignored. "Tell me more about you getting your kit off for cash."

"Think the idea is I put the kit on. But I ain't doin' it."

Seb bit his bottom lip, nodding. He'd run out of ways to make Jay see his worth. Maybe try for a different tack.

"Hey, listen, I was thinking of going for a run tomorrow. Before I have to go collect my suit."

Jay furrowed his brow. "Suit?"

"The charity gig." He paused, wondering if he should say the next bit. "You could come along?"

"Oh, right, I ain't sure…"

"We're performing. First up and I planned something epic. I got Ann a ticket too."

Jay nodded and made his way to leave.

"So the run?" Seb called, hoping to hit something. Whether he was on target or not. "You want to come? Show me your route? Ewa recommended you start light jogging. And believe me, I'll still be sprinting to keep up."

"I ain't sure —"

Seb's phone vibrated against the counter, drilling a hole through the stilted conversation. He dropped his gaze from Jay and covered his hand over the display to mask the thrumming.

"Just answer it, babe. I'm going a bed."

With that, Jay limped off. Seb deflated into the seat, crushed that another night had him left alone with only his unravelling thoughts for company. It didn't seem to matter what he said, or did. Jay seemed unreachable at the moment. At least to him, anyway. The man he loved was too pained, physically and mentally, to just open up. He understood, he did. It just hurt so much to be brushed aside, to not be given the chance to make things better, to prove he could be the stability that Jay needed. Jay was lost in the whirlwind of the past year and Seb so wanted to find him. The way Jay had found him in New York.

He waited a while with just the whirring from the fridge-freezer to hide his thumping heart, until the phone buzzed again. He rolled his eyes, then swiped to take the call. Least it might stop the incessant ringing. "What?"

153

"*Sparky.*"

Seb ripped the phone from his ear and checked the display. English number. London. *What the fuck?* He slammed the phone back. "Stop fucking calling me, you utter—"

"Sebastian, before you hang up. I'm calling on behalf of your father. Believe me, I wouldn't be continuing to chase you for anything else."

Seb stood from the stool and scraped a hand through his hair. "If he wants to talk to me, he knows where I am. I don't need his lapdog calling me every fucking second of every goddamn *shitting* day!"

"He wants to see you. Mutual ground."

"Bore off."

"It'll be worth your while."

Seb paused, his mind on overdrive. A thought struck. "Is he *dying*?"

Stephen's chilling laughter sent Seb's teeth on edge. "No."

"Unwell, hospitalised?"

"No."

"Bankrupt?"

"No."

"Is he getting married and has an extended family he wishes me to meet?"

"No."

Seb paused, racking his brains. "Then I've nothing further."

"Thursday. One p.m. The Royal. You remember where that is, I'll assume?"

Seb gripped the phone harder, his blood boiling and replied through gritted teeth, "I recall, yes."

"If you're there, you're there. If you're not, well, that will be a crying shame."

Seb opened his mouth to reply, but the whirring through the phone speakers indicated he'd been cut off.

"*Fuck!*" Seb threw the mobile on the island, the already shattered glass spreading. Then he turned and met with Jay stood at the archway, topless, his jeans hung low on his hips. How long had he been there? Seb swallowed with unease.

"Couldn't gis a hand with the shower, could ya?" The slight tinge to Jay's cheeks made Seb melt.

"You mean?" Seb didn't really want to think if there was a subtext to Jay's request, he'd only be disappointed.

Jay's chest rose with his inhalation. He nodded.

Seb rushed over, draping his arms around Jay's neck and kissed him. "Thought you'd never ask."

CHAPTER TEN
Chasing Shadows

To be honest, Jay didn't think he'd ask either. It wasn't like he needed a shower, having coped with one by himself earlier that day. But what Ann had said at the pub niggled his mind, especially when seeing Seb so deflated. He'd thought he better throw the bloke a bone. One he hoped would stay hard this time.

Seb took his hand and led him up the stairs, allowing the extra time Jay needed. He didn't complain. He didn't demand to go faster, and amazingly he didn't say anything either. He remained quiet, tugging Jay into the main bathroom and switching on the waterfall shower. He waggled his fingers under the spray, checking the temperature while Jay fumbled out of his gear.

Trying to close off his mind, Jay willed with every fibre of his being for this to go well. Too many attempts and too many let downs had him already fearing the worst. It wasn't down to his mood. It hadn't been down to the pain either, nor so much the not wanting to. He'd been told using the high dosage of pain-killers could affect his performance, and not the one on the pitch. He'd refrained for a couple of days. Dealing with the pain, if only to see what would happen. Now he needed to not think, and to just feel.

When Seb turned, Jay sucked in a breath. Those dark eyes found his and Jay saw everything behind them. Everything that had always been there. The lust, the passion, the man he was and had become. *For me.* But most of all he could see the love hadn't faltered. It hurt to think he'd pushed this man away so often. He had to make that up to him. He had to prove he wasn't finished, he wasn't over, he was Jay—his Champ, even if Seb hadn't used the pet name for some time. *I gotta give him a reason to come back.*

"Water's hot." Seb unfastened the buttons on his shirt, revealing the plectrum pendant that hung down to his sternum.

Jay licked his lips and stepped forward. He took hold of the necklace, stroking the platinum between a thumb and forefinger. Seb never took it off. Not even to shower, and Jay should cling to that if nothing else. Letting it go to rest against the coarse dark hairs scattered across Seb's chest, Jay breathed in and slid his hands beneath Seb's shirt to shrug him out of it. The top drifted to the floor and Seb took over the rest, unfastening his belt and hopping out of his tight jeans. He stood there almost vulnerable, naked with only the tattoos covering his skin. The tattoos that showed who he was, and who he had been—musician, poet, dreamer and a *lover*. And that suddenly brought Jay to a haunting reality. Seb had so much past, had had so many lovers, and a wealth of sexual experience. Seb craved it, and it had signified who he was for so long. But now Jay was who he had to live with—a man who couldn't match up.

"How you wanna do this?" Seb asked, lightly, almost as though he feared the answer. "And are you sure you can?" His gaze drifted to Jay's groin, or perhaps it was lower, Jay wasn't sure. So he quirked an eyebrow for confirmation.

"I mean the knee," Seb rushed out. "The pain?"

Swiping away the metaphorical slap to his face, Jay kissed Seb for what felt like forever. He didn't want to stop, and Seb allowed it, twirling his tongue inside Jay's mouth in reunion. Jay did his best to switch off, to leave Seb to refuel their spark. The way Seb had done so many times previously—from Jay's first time with a man, to the moment Jay knew he couldn't ever be with anyone else. Seb was ready, willing, and hard. Jay reluctantly pulled away and looked down. The glorious sight of Seb's cock pointing back at him, seeping precum from the head in impatience, sent Jay reeling through conflicting emotions. He wanted to devour it, to be able to lower to his knees and honour it the way it deserved to be. Not only was that impossible for him right then, but the effortless way Seb's cock demanded attention, like the man himself, only proved how inferior Jay was beside him.

"C'mon, handsome. Let's get you dirty before I clean you up." Seb smirked and reached over Jay's shoulder to open the bathroom cupboard, taking out the lube. "I've waited so long for this."

And there it was. Proof that Seb needed this. Needed sex. And Jay hadn't been providing it for him. He quivered. *Why is this so terrifying?* Was it the fear that it could hurt? That it might do more damage to his knee and prevent recovery? Was it that he wouldn't be able to fuck hard, something Seb encouraged every now and then? Or was it something else? Something more inherent? Whatever it was, he had to get the fuck over it. So he watched Seb squeezing lube onto his fingers in preparation, hoping just the sight would be enough to dial up his desire.

"Seb—"

"Shh." Seb threw the tube into the sink, the steam from the pelting hot shower hazing around the bathroom and clouding his features. "Just let me."

Jay didn't have much of a choice as Seb slapped his mouth onto his and kissed him with an appetite that was far greater than his need for Pralines and Cream. It fired Jay's gut, and he willed it down to his groin so he could prove he yearned for this as much as Seb obviously did. Impatience overtook and Seb cupped Jay's balls, fondling them between his fingers, ignoring the fact that Jay's dick still remained unprovoked. Jay fluttered his eyes closed and Seb slithered his wet fingers through Jay's legs, coating Jay's taint with the lube. It felt good, it did. Like a low tide rippling along the surface, before a crash of wave raged over his mind.

Seb kissed him, eagerness sparking his darkened eyes. "There you are." Hovering to Jay's side, he slipped a hand around Jay's back and stroking along his buttocks before gliding a sodden finger between the crevice of his cheeks. "Whichever way you want it, baby."

"Shit." Jay closed his eyes as Seb bit down on his lip and teased his hole. He had no idea how he wanted it. Just wanting it was enough at this point. Gripping the edge of the sink beside him, he urged the dull ache niggling along his left leg to piss off and make way for the swelling of pleasure to flow freely. To set *him* free.

"Missed you, baby." Seb nipped at Jay's earlobe and trailed kisses along his neck while working his way closer, and closer, until —

Jay gasped. Seb edged his finger through the ring of muscle and thrust in, crooking to stroke at the right spot that Seb always managed to find so quickly, so easily. He ghosted his other hand over Jay's balls and rubbed along his shaft, enticing it to come up to play.

When only a flicker of a response was met from Seb's hand alone, he slapped his mouth from Jay's and lowered to a crouch. He buried his face in Jay's groin and licked everywhere, teasing with an urgency Jay knew he must be feeling. 'Cause he was too. Frustration apparent, Seb wrapped his dripping hand around his own cock and stroked, taking Jay's into his mouth and easing the soft flesh in and out.

Water dripped from the open door of the shower and spilled onto the floor, pooling around Seb's feet. Jay grunted as the rush of blood finally went to where it was needed more. His cock inflated in Seb's mouth and Seb hummed, sucking in the extra girth with greed.

"That's it. Fuck, yeah, don't stop." Jay gripped the sink tighter with one hand, curling his other into a ball. He trembled, anticipation surging through his entire body and clung onto the porcelain, along with the hope that this was the release he needed. That this was would be where his recovery could begin.

Burying his nose into the trimmed hairs of Jay's groin, Seb peered up and Jay was now fairly certain Seb was getting somewhere. A groan vibrated his throat. He so wanted to let go of the sink and trail his fingers through Seb's hair — to help him along, to guide him, to show him he wanted it. But all he had was his words.

"*Seb.*"

Seb muffled a response, a slight curve of his lips around the hardening cock and met with Jay's gaze. Speeding up, Seb shifted his position, trailing a hand between Jay's legs to tease his balls. This was it, this was fucking good and Jay was there, ready, able...*willing*.

Then Seb slipped, his feet sliding into the puddle of shower water. Making a grab for the sink, his mouth fell from Jay's dick and he flailed, falling forward onto his knees and bashed his shoulder against Jay's leg. Pain wrenched through Jay's knee and he fell back, floundering for something to hold him up. Finding nothing but the metal towel rail behind him, he sucked in through gritted teeth as the heat scorched his palm.

"Shit, baby, no." Seb stood and pulled Jay away, holding him upright.

Jay clung onto him, panting.

"Stupid move. We'll take this to the bedroom." Seb draped Jay's arm around his shoulders and attempted to drag him out.

Jay hobbled, throbbing pain making it difficult to even limp. He hung his head and slapped a hand along the wall to hop the rest of the way to their bedroom. Seb lowered him to the mattress and Jay flopped back, throwing an arm over his eyes to prevent Seb from seeing the tormented tears. He'd think it was for the pain. It wasn't. It was for not being able to do the most basic of needs for his boyfriend. The moment gone, passed, and Jay couldn't muster the energy to try again.

"Sorry." The apology was muffled into Jay's arm.

"No, I am." Seb crawled on the bed beside him and cuddled up. "Just give it a minute and we'll try again."

"I can't, Seb. I can't."

161

"Okay, okay." Seb kissed the falling tears that escaped from under Jay's arm. He pushed it away to look him in the eye. "Baby…"

"I'm sorry."

"You don't need to be sorry." Curling an arm around Jay's face, Seb hugged him to his chest.

"What if this is it, Seb? This. Me? A man who can't fuck you the way you need, who can't get on his knees for you anymore."

"Jay," Seb breathed out. "I don't need you on your knees. I need you in my arms."

That was all it took, and the tears fell freely. Jay swivelled on his side and buried his face into Seb's chest. "Just lie with me." He sniffled. "For a bit, at least." His tousled hair fell into his stinging eyes.

Seb scraped it back and planted a soft kiss to Jay's forehead. "Always."

If Seb had left him, Jay wasn't aware as he passed out in a comatose state of pain.

* * * *

Seb awoke early and slipped out of bed, a shame to leave Jay there but he thought it best to give the bloke the rest he needed after last night's clusterfuck of a fuck attempt. And because the embarrassment of it all still lingered on his mind, itching him like a skin blemish. He shouldn't have been so demanding. He should have taken it easy. They should have just showered, properly, and bathed in love rather than Seb going straight for sex. He'd thought that was what Jay had meant, had wanted. Maybe it had been, until the slapstick slipping incident. It still made him feel like crap that he'd resorted to type

162

rather than stepping up and taking care of his man the way he should.

He didn't bother going for the run he'd mentioned. It had been a feeble attempt at reaching Jay. Instead he went out to collect his suit from the tailors down the high street and purchased a couple of takeout coffees and pastries on the way back. At least that might soften the awkwardness of the night before.

The echoing grunts and yelps that bounced off the walls as Seb returned home put him on edge. He winced. Those painful cries coming from his boyfriend had become an all-too-familiar sound. With unease in his gut, he clipped his suit over the living room door, threw the breakfast peace offerings in the kitchen and bounded up the stairs two at a time. Their bedroom was empty, covers in a sprawled mess, but the door down the hall to Jay's gym, which had become more a therapy room, was slightly ajar. Seb tiptoed to the end and peered in.

Jay lay on his back on the floor matt, Ewa kneeling in front of him and lifting his leg, bending it at the joint, and looking every bit like she was torturing his boyfriend. Apparently keeping active was key to Jay's recovery.

Biting a thumbnail, Seb stepped back. And for some reason, thought it was a good idea to listen through the gap.

"Are you running yet?" Ewa asked, which was immediately followed by a grunt from Jay.

"Light jogging, yeah." Jay's stifled voice told the blatant lie.

Seb shook his head.

"Good. That'll help. But this still feels stiff." Ewa tapped his knee and Jay grimaced, sucking in between gritted teeth. "And feels a bit tender today. Have you knocked it?"

163

Seb winced.

"Yeah, a bit. Last night," Jay replied. "Tried something stupid. Doubt that'll happen again."

Closing his eyes, Seb hefted out a sigh. All his goddamn fault.

"What did you try?" Ewa's voice had an air of concern in her elevation.

Jay breathed out, heavily, and the silence made Seb assume he was communicating via other means to the woman who was getting more intimate with Jay than Seb had for the last few months.

"I see." Ewa chuckled. "Well, the road to recovery can be a lonely one, so sometimes it's a good idea to allow someone to walk alongside you."

"Is that some kinda physio poetry?"

"No. Although, I seem to recall a song might have said something similar." Ewa pushed back on Jay's leg, bending it at the knee.

"Don't say it's a Drops song."

"Surely you would know." Ewa set Jay's leg to the floor and stepped back, hands on her hips. "All I'll say is that I've dealt with these injuries a long time. I've dealt with sportsmen and women who are out of the game for a while. I know how it affects them. Let him in. Let him know how you feel. Let him take some of the pressure off you."

Seb didn't wait for Jay's reply as Ewa started packing away her things into her duffel bag, so he scarpered, quietly, back down the stairs and into the kitchen. He set up the plates for the pastries and sat at the island, flipping through the various papers and magazines that had been delivered that morning. Ewa joined him a short time after, giving a brief nod of greeting and filled her water bottle at the sink.

164

"I don't know how he resists those sad puppy eyes." Ewa smiled, screwing the top on her bottle.

Seb snorted. He hadn't been aware he'd been staring at her, willing for her to give him some good news. "How is he?"

"Surely you know the answer to that?"

"I'll rephrase. How is the knee? Really?"

"It's okay. It takes time to heal and get full range of movement. But it looks healthy enough. The last operation has done its job."

"Is there a but in there?"

"Recuperation is as much about the mind as it is the damaged ligaments."

Seb nodded, understanding. All too well. "What can I do to help?"

"Well." Ewa pushed away from the sink and slung her bag over her shoulder. "Stretches, gentle exercise, lay off the painkillers. All of which he's been told. You can ensure he does them." She headed toward the archway. "And maybe a night out?"

Seb smiled. "I got one planned."

"Good. I'm due again in a couple of days."

"Thanks, Ewa."

As she left, Jay entered. Seb pushed over the takeout coffee and pastry toward him, which he took with a grateful nod and tucked in straight away. Seb smiled, mostly to himself and soaked up the remaining news.

"Seb?" Jay cut the silence, wiping the crumbs from his fingertips down his shorts.

"Hmm?" Seb peered up from the paper, meeting crystal-clear blue eyes.

"About last night…"

"Hey, forget it. I'm sorry, completely my fault. I took things a bit far. I just couldn't help it. Never can with

165

you." He winked. "So, we'll chalk it up to my stupidity and just see where things go from here, right?" That was light, carefree, whilst also heartfelt. He was rather proud of himself.

Jay nodded. "The bathroom's a bit of a mess."

"Luckily, I booked the cleaner for tomorrow morning."

"Soon as I'm better, she goes."

"Ooo, you drive a hard bargain." Seb grinned. Jay's sudden positivity was infectious. Perhaps it was time for something more. "I got an hour before I need to go rehearse. Fancy a proper brunch?" He twisted from the stool and headed over to the fridge, pulling open the double doors.

"Like what?"

Scanning the limited contents in the fridge, Seb furrowed his brow. Cooking hadn't ever been something he was interested in. But perhaps he needed to start making an effort. "Eggs?"

"I can't eat your scrambled shit again."

Seb peered over his shoulder, and added a mocking expression of hurt, then turned back to the fridge. "We got some cheese. Leftover salmon. Oily fish good for the prostate." He winked. "Omelette?"

"You're gonna have a bash at an omelette?"

"I'll have you know, James 'Rutters' Ruttman, that when I have a bash at anything, I usually come out on top."

Jay snorted. "All right, I'm game if you are."

Was that a come on? As much as Seb hoped it was, he wasn't going to make the same mistake twice. This was all about the cooking. And proving to Jay that they could do all the normal things, that they could get back to being a couple. So he set to pulling out the ingredients he assumed he needed, spreading them along the kitchen counter and finding where in all the units the frying pan would be kept.

"Last drawer on the right." Jay pointed to a what appeared to be the end of the built-in units.

"That's a drawer?" Seb's elevated his voice as he stumbled upon the hidden cove. On pulling a drawer free, he gasped. "When the fuck do we ever use all this shit?" He rummaged through the baskets of pristine aluminium saucepans, griddles and frying pans that he swore he hadn't seen in all their time living here, or in the flat in Limehouse.

"You know when you said you unpacked?" Jay tapped his hands against the island. "Did you not notice them?"

"I believe your mother was in charge of the kitchen." He tugged out a deep-dished frying pan and clanged it onto one of the farmhouse range cooker hobs. "Right. Bowl." Seb slapped his hands to his thighs, glancing up at the rest of the units.

"If you ain't got a clue where the bowls are, I'm gonna start to worry."

"I do. I do." He didn't and hovered over to a cupboard below him.

Jay shook his head. Seb side-stepped to the next, hand in the air to the door above. Jay pinched the bridge of his nose and Seb had to bite his bottom lip through a smile. Jay stood, then limped toward the L-shape units. He pulled the bottom drawer open and produced a porcelain mixing bowl which he handed over to Seb.

"Much obliged." Seb set it down and cracked a couple of eggs into it. Seasoning, he knew that one, and ground salt and pepper on top. The cooking utensils stuck out from the shiny black holder on the counter and Seb hummed before pulling the wooden spoon free.

"Hold up." Jay stepped behind him and grabbed the spoon from his hand. "I don't know how someone who was brought up with as much privilege as you, yet you don't know your arse from your elbow."

"That's catastrophically unfair." Seb pouted. "This is my elbow." He nudged Jay with it, then grabbed Jay's hand and slapped it to his backside. "And that, there, is my arse. I'd show you it but I'm cooking."

Smiling, Jay squeezed. Then leaned over to tug out a whisk from the utensil pot. He shoved it in Seb's hand, but instead of letting him get on with it, Jay stepped in closer behind Seb and curled his fingers around his wrist.

"Pick up the bowl." Jay's breath tingled down Seb's neck, and he shivered before doing what he was told. "Hold it at an angle, then loosen your wrist."

"You telling me I'm limp-wristed?" Seb tutted.

"Not always." Jay's voice rumbled deep in Seb's ear.

Seb smiled, the hairs on the back of his neck prickling. This was more like it. How it had been. Jay guided Seb's hand to whisk through the eggs and Seb's chest burst with unbridled yearning at the intimacy of Jay's touch. He closed his eyes for a moment and leant his head back onto Jay's shoulder, allowing Jay to take over. The cooking, and Seb's body, mind and soul. Jay pressed in closer, crushing Seb against the counter, almost as though he wanted to slide inside of him. Maybe he did? *Should I let him?*

Slowly, Seb tilted his neck and captured Jay's lips for a contorted kiss. Continuing to whizz through the eggs, Jay opened his mouth and slipped his cool tongue inside Seb's mouth. Seb was stuck where he was, compressed by Jay's body against him but also not allowed to stop stirring. He did his best to keep up the kiss. He couldn't not. The very act sent tingles along Seb's spine, and if he didn't know better, he'd think he could feel something against him, prodding him. *Just don't acknowledge it. Just keep kissing him.*

A splat onto Seb's shirt made him gasp. "Fuck." Some of the egg had sloshed out of the bowl and down his front.

Chuckling, Jay released Seb's hand and leaned over to pull the roll of kitchen towel from its holder. Seb attempted to clear it up, but the gooey contents stuck to the cotton of his top. He whipped it off and handed it to Jay.

"Now let me finish this, will you?" Seb wriggled away from Jay. As much as he'd love to step up their foreplay, he was mindful that a step would lead to a stride, then a leap and before he knew it they'd crash and burn. Seb had to prove he could be more than just sex. "Sit down." He nodded to the chair.

Jay hobbled back to his stool and sank onto it. Seb could feel Jay's lingering gaze on him as he began the task of lighting the gas hob and attempting to actually cook. Topless. But he didn't honour him with a look over his shoulder. His grinning face would have given him away.

His first attempt wasn't too bad. Not exactly a perfectly folded semi-circle and more a mush of scrambled eggs with flakes of pink salmon dotted in it, but it was still the best he'd ever done. And Jay tucked in as soon as Seb handed him a plate.

"So what's your plan for tonight?" Jay forked through the rubbery eggs.

"Car coming at six. So I'll be suited and booted by then. We're on at eight." Suddenly, a thought struck.

169

Could he really go with it? *Should I push for it?* "Why don't you come with me? Like, go together. Show our faces for real."

"What, in the media? Televised?"

"Yes."

Jay chewed his bottom lip.

"I think it'd be good for you. For both of us. To face all this, once and for all. Be a united front. Show them we aren't scared. That you aren't hiding. That you're on your way to a full recovery. You don't need to do any interviews. We don't need to pose for photos. We just go, together. Like any other couple."

Jay inhaled a deep breath. Eventually, and unexpectedly, he nodded. "All right."

Seb smiled. "That's my boy." He stood, scraping away the empty plates and planted a chaste kiss to Jay's lips.

He was now more than a little excited for tonight. Not only was the band doing something a little different on stage, and were in the running to receive an award for their latest album, but now he had Jay coming. As his date. To a media-fuelled event. If things went well, this could spell the end of them living their life in the shadows.

CHAPTER ELEVEN
Victory Dance

The blacked-out Mercedes pulled up beside the illuminated front of the Roundhouse in North West London. The charity and awards dinner was certainly pulling out all the stops to prove it would be the top of the celebrity calendar for years to come. Not even the football awards dos that Jay had attended in his time had flaunted this much lavish decoration. In the back of the chauffeur-driven car Jay twisted his clammy hands in his lap and adjusted his suit jacket.

Whilst Seb had gone all-new for his whistle and flute, Jay was stuck wearing the suit the club had got for him for their last football bash. It still fit, if a little loose where it counted, but Seb had insisted it didn't show. He,

171

of course, was decked out perfectly in a slim-fitting black Hugo Boss that hugged his slender frame, and his tight black shirt finished off with a thin ruby-red tie gave him a more sophisticated rock look. If Seb was nervous about the night ahead, he didn't show it. He just bounced beside Jay with relentless energy.

Someone opened the car door from the outside, and Seb slapped on his smile for the flashing of cameras, screaming of fans, and eager news reporters waiting along the path, forming an aisle leading up to the entrance. The red carpet draped over the concrete flowed up the front steps, toward the open glass doors. *Steps. Four of them. Fucking great.* Slipping along the back seats, Jay attempted to vacate the car without a grimace. 'Cause that wouldn't produce a particularly great photo for the waiting media. He now wondered why he'd agreed to this at all. Normally, during Seb's gigs, he snuck in the back and left Seb to do his schmoozing with the band, or alone. Mainly it would have coincided with Jay's football fixtures, his rest days where he was confined to the house, or some other commitment to West Ham. But this wasn't any old gig. This was Seb's first awards do, and Jay being out on injury meant he'd run out of excuses not to be in front of a camera with him.

Seb was already shaking hands with the first reporter, laughing and answering the questions fired at him. Jay felt as awkward as fuck, standing there, behind him, waiting to be told where to go. Seb shot him a wink. No doubt that would be captured on camera and would go viral by the morning. Seb thanked one news crew only to be called over to the next. The drone from the cheering fans and the chatter from the organisers as they shoved people through doors or in front of various press felt like a circus. And the snaps from cameras left flickering yellow dots in Jay's eyes. He tried to zone it out, like he would have on a football pitch, but it was only making the dull ache in his knee more prominent in his mind. Fluttering his eyes to a close, he focused on getting up the steps unaided. He couldn't bear looking like a tit in front of the UK media who already called him names he had to look up on Google.

"Jay! Jay! Over here!" The frantic waving from a female reporter the other side to where Seb stood caught Jay's eye. He didn't want to give interviews. This wasn't his event. This wasn't football and therefore he wasn't contracted to speak to the press.

"How's the recovery? Is Seb looking after you?" Another voice heckled over the crowd, ushering for him to come closer.

No one was picking up on his mental memo. He knew it was rude to ignore them, and that he'd be called any number of things by the papers tomorrow but he couldn't bring himself to care all that much.

"When do you expect to be back on the pitch?"

Jay drifted his gaze to the first reporter, and that was when all the other news crews must have cottoned on to what they were missing and aimed their huge microphones and camera lenses on him. His name, both the Rutters nickname and the more intimate Jay, was blurted out all over the place. Along with a demand they get the first posed photograph of the couple.

Jay had never wanted to get inside faster. He stepped over to where Seb was still ranting into an outstretched microphone about some political stance or other and slid a hand on the small of his back, leaning in to whisper in his ear. He was more than aware the flashes had increased with him doing that. It rang in his ears as well as wrecking his retina.

"I'm heading in."

Seb looked him the eye. He nodded, then held out a hand to the reporter. "Sorry, duty calls." He nudged Jay forward and walked by his side, shoulders brushing, but no hands held, toward the Roundhouse entrance. Seb motioned for Jay to take the steps first, using the moment to wave at the clicking of cameras.

With it much calmer inside, Jay could breathe again. A fifty-thousand-strong crowd of football fans seemed far easier to block out than a handful of tabloid journalists asking difficult questions.

"You okay?" Seb asked, squeezing the top of his arm.

"Yeah." Jay shook his head. "Just didn't expect that, and I was shitting myself that I'd fall arse over tit and be on Britain's Funniest Celebrity Gaffs by Monday."

Seb chuckled, sliding his hand down to tug on Jay's fingers. "Thank you."

"For what?"

"For being here at all. I know you find all this difficult."

Jay nodded. "I just ain't good with the press. I got no idea why they have such interest."

"Because lives of other people always are, right?"

Jay went to speak, but a clipboard holding and headpiece wearing bloke rushed up to Seb and demanded he go to the dressing rooms.

"Break a leg." Jay winked.

Seb narrowed his eyes, then laughed and jogged off down some corridor while Jay was shown through to the main arena. Round tables were set up in the decorated hall in front of the stage, with the cheap seats at the back filling up with the ticketed-only audience. A penguin-suited usher showed Jay to his table near the front. Leah,

Martin's girlfriend, with her pink hair tousled to below her waist, smiled in greeting, along with another girl, stick-thin and made up to the nines one chair removed from her. Jay guessed that was Noah's plus one. The men the other side of the table were part of the record label, heads together discussing business. Then, by herself, in a glittery black dress, sat Ann. Jay smiled. *Thank fuck for a familiar face.*

"Hey." Jay sat beside her, stretching out his leg.

"Hi." She attempted a smile in return, but Jay could tell it hadn't reached her eyes.

"How'd he rope you into this?"

"I think at the time he asked, I was glad to come. Now," Ann's gaze flickered momentarily to the girl opposite, "I know I shouldn't have."

"Want some wine?" Jay reached to the middle of the table for the bottles of red and white.

"No." She held up a glass of water. "My drink for tonight."

Jay blinked. "Why? What's up with you? Bun in the oven, is it?" When Ann didn't respond, Jay midway to pouring some red into his glass, paused. "You ain't?"

"Shhh." Ann lowered her head.

"Are you?" Jay set the bottle back on the table.

"Fuck, Jay." Ann screwed her eyes shut. "I really, really should not have drunk that wine with you the other night."

"Fuck, Ann! What? When did you find out?"

"This morning. I did a test to kinda put me at ease, y'know? I was late, yeah, but I did not think I was acts preggers. Turned out, the thin blue line got me good and proper."

"Wow. So, Lucas? Does he know?"

Ann's body deflated and she closed her eyes. "No. Which is probably a good thing because it ain't his." She peered up at Jay, sad brown eyes glistening.

"You slept with someone else? When?"

"Look, don't go all moral high ground on me. I am aware I am the stupid fucking cliché of a poor girl from the East London council estates. Knocked up at twenty-four and currently single. Thank you, British statistics." She held up her glass of lemon water in cheers. "I feel as much of a bitch as your eyes are telling me I am. I'm an idiot. I wish it was Lucas's. But he would never have allowed this to happen, so that's my lesson learnt, ain't it?"

Jay had to let that process for a moment. Ann, pregnant. But not only that, the father wasn't the man she'd been seeing for the past couple of years. The man who didn't believe in sex before marriage, the man she thought didn't want her sexually. Like he hadn't. Was that what people did? Go find it somewhere else if they weren't getting any? Jay swallowed a glug of red with unease. "Whose is it?" he finally asked.

Ann tilted her neck, her whole body sinking into the seat. But a bursting drum roll interrupted the moment and the evening's host bounded up onto the stage, hushing the room for his introduction.

Jay leaned over to Ann. "Seb's on first. We'll talk later."

Ann sipped from her water, gaze focused ahead to the stage. The compère did his speech, introducing the night and the awards that were on offer along with how any money raised through auctions and various other means would all be going to the Teenage Cancer Trust. Jay settled back as the first act was announced. The Drops. Red curtains slithered to an open and revealed a rather strange set-up. Especially for a Drops performance. It wasn't the usual three-piece band with Seb out front. It looked more like a set for a West End stage, dressed up to appear like a bar tavern in the Wild West, with men in cowboy hats and women dressed in over flowing ball gowns.

A single tinny drum roll started up first, and a spotlight focused on Noah to the left behind a smaller kit than his usual. Following that, a vibrating bass line punched through the rhythm, and Martin's silhouette lit up on the right of the stage. Then came that voice. The deep, husky, tones ricocheting around the whistling hall and a stream of light flowed down on Seb, up front, guitar around his neck as he sang into a headset mic. Jay's stomach fluttered, the hairs on his arms standing to attention. This wasn't their usual set-up. This was something else. Jay would have chuckled at the wording, if he wasn't in awe of what happened next.

It was like a rock-opera. A story sung in chorus and verse detailing murder, mayhem and entangled lovers, and re-enacted on stage by the dancing performers. Seb, Martin and Noah remained focused out front, ignoring the dramatics around them, even when Seb received a few backside pinches and a red kiss mark left on his cheek by a roaming dancer. The audience whistled and all clapped along with relish.

Jay had seen Seb perform dozens of times. Sometimes physically there, many times just the catch-up on live video. And each time he was in awe of him. Each time he was hurtled back to that very first moment, in the dingy Underground bar, when Jay hadn't known where that rocker would take him.

Then Seb's singing stopped, making way for an instrumental solo and Jay sat forward in his seat. There

177

must have been other musicians in on the performance, unseen from the seats, as Seb whipped his guitar off from around his neck, handing it to a roving performer all the while the music increased. Seb held out a hand, and a pirouetting dancer in floating red ballgown slapped her palm into it and he dragged her forward to him, sliding his other hand onto her hip. Jay's eyes could have popped from his head as he leaned forward and watched his boyfriend serenade the woman around the stage in a perfected tango. Seb could dance. *Really* dance. And pretty damn good.

And Jay hadn't known about any of it. *How could I have not?*

"Fuckin' hell." Ann exclaimed. "You so know he's gonna be picked for *Strictly* after this."

Jay heard her, but couldn't tear his eyes away from the stage. He'd known Seb could move to a rhythm, being musically talented and all, and on occasion Jay had danced with him, but that had been slower and more sensual, with only really one thing on their mind. This, this was something else. This was professional standards. Seb roamed that stage, gracefully so, launching through various swings and twists. And his partner was attached to him, eyes focused on him, looking ever the woman in love.

Jay envied her. He could never be her.

As the instrumental part increased, speeding up to a climax, the woman was ripped from Seb's arms to fall into another dancer's, and Seb was handed back his guitar and continued singing, with no fault in his voice. The crowd, needless to say, went fucking wild. Jay couldn't even clap. He'd been stunned, frozen.

A table across from theirs claimed by some boy band that Jay recognised but couldn't have cared less what their name was erupted into cheers. One of them launched to stand on his seat and wolf-whistled up at Seb. Jay narrowed his eyes, jealousy stabbing his conscience. Seb grinned, winked at the bloke, and sang the last line to the performance. The entire audience consisting of musicians, celebrities, and those lucky enough to have held on the phone at 8 a.m. to claim the couple of thousand civilian tickets, roared.

Jay stood, his heart pounding. All he wanted was to leap on that stage, take Seb in his arms and kiss him. But he *couldn't*. With his heart in his throat, he limped out of the hall, finding the nearest fire exit.

* * * *

Still buzzing, Seb ran off the stage to stand in the wings. The performance had gone better than he'd imagined on devising it only a couple of weeks ago. He had his mother to thank for having given him his theatrical musical background and the contacts to seek out a dance crew that had been open to his last-minute ideas. Seb peered past the curtains, out to the front stage with Martin and Noah huddled behind him as the backline tech crew cleared away their set, making room for the first awards announcement.

He didn't really think he had a chance. The category of debut album was a tough one. All the albums, bar one, in Seb's opinion, were front runners. But if the Drops won this, then they'd finally get noticed by those in the industry that mattered—the critics. These awards were independently judged by a panel of music professionals, and not voted on by the public. And that meant more to Seb, knowing that his popularity for being

Jay "Rutters" Ruttman's boyfriend seemed to outweigh his musical talent. Yeah, the band was rising up the charts, gaining mainstream fans, but they all still focused on his celebrity status rather than the music he consistently produced. Here, things might change.

He bit his thumbnail, trembling with anticipation as the screens around the venue showed each of the bands in the running. The Drops' *Breaking Through* video popped up first, Seb on his back in the water singing to the camera, which then cut to the next band, Attax. *Not a chance.* Then the next.

"I'm gonna have to light this thing, they don't hurry the fuck up." Noah slipped out the cigarette tucked from behind his ear.

"Shhh," Seb shot over his shoulder.

"And the winners are…" The compère opened the envelope in front of him, and dragged out the anticipatory wait.

"Come the fuck on!" Noah yelled.

"Attax."

The audience burst into thunderous applause. Seb hung his head, disappointment surging through his entire body. Any of them. Any single one of them, but that fucking band.

"Bollocks to it." Noah stomped off and after a brief squeeze of Seb's arm, Martin followed behind him.

Seb stayed grounded, watching the band receive their shiny trophy and giving a speech about how humbled they were, *blah blah, fucking, blah.* Every clap from the crowd as the band returned to their table felt like someone banging Seb's head against a brick wall. He wanted to stamp his foot and demand a recount, but instead he watched each of the Attax band members shaking hands with whoever sat at their table. Trailing his gaze along the rest of the venue, it was then that he noticed the absence of a certain young blond.

Pulling himself together, he bundled off backstage and through the swinging doors that led to the adjoining corridors of dressing rooms and rehearsal space. He searched for an exit, biting down the hurt and slight feelings of betrayal as he focused on finding Jay in the hope there was a better excuse for his departure than the ones Seb was currently thinking up. A set of fire doors were clanged shut at the end of the corridor, and Seb bounded toward them before a call of his name made him stop in his tracks.

"Sebastian?" The guy was suited, as most that evening were. But his one screamed all money and top executive. As he stepped closer, Seb noted the suit was a Prada special. *Nice.* "Kenneth Larson."

Seb instantly slapped his palm into the man's outstretched hand.

"A&R Director for Sony Music."

"I know, I know." Seb nodded as though he was the fucking Churchill dog.

Smiling, Kenneth stepped back and tucked his hands into his trouser pockets. "That was some performance back there."

"Thank you." Seb was aware he was acting like a startled fanboy, but he couldn't not. This guy had been the driving force behind many of the bands that Seb himself had listened to for most of his adolescent life. Kenneth Larson was God in the music industry.

"You devised all that yourself?"

"Yes."

"And you're currently signed with Armstrong Records?"

"Yes." *And also currently unable to say more than one fucking syllable!*

"How are you finding them?"

"Honestly?" Seb rubbed his forehead, invigorating his speech to come to life. "I mostly do it all myself. I give them a percentage of my royalties for them to stick their fingers up their arses. They have no clue. I believe they're more interested in my celebrity exposure than my music."

Kenneth chuckled. "Yes. I can imagine. They are a small outfit. That comes with the territory. I can see they are clinging onto your more...unprecedented interest in the hope it gains them sales."

That was a new one for fucking a gay footballer.

"I think we might be able to help." Kenneth produced a business card from his jacket pocket and handed it over. "I was at V Fest. I was impressed and I've followed you ever since. You're talented, Seb. More than you're given credit for. And tonight, I think you might have just proven that to the naysayers. Those who think you're riding on this wave of hysteria around you."

Seb flipped over the card. Pristine white matt with just Kenneth's name and a personal mobile number printed in jet black ink. Elegant. *Minimalist.* Except Seb held in his hand the thing he had wanted most in his entire life. This made up for losing the award to fucking Attax.

"And an FYI. Money in music isn't found in royalties anymore. I'm sure you're aware of that, what with you having utilised the free market to gain exposure from the outset."

"I am aware. Sales of physical CDs have reduced drastically since the introduction of music streaming. No one cares to hold a record in their hands anymore." Seb tutted. "Whereas I think that's the beauty of it. A brand-new limited-edition LP is an artwork."

"Agreed. But for the majority, it's the tours, the live performances, that bring in the fans. And fans bring in the dollars. People now pay to *see* you, not just to hear you." Kenneth smiled and pointed a finger. "And you just gave the world a reason to seek out your next tour date. Which is when, by the way?"

"Unplanned. On hold."

"Reasons?"

Seb sighed. "Personal ones."

"Unpersonalise them. America awaits you, Seb. I can have you touring the states and cracking America in no time. If you want to hit the big time, if you want to know how to make money in music, then America is the first step to global success. And you do not want to be doing that with a three-man team making up Armstrong Records, or, as you say, by yourself."

"You'd sign us?" Seb's voice warbled with the revelation.

"I'd sign *you*. If you come with band members already in tow, so be it. But just so we're clear, it's you I want." Kenneth tapped the top of Seb's arm. "Call me, we'll arrange a meeting and go through things. Enjoy the rest of the evening, regardless that the Awards committee have no idea what they've just missed out on."

Seb tapped the card in his hand, then nodded. "I will. Thank you."

Kenneth sauntered away, finding the double doors that lead through into the main hall. Seb's chest tingled. He had to find the lads. *Asap.* Grinning, he ran back toward the hall.

* * * *

Leaning his elbows on the railing separating the smoker's area from the back alley, Jay stared up at the night sky. A full moon lit up the darkened city and he exhaled a steam of condensation into the air. Least it was quiet out there, except for the occasional thunderous round of applause that drifted through the bulky fire doors. He felt a git for bailing, especially as the announcement for best debut indie album was due up first. Jay wouldn't know if Seb had just landed his first accolade.

The doors behind him clanged open and Jay angled his head to see who the outcoming was. Ann smiled, and teetered down the steps, having to side-step them due to her tight pencil skirt.

"Been looking for you everywhere." She bumped his shoulder. "Taking up smoking?"

Jay hung his head.

"Didn't know Seb could tango." Ann twisted and leaned back on the railing to face him, her smile filled with sincere sympathy.

"Nor did I."

Nodding, Ann scraped her peep-toe heel along the pavement. "I'm sure he did it to impress you."

Jay shrugged. Maybe Seb had. Maybe he'd kept his ballroom dancing skills a secret to one day show them off to Jay. Maybe he'd been waiting for the right moment. Jay wasn't sure that tonight, when Jay could hardly walk, was the best time. But he was also aware that not everything needed to revolve around him. He just couldn't help thinking it was a kick in the teeth when he was already down.

"Don't go doing that." Ann pushed him gently on the arm.

"Doing what?"

"Thinking you ain't good enough for him."

Jay didn't reply. Instead, he eyed Ann's skin-tight dress. "What are you gonna do?"

Ann shrugged. "Fuck knows."

"How long you been sleeping with the bloke?"

"On and off for a while. More off than on, I'd say. Until a couple months back when I thought things were definitely over with Lucas. Then it was more on." Ann sighed and adjusted the pins in her up-do. "I know I'm a cow. I know I'm going straight to hell. I know everyone will think I'm a bitch. I don't know how to explain it, but I guess I needed to know I was desirable. He did that for me."

Jay tried not to let disappointment seep into his expression. It wasn't his place to judge. It was his place to be the mate Ann needed. The way she had been for him so many times before.

"Have you told him?"

"God no." Ann shook her head with a vicious frown. "To be fair, I only found out this morning and, well, the bloke ain't really the marriage-and-kids type, so I'm fairly certain he won't take the news too great. Might ruin his rep."

"Could always tell Lucas it's his, then he'll have to marry ya."

Ann laughed, glistening tears in her eyes. "Spontaneous conception? Don't think that'd work to be honest."

"I weren't being serious."

"I know."

After a pause, Jay nudged her shoulder with his. "I think you'd make a great mum." He smiled, hoping he was saying the right thing. He didn't know anymore. He'd lost more than his ability to play football. He'd lost

185

his ability to be able to assess what people were thinking, *feeling*. So drowned in his own drama, he'd lost his empathy for others.

"Really? I thought I wouldn't have kids. Like, ever."

"Why not?"

Ann picked a piece of fluff from Jay's jacket. "'Cause remember back when we was kids? And we snuck out to go to that shitty travelling fair down Plaistow Park?"

Jay racked his brains, vague memories teetering on the surface. Then, he chuckled. "We were, what, fifteen?"

"Yeah, 'bout that. You threw up on the Waltzer." Ann laughed.

"'Cause you made me eat the whole bag of candyfloss."

"No-one made you, Rutters. You just hadn't ever eaten than much sugar in one sitting before."

"What's this gotta do with you not wanting sprogs?"

"I didn't say I never wanted them. Just, I had a different vision of having kids." Ann sniffed, and she had trouble swallowing. "'Cause, remember that little boy we found? Crying that he'd lost his mum?"

"Oh, yeah. We waited with him, then walked him around and found his mum in a panic."

"Yeah. She was so grateful. And I always remember 'cause she said to me 'don't ever let that one go. You'll make fantastic parents.' And that was when we'd only kissed a couple of times. But I was so in love with you. How you were with that kid, too. My ovaries were knocking to be let out."

Jay's shoulders dropped and he pushed away from the railing. "Ann—"

186

"Look, it ain't that I'm upset about it or nothing. I mean, shit, I came to terms with it years ago. But this…" She stroked her stomach. "Kinda brought that all back. If I was going to have kids with anyone, it was going to be you. Like I thought we might have back when we was fumbling around trying to make it work. When contraception was you faking it."

"I didn't—"

"Don't try convincing me anymore. I ain't as stupid as I was back then. I'd've loved to have your baby. Still would. I'd give it to you and Seb in a heartbeat."

"I think you'd feel differently about that when you hold it in your arms."

"Maybe. But this isn't yours. And it isn't Lucas's. And I'm such an idiot to have chased anyone who'd have me just because of all the old feelings of rejection. Now I'm gonna be a single mum, forever, 'cause no one is gonna want me now." Tears streamed down Ann's cheeks and she tried to clear them with her thumb.

Jay had no idea what to do. Or to say. He rooted in his pocket and found a cloth that he supposed should have been tucked into his lapel. Handing it over, he wondered how much about Ann's behaviour was down to him.

"Who's the father?"

The fire escape doors behind them clanged open and out stumbled Noah, customary cigarette clenched between his lips. "Fuck this shit. Coming outside for a fag is doing my nut in." He nodded down to Jay and lit the cigarette, blowing smoke into the air. "Jay. Ann."

"Noah." Ann folded her arms.

"Babe, move over." The girl from the table curled a manicured hand around Noah's arm and pushed him aside. Noah lit her cigarette for her, holding her hand as he did so, then peered down to ground level.

Then Jay realised he didn't know the outcome of the awards. "You win?"

Noah blew another lungful of smoke into the air. "Nah. Attax did."

"Sorry."

The girl kissed Noah's cheek. "Don't worry, babe, you'll win drummer of the year."

Ann shivered beside Jay. "I'm heading back in. You coming?"

"Give me a minute."

Ann squeezed his arm, then teetered back up the steps, slipping through Noah and the girl and slammed the doors after her. Jay twisted around, ignoring the sound of lips smacking against each other and took a deep breath. Until—

"Watch it, Saunders." Noah flicked his cigarette over the barrier as Seb bashed the door into his girlfriend.

"Sorry, Martin with you?" Seb baulked on catching Jay's gaze. "Baby!" He bundled down the steps to stand in front of him. "You okay?"

"Yeah." Jay nodded. "Sorry, I just needed air. The knee seized up." It wasn't right to lie, but nor was it right to offload all the crap on Seb just then. Not when he'd just lost out on his first award.

"Right." Seb bit his lip.

"And, well, Ann needed a chat." *Even better, blame Ann.* "She's pregnant."

"For serious?"

"Yeah."

"Wow. I thought she and Lucas—"

"It ain't his."

"*Shit.*"

"Yeah."

"She keeping it?"

Jay shrugged. The clang of the fire doors above jolted them both. *Shit.* He'd forgotten that they hadn't been alone in the darkened alley. Jay didn't suppose it would matter. It had only been Noah. He wouldn't have cared to listen when sucking face with the model he'd brought along.

Seb brushed his shoulder with Jay's. "I'm sure she'll be fine. She's tough. And feisty. And she'll have your, our, support whatever she decides, right?"

Jay nodded.

Smiling, Seb tugged Jay's fingers. "Come on, let's go in. I need to speak to the guys." He went to head up the steps toward the doors, but Jay tightened his fingers around Seb's and pulled him back.

"You all right?" Seb asked, looking down at their entwined hands.

Jay hated what he was going to say, but right then, he couldn't stop himself. He just wanted to be alone. With Seb. Like how they'd been earlier. "Can we just go home? I ain't feeling it."

Seb hung his head, inhaling a sharp breath but when he looked back up, he slapped on a smile. "Sure."

Boyfriend Goals!

Seb Saunders and Jay Ruttman make their first public appearance together.

Last night saw the long-awaited public confirmation that Jay Ruttman, West Ham footballer, and Seb Saunders, front man of the Drops, are a couple.

They arrived at the Charity Music Awards where the Drops were performing, together, with Seb even stopping to talk to press.

Jay, who is currently out in injury, remained behind him, noticeably uncomfortable in the limelight, but did huddle close to the lead guitarist and lead singer.

Since coming out at a press conference last year, Jay has remained tight-lipped on his romance and neither have appeared at any public engagements together.

Seb Saunders, whose band was up for the award for best debut album, spoke to us before entering the glitzy do. "It's great having him here. He can pick me up when I've downed all this free champagne."

When asked about Jay's injury, there was a noticeable anguish on the usual brazen front man. "He's in recovery. He's doing good."

Jay refused any interviews, shunning any media attention, and the couple were seen to leave the venue together directly after the Drops outstanding performance. They subsequently lost out on the debut album award.

CHAPTER TWELVE
Alternate Picking

A honking of a car horn from outside the house woke Seb up the next morning. Lifting his head from face down on the pillow, he squinted. "The fuck?"

A piping-hot mug of coffee clunked onto the bedside table beside him, followed by his mobile phone and the slap of a newspaper on his back.

"I just been on the dog with the club, they calling me in." Jay was dressed. Which, yeah, was an odd sight already. But even more strange was that he'd donned the West Ham training tracksuit that hadn't seen the light of day in a few months now.

"Right." Seb swivelled onto his back, rubbing his eyes and fell against the upholstered winged headboard.

The newspaper crumpled on his lap, so he unfolded it to the front page. "Didn't have you down as a *Sun* subscriber."

"Courtesy of your cleaner this mornin'."

Seb snorted. "Out of all the posed photos of celeb couples from last night, they choose this papped one of us, huh?" He cocked his head taking in the photograph that had been blown up to fit most of the tabloid front page. It was of them, at the entrance to the Roundhouse, with Jay's hand on the small of Seb's back and leaning into his ear. Fuzzy around the edges, too. The headline in bold made him chuckle. *Boyfriend Goals.* Until he peered up over the paper and met with Jay staring down at him, chewing his bottom lip. "You pissed?"

"No." Jay shook his head.

"Is the club?"

"Can't see why. Ain't exactly news, is it?"

"So, why they calling you in?"

Jay shrugged. "I dunno. My guess, they're gonna tell me how long I got. Ultimatum, maybe. For the knee."

"Right." Seb shuffled up in the bed. "Do you need me to drive you? I can be ready in a jiffy."

Jay arched an amused eyebrow. "A jiffy?"

Seb tutted. "It's too early for me to mockney, right now."

Jay chuckled. "Lucky I love you plummy." He leaned down and planted a kiss to Seb's lips. It wasn't rushed either. He stayed there, for a good few seconds, regardless that Seb's breath must have tasted like a day-old dog's dinner.

"Minty." Seb smiled.

"Stay in bed. My dad's coming to this one."

"Right." Seb hid the disappointment. "You want me to stay here all day?"

"You got anything on?"

"Under here?" Seb lifted the duvet to display his morning salute.

Jay laughed. Which wasn't the reaction Seb had been hoping for. "Nah, I mean you doing anything?"

"Oh." Seb slapped the duvet back down, sending a memo below that he'd take care of it himself later. "Not that I recall."

"Sweet. I'll see ya laters, then."

"That you will." Seb reached for the coffee. He took a sip, cocking his head and enjoying the view of Jay back in his usual attire.

"Oh, by the way." Jay stopped at the door and pointed down at Seb's mobile. "Brought that up 'cause it kept beeping."

Seb darted his gaze to his mobile screen. "Anyone interesting?"

"I didn't check it." Jay grabbed a baseball cap from the back of the door, scraped his floppy hair back and slipped the cap on his head. "Random number anyway. Laters."

Seb took another sip from his mug and listened out for the front door, followed by the scratching of tyres on gravel before plonking the mug back down, shoving the paper from his lap and reaching beneath the duvet. He wrapped a hand around his begging cock and visualised Jay in his sweat-induced and mud-splattered football kit. *Is it a fetish?* He wasn't sure. But it always got the job done.

His phone vibrating against the bedside table jolted him. He was about to ignore it and fulfil the job in hand, but a sudden thought struck. *Could it be Kenneth?* No one should ignore Sony's A&R Director. Snatching the phone, he checked the incoming message.

Today. The Royal. 1p.m.

He threw the mobile away as if it was on fire and slammed back against the headboard. His fucking father. What could the man want? *It's been over a year.* Seb shut his eyes, attempting to stave off the overriding curiosity. Irritated, he picked the phone back up and scrolled through the latest news reports. There he was. Every single entertainment section. With Jay, his hand on his back and leaning into his ear. That photo must have earned the pap a fortune as it was everywhere. He wanted to smile, enjoy the moment of step one celebrity couple status. But he clicked out of the phone and shuddered.

He hadn't missed a single thing since walking out on his old life. And nor did he want any of it back. He wasn't going to attend his father's meeting. He didn't *need* to go. He had no interest in what Will Saunders could be reaching out to him for. *I have a potential touring deal with Sony Music, for fuck's sake!* He was climbing to the top, reaching the dizzy heights of international rock stardom. Everything his father had always told him he would never achieve. So, fuck him. And fuck Steven. And fuck the fucking Royal.

Mumbling obscenities under his breath, he stomped over to the en-suite bathroom and showered.

* * * *

"It ain't all bad news." John slapped a hand on Jay's shoulder as they emerged out into the parking lot of Upton Park Stadium after a being holed up in their boardroom for a good couple of hours.

197

"I know. Cheers for coming." He could hardly look his dad in the eye. He hated that the bloke who'd given up everything for Jay to get to this level now had to hear the bad news that it might have all been for nothing. And the papers that had once again been spread all over the tables regaling Jay's public display of affection to his boyfriend. No-one had mentioned that, but it was a definite elephant in the room.

"They just sayin' don't go straight back into team training." John loosened his tie, relaxing after having been done up to the nines for the meeting with the bosses. His dad was much more comfortable in paint-splattered decorating gear. "There's a chance that you could undo the repair if you do. It's all looking good, so take it light, train by yourself."

"How long do you think they'll keep throwing money at this?"

John shrugged. "Money stuff ain't me forte. You know that. I'm here to make sure they got your best interests at heart. And I'd say, they do. You got time, son, don't rush it."

Jay understood. Any impact on his lower limbs at this stage in his recovery might regress him back to square one. He needed to build up his strength first, by himself, which he found so bloody difficult. He was a team sportsman, a footballer, training all his life with others. Yeah, he could do light jogging by himself, a few weights, swimming, all those other things that the club suggested. But he itched to get back into the game, to the point he was so fucking frustrated with it all. He didn't know what else he could do to speed things up. He was a caged animal, ready to burst free. He needed to do something. *Anything.* He *had* to get back on the football pitch, because he was slowly losing himself in all this recovery.

"Do you think I was wrong?" Jay hadn't ever asked the question outright to his dad before, believing he knew the answer already. John had warned him what his coming out could do to him. Now it seemed that John's fears had been confirmed.

Pressing his meaty palm down on Jay's shoulder, John stared into Jay's eyes. Jay swallowed. This man, this man had seen Jay at his best and at his very worst. His opinion was paramount. "I'm proud of ya, son. You know that."

Jay nodded, biting his lip. "Ewa said it's all in my head. That somehow I'm manifesting the pain out of fear or some shit. I thought that was all bollocks. But I dunno, Dad, I thought I could handle all this."

Stepping back, John smiled, the crows-feet around his blue eyes slicing down his cheeks.

"Maybe you need to stop thinking about what other people are thinking. You know what football's like. You know what fans are like. You been coming here since you were five. You been playing football just as long. That's you, Jay. That's who you are. What other people think is, well, mute, innit?"

"Moot?"

"Yeah, as in they should keep shtum about things that don't concern them."

"Right." Jay nodded.

"But they won't, 'cause they gobby arseholes. So whatever they say don't matter. 'Cause they have to flap their gums to keep warm in the terraces. Tha's all it is, son."

"Okay…"

"What you need to remember is who you are. Remember the kid who kicked a ball against a concrete wall until it was too dark to see. Remember the kid who saved every last penny of his pocket money to buy the best studs that we couldn't afford. Remember the kid who went running every morning before school and every evening after, even in the snow. The kid who practiced ball skills instead of hanging out with his mates, chasing skirt. And the kid who didn't take any shit on the pitch." John smiled. "And remember the man who a year ago stood up for what he believed in."

Jay nodded.

"I don't think I've helped, have I?" John scrubbed his protruding stubble. "I been as bad as those in there." He angled his head toward the stadium. "You fell in love, son. And I ain't too old to know what that feels like. And you having to hide that? To keep shtum about it. Nah, that ain't right. It ain't right for you and it ain't right for Seb. And I see what he's being doing for you these past few months. I have to admit, I was wary at first. I thought he'd scarper off, that he wouldn't deal. But look at him. He's there for you, ain't he? He's not mucking about."

Jay bit his bottom lip and glanced up to the sky. His dad, for once, was speaking sense. Seb had been there for him. This whole time. *Hadn't he?*

"You need a lift back?" John squirmed out of his jacket and threw it into the back seat of his Fiesta. "I'm kinda going the other way, though. Gotta pick up the van and get to a job."

"You should retire."

"Ha. Yeah, all right, mate. Your mum'll go barking if I'm at home all the time getting under her feet. We have talked about moving, away from the council-run gaff. Getting a house that we can do up ourselves. But, a mortgage is out the question at our age and landlords are bastards about that sorta thing."

"I'll have a look around for somewhere for ya. Maybe I can get a second mortgage?"

John tapped Jay's cheek. "You worry about you. We're fine. Getting in?"

"Nah, don't worry. I'll bell Seb."

"All right, catch ya laters." With that, John slipped into his car and skidded out of the stadium car park.

Jay hobbled to the gates, fishing his phone from his back pocket. Right, so he needed a confidence boost. He needed to get all the voices out of his head that told him he didn't belong on the pitch, that he wasn't a man, or worthy of his position in the team all because of who he chose to share a bed with. He needed to show the world who he was, no fear. Exactly how he should have been at the awards gig last night. Instead of a papped photo of him discreetly whispering in his boyfriend's ear, it should have been a posed shot. A happy shot. The two of them. No hiding, no shying away, no 'no rocking the boat' mentality. A massive shout out to the world that, fuck them all, he was Jay "Rutters" Ruttman. *You can knock me down, but I'll get straight back up and in your fucking face again!*

And who better to help him with that?

He swiped his phone, hit the Call button and waited. It rang. And rang. And rang. *Lazy bastard.* Tucking the phone into his front pocket, he resigned himself to a limp to the tube station. Actually, on second thoughts, he'd best get a taxi. Rummaging through his wallet for a minicab number he could rely on, a different card caught his eye. He tugged it out, flipping it over and clucked his tongue in contemplation. Should he? *What the fuck have I got to lose?* Tapping in the unfamiliar number, he waited.

"Riley Burton."

"Riley, it's Jay." He shut his eyes. *What the fuck am I doing?* This went into the 'all things absurd' column of the 'stupid things he'd ever done' listings.

"*Rutters?*"

"Yeah, you said call. But if you're busy, no sweat."

"No, no, not busy." Riley's voice perked up a notch. "Well, I am. But don't tell the boss, eh? How ya doing?"

"Recovering. Slowly. Just been at the club, actually. Starting me on light duty."

"Sweet. That's good, but I know you, Ruts, bet you can't wait to get back on the team, right? And I mean that with no pun intended." Riley chuckled. "Listen, did you have a chance to think about my offer? Talk it over with that fella of yours? Please tell me he didn't persuade you out of it, 'cause I been chewing the CEO's ear off about you, and I have to say, you're the current hot favourite."

"Really?" Jay didn't believe that. *Couldn't* believe that. Not with all the stuff he read about himself in the press.

"For sure. Look, you're a catch. Girls all fancy the fucking pants of you, and the blokes seem to want to buy you a pint. If that don't scream mainstream appeal, I don't know what does. So, come on, let *me* buy you a pint and we'll talk it over?"

Jay scrubbed his fingers across his brow. He'd got this far, might as well go the whole hog. What harm could it do? "All right."

"Excellent." A loud clap burst down the phone. "Feel free to ask the boyfriend to come along. I did ask the company what they thought of him, but a no go on that,

I'm afraid. Not their target clientele. Too edgy. *Particular.* But happy to meet him. The geezer's everywhere this morning."

"Tell me about it. I'll give him another bell, but looks like he's still in uncle ned."

"I hope that's all right with you."

"*Bed.* He had a late-night last night."

"So I saw. All right. You at the club now? I can come pick you up, if you like? That way, I can do some more convincing and show you their company warehouse. It ain't far from the Boleyn."

After a brief pause, Jay made the most surreal decision of his life. "Sure. I'm at the gates."

CHAPTER TWELVE
When it Comes Around

Seb had been in many hotels during his twenty-six years. From the bog-standard side-of-a-motorway Travel Lodge deals that he'd endured when road tripping with his band to the most sophisticated home-from-home five-star luxury that had been his staple in holiday stays when he'd had access to Daddy's credit card. He'd been on skiing trips, city breaks, exclusive beach resorts, and chowed down in some of the finest hotel restaurants that the country's hospitality and tourism industry had to offer. He'd even been allowed a splash of extravagance with Jay on a couple of occasions.

But the Royal, situated in the heart of Piccadilly in London and practically overlooking the Queen's back garden, was still the most lavish hotel he'd ever had the misfortune to lay his head down in. With its Grade II listed status, Michelin-starred restaurant and grandiose surroundings that matched the magnificence of its internal decor, the Royal screamed to those begging to be part of high society and immerse themselves in gluttonous opulence. Seb hated it, having had to endure many an afternoon tea and evening meal there, courtesy of his father who once upon a time wouldn't let Seb out of his sight, even when conducting a business meeting. But they weren't the only memories of the Royal that produced the stale, bitter taste in his mouth. The bedrooms brought forth the internal shudders.

Jiggling on the spot outside the entrance, Seb couldn't fathom what it was that had brought him here. It was as if he'd been on autopilot. His conscious mind ran through streams of obscenities, claiming he wanted no involvement in any Saunders business—personal or otherwise. But his subconscious had him boarding the District Line and stomping the London streets at his father's instant request. Maybe it was to show the man who Seb had become, without his father's approval or support.

The top hat-and-tails door attendant nodded politely, ushering his white glove toward the glass door. Seb sighed, then shook his head and turned away toward the traffic. He tugged out a pristine pack of Marlboros from his back pocket, twirled open the plastic casing and cracked open the lid. He hadn't craved cigarettes without the use of alcohol for a good long time, but that had been another instinctive impulse as he'd made his way here from St James's Park tube station. He'd most definitely needed his dark shades at the open newsstands when purchasing the pack, as every piled-up newspaper boasted his picture alongside the paparazzi shot of him and Jay.

After sucking the toxins of the first cigarette, the rush went straight to his head and surged through his veins. Dangerous, really, how something so cheap could

205

give such a high. He took another drag and blew the smoke out into the air, getting all the old feelings back. Another draw in and his lungs swelled. He held the nicotine down as a passing red Routemaster blew his hair to the side, then exhaled the smoke as the vacating bus revealed the bright lights of the advertising billboards over the road. Seb swallowed. The Nike emblem blinking in the distance advertised the latest in on-trend football studs — *for a professional hit.*

Jolted to reality, he searched the pavement for somewhere to throw the butt and stamp it out.

"Not got a spare one, have ya?" A doddery old homeless man pointed his fingerless gloves at the half-chomped-down end.

"Sure." Seb tucked the lit cigarette into the man's outstretched fingers, then handed over the entire pack. "Yours."

"Bless ya heart."

Seb passed over the bright pink lighter he'd also had to purchase at the newsstand and, feeling mildly more at ease, twisted back to the hotel front and allowed the doorman to usher him in. He made his way to the back restaurant, his hands shaking, but he clenched his fists to stave it off. Lavish decadence dripped down the gold-embellished vinyl wallpaper and oozed from every handmade soft chair covered in the custom design patchwork. All the men wore suits and sipped coffee from espresso cups, and every woman had perfectly styled hair and manicured nails. *Nothing changes.* Except Seb now didn't care that his dress code of skin-tight and designer-ripped black jeans, T-shirt and leather jacket would be deemed inappropriate for such a high-class venue. *Let my father disapprove.*

His glance hit the table at the far window facing the grounds of Green Park. *The usual table.* Except the man, back to him and flicking through a broadsheet, hadn't been the one Seb had been expecting. Seb nearly twisted to walk out, but infuriated anger exceeded any rationalised response and he stomped ever closer.

"The fuck are you doing here?" Seb didn't bother to lower his voice, regardless of all the other diners hovering china tea cups at their lips and peering disapprovingly over.

Stephen Coles swallowed his mouthful of no-doubt espresso coffee, rapped the cup onto the saucer and folded the newspaper with graceful ease and control. "Good to see you too, Sebastian."

"I came to see my father, not you."

"Curiosity killed the cat, you know."

"Yeah, and you can keep your fucking distance."

Stephen chuckled. "Sit down, Sebastian." He kicked out the opposite chair with his tan leather Oxfords. "Your father had to take a rather important telephone call. He asked me to wait for you, in case you thought he hadn't arrived."

"I still fail to see why *you* are here. In London." Seb gripped the back of the chair and it took all his effort not to launch it at Stephen. If he'd been able to lift the heavy-duty handmade upholstered lounge seat, he might have had to dig harder into his resolve. Still, the act might go in the rock and roll hall of fame. *Put that image on the front fucking page!*

"Your father and I are in meetings regarding the development opportunities after twenty-twelve."

"Of course you are." Seb sneered and was undecided whether he should sit or knock this all on the head — *Stephen's head.*

207

"You must have a stake in all that now, hmm?" Stephen raised his eyebrows.

"In what?"

"The redevelopment of the East London area. Didn't you go over to the dark side?"

Seb snorted, glancing away but noted the side of Stephen's mouth twitching amusedly. That scar trailing his left lip still produced more of a lopsided smirk than a comforting smile.

"Please do sit down, Sebastian. You are causing an unnecessary scene. Especially with your heightened celebrity status this morning."

Seb looked around at all the other diners. At least the clientele was sophisticated enough not to produce their iPhones and take a few snaps. Half those in here were celebrity in one way or another.

"What can I get for you, sir?" A waiter rushed over, obviously trying to diffuse the obvious animosity.

"Glass of the Margaux." Seb yanked out the chair and sat, folding his arms. Might as well order the overpriced wine considering it wouldn't be him footing the bill.

Nodding, the waiter trundled off.

"Still have expensive taste, I see." Stephen brushed down his silken tie, firmly knotted in the classic Windsor.

Seb had a sudden urge to yank it and peanut the man. Instead, he wriggled out of his jacket, draped it over the back of the chair and clasped his hands on the table top all while Stephen's lecherous gaze roamed over him to the point it was invasive.

"You look good, Sparky."

Seb snorted. "Success suits me."

"I had no doubt that it wouldn't."

Stephen's smile brightened his dark eyes and Seb had to shift in the seat. He hadn't seen or heard from Stephen in two years, the last being when Jay had chucked him out of Seb's New York apartment declaring he should inform Seb's father of the multitude of reasons why Seb would want to leave the company — aka, because Stephen had fucked over the boss's son in more ways than one. And whilst Seb had written a resignation email to his father, he'd left out any of the details pertaining to his unconventional relationship with his business partner. He hadn't thought it necessary. What would be the point of dragging all that back up again? Stephen would have wormed his way out of any wrongdoing and smeared Seb's name in the mud as he'd done it, which, in turn, would have affected Jay. It had all been best left unsaid.

"How is the cohabiting?" Stephen added a sugar lump to his cup and stirred, the spoon clanging against the china.

"Blissful." Seb couldn't help but silently add *'for the most part',* until Jay's injury had got between them, but it wasn't like he would be admitting that to the man in front of him. Or anyone for that matter.

"So I saw. I'm quite surprised the *FT* didn't cash in on the happy couple's first stint in the public eye."

"Jealous?" Seb elevated his voice in mockery.

"On the contrary, Sebastian. Where is it you live, now? Just so I know where not to direct our property plans in the east."

Seb cocked his head. "If you're getting in on the Olympic development, you must be moving back here? Lisbeth will be delighted." Seb wasn't.

Stephen gave off that smile again, the one where it could be misconstrued as serene. Or perhaps it was?

"Undecided. I'm interested in the opportunity. Who wouldn't be? But I have a life in New York, one I like."

"Screw Lisbeth and your daughter, then?"

Stephen sipped from his cup, eyes fixed on Seb. "I do believe it is the other way around."

Seb moved his elbow for the returning waiter to place his glass of wine on the table. He must have accidentally given the faintest intrigued expression, as Stephen sighed and placed the cup on the surface to elaborate.

"She has been having an affair for quite some time."

Seb nearly choked on the wine he'd sipped and grabbed for the napkin to dab at his lips. "Really? How do you know?"

"She fell pregnant."

"Ah." Seb rested his lips against the glass, attempting to curtail his amused grin. "Not yours then, I take it?"

"Not when I was in New York and she here."

Seb couldn't help it: the laughter burst out unannounced. "Oh, that is fantastic news. I think I love her after all. An absolute darling." He held up his glass in cheers. "Was it anyone we know?"

"Monty's son."

"The mayor?"

"Yes."

Seb furrowed his brow. He'd been out of these circles too long to remember all the old high society elite. "Jude!" He slapped his leg in recollection. "Fuck. Wasn't he about seventeen?"

"When you were, yes."

Seb chuckled. "And the baby?"

"She lost it."

Seb twisted the stem of the wine glass and didn't falter under Stephen's gaze. He didn't have to be a mind reader to know that meant she'd been forced to terminate. Poor Lisbeth. *At least Ann can make her own decision.*

"Well." Seb took a sip of wine. "That all sounds like a terrible bind."

"Indeed."

Seb winced. "The divorce could set you back quite a bit, eh?"

Stephen laughed, the deep chortle ringing around the restaurant. "What makes you think we'll divorce?"

"Adultery? Sex scandal among the high society? Cheating?" Seb waved a nonchalant hand.

"As I keep telling you, Sebastian, love and sex are two different things."

"Not to me, they aren't."

"Really? You? Sparky, the man who slept his way through London and then started on New York—"

"One man in New York. One!" Seb pointed an angry finger. He knew the outburst came mostly from his guilt at having slept with anyone when estranged from Jay. But back then, he'd been a different person. One who could still be influenced by the utter arsehole in front of him.

"Whilst claiming to be in love with another? I think that proves my point, does it not?" Stephen gave a triumphant wink, twirling the contents in his espresso cup.

"You haven't changed a bit." It wasn't a compliment, even if Stephen's smirk suggested as much. "Actually, you have. You've gone grey."

Stephen laughed. Guffawed, rather. "Come on, Sparky. You used to insult me far better than that. If this is what love does to you, you can keep it."

Seb opened his mouth to refute, to argue, to say something, anything to prove he hadn't lost his edge, but nothing came to the forefront and a hand clamping down on his shoulder from above prevented any comeback either way.

"Apologies, Sebastian." Will Saunders unfastened the last button on his fitted blazer and gave a curt nod of greeting to both table occupants.

He hadn't changed much either. Slightly more silvery flecks, possibly a few more lines around the eyes, but mostly he was still the same nondescript persona. *Cardboard cut-out.*

"I had to take that call." Will slipped into the seat between Seb and Stephen and tucked himself under the table. "Thank you for waiting. And for coming."

Seb's mouth had gone dry and he found it difficult to form words. So he nodded and sipped from his glass of wine. He'd need the alcohol to get through whatever was coming next.

"I suspect you are eager to learn of my reasons for extending this invitation to you?" Will reached for the pot of coffee in front of Stephen and poured himself a cup, seeming to forget to refill Stephen's. Perhaps it was a boss thing. *Never pour beverages for those below you on the company chart.*

Seb had to clear his throat to speak. "It was rather a surprise to hear from you. Well, not you exactly." He drifted his scornful gaze to Stephen.

"Yes, initially I had thought you would be persuaded more by him than by me."

It really was a marvel how little his father had picked up on over the years, from the once lingering looks between his son and his executive assistant, to the behind-the-back laughing about their secret liaisons, to the final argument and following years of Seb's utter contempt for the man his father had bestowed his international business venture on.

"I have since discovered that not to be quite true. So once again, I am grateful for your attendance."

Seb furrowed his brow and noted Stephen's slight twitch opposite him. Had his father overheard their conversation?

"I think it's best all round if I just cut to the chase? Sweep over the pleasantries?"

"Please do." Seb toyed with his wine at his lips, the taste of wild berries bursting on his tongue. He had a sudden urge to knock the whole lot back.

"I had been informed that you had an infatuation with Stephen." Will met Seb's gaze, unfaltering. And he spoke as if he was reciting the evening news, not declaring something so profoundly ridiculous. "On first sighting, I believed you to be a young boy with a first crush."

"What? I'm not—"

Will held up a hand. "Let me finish."

"Sir?" Stephen wriggled forward.

"Not now, Stephen. I am discussing things with my son."

"Perhaps I should leave you two to it." Stephen pushed his chair back and made to stand.

"On the contrary. Please, sit. I will need your input."

Stephen lowered back into the chair, albeit reluctantly, and Seb slid his confused gaze from Stephen to his father.

"Now, where was we?" Will sipped his coffee. "You were, what, a seventeen-year-old boy when I hired Stephen? And even though it was obvious from the

213

outset, you were living openly as a...homosexual. Well, you couldn't not after that disastrous incident at Winchester, no?"

Seb bit his lip. His first kiss, back at boarding school, with the Head Boy. *Fond memories.*

"So I believed your interest in Stephen came from simply being more open to your attractions. I discussed this with Stephen, in fact. Did I not, Mr. Coles?"

Stephen inhaled, sharply. "Yes, I do seem to recall—"

"I'd said, 'be careful, dear chap, I think my son may have taken a shine to you'. We didn't want to cause you any unnecessary angst, so I suggested he be more..." Will wafted his cup in the air. "Avuncular."

Seb snorted at the word. And it was only being intrigued at where this was all going that kept him listening.

"Yulia had said you two were getting closer." Will sipped his coffee, his oversized hands almost burying the cup. "She relayed that Stephen had been in your room. That garments had been found there. On confrontation, Stephen had convinced me it was all platonic. A friendship. You were borrowing his clothes. But I felt we needed to put up a barrier. For your protection. Because I knew you were in a vulnerable position, and it was common knowledge that Stephen was not, how do you say? Batting for your team?"

Seb shook his head. He wasn't sure how much more he wanted to hear and now wished he'd stuck to his guns and not bothered coming. If this was all so his father could declare he'd found out about Seb and Stephen's affair, then Seb had no interest in being there for the explosion. It made no odds to him anymore. Nothing at all. Stephen was a mere fleck on his distant past. No,

214

worse than that. The leftover scar from a skin blemish that had now been treated, to never return.

"So we encouraged the wedding," his father continued on, oblivious to Seb's reluctance to offer any contribution to the conversation. "And, well, I thought that would be the end of it." Will leaned back, waving a hand to a waiter. "We'll have a bottle of the Margaux, thank you."

"Certainly, sir."

"Good man." Will tapped the waiter's back then readdressed the table, his polished smile diminishing. "Little did I know how far back this thing between the two of you went. *Infatuation*?" Will's deep gruff vibrated through Seb's chest, and by the looks of it he wasn't the only one affected. "What was it you said, Stephen? That Sebastian found it impossible to work with you due to his *infatuation*? That your continued rejection of his advances had caused him to go 'off the rails?'"

"You said *what*?" Seb gripped his empty glass, his fingernails whitening.

"Sir, I—" Stephen's cheeks reddened beneath his dark stubble.

"And yet on clearing the house this morning, I find these." Will pulled an envelope from his inside jacket pocket and threw it onto the table.

Seb stared at it. Distressed edges, ripped fold, his own scrawled handwriting on the front, *private shit*. He closed his eyes in realisation.

"I don't know about you, Stephen, but I haven't seen my son naked in a fair few years, so I had to keep checking it was him. Feel free to peruse at your leisure." Will pushed the envelope closer to Stephen. "The ones of you together were particularly off putting. One wasn't aware you were that bendy."

"Sir, allow me to —"

Will held up a hand, and nearly struck the returning waiter. "Apologies, dear boy. Please, pour." He gestured to his and Seb's glasses.

The waiter did, then scurried off as silently as he arrived.

"One can assume from those developed photographs that an infatuation could only have come by encouragement?" Will raised his glass to his lips, his eyebrows scaling his forehead. "Would you agree, Stephen?" He stared, unflinching. Seb knew that authoritative glare, having been on the receiving end of it many a time. He held his breath in wait.

"We had a relationship." Stephen swallowed.

"So I saw." Will nodded to the envelope. "A rather active one. Paris, Edinburgh, Milan. And on cross checking, all on company time and credit. What a marvellous time you must have had on Saunders & Son." Will sipped from his wine. "Quite literally."

"We deemed it unnecessary to tell you at the time."

Stephen might as well dig himself a massive hole, one he would hopefully go bury himself in. Will had that knack, keeping up the stare until the recipient spilled all and everything, and threw in a false confession for good measure. Will Saunders should have been a detective.

"One rather would." Will nodded. "He is your employer's son. And barely legal at that."

"He was eighteen when it started."

"Well, that is jolly good to know."

Seb felt like he was at tennis match, snapping his gaze from one to the other and having no clue what the score was, or if he should cut in at any time.

"Of course I ended things when I got with Lisbeth."

"As one should." Will plonked the wine glass back on the table. "But, you see, Stephen, what I find an awfully perplexing conundrum, is why you would continue to harass him after your marriage, and the birth of your daughter?"

Stephen furrowed his brow.

"Yes. That's in there too." Will pointed to the unopened envelope. "Or did you forget that my son is a poet and a dreamer? Surely, with how close you both were, you would know he writes things down, often turning those words into song and verse?"

Stephen breathed out a laugh, if a nervous one. "Sir, with all due respect, they are the ramblings of a heartbroken teenager. I wouldn't put too much faith into what he writes in his songs."

"Oh, you are absolutely right." Chuckling, Will snatched his glass and took a lingering sip. "But forgive me if I am misunderstanding. I'm just trying to get my head around all this new information. Why would you have requested the New York position? I gave you the option to be promoted here, London, where your wife and child reside, or to New York, where my son was taking over. Where was it you chose again?"

"It was simply a matter of where I felt I could achieve more."

"Yes, of course. And nothing to do with wanting to seduce my son for your own gains?"

"No, sir. Like I said, it was a relationship. One I ended. One I deeply regret. I guess it was a matter of giving in to his continued advances. I thought we could have been friends. I guess Sebastian was my experiment, and for that I am sorry that his feelings ran deeper than mine."

"Go fuck yourself, Stephen," Seb scoffed.

Will held up a finger, settling the unrest. "Experiment? My son was an experiment to you?"

"For want of a better word, sir."

"And is my accountant an experiment? My new architect?"

"What?" Seb slammed his glass on the surface. "You didn't?"

"Oh, he did, Sebastian." Will nodded. "I have a sexual harassment complaint on my hands from one Xavier Konchetsky. It is the reason why I flew Stephen back here. Truth be told, I suspected that perhaps this wasn't Stephen's first homosexual relationship turned sour. On finding these" — he pointed to the envelope — "I suspected correctly. I just didn't want to believe that I could have missed it. Or that you wouldn't have told me."

First off, Seb was a little stunned at how his father had gone through the entire contents of his bedroom back in Kensington and not just bulldozed it to shreds like Seb had expected. That envelope had been discarded at the back of his wardrobe some time ago. The only reason he hadn't set fire to those photographs, or the several letters he'd written but never sent to Stephen explaining how much of an arsehole he was, was all down to good old-fashioned blackmailing possibilities.

Second of all, Seb wasn't here to relive the past. To explain himself. To explain Stephen. So, he stood.

"I thought this would be about the house. Or Yulia. Or something else. Something I care about." Seb waved a hand at Stephen. "I have no interest in this." He scraped his jacket from the back of the chair.

"Sebastian, please." Will leaned forward, hand spread on the table.

Having never heard the man beg before, Seb was a little startled to hear his father's plea.

"I have more to say and I would like you to hear it."

I should walk out. I don't need this. I have my own life now. He was free of all the high society scandals, suffocating Saunders wealth and birthright nonsense. But something in his father's eyes made him sit back down, hugging his jacket to his lap.

"Thank you." Will turned to Stephen. "Lisbeth will be requesting a divorce, handled by my lawyers. I don't see you having an awful lot of your assets left after they are finished with you."

"With all due respect, sir, that would be Lisbeth's decision."

"Which she has already made. I was aware of her seeking out a private solicitor some time back. I urged her to rethink. However, in light of things now, I have given her full access to Saunders & Son's legal team."

Stephen's chest rose with the force of his harried inhalation.

"I would also suggest you search for new employment, because as of today you are suspended from Saunders & Son, pending an investigation into the allegation from Xavier Konchestsky."

"Xavier came onto me. Whatever he has insinuated, he's lying." Stephen's usual calm composure diminished with every word spoken.

"Like my son did?"

Stephen darted his gaze to Seb. "It was a platonic relationship."

"For some of the time." Seb shrugged. "But, honestly, I don't care anymore. I'm beyond caring."

"I am sure you can appreciate my predicament here, Stephen. I fail to know if what is coming out of your mouth is truth or lies. Therefore, I suggest you find a reputable solicitor, as this could be a lengthy proceeding. All your security clearances for the business accounts have been revoked, as per my instructions to the IT department—that very important phone call I had to take. I have also arranged for Natalie to clear your desk and your New York apartment will be rescinded forthwith." Will shot back a glug of wine. "Please do not let us keep you any further, Mr. Coles. I am sure you have a frightfully long day ahead of you."

Seb had to bite his lip to hide the smile. His father could be an absolute brick when he wanted to. *Yeah, I said brick. This time.* Seb chuckled.

"Sir, if I could just have one minute to explain my side of things?" Stephen shuffled forward in an attempt to come across less threatening, less evasive, Seb assumed. It wouldn't work on Will Saunders. He'd clearly already made up his mind.

"No. You had your chance when I asked you why Sebastian had fled, why he didn't talk to me first about leaving. That cock-and-bull story you told me back then leaves this bitter taste in my mouth that I cannot seem to be rid of, even drinking this delightful tipple. You betrayed my trust. And that isn't something you can gain back, regardless of what beastly, vile lie comes out of your mouth next."

"I love him."

Seb widened his eyes so much that the air conditioning dried out his pupils. Will sighed. Then he laughed but composed himself quickly enough.

"Which one? Sebastian or Xavier? Leave, Stephen. Now. Please don't make me ask Cuthbert to call security."

Will leaned in closer, lowering his voice to a hushed baritone. "We really would like to keep up appearances here. Let us not cause an *unnecessary scene*."

Seb watched Stephen's rise from his seat, but he didn't say anything. There really wasn't any more to be said between them. It had all been over and done with some time ago. Seb had never had any intention of calling it all out to his father. Perhaps if he had, Xavier would have been spared the same treatment. But he didn't know the truth of that one, either. Nor did he really care to.

Will grabbed the bottle of red and refilled their glasses, remaining silent until Stephen had vacated the dining area.

"I think we need this, don't you?"

Seb breathed through a nervous laugh. Not through fear of anything his father could say or do to him. Seb had already relinquished everything he ever had a right to, and he still didn't want any of it.

"I wish you'd told me." Will picked up his glass.

"You would never have listened."

"Quite possibly true. But I wish you had."

Seb nodded. "I sometimes wish I had too. Then I could lay most of the blame on you rather than my own bad judgement and weak will."

His father took his time to swallow the wine, gazing up at the ceiling in pensive thought. "Were you in love with him?"

"No." Seb picked his thumb nail. "I think at the start I confused what I felt for love. But I now know what real love is, and no, Stephen neither deserved nor ever had my love. He took every bit of my hope that there could ever be love in my life each and every time he came into my room and left straight after. It was Jay who gave it back to me."

221

"I'm sorry." Will stared Seb in the eye. "I have always been able to admit my failings to do with business affairs. But with you, I really did fail terribly."

Seb couldn't believe what he was hearing. His father admitting a mistake, and not just any mistake but that his nonchalant, and often disregarded, treatment of Seb had been a failing. Seb hadn't ever believed that his father would even care enough to think that their strained relationship had been his fault. Seb ran finger around the rim of his glass and all the hurt, the bitterness, the anger and resentment left him. All he had left was pity.

"It's understandable." Seb threw half the wine down his throat. "You were, what, my age, late twenties, when Mum walked out and you were left to raise a son you didn't have a single thing in common with? I can understand why you gave me to Yulia, and why when Stephen turned up and levelled me out a little, you couldn't bear for anything to rock the boat again. That's probably why I didn't tell you. I knew you wouldn't be able to handle it."

Will tapped a fingernail on the glass, the rhythmic ting like a metronome to the conversation. After a moment, he nodded.

"How very observant, Sebastian."

Seb shrugged. "I write crappy songs about the human condition. Observing people and emotions are all part of the music."

"I hardly think sixteen million copies sold of your last album constitute you calling the songs crappy." Will smiled, and his whole face lifted to the point Seb could have mistaken it for pride. "Yes, I follow your career. And, maybe, I can take a little credit for who you have become. Us Saunders are always a success. Perhaps you took a different path, but you are a success nonetheless. So we'll have less of the crappy, thank you."

"I'll let you into a secret. A few of them are crappy. Especially when you're told to write two more to complete an album and you've got an hour to do it. Jay will never forgive me for the *Fuck Me Blue Eyes* B-side." Seb chuckled, but his face soon dropped.

"How is he?"

"In recovery. It's hard. All he's known is playing football. Imagine if you couldn't run your business, or I couldn't play guitar. That's got to hit where it hurts, right?"

"I believe so."

"He'll bounce back, I'm sure of it." He wasn't totally convinced, but he was getting there.

"And if he doesn't?"

"What do you mean?"

"Falling from grace often drags others along for the ride. Are you prepared for that? To be the one out front? Alone?"

Seb chewed the inside of his cheek. He wasn't entirely sure what his father was getting at. That Seb should discard Jay if he ends up retired from football? That being with an injured ex-professional would drag his career down?

"Just be careful, Sebastian. One-sided success can often make the injured party quite bitter."

"Are you talking from experience there?"

"Why do you think your mother left? She needed her own success. Being with me prevented that." Will had a wistful gaze in his eye, but it soon levelled out to his more accustomed austerity. "I should probably explain. This reunion was never meant to be about Stephen. It's about the house. I'm selling it. I was offering for you to come and collect anything you want. I apologise about my hasty treatment of you after leaving the business."

"Where are you going?"

"New York. I'll be taking the helm over there. Originally, I was bringing Stephen back here to give him the twenty-twelve development in order to work things out with his wife. New York now clearly needs me in the driving seat."

"What about the Olympic development? Who'll take that on?"

"I will have to pass that opportunity up. Unless, of course, you would like a side project?"

"No." Seb rushed that out.

Smiling, Will stood and brushed down his tie. "Come by the house whenever you would like. I'm selling privately, so no rush." He buttoned his jacket, then laid a hand on Seb's shoulder. "I know our relationship can never be fully repaired, but I am willing to listen to you. Any time. You are always my son."

Peering up, Seb met with sincere eyes. "Thank you."

Will tapped twice. "Perhaps you've even shown me that there is a little room in my life for a love story. If there's still time, of course."

Seb breathed through a laugh. "You know Sylvia never remarried either."

"Is that a fact?" Will smiled. "Take care, Sebastian."

His father took off and shook hands with the maître d', no doubt footing the bill, then vacated the restaurant. Seb felt as if he'd been whacked in the head with a sledgehammer and wondered if the cigarette he'd chugged earlier was actually something more, because everything that had just happened felt as surreal as that time he, Martin and Noah had got stoned before the Winchester gig.

"Fuck," he mumbled to his lap.

"I beg your pardon, sir?" the waiter asked, clearing up the empty cups and glasses.

"Sorry, nothing." Standing, Seb clipped out a tenner from his wallet and handed it to the waiter, then made his way out of the restaurant, through the grand lobby, toward the foyer and excited the Royal for what he promised himself would be the last ever time.

The fresh air stung his heated cheeks, and he inhaled a deep breath. Euphoria. *Total freedom.* Chuckling, he held out a hand to the oncoming black cab.

CHAPTER FOURTEEN
Take the Shot

During the twenty or so minutes wait, Jay tried Seb's phone twice. No more ringing and straight to answer phone.

"Oi, lazy git. I got called to somethin'. Thought you'd wanna tag along. But fuck you, I'll catch ya laters." He switched off just as Riley pulled up in a pristine white Range Rover. The window lowered and Jay poked his nose in.

"They let you rough nuts just loiter round here?" Riley grinned, then angled his head. "Get in. I think that's a pap on the other side of the road."

"Great." Jay slipped into the passenger side, *clunk-click*, and they were off joining the bumper-to-bumper traffic through the Upton Park outdoor market. To say it felt weird was an understatement. Riley's over-potent deodorant spray wafted under Jay's nostrils and it was like being transported back in time. And with the speed

Riley was driving, they weren't far off the eighty-eight miles per hour to achieve it.

Gripping the steering wheel with one hand, Riley rolled his shirt sleeve up to reveal a scribed tattoo on his forearm. Jay tilted his neck to decipher the words.

"Carpe Diem." Riley wriggled his arm.

"Seize the day. Nice."

"Like tattoos, Jay?" Riley scrubbed his fingers through his light brown hair, shunting the car toward the parked bays to avoid an oncoming replacement bus service.

Tightening his hold on the door handle, Jay thought that perhaps Riley shouldn't put his trust in tomorrow, as it might not come at all with the way he drove. "I like 'em on other people."

Riley smiled. "By that, I'll assume you mean your man."

"He's got an obsession with 'em, yeah."

"How many he got?"

Jay glanced out of the window, attempted to count the ink on Seb's body without recalling each time he'd licked them. "A lot."

"He not convinced you to ruin that pasty skin of yours yet then?"

"Nah. Think he accepts me without." Jay shrugged. "He did ask once, but I got some stupid thing about needles."

"Ha. Why is it the tough guys always do, eh?"

"Yeah. I know. Stupid. Back at uni, the scholars all wanted to get a matching tatt. Like a camaraderie thing. I went along to the parlour down docklands, then shit myself and bailed. Did fuck all for my street cred, I can tell ya."

Riley laughed. "I'll bet. Probably a good thing, though. It's a novelty now, ink-free skin. I blame that Beckham. He just can't stop. 'Ere, you ever played him?"

"Nah. And now he's at Real Madrid, I doubt I will. Did meet him a couple times though. Talked about how east London's changed since he was a kid."

"Yeah. Sure has. We're here."

Riley pulled into an industrial estate on the borders of Newham and Hackney, home to builder's merchants and other businesses needing larger scale premises. Most of the warehouses were boarded up with a *Land Now Occupied* sign hanging on the shutters. It was just the greasy spoon shack and the building that Riley pointed up to that appeared to be open for business.

"The Olympic development." Riley stepped out of the car and flicked his keys around his finger, heading toward the outhouse. "Don't get me wrong, twenty-twelve is gonna rock shit and it'll certainly do wonders for this place. But it means many of the businesses round here have had to find new premises, most out of the area and costing a helluva lot more. This setup is mostly an online retailer. So they're coping with a warehouse, not a shop front." He unlocked the rusty shutter, the metal crackling like thunder as he slipped it up. "They store their stock here, and it doubles up as a photo studio. I called ahead. The CEO is out at a meeting but I had the keys and said I'd give you a look-see."

Jay wasn't sure what he had been expecting, but from the outside it hadn't seemed all that impressive. Inside was a different story. There were railings upon railings of clothes stacked up around the walls of a wide-open-plan space with a curved grey screen in the centre that Jay guessed was where they did the photo shoots. Spot lights, umbrella shades and various props were set

228

up around it, along with boxes upon boxes of sports equipment, from footballs to boxing gloves, to cricket bats.

Riley flicked on all the lights, illuminating the darkened space and allowing for Jay to mosey around. He stopped at a few framed posters on the wall, minor celebrities that Jay recognised but couldn't place, showing their love for Tyrant Sports & Leisure Wear Inc through smiles and various poses.

"Told you they need to update the marketing." Riley came up behind him. "Not sure that fella's been in the news since the last *Big Brother*."

"That's who he is then."

"Yeah." Riley rocked back on his heels. "Can see why the company hired me, right? They need a better image. At least a sports personality if they selling sports clothing. And you, my old friend, could be just it."

Jay snorted. For one, he wasn't sure he'd consider himself an old friend of Riley's, but still, *bygones be bygones, and don't look a gift horse in the mouth and all that.* And two, he had no idea how he could be the image for an entire clothing brand, considering he lived day in, day out in what West Ham provided for him or what Ann suggested he wear. *Why didn't I bring Ann?*

"Take a look at the gear. If you like it, try some on. If you don't, then we'll fuck all this off and just go to the pub. Either way, I win." Riley slapped Jay's shoulder and chuckled.

Considering he was there, he might as well take a look. Scraping back the clothes on the first rail, he thought they were decent enough. Good quality for leisure wear. Amazing he had an opinion, really. This wasn't like when Seb made him shop, or Ann chose his clothes. This was sportswear. Plain T-shirts, work-out vests, tracksuits, hoodies...

"Go on, try something on." Riley nudged him. "And I'll get the camera ready."

"Camera?"

"Yeah. Take a few snaps, show the CEO. She's got to confirm it. If you're not photogenic, there'd be no point signing you, right? Although, that pic in the papers this morning was all right. I quote from her, 'nice suit, hugs him well'."

Jay burst out a laugh and Riley scurried off to ransack a locked cabinet. That suit had hugged him well, last year. When he was at his fittest. This year, there'd been a bit of give. But he guessed no one could tell that on a stolen shot from a pap. Heaving a resigned breath, Jay yanked his top over his head and looked around for somewhere to put it.

"Just hang it up." Riley smiled, fixing together what Jay assumed was a focus lens and flash to a Canon camera before taking a few shots at the floor. "They also do an underwear range, if you fancy a go at that first? They hug the right bits an' all."

"Let's just start with the overwear, yeah?"

Riley chuckled. "All right. Grab a few bits, put 'em on, then when you're ready, stand there." He pointed at the plane grey backdrop. "These are just test shots. For the real thing, we'll have you out somewhere a bit more stylish. Somewhere that screams all you."

Nerves suddenly crept up on Jay, mostly 'cause he felt like a bit of a tit. Grabbing hold of the railing, he managed to free himself of his trainers, socks and tracksuit trousers, relieved that he'd shoved on his better boxers that morning, with only a slight wince from his aching knee.

"You all right?" Riley nodded to his leg.

"Yeah, yeah. Just certain positions, y'know?"

"Ha. I'll bet your boyfriend ain't pleased with that." Riley winked and Jay wondered when all these double entendres about his sexuality were going to end. "No problem, mate. I'll grab you a chair in a bit. And, don't take this the wrong way, but looking at you now, I think the underwear might be top dollar. Don't panic, though. I'm a gentleman. I'll buy you dinner before asking you to get all your kit off."

Jay arched an eyebrow. "Better be somewhere nice, then. I don't take me kecks off for a cheeky Nando's."

"Ha. Sure." Riley stumbled back, eyes firmly fixed on the camera.

So the guy could dish it out but not take it. *Noted.*

"Let's start with the trackies." Riley pointed toward a pair of lounge joggers draped over a railing. "Hang 'em low on your hips, show a bit of boxer and that'll flaunt that six pack you got goin' on. What's that, eight hours a day in the gym?"

"Something like that." Jay fumbled into the bottoms, adjusting them at the waist, and held out his arms in display.

"Perfect. Now stand over there." Riley pointed toward the backdrop.

Jay took one step and his knee shot out a painful spasm. Riley grabbed his elbow, which was lucky or Jay would have made an even bigger twat of himself by collapsing to the floor. "Cheers."

"No probs. Must be a bitch, that." Riley steadied him up and steered him over to the marked-out position in front of the grey screen.

"Yeah, one minute it feels fine, next I'm on the floor. Crying." Shaking himself out, Jay faced front and waited for the next instruction.

Riley hovered back and lifted the camera to look through the lens. "All right. Do something."

"Like what?"

Riley chuckled, then peered around the camera. "Most people smile. Or not. Moody might work best with you, actually. You got that rough, tough, East End, don't mess with me vibe going on. That's what we should go for. Play on that image."

"Hardly feel rough and tough with a gammy knee, right now."

"Sure, but how did you get it? 'Cause you kicked some fella last season. And from watching the replays, mate, I reckon he deserved it."

Jay hung his head. Maybe the bloke had, but Jay should have learned his lesson from the first time. A sudden rush of shame swarmed over him. The last time it had been Riley on the receiving end.

"Much like I did." Riley broke the awkward silence. "Back in the day."

Jay met with Riley's sullen expression behind the camera.

"There. That." Riley waggled his finger and instantly fired a few snaps. "Yeah. Definitely better moody. Look off to the side. Think about something."

Jay turned his head. "Think about what?"

"Something that pisses you right off. Chelsea scum?"

Jay laughed and Riley lowered the camera.

"You got a nice smile, too. I'll give you that. We'll capture those eyes at some point as well. But for now, let's try irritated. Angry. Imagine some geezer coming on to your fella?"

Jay didn't have to think too hard about that as it had become a far too often occurrence since Seb's popularity had soured.

"Good, good. Narrow the eyes. That's it." *Click, click, click.* "Face me again. Yes. Like it. Shit, you ever done this before?"

"Once, for Ann when she was doing her BTEC fashion entry coursework. I swore I'd never do it again. Yet here I am."

"Easily persuaded."

"Tell me about it."

Riley dropped the camera away from his face. "Ann? Oh, Ann! That's the girl from the bar? She's your ex, from school?"

"Yeah."

"And you're still friends?"

"Yeah. She keeps me grounded, y'know? Reminds me who I was before all this." Jay waved a hand, indicating the strange setup of him being asked to model for a clothing line simply for playing football.

Flicking through the images on his camera screen, Riley nodded. "These are pretty good. Bit of stylish touch-up on it and they'll look a treat." He rushed over to a chair by the wall and dragged it toward Jay. "Straddle it, drape your arms over the back and clench the biceps. Make it look like you can't get a hand around 'em."

Jay slipped into the seat, straightening out his bad leg while Riley adjusted the spotlights overhead and hurried back in front of him. He draped his arms over the back of the chair and balled his fists to flex his biceps.

"Still remember those punches you laid on me." Riley's voice was distant even if he were only a few inches away from Jay. "I've received a fair few whacks in my time. Being a little shit never did me any favours. But yours." He shook his head through a laugh. "Hurt. And I've never seen a man so fucking angry."

Jay didn't know how to respond to that. He just stared, straight into Riley's hazel eyes.

"It must have been hard."

Jay wasn't sure if that was a question or statement. "What must've been?"

"Dealing with all that shit growing up. I remember the academy days. Shit, a training session weren't standard without some homophobic banter being thrown around."

"Banter I can handle. Everyone has the shit taken out of them for something or other. It's team mentality, try and sniff out the weakest. You learn to deal with it, to ignore it, to pretend you ain't heard it. But what I can't stand is when people think it's a reason for you not to be on the pitch at all."

"Yeah." Riley shoved the camera closer to Jay and snapped. "Sorry, mate, was a perfect pose. Your natural look is pretty damn fucking perfect. You ever retire, you got a job here." He checked through the images. "So, did it get easier once you came out? Like, did that stop all the shit?"

"A little. Took me a while to get the courage to do it though." Jay shrugged. "To be honest, I don't think I would have if it hadn't been for Seb."

Another quick snap and Jay had to blink back the yellow flashes.

Riley smiled, checking the image. "You mean you'd have stayed in the closet?"

"Probably. There weren't no reason to tell 'em before him. As long as the gaffer knew, and maybe the club execs, then it didn't need the big announcement that it had."

"So why?"

Jay breathed through a laugh. "'Cause Seb ain't one to stay locked up in a closet. It weren't fair on him."

"Yeah. So I see. D'you reckon if he had though, if he'd been some normal geezer, a fucking shop assistant or librarian or something, that you wouldn't be sat here now, injured?"

Jay chewed his bottom lip. He'd been thinking that a lot himself lately. That if he hadn't come out, that if Seb hadn't become the big shot that he was, if he'd kept to their promise to stay out of the media, then perhaps he wouldn't have been targeted on the pitch. No-one would know. He wouldn't have the apprehension before every game, worry about how he acted, worry about how Seb acted. He wouldn't have to check over his shoulder when walking down the street just in case there was someone taking his picture. He'd be playing football. The way he'd always wanted. He glanced away and wondered if, deep down, that was his real problem.

Snap.

"Sorry. Natural." Riley grinned. "Why don't we try on some of the other gear? Different poses. I'll put some music on, might help you relax."

Riley switched a large plasma screen to MTV and upped the volume. And, after a few more trial shots in various different styles of clothing and poses, Jay did loosen up. He was even allowed to smile at one point. It wasn't half bad, just standing there, or sitting, or lying down at one point, whilst someone took his picture. No wonder Seb enjoyed doing his press shots. It was like becoming a different him. A more confident him. Through Riley's camera lens, Jay got a smidgen of himself

235

back and he was certain that boost would last until he got home to Seb. Just the thought made him tingle with anticipation.

"I'll call that a wrap." Riley switched off the spot lamps and attached the camera via a cable into an open laptop plugged into the wall. "I'm going to start uploading these and send 'em off to the boss, see what she thinks. But I'm pretty sure it'll be a goer."

Jay shoved his own clothes back on and made his way over to Riley. He peeped over Riley's shoulder, expecting to cringe at the photographs. Instead, he nodded in approval. Not half bad at all. Riley had a knack for atmospheric photo taking.

"I also gotta get you to sign something. It's printing off in the next room."

"What is it?" Jay narrowed his eyes. "I thought this was all just a test shot?"

"It is. But we've now got your images on file. So, we kinda need your consent for that. It's all legal crap. Sure your boyfriend gets it all the time, huh?"

"Yeah. I guess." Jay bit his bottom lip, eyes darting across the words on the laptop screen. "Maybe I need him to take a look."

"Why? He your keeper as well as your bed warmer?"

"Nah, it's just he's got a background in all that contract stuff. Be better for him to take a squizz."

"He here?" Riley looked around, eyes wide. "Seriously, Jay, it's bog standard shit. And if I was your agent I'd be telling you not to turn this down. This could be your meal ticket, to show the world who you are. And if you don't sign this, well, these awesome snaps will go to waste and no doubt the boss'll have me chasing some other celeb for the fifty-grand endorsement deal." He slapped Jay's arm and squeezed. "It's just a signature and we could have this signed off by Friday. Make a great weekend gift for the other half, right?"

Jay knew he should say no. Seb would kill him for signing something without it being checked over. But they were only a couple of images, right? The paps took his photo all the time and shoved it all over media without his knowledge, or permission. Perhaps it was 'cause he was still on a bit of a high and eager to get home to Seb that made him nod.

"And, ha, look at that." Riley pointed up to the television screen. The latest Drops video blasted out. "It's like he's looking down on ya."

Jay snorted. *Fucking typical.*

"Back in a sec. I'll just grab the contract from the printer."

Shoving his hands in his pocket, Jay watched the video and smiled. If he hadn't been itching to get home before, he was now. No wonder Seb had been voted Sexiest Man in Rock according to the MTV poll. As the video faded to a close, a female presenter popped up on the side of the screen with the latest in entertainment news headlines scrolling above.

"That was the latest from the Drops. And did you see the performance last night? Phew." She fanned herself, her red lips forming an O. "Hot stuff. And speaking of which, the first photograph of Seb Saunders with West Ham's Jay Ruttman has been all over the papers, finally confirming that they are a couple, having remained tight-lipped on their romance for over a year."

The same image that had been plastered on every newspaper that morning shot up on the screen. Jay shook his head. He still couldn't understand why there was so much interest in it all.

"But, then who is this?" The presenter slapped a hand over her mouth as another photograph popped up beside her. "Is our Seb *playing away* from his man? This was taken earlier today at the Royal hotel in London, renowned for their plush bedroom suites. Tut-tut, Sebastian."

It was as if someone had just ripped out Jay's heart and stamped on it with his brother's steel toe-capped boots, then stabbed it like the dart board up in The Court Yard. A rush of blood drained from his face, and his entire body shivered. He felt sick. And angry. Really fucking angry. The photograph, blown up on the screen for the entire fucking world to see, was a little fuzzy, taken through a window pane and distorting the faces somewhat, but there was no doubt that was Seb, throwing his head back and laughing. Jay would recognise his boyfriend in silhouette.

"Right, here we go." Riley stepped up behind him and held out a bunch of papers. "What? Now you go give me the best fucking pissed-off pose?" He glanced up to the screen. "Shit. Who's that?"

Edging closer to the screen, Jay balled his hands into tight fists and clenched his jaw so tight that his teeth might rip back through his gums. "Stephen fucking Coles."

CHAPTER FIFTEEN
Sliding Tackle

"Shit." Seb tapped the screen on his mobile phone. Dead. Nothing. He'd run the blasted battery down and still had a couple more phone calls to make. That last chat to Kenneth had obviously gone on for far longer than he'd realised. *Might be time to fit a landline!*

Since getting home from the Royal, Seb had focused all his energy on finding out if the Drops could be released from their Armstrong Records contract to be free to sign with someone else. A partnership with Sony would elevate him, and the Drops, right to the top. Mainstream, mass appeal. Amazingly, those at AR had agreed to let Seb out of their contract early, making it even easier to sign his rights over to Kenneth. An American tour looked ready to go. He just had to get the agreement from the other two, which would be easy enough. Wave a few pound signs under their noses and they'd be up for it.

He rummaged through the drawer in his music room, finding a charger and plugged it into the socket on the wall. Then he noted the time on the clock above the door. The timepiece that Jay had insisted on in order for Seb to realise how long he spent in there. Except, this time, it spelt more of a concern as to how long Jay had been missing. Could it be a good sign that he'd been at the club for most of the day? Perhaps even training with the squad? Or, it could be West Ham sending Jay on his marching orders, retirement at twenty-four. Which, actually, wouldn't be the disaster that Seb had been led to believe. Without football in the way, both of them were free to live their lives the way they wanted, no constraints. But either way, Seb was buzzing to tell Jay his news.

Humming a tuneful melody, he danced his way across the hallway into the kitchen. He might as well get a start on the preparations. When he opened the fridge, the two bottles of Bollinger wedged in the door and nicely chilled clanged against each other. Seb smiled, floating on a woozy high. It seemed like everything was coming together. Finally. Tonight was a celebration. Not quite the one Seb had planned on using the champagne he'd ordered from Reg at the Court Yard for, but a celebration nonetheless. Not only had all the crap from his past been put into some kind of box with the lid firmly closed, and not only had Seb just landed one of the most lucrative deals of his musical career, but that Jay was stepping out with him. *Okay, bad analogy, what with his injured knee and everything.* But Jay *had* taken inches to brave the media with him. Their photo had been everywhere. Their relationship had been talked about on chat shows, radio programmes and online forums. Seb wasn't being hushed anymore. And that meant more to him than anything.

240

He rummaged through the food contents; his brief flick through Jamie Oliver's cookbook earlier had inspired him to attempt an actual dinner. Normally, he'd have suggested a takeaway and got the eye roll from Jay about it. So he figured a home-cooked meal would suffice in offering Jay condolences if his day at West Ham hadn't been a successful one, and nothing said 'I love you' like a home-seared rib-eye steak. It seemed easy enough for even him to manage. Whack a bit of salad leaves beside it and Jay couldn't complain. And if Jay came home with good news, all the better. They'd both be celebrating.

He'd got as far as taking the griddle pan out of the newly found hidden drawer when the front door clanged open.

"Hey," Seb called out to the hallway. "You better be hungry, as I'm starting dinner. And, no, before you make the jibe, your boyfriend has not been abducted by aliens and replaced with an upgraded model." He scanned through the other cupboards above his head for the herbs, spices, and other whatnot he needed, when Jay appeared at the archway. "Take a seat. We're celebrating. I got some fucking awesome news. Have you been at the club all this time?"

When Jay didn't move, Seb peeped out from behind the cupboard door. *Oh shit.* That look on Jay's face meant that scenario one was obviously in play. Bad news was affront. Seb would have to try his damnedest to make Jay see that it wasn't the end of the world. That there was more to life than football, and that he was going to offer him the chance of a lifetime.

"No." Jay's voice was deep, eerily so.

"Oh, right. Where you been? And you're okay with steak, right? Rib-eye? I know it's the fatty one, but it's a top-quality cut from the butcher's. And I've checked the

241

Jamie Oliver recipe and apparently the man says it's fool proof, so if a guy from Essex can do it, so can a public schoolboy drop-out from West Kensington. Of course, we all know that means I will now fuck it up. But you'll smile sweetly and love me anyway, right?"

"Which question do you want me to answer first?"

"Huh?" Seb ripped open the plastic butcher's bags and prodded the tender meat. That was proper steak. Thick cut, locally sourced, and cost as much as the Bollinger. *Let's seriously hope I do not ruin this.*

"I called you."

Seb ground salt and pepper over each rib-eye, turning them over and slapping each on the chunky wooden chopping board. "You did? Sorry, I've been on that phone all bloody day. It's just run out of battery. Did you need a lift? Rare or medium? And, what did the club say?"

"I'd tell ya if you stop firing questions at me."

Seb darted his gaze to Jay still hovering at the doorway. "Sorry." He smiled and wriggled his shoulders, trying to ruffle out his antsy pants or he'd never let Jay speak. "I'm just a little psyched."

"Why?"

"All in good time, baby." Seb winked, then sprinkled the olive oil into the griddle pan. "What happened at the club?" He needed to know Jay's outcome first in order to choose which way he was going to deliver his epic newsflash.

"Much the same. Light training by myself. Slow and steady. Build up to full fitness."

"Okay, well, that's positive, surely?"

"I guess."

Seb washed his hands in the sink, shooting a concerned glance over his shoulder. That wasn't the look of a man who had received good news. And Jay still hadn't ventured into the kitchen. It made things a little awkward to figure out the best way to explain what Seb was so excitably restless about. "That took all day?"

Jay's sudden burst of laughter bounced off the kitchen units and he scraped his cap off, ruffling out his hair and spun it onto the island. "No."

"Okay…" Seb twisted, leaning back against the counter. Was there some joke he was missing out on? "Care to elaborate?"

"I met up with Riley."

"Who's Riley?"

"That old mate of mine who wanted to tap me up for the clothing endorsement deal."

"You didn't tell me he was an 'old mate.' How'd you know him?"

"Football."

Seb tutted through a fond smile. "Naturally. Wait, does that mean you're considering it?"

Jay shrugged. "I went to a studio. Did a few test shots."

"Wow. My boyfriend wants to be a model. And what's that?" Seb pointed to a bunch of papers Jay held in his hand.

"The contract." Jay hobbled into the kitchen and slapped the papers down on the island.

Seb scraped his bottom lip. Jay's non-conversational tones was making him edgy. "You want me to check over it after dinner?"

"Don't bother. I signed it already."

Seb leaped away from the sideboard and stumbled forward. "You what?"

Pinching the bridge of his nose, Seb tried to get a handle on his seeping annoyance. After everything. All

243

the talks about staying away from the media, being careful what they said, or did, living in the shadows. Had Jay just gone and signed over his image? Without talking it through?

"Why didn't you check it over with me first?" Seb aimed for keeping his voice calm, collected. He was sure he pulled it off. Until he met with Jay's steely glare back at him.

"You didn't answer your phone."

Seb gritted his teeth and took a deep breath. "So you bring it home and I check it."

"Couldn't be too sure you'd be here, could I?"

"So you wait! Jay, for fuck's sake! Do you even know what you've signed? Did you read it?"

"I ain't a fucking imbecile, Seb. I can fucking read. No matter what everyone thinks of us footballers."

Seb was a little taken aback by how Jay spat that at him. This evening was not going to plan, and it seemed, if Seb didn't know any better, that Jay had been gunning for an argument from the moment he'd stepped into the kitchen.

"Are you all right?" Seb had to ask, regardless of any outcome.

"Why wouldn't I be?" Jay folded his arms, and shrugged, a stance full of evasive ambivalence. What the fuck was going on?

"I don't know. You're all...tense." Seb waved a hand over Jay's rigid form. He didn't want an argument. Not tonight. Not ever, really. But tonight had meant to go so differently. "Look, I'll read it later, find a small print clause or something so they can't use your image for certain things."

"Like what? It was a few test shots, Seb. That was it."

"Jay, baby, you've have no idea what you've just allowed them to do with your fucking image, do you? No-one signs something on the first show! You take it home, you consult your legal team, and you cross check. Surely, you know better than that! Fuck, Jay! What happens when your face gets plastered everywhere, nice little quote next to it slagging off something or other. 'Vote BNP and fuck everyone who don't agree', Jay Ruttman, West Ham. Shitting, fucking, bollocks, Jay! How well do you even know this guy?"

"West Ham recommended him as my agent. But I knew him from back in the Academy."

"The Academy?"

"Yeah. I played him a few times on the circuit."

"Played him? Like, he was on your team?"

"No. He was an opposition. He got dropped same time as me."

"Why'd he get dropped?"

Jay heaved a deep breath. "'Cause we had a fight."

"We? As in the royal we? Or you and him?"

There was a brief pause where Seb couldn't get his eyes wide enough and Jay stared back, those usually beatific blue eyes darkening with each passing moment.

"He's the bloke I beat up. Over Tom."

Seb's mouth dropped open. "What the actual fuck?"

"Don't start." Jay turned away and if he felt guilty about what he'd just admitted, it didn't show. Instead it was pure frustrated anger flickering across his pale features. "I ain't in any mood for it."

"I will fucking start!" Seb flapped his hand, irritation surging through him. Fuck trying to be calm and defuse the situation. What Jay had just done was beyond dumb. And he couldn't fathom why Jay would

245

have done all this without consulting him. "You just signed an Image Rights contract, a fucking Use of Likeness legal binding fucking document that allows a man access to use your face for his goddamn, fucking pleasure and then you tell me it's the homophobic wanker that you beat the shit out of, earning you both a place on the dole queue."

"I was seventeen. It earned me a place back at school."

"Details!" Seb's voice hit higher decibels than his professional standard amps would have and he couldn't control his rage. "Did you not think this bloke might want some kind of retaliation? Get back at you for not making it as a professional? Because of you, queer boy, he might have a fucking vendetta! Like that arse hole who fucked up your knee? Why the shitting, *fuck* did you not tell me all this before you fucking went?"

Eerily calm, Jay stepped forward. A breath away from Seb, he asked, "Do we tell each other everything, then?"

"Of course we fucking do!"

Jay cocked his head. "Where were you today?"

"Here. Sorting out my deal with Sony."

"Really?"

"Yes. And I was going to tell you all about it whilst we ate this fucking romantic dinner that you have subsequently ruined, FY fucking I."

In a childish sulk, Seb grabbed the steaks and threw them slap-bang into the swing bin. He paced the end of the kitchen, his chest ready to explode, all while Jay's blue glare followed every vexed stomp. *How had this gone so fucking wrong?* This morning, everything had seemed rosy, golden, bright rainbow colours floating around them both as their unified image had been seen in every tabloid. Now this clusterfuck of epic proportions, and Seb had no idea what had brought them here.

Seb paused, hands on hips. "What's happened? Is it because of the picture in the paper? Did the club tell you it was wrong? Did they say you need to ditch me? Is it because of your knee? Because you can't play football?"

"You tell me, Seb." Jay stared at him. Challenging him. And he might as well have slapped Seb around the face.

It was the picture. It had to be. So Jay hadn't been happy about stepping out in the media? That had all been a front. Football was clearly still more important to him than their relationship was. One day back at the club and Jay was, what, running back to the closet? *Fucking aces!* That's why he'd gone and done the photo shoot. To get him back in the football limelight. To segregate himself from Seb. From who he was and had made inroads to being. Jay could be a fucking icon! Instead, he shied away. Didn't talk about it, didn't include Seb. Hurt didn't even begin to describe this one.

Jay opened his mouth to speak, but the doorbell cut between them.

"Ignore it." Seb stared at him. He needed this argument over and done. He had to know where he stood, if being swept under the carpet would be his entire life.

"Like everything, huh?" Jay pushed away from the counter and headed toward the front door.

Seb followed him and was about to yell a dozen more obscenities at Jay's back, but after Jay had yanked open the front door, a sobbing Ann collapsed onto Jay's chest.

"Hey, hey." Jay hugged Ann, stroking a hand through her hair. "What's up? What's happened?"

247

Seb staggered closer and met Jay's concerned stare back at him. Breathing out his annoyance, Seb shut the door behind Ann.

"I told my mum." She sniffled. "I told her I was keeping the baby. I can't get rid of it, Jay, I can't."

"Shit." Jay tugged Ann away to look her in the eye. "It's all right. It is."

"Is it?" Ann hiccupped.

Jay raised his chin toward Seb and mouthed the word 'tissue'. Seb ran off, then returned with a bunch of toilet paper from the downstairs loo and handed it over. The trumpeting blow of Ann's nose put things between he and Jay into some kind of perspective. Perhaps her intrusion might smooth things over for them? Make them realise there were bigger problems to have.

"How am I going to manage?" Ann shook her head and her brown eyes filled with tears. "My mum said I was stupid. That I'd never cope on my own. That I was going to end up like her. She wanted much better for me, not to live in some rundown council estate in east London, single with child, like she had. That I should have stayed with Lucas as he could've given me a right, proper life. She's right."

"She ain't right." Jay gripped the top of her arms. "And you ain't alone. You got me."

"And me." Seb ran a soothing hand across Ann's back.

Jay's blue eyes over her head were filled with something Seb couldn't place. Was it remorse? Regret for their stern words earlier? He couldn't tell, and ached to find out, but Ann had to come first right then.

"Come on." Jay slipped a hand around Ann's shoulders and steered her through to the kitchen, setting her down on one of the island stools. "What about the dad?"

Thinking it best to leave them to it, Seb slid the contract from under Jay's arms and leaned on his elbows to read through. Might as well look for some hope within the right to privacy clause.

"I have to tell him, I know." Ann sniffled into the tissue and grunted. "I just don't want to be that bitch who ruins his life as well."

"Why would it ruin his life?" Jay reached for the kitchen roll, tearing a piece off and handing it to her.

"Because he won't want this. Me."

Straightening, Seb rested his hip on the island and folded his arms. "I think you might be surprised there."

"About what?" Ann peered up, her puffy brown eyes glistening.

Seb felt for her, he did. He knew a little of what she must be going through. Perhaps without the added pressure of a baby. But he knew what it was like to feel unwanted. "You never really know what someone wants."

Ann snorted. "Cryptic."

Jay twisted, facing Seb. "That a fact?"

"Seems to be." Seb didn't falter his stare.

"Have I interrupted something?" Ann darted her bloodshot eyes from Seb to Jay.

It looked like Jay was about to respond, and Seb would have quite liked to know what that response would have been. But the doorbell sang out again and Seb decided to go answer it this time. It wasn't like he was needed where he was.

"Why are you not answering your fucking phone?" Noah demanded after Seb had opened the door.

"Sorry, dude." Martin poked his head above Noah's. "We've been trying to call you all day."

Seb ushered them both in. "Phone out of battery and in the other room. I said I'd call you back."

"I know, but Noah needed to talk to you. Like, stat." Martin hopped his gangly legs into the house.

Noah had already made strides toward the kitchen and Seb slammed the door, following them both through the hallway before practically bumping into the back of Noah hovering at the entrance archway.

"Maybe we should just go into the next room?" Seb suggested, waving his arms to get them both to move away from the desperate scene in the kitchen.

Ann stood and brushed down her crumpled top, then addressed Jay as she spoke. "Don't worry, I'll go. I'll speak to you later."

As she tried to slide past, Noah grabbed her wrist. "Don't." He focussed wide, pleading blue-grey eyes on Ann. "Don't leave. I know."

Ann swallowed. "What? How?"

"Him." Noah nodded to Seb behind him

Seb's mouth hung open for the second time and he tried to find some words, but was oddly fascinated at the scene in front of him. So he shut up, and listened.

"I'm guessing I'm your only bit on the side, so the baby is mine?" Noah rubbed his thumb along Ann's wrist.

"What?" Jay stood, brow furrowing.

Ann spun back. "Jay—"

"He's the father?" Jay flapped a hand at Noah. "*Him*?"

Ann pursed her lips, nodding with a shameful hang of her head.

Jay directed his attention back to Seb and Seb was hard-pressed not to flinch at the sight. "And you *knew*?"

"No." Seb shook his head. "No. I suspected. I didn't know for sure."

"And, what, you kept that from me?" Jay's glare was hard, to the point Seb thought daggers might spring from each eye.

"It wasn't my place to tell you. It was a suspicion. That's all."

Jay snorted. "How long have you suspected?"

Seb shrugged. "A while. When the dude said he didn't have her number back in New York. He only deletes the ones who dump him. He keeps the others just in case."

"New York? That's two years ago. My best mate, fucking about behind her boyfriend's back with your drummer? You didn't think that would be something I might wanna be clued in on? That I might wanna help her with?"

"She's a consenting adult, Jay."

"She had a boyfriend!"

"Love and sex are two different things." Seb couldn't believe he'd let that slip out. It hadn't even sounded like his own voice that had said it. *Stephen's.* Seb shuddered.

"Is it now?" Jay glared at him, face reddening.

"Jay—" Ann wriggled her wrist free from Noah's grip. "Calm down. I'm sorry. It ain't Seb's fault. It's mine. And now I have to face the consequences."

"We both do." Noah grabbed her hand and held it to his lips. "I want this, Ann. All of it. I always did, but you never let me prove myself. You always went back to him. That's the only reason I ever went with those other girls. To make you jealous. So that's why I'm here. To tell

251

Seb I can't do this American tour. I don't want to leave you and not be here for our baby for two years of its life. It just ain't right."

"What?" Jay stumbled back.

"Hang on, hang on." Seb held out his hands to calm the situation down. This was racing forward so fast he had a bigger head rush than when he'd downed a bottle of Jack before a gig. *Could do with some of that now.* "We've not even discussed the US tour. Not the details."

"You said two years." Noah nodded to Martin for confirmation.

"Yeah, dude, your phone call said a two-year round tour." At least Martin had the decency to cringe a little. "I had to tell him, 'cause he'd told me about Ann."

"Yes, okay, I did." Seb stuttered. This was not how he had wanted to deliver the news. "The finer details haven't been planned. That's the next stage. Once we sign."

"But you didn't discuss it with us." Martin gained an inch of confidence to match his height to deliver that. "You should have asked us first, if we wanted to leave AR and go with Sony. I mean, I've got Leah. We're going good, y'know? I'm not sure about buggering off for an extended tour of the states. And Noah's now got a baby on the way…"

"And, so?" Seb rammed his hands on his hips. "That means we shouldn't tour? We shouldn't aim for the top? We were going nowhere fast with Armstrong. This is our meal ticket to everything we ever wanted."

"We were doing all right as it was, weren't we?" Martin asked rather than stated. "We had creative control. Like *you* wanted. We had the yay or nay on stuff. We took it easy. The Drops were never mainstream appeal. We never wanted to be, right? We wanted to stay true to ourselves. The outcasts, the misfits, the drop-outs!"

"Exactly," Noah piped up, his hand still stroking the small of Ann's back. "We've followed you wherever you wanted. Done everything you ever wanted of us. From that fucking death threat Winchester gig to the New York shit to V Fest. Now it's time to listen to us, let the band be a democracy. And my life, right now, is here. With Ann and the baby."

"And mine's with Leah right now." Martin flinched, obviously not feeling as confident as before. But he continued nonetheless. "Why do we need to do this right now? We just got established. Let's ride the wave for a bit? Why do you always have to climb higher, go one better, be bigger?"

"Because that's me, Martin!" Seb punched his chest. He couldn't believe this was happening. He was sure Martin and Noah would have been up for the tour. How couldn't they be? Why wouldn't they want to be the best version of themselves that they could? Why wouldn't they want the ultimate success? "I'm a Saunders!"

The kitchen hushed into a silence and Seb glared at each so-called friend individually. His gaze landed on Jay, and it was as if he couldn't hold it in anymore. He begged for Jay to understand this, and why he needed to do this, and how it meant so much to him. But the look on his face said otherwise.

"And what does that mean, Seb?" Jay was calm, but his clenched fists trembled.

"What do *you* mean?"

"You're fucking off for two years? To the US? And you hadn't even told me that, either? Déjà fucking vu, Seb!"

"I was going to!" Seb exploded, unable to keep himself in check. This had all gone horribly wrong. All of it. And he still had no idea why. "But you came in pissing and moaning about some shit or other and didn't give me a fucking chance."

"So that's what you did today." Jay's blue icy stare delving right into the pits of Seb's resolve. "Made sure you'd be all right while you're out there?"

"What the fuck are you talking about?"

Hanging his head, Jay mumbled to the floor. "I can't believe it."

"I can't believe you're being such a passive-aggressive bitch! What the fuck is up with you?"

Jay looked up, blue eyes sparking. "What were you doing at the Royal, Seb?"

Acid burned in Seb's chest and up to his throat, bubbling over his skin. So that was what this was all about. He had no idea how Jay could have known he'd been at the Royal earlier. Maybe Jay had seen the message on his phone and been stewing about it all day, thinking Seb had gone to meet Stephen. But then instead of actually asking Seb about it, he'd fucked off and got his kit off for another bloke! Seb wasn't even sure if he would have mentioned the meeting with his father to Jay at all. The whole thing was so insignificant in his life right then that it hadn't made it passed the forefront of his brain. There hadn't been anything to tell!

Seb heaved a deep breath. This was because Jay thought Seb had been going behind his back. Doing what Ann had done to Lucas? And yet he hadn't the decency to just ask Seb the damn question. That look on Jay's face said it all. He thought Seb was a cheater, a man-whore, someone who would risk their precious relationship that had meant more to him than anything in his entire life for

254

a quick fuck. Or even that he would think Seb could bounce back to an utter arse wipe like Stephen Coles just because he hadn't been getting some for a while. After everything, Jay didn't trust him.

Storming past, Seb couldn't look at him. He yanked open the glass liquor cabinet at the end of the units, grabbed a bottle of unopened Jack Daniels, then bundled past all the bastards who just stood there staring at him. He'd made it to the front door when Martin's yell made him stop for a miniscule moment.

"Seb! Don't be a dick. We need to talk about this!"

"Go fuck yourselves. You all take me for a fucking bastard. I'll go it alone. All of it. I should have remembered *my* motto — everyone, *always*, buggers off in the end!"

CHAPTER SIXTEEN
Out of Sight

The entire house rattled on its hinges as the door slammed shut. Jay didn't know what to do first—run after Seb and demand he tell him what the hell was going on, throttle Noah for causing all this, or scream at Ann for keeping everything from him. The unified exhale of breaths from all those still left in his kitchen gave off a stagnant atmosphere and Jay's head rushed through a dozen emotions at once. He couldn't clear it. He couldn't think straight. He couldn't figure out what had gone so wrong. Had Seb's reaction been an admission of guilt? Or was it a hasty retreat from having been wedged into a corner by everyone's accusations? Jay needed to talk. He had to get all the squirming, confusing, relenting thoughts out of his head and sort through them. To make some kind of sense over what had just happened. And there was only one person in the vicinity who could help him with that.

"Ann, can we talk?" Noah got there first, though.

Ann sniffled and nodded. "I think we should." She peered up to Jay with concerned eyes. "Jay, I'm sorry."

"Yeah. Me too." He was. He knew his reaction to her news hadn't been fair. Ann *was* an adult. She didn't need to tell him everything. She wasn't his property. She wasn't even his girlfriend in order for his betrayal to feel justified. Deep down, he knew that had all been about Seb. He wanted to ask Ann to stay with him. To talk to him. For her to tell him that he was being an idiot, that none of that stuff with Seb and Stephen could even be remotely true. He had a sudden urge to go back to how things used to be, before all the adulting. When he and Ann had used to sit on the park swings and make plans for their future, not actually be living it. When football, relationships, media-frenzies and babies hadn't even been a faint line on the horizon. "Go on." He nudged his chin toward the door. "You two gotta lot to sort out."

She looked as guilty as hell, but smiled through the tears. "Are you okay, though? What was all that about, with Seb?"

It wasn't fair to offload his own woes on her. Not when Ann had so much stuff to deal with. Regardless of how he felt about her situation, she clearly needed a chance to figure out her next steps. And that wasn't with him. And whatever he thought of Noah, at least the man had stepped up when he needed to.

"I'm all right. And, honestly, I'm not sure." It was the truth, sort of.

Ann squeezed his arm. "I'll call you. Later."

After walking them out, putting on a brave front, and closing the door, he came face to face with Martin standing awkwardly behind him.

"Dude, I'm sorry. Had no idea he wouldn't have discussed it with you either."

"Yeah, well, it seems he likes to keep secrets." Jay fished his phone out from his back pocket, opened the Safari App where he'd stored the MTV news report, image and all, and showed it up to Martin. "Tell me that ain't him."

Martin squinted, leaning forward. "There'll be an explanation for that."

"Which is?"

Martin shrugged. "I don't know. But the Royal?" He shook his head, disbelief written all over his face. "There would have to be a pretty damn good reason for Seb to have been there. Even more so with that." He pointed an angry digit at the phone.

Jay looked at the picture again, clicked it off and sighed. "Why? What's so special about the Royal?"

Martin blanked. "Oh. Well, that's where it happened, y'know…"

"Exactly!" Jay's heart, already crushed, felt like it'd splatter all over the cream walls. "All the more reason."

"No, no, he wouldn't. Not after that last time…" Martin trailed off, eyes darting to the floor before finally focusing back on Jay. "Trust me. He wouldn't."

"What aren't you tellin' me? And what hasn't Seb told me? Again."

"It's not my place if you don't know already."

"Martin, I swear to fuckin' God, I'll smash your entire kit in there." Jay jerked his thumb over his shoulder at the music room. "Tell me what you already thought I knew."

Martin heaved out a sigh. "That's where Stephen got a bit…fist happy, shall we say? Seb ended it, he got a whack. I had to come pick him up after he'd tallied up the bar bill to such heights even Will's credit card couldn't bail him out. I had to tap my dad up for a loan. It's why

258

Seb bought me the guitar. To say thanks. And sorry, I guess."

"Shit." Jay hung his head. He'd known Stephen had been rough. Seb had admitted to that. He'd also been a witness to Stephen going off the rails in New York. But he hadn't known it had ever been as bad as proper beatings. "Stephen used to beat him?"

"Once. He did it once. Because Seb ended it. Stephen kept coming into Seb's room after that, but Seb managed to get him out. Lock on the door. Then you."

"I'll never understand why he didn't tell his dad."

Martin shook his head. "'Cause the guy is manipulative, man. A real sleaze. There was blackmail, there was bribery, there was a lot of fucking shit that went down back then. It took a lot for him to do what he did. To stand up to him. It was you who gave him the ultimate courage, though. Like, no disrespect here or anything, mate, but I don't think you quite know the circles he roamed in. That Stephen and his dad roam in. The pressures of that world to be something when you're not is pretty hard."

Jay inhaled a deep breath. "I understand that more than you'd think."

Martin nodded. "Yeah. Guess you would."

"So why would he be there? That's him, Martin. We both know it."

"I don't know. I honestly don't know." Martin squeezed his arm. "Talk to him. Listen to him. That's all he's ever asked people to do. Why d'you think he writes it all in songs? 'Cause no one ever listened to him otherwise."

Jay was now even more confused than before. He'd no idea why Seb had gone to meet Stephen. He'd attempted to run through all the rational scenarios when

259

Riley had driven him home earlier and he'd concluded that he should give Seb the chance to tell him without prompting, without Jay having to say he'd seen the picture. But when Seb hadn't even mentioned it, then outright lied when Jay had asked him where he'd been, and then storming out when Jay had posed the question of the Royal at all, everything pointed to the worst. If Seb had been planning a two-year trip to America, would he have contacted Stephen for some sort of rekindling? Deep down, Jay couldn't believe it to be true, but his crippled self-esteem knocked his confidence. Jay wasn't good enough, he hadn't been giving Seb what he needed. Seb had been a highly sex-charged bloke before Jay, one-night stands second nature. Why wouldn't Seb go elsewhere if he wasn't getting his basic needs met by Jay? Unlike Jay, Seb could have sex without making love. *Love and sex are two different things.*

"I'm going to shoot off." Martin opened the front door. "Call him. Talk to him. Do not let him down that bottle before you do. I'd been happy those days were over."

As the door closed for the third time, the house shunted into complete silence, which didn't help the thoughts still swimming in Jay's head. He scraped back his hair and paced the corridor, trying to decide what to do. Where would Seb have gone? Why had he gone? Was he gone for good? The very thought made Jay sick to his stomach. He pulled out his phone and clicked on Seb's name, setting off a delicate buzzing in rhythmic timing with the ringing in his ear. He followed the vibrations and peeped in to Seb's music room. Seb's phone, on the floor and plugged into his laptop, was no doubt downloading his music as well as charging the battery. Switching his off, Jay stomped in and tugged Seb's phone from the wire.

Was it committing the ultimate sin to check through his boyfriend's messages? *Can I be forgiven for needing to do it, having to see for myself?*

He'd got as far opening the iPhone to the main screen when his own phone buzzed in his hand and made his heart leap into his throat. He dropped Seb's, shattering the already broken screen and threw a guilty glance over his shoulder, checking if someone had seen his betrayal of trust. When only the ticking clock stared back at him, Jay checked the message.

Mate, it's Riley, I'm down that pub near you. Tap me up if you want a drink.

At that moment, Jay couldn't think of a better idea. He tucked his phone back into his pocket, grabbed his keys and left the house.

* * * *

Dangling the bottle between his legs, Seb lowered his head to shield his face from the passenger's opposite. He should have picked up his shades on the way out, or hailed a cab rather than riding the train. But his head wasn't thinking straight. His trembling legs had stalked toward the Docklands Light Railway, leaped over the turnstiles and he now found himself sitting in a carriage hurtling him back over the river.

The whisky remained unopened. He yearned to down the entire thing and scorch his insides. Like the good old days. Always trust in Jack to give him what he needed. But now knowing that he was on display, a photograph waiting to happen, a headline ready to be sold, he thought better of it than chuck back the stuff in public. He needed privacy. He needed somewhere he

261

knew, and could trust in. *Beneath the duvet, entwined with Jay.* Seb snorted. No such luck.

Looking up, he checked which stations he'd be passing. He stood, grabbed the rail overhead and leaned in closer. The plan materialised in his head without much thinking. Gripping the bottle, he stood by the exit doors and bundled out at Bow Church. Ignoring the high-pitched bleeps from those who had Oyster Cards, he trundled down the steps, out into the street and headed left toward the underground. He managed to sneak in through the disabled entry behind a mother with buggy and boarded the District Line, Westbound, trying not to let his gaze settle on the stations leading eastward. *Plaistow. Jay's side.* He'd obviously been merely a visitor there.

Leaning against the glass pane by the doors, he tapped his fingernails on the bottle, impatiently willing the tube ride to go quicker. He avoided eye contact with those passengers alighting and boarding. It wasn't too hard; Londoners barely acknowledged one another's presence as it was. But him, having been in the media twice already that day, he couldn't risk anyone calling him out. Nor did he want it. He wanted to be in the shadows this time. Alone. *The way I've always been.*

When the carriage doors swished open at Victoria, he jumped off and his legs knew the way. Holding the JD by the neck, he departed into the bustling west end. Without looking, he paced the same pavement he'd stepped on when he'd been a fervent teenager, a heartbroken young adult, and a cynical new man. The darkened sky matched his mood. Except for the occasional flicker from the street lamps or the dim haze from the late-night coffee shops and packed-out wine bars, the gloom shrouded him. Here, he could hide in the shadows.

Hitting the fork in the road, he stopped and breathed in the exhaust fumes from the city. Across stood his old haunt, and the low drone of chatter even sounded the same. Except, back then, there wouldn't have been as many gatherings on the narrow path, considering smoking had been permitted inside. He glanced up to the sign and the huge Stag's head above the door welcomed him back. As much as he craved a cigarette, he knew better than to ask for one from those huddled under the veranda and so thrashed through the doors and into the bar.

All men, mostly suited, with a couple of females dotted among the many that stuck out like a sore thumb, filled up the traditional tavern. Seb headed straight for the bar stool at the end and dumped his bottle of Jack on the matt with a vicious thud.

* * * *

When Jay arrived at the Court Yard, Riley was propping up the bar and laughing with the bird serving him. Perhaps this hadn't been his best idea. Watching Riley trying to cop off with the staff hadn't been number one on his to-do list. He was just about to twist around when Riley caught his eye and held up his pint.

"Jay! Mate. Come on. Don't let the draught in." He ushered him over, pulling out a stool from beneath the bar. "Go on, park your arse."

Jay limped over, his knee aching from not having been able to rest that day. He settled down in the seat, offering a firm nod in greeting to the bar girl. "Corona, please, love."

263

She nodded and leaned down to the chillers. But Jay glanced up to the spirit section and for some reason a stupid thought struck.

"Actually. JD." *Seb's poison of choice.*

"Nice." Riley tapped him on the back and gulped from his full pint. "I'll join you on that. Make that two, Christie."

"Single?" the girl asked with the glass already tucked under the Jack Daniel spout.

"I am, he's not." Riley cackled and shoved Jay on the arm.

"Wouldn't be too sure about that, mate."

"Right." Riley's face dropped. "Sorry. Make it two doubles."

Two tumblers of Jack landed in front of them and Riley shoved the girl a tenner, waving her off. Jay lifted the glass to his lips, the pungent musky scent hitting his nostrils and sending him on a whirlwind of nostalgia. That was Seb in a glass—rich, aromatic and smooth. For all of Jay's avoidance of hard spirits, whenever Seb had been on the JD, Jay hankered for his intoxicated kisses— almost as though Jay could get high from the droplets still left on Seb's tongue. *Maybe it was just Seb?* The morning after a night's drinking had always dissuaded Jay from overindulging, but right then, he felt like he had a hangover from Seb.

"You wanna talk about it?" Riley leaned his forearms on the bar counter, wrapping both hands around his pint.

Jay did, but he wasn't sure Riley was the right person. *Who else is there?*

"He walked out." Jay hovered the glass at his lips, still unsure whether to drink.

"For good?"

264

"I don't know. When I asked him where he'd been, he lied."

Riley whistled, taking a swig of beer. "Shit. So, the fella? The one in the picture? Who is he?"

Jay's eyes fluttered to a close. He still couldn't bring himself to think it could be true. Trouble was, no one had given him any other explanation. "His ex. Lover. But it's more complicated than that." Downing the JD, the hit caught in his throat and burned his chest. He coughed into a balled fist and his eyes streamed. "Fuck." His voice was as hoarse as his forty-a-day grandmother's. "That's why I don't drink."

"Ha, and that ain't done much for your street cred neither." Riley chuckled and clapped Jay on the back. "I'm sorry, mate. The bloke's an idiot. You're better off without him, if you ask me."

Jay shook his head, undecided whether he was disputing the accusation or just doing it for want of anything else to reply. "I dunno. Maybe it's all my fault."

"How'd'you figure that?" Riley finished his pint, then went onto the glass of Jack.

"I've been a prick recently. Since this." Jay tapped his knee. "It's got in the way, of us. I haven't been able to…" He met Riley's gaze, wondering how to put it. "Perform."

Riley furrowed his brow, then after a moment, "Oh! Right. No going bump in the night, I get it. 'Cause of the pain?"

"Yeah, and the pills, and the ops, and, well, me. It's all in here." Jay tapped his head, and the realisation struck for the first time. This was his fault. All of it. Even before the injury, Jay had been pushing Seb away. "It's all because I just never let us be free. I wouldn't let us be seen, be talked about. As much as I was out, I still hid it. I

265

told the world I was gay. Then I ran away and shut the door and asked Seb not to open it. I didn't come out, as much as just peep my head through the window. Then getting this injury, I didn't challenge it. Seb told me to. I wouldn't. It's football. You leave it on the pitch."

"Yeah. I know." Riley downed his JD and waggled the glass at the server.

Jay had still yet to take another sip. The first lot had burned his chest and seared his taste buds. The girl passed over another glass to Riley, offering Jay the same. He refused. He might be able to nurse this one all night.

"You know what you need?" Riley bumped his shoulder. "A good, old-fashioned, night on the town. One where no one knows you. Where you're not looking over your shoulder. Where did you used to go before you met Seb? To hook up, I mean?"

Jay furrowed his brow and attempted another sip. "Nowhere."

"What? You met all your old conquests on the pitch? I doubt it, mate."

"No, I mean, I didn't. Hook up. Go anywhere."

"You're kidding?" Riley shook his head and knocked back half the whisky. "You never had anyone, before Seb?"

"No. Well, there was Tom. But that wasn't, y'know…"

"Tom?" Riley scrubbed a hand over his face, his dry fingertips rasping against his stubble. The scratching reminded Jay of Seb's hands over his skin—years of playing guitar had given Seb's fingertips their calloused edges. "Oh, right, the American. Yeah, I remember."

Jay didn't prompt him again. Riley should remember Tom, considering he'd been one of the ones to give him a smack in the mouth. It wasn't worth dredging up and would only highlight what a surreal situation this all was. Jay, here, drinking with the bloke who'd sent his life down the fork in the road. *What would Tom say if he knew?*

"So what you're saying is that Seb, he was your first?"

Jay knocked back the rest of the JD and slammed it on the surface, his chest on fire. "Man, yeah. I'd slept with girls."

"Right. Wow." Riley ponderously sipped from his whisky. "That's, shit, I don't know what to say, mate. That, there, might be your problem."

"What?"

"You've only been with one man? One bloke? How do you know he was even the one for you? You gotta fuck a lot of frogs before you find your prince."

"That so?" Jay waved his glass at the serving girl and she refreshed it quick smart. The whisky, like Seb's Jack'd-up kisses, was quite addictive once the initial burn had worn off. That was like a euphemism for the man himself. "I think if you know, you know. Don't matter if you've fucked a dozen or none. The feeling's gotta be the same, right?"

"Maybe." Riley shrugged, then lingered his glass at his lips and held Jay's gaze. "Maybe it's time you found out."

* * * *

"You can't drink that in here." The above strobe lights shone off the barman's bald head.

Seb stared the bloke in the eye, wandering his gaze down the man's checked trousers, white vest and braces. *Nothing changes.*

267

"Sebastian?" The barman grinned, cocked his head and slammed a hand on his slender hip. "Long time, no visit. Thought you'd outgrown us."

"Donnie." Seb greeted the owner with modest enthusiasm. "Glass. Ice."

"You know I can't let you drink that in here." He pointed to the full bottle of unopened Jack.

"You want me to go outside and drink it? I'll still need a glass." Seb wriggled out of his jacket. "And ice."

"We've got security now." Donnie angled his head toward the beefcake folding his arms at the end of the bar and staring at Seb as though he'd just taken a shit on the counter.

Seb sighed. The last thing he needed was to be chucked out. He slipped the bottle across the smooth wood. "Gift. For you."

Smiling, Donnie curled his fingers around the bottle's neck and dragged it to his chest. "What can I get you?"

"JD. Bottle." Seb squared his shoulders. "Glass and ice."

Donnie chuckled and dumped the bottle back down in front of him. "That'll be fifty. For you."

Seb tugged out his bank card from his pocket and handed it to Donnie to swipe through the till. Slipping it back into his jeans, Seb nodded a thanks for the glass plonked in front of him while Donnie sprinkled ice from the scoop into it.

"You looking for something tonight?" Donnie's green eyes twinkled. "I know a few of the regulars miss your visits. But we've been playing your records and keeping your stool warm for you."

Seb stared across the counter, his face a blank expression. Donnie smiled, leaned forward and his once youthful complexion was now sprinkled with deep lines.

"Although, I think most people in here would be very interested in watching your boyfriend fuck you." He stood straight. "I know I would. And might I say, Sebastian, I was very surprised to hear how that turned out. You were never really the marriage-and-kids type. Not when you used to drink in here."

"People change." *Do they? Jay didn't think so.*

"I'd certainly change to be on the receiving end of a footballer. Nice catch by the way. How does one score that sort of discreet gym Queen?"

"Fuck off." Seb twisted open the cap on the bottle, filled his glass to the brim and his chest tightened like a vice grip. Why the fuck had he come here? What could he possibly gain from going backwards? That's what he'd told the others. Always move forward, always aim high.

He could get himself back, that's what. He *had* changed. After vowing never to be controlled again, it had happened without him knowing it. He'd been censored. Like when the radio bleeped over the obscenities to play his tracks, Jay had clamped a gag on him. And for what? For 'survival on the pitch'? *Didn't work, did it?* He'd been targeted and injured anyway, sinking him into depression and clearly blaming Seb for what had happened, to the point Jay couldn't see past his paranoia anymore. Seb had tried to understand, had accepted everything Jay had asked of him, and had been the dutiful, and fucking faithful, boyfriend. Okay, so on a couple of occasions, he'd slipped up and mentioned them in the media or on stage. He couldn't help it. He was so goddamn in love with that man it had been hard to keep schtum. Maybe Jay was rethinking everything and had realised that having a boyfriend in the public eye wasn't what he wanted. That look on his face as he'd asked about the Royal...

Seb tapped his pockets. *Shit*. He'd left his phone at home. *Is it my home?* Where was his home? Cupping his palms against the glass of JD, Seb hung his head and the ice melted through the warmth still in his hands. His father was currently clearing out his childhood home, ready to sell to the highest bidder, and whilst Seb wouldn't have cared a few weeks ago, suddenly the thought of not being able to go back there caused a dull ache in his heart. Or was that just what Jay had left him with?

Seb clenched his jaw. His father—this was all his fucking father's fault! Why couldn't his dad have just left things as they were? Not once in Seb's miserable upbringing did he think that his father had really cared for him. Seb had been his commodity, his heir, not his son. But what he had done earlier—calling a truce, confronting Stephen and apologising for not having been there, telling Seb he was proud of him, offering his possessions back—what had that all been for? For Seb? Or to relinquish the guilt Will carried around? *Selfish bastard.*

If Will had just let things be, the way Seb had done, Seb wouldn't be here right now. Alone, cold, and inhaling the stale odour of the past. Jay wouldn't have accused him of cheating, and Seb would have had time to convince the band that the tour was right. Once again, his father had prevented Seb's happiness.

Pushing his glass away, Seb stood.

"Leaving so soon, Sebastian?" Donnie wiped down the bar, and dragged the bottle of JD over to his side.

Seb didn't respond. He just left the bar. Sans his bottle, with not a single drop having touched his lips. *See, people do change.*

* * * *

"I think that's the last thing that should be on my mind, right now." Jay knocked back another swig of whisky, the fuzzy haze now hitting his mashed mind and relinquishing his knee to a mere distant, dull ache. "Not least forgetting that the paps follow me like flies round a shit heap."

"See, that's where I think you went wrong." Riley swivelled to face him, leaning his hip on the counter. "Don't get me wrong, I think you're as brave as fuck to come out like you did. As a professional. I mean, shit, that had to affect more than just your performance on the pitch. That's hit your profitability, your transfer possibilities and the club's marketing. There's a reason no-one ain't come out before. Because it's a risk, business-wise. What club would want to take on a liability and a potential hostile crowd?"

Jay listened with one ear, the other trying to drown Riley out. Jay had lived all this. He didn't need reminding that his coming out had affected his career potential—regardless of what any Kick It Out campaign fought against. He knew West Ham couldn't sell him, not that he'd want to go anyway. What club would make a play for a bloke who caused trouble? Even if his knee wasn't an issue, he'd struggle to make the national side. England wouldn't risk taking an out gay player to a hostile country, rendering him not worth the aggravation. He'd been through all of this with management and with those running the campaign. He'd taken the first steps, yeah, paved the way for others to step out into the limelight—

271

except none had. And why? Was it because they could see how it had affected him? He unconsciously rubbed his knee.

"You should have stayed in the closet." Riley tipped his glass toward Jay. "And, yeah, before you ask, that would have been my advice if I'd been your agent."

Jay had heard that over and over as well. To the point he'd started wondering it himself.

"You could have had a sweet life then. Found a bloke who didn't want to be in the limelight, didn't harass you to come out, didn't take on the media as some kind of fucking mission to change the world. You could have just had a regular hook up, with a guy who understands why you have to keep it all in."

"Really?" Jay rolled his eyes. "I ain't sure there are many blokes out there who would understand or accept being swept under the carpet. It ain't fair on them, like it ain't fair on Seb."

"I don't know, mate. I think you'd be surprised." Riley swigged from his glass. "You're not the only one to have feared coming out. Some of us stayed in, and let it ruin us anyway. Then ran away to another country, so as not have to face it."

Jay turned to meet with Riley's gaze. He narrowed his eyes. Had he heard right? He couldn't have. Not Riley. Not the man who'd called him faggot on the pitch? "Are you sayin'—"

"That I'm gay?" Riley laughed, then shrugged. "Bi. And it took me a long time to get to that point."

"But—"

"Come on, Jay, you did psychology."

"How did you know that?"

"I know more about you than I should. Or than I want." Riley chugged back his remaining whisky and

272

slammed the empty glass on the counter. He dipped forward, resting his forearms on the counter and hung his head.

Shame? Was that shame? Remorse? Regret... Jay had no clue. Nor did he know what to ask. So he didn't say anything.

"Back in the Academy, how many times do you think we played each other on the circuit?" Riley didn't look at him when he spoke, but the pause indicated he expected Jay to answer.

"No idea. A fair few. Local teams. I'd been at West Ham since eight. London tournaments each year, plus at least two games a year."

"Yeah. A lot." Riley nodded at the returning girl, pushing his glass over and she added another refill, which he knocked back. "I started noticing you pretty early on. You had skill. I was a scrappy defender, used my bulk rather than my brain. You seemed to be able to get around me even though you were smaller, skinnier. You could showboat, too. But you never did it for effect." Riley shook his head through a fond smile. "And you were quiet. Really fucking quiet. Then suddenly you'd burst across the pitch like someone had lit a firework up your arse, with that platinum blond hair flopping all over the place. You set me on edge every time I played you. I liked you. First, I thought you were a great footballer, with real potential. Someone to learn from, to aspire to. Then, I don't know, I started seeing you differently."

Jay's chest rose with the realisation. Maybe it was the whisky that had caught in his throat, but something prevented him from being able to speak. He just sat there, blank.

"I tried to talk to you a couple of times. You probably don't remember. I think we both got a lot of

273

stick back then and conversing with the enemy only got you more. So I admired you from afar. I figured, if you were like me, and I had suspicions that you were, then we could be friends. Tough it out together. So when I got picked for that tournament at West Ham, I'd sort of understood what my feelings were and I wanted to tell you. To ask if you were hiding and struggling with it all too."

Riley threw the remainder in his glass down his throat, grimaced and shook out his shoulders. Jay's phone vibrated in his pocket, so he tugged it out while Riley wasn't paying attention and set it on the counter. He clicked the screen and his heart sank.

How's things, Squirt? Ax

Shutting his eyes, he covered the screen with his hand as Riley continued.

"Then I saw you. With that American. Not just me. A couple in my team were with me. And fucking hell, did they let rip." Riley searched Jay's gaze. "I didn't touch him, honest. I didn't. But I didn't stop it either. Because I couldn't, if I did, I'd be called out. And right then, I was so fucking angry. How could you be so fucking stupid? So careless? I couldn't understand why you'd do that, there, then! Why hadn't you been hiding in fear, like me? And what the hell did that guy have that you couldn't have seen in me."

"Riley, I—" Jay found his voice, but he was cut off anyway.

"Let me finish, Jay. I've carried this around a long fucking time. I'm sorry for what I did. I'm sorry for allowing that to happen to him. And when I was on the pitch, I took it all out on you. Everything. My anger, my

274

hatred, my fear, my shame. It was all there in every tackle. I didn't want what happened to your bloke, happen to me. I wanted to play football, be accepted, be part of the team. But after seeing that, I knew if anyone found out, I'd never be able to. So I took you down. And believe me, I have regretted it every day since. Because if I hadn't, maybe, just maybe, I'd've had the balls to tell you how I felt. Then we could both be playing football. Together. And, perhaps, we'd be each other's closet."

Jay wasn't sure if Riley was finished, so he held his gaze for longer than it was comfortable. He wriggled in his seat to give him time to gather some thoughts. That was a hell of a lot to take in. Nor had Jay suspected any of it. That moment, on the pitch, had changed his life so drastically, and defined who he had been for so long. And it was all fake. It hadn't happened because someone had called him out, didn't believe he belonged on a pitch. It had been because Riley had been defending himself.

"So now we have a chance." Riley lowered his voice. "You don't need Seb, Jay. He makes your life more difficult. I see that. You need someone who understands. I understand. I can be what you need. I could've been back then, but I was scared. So let's shove that under the carpet and start over. And I promise, one night with me, and you'll realise that there is a better fit out there." He slipped a hand up Jay's back, stroking his fingers along Jay's neck and tugged him across to whisper in his ear. "We both want it. Why else would you have done what you did today? I saw you getting ready for those pictures and, fuck me, Jay, I can't wait to get a taste of you in my mouth."

CHAPTER SEVENTEEN
Memory Lane

Jiggling on the entrance porch to his old house in Kensington, Seb shoved his hands deep in his pockets and tried to control his racing heartbeat. This was where he'd been brought up. Among the elite, among those *Made in Chelsea*, and among those who wouldn't know what a breadline was if they stumbled on it. These mansions sat away from the road, separated from the other oversized city properties owned by the wealthiest in London, on one of the most expensive areas in the UK. Most of the terrace town houses were no bigger than his and Jay's detached five-bed in Greenwich, but the social climbers would pay through the nose to live in SW10. Seb? He'd given it up and would have lived on Jay's old council estate in one of the poorest postcodes in London if that had been the only choice a year ago.

There had been some 'new money' injected into the area — those who had probably made their millions from e-commerce projects, whirlwind celebrity stints, or got lucky on the stock markets. But mostly it was still the same old circle of elite families handing their wealth down from generation to generation that Seb had grown up with. And grown up he had. From the age of nine, when his mother had walked out, he'd morphed from a happy, privileged child to an abandoned youth and into an insolent teen.

The place seemed larger than he remembered, more foreboding. Perhaps it was the lack of any illumination, except for the outside security spot lights, or no movement from within to welcome him home. Not that it ever really had, but a year living with Jay and Seb had been used to someone being there for his return, to smile at him when he walked in the door, or reprimand him for being later than he'd said. The mainly gravel sweeping driveway was vacant of any cars too, and the side-by-side garages were locked and sealed with pristine padlocks, including the one that had used to be his band's rehearsal space.

He peered in through the left bay window and breathed a sigh of relief that the sparkling white grand piano was still perched in its place of worship. His father was either planning to sell it along with the house or hadn't yet found someone to take it away. Seb had a sudden urge to save the piano that his fingers had ridden the ebony and ivory on for the best part of eighteen years. *Maybe I could just wheel it out the door?* Untucking a hand from his pocket, he tried the handle. Locked. He'd expected as much. And considering it needed several sets of keys to open it, and Seb had discarded them all some time ago, he only had one option.

With a deep breath, he pressed his finger on the doorbell and the grand *ding-dong* echoed through the chunky wood. Shoving his hands back in his jeans, he did

277

a quick sweep of the surroundings. No *For Sale* sign, so his father really was attempting a private sale. *Trust him.* If his father's business contacts were anything to go by, this house would be bulldozed to the ground to make way for a leisure complex by the New Year. Muttering obscenities under his breath, he stood to attention when the scuffling from behind the front door surprised him.

"Sebastian!" Yulia threw her hands to her mouth. "Oh, my goodness!" Waving frantically, she ushered him in for a bear hug. "I have missed you too much!"

It took a moment, but Seb soon wrapped his arms around his old housekeeper's slender waist, nuzzled his nose into her neck and the familiar floral, powdery perfume sent him on a nostalgic rollercoaster of emotions. This wasn't his mother, although she had acted as such, minus the real love and attention a young boy craved. He still clung to her as if she had been. From the age of nine, Seb had been fed, clothed and often berated for his rebellious misdeeds by Yulia alone and he'd begged for her to take him to Poland when she took her annual visits because being alone for the summer, regardless of where in the world his father had carted him off to, had been unbearable. She had smiled, though, and ruffled his hair, and told him better things were in wait for him here. He'd never believed her. *Until Jay.*

As he stood there, hugging the old lady and gently rocking her from side to side, he cursed himself for having walked away from her when he'd turned his back on his father. Suddenly he realised what he had missed out one—the unconditional love of a mother, a decent role model for a father, and the absence of any sibling to share his childhood with. All those things that Jay had, and he often took for granted. Was that why Seb was such a fuck-up? Was that why he was so goddamn selfish? Was that why he always reached so high, when really it was a home and a family that he craved? *I'm just like Sylvia. I walk away from everyone who loves me. And for what?* He choked.

"None of that, now." Yulia stroked his neck in comfort, then tugged him away and held him at arm's length. "No tears. This is happy time. Come in. Your father not here, but he said you may stop by and I so hoped that you would. I am leaving after today."

Stepping into the house, Seb flinched at the deep boom of the door closing behind him. The entrance hallway, where he'd roamed most of his adolescence, had always been void of detail, but he noticed even the very few hanging pictures, antique paintings and handmade furniture were now all missing. The whole place was a vacant cavern of nothingness. *Replicating a Saunders soul, perhaps?*

"Do you know when my father will be back?" Seb faced the old lady's comforting smile and her small grey eyes filled with sympathy.

"Did we ever?"

Seb snorted. Wasn't that the damn truth?

"Most things I have cleared away." Yulia nodded up at the sweeping spiral staircase. "Your room is in boxes. Take what you want. Anything left after sale goes to the charity pick-up." She pushed his back, urging him up the stairs.

Seb climbed each step with a sinking heart and crossed the sterile landing to the end where his old bedroom door remained closed. As he curled his fingers around the handle, he brushed his thumb over the makeshift lock he'd had fitted a few years back. He shuddered with a prickle of doubt. Shaking himself out, he opened the door and stepped inside his childhood.

279

The room was bare—no sheets on the bed, no artwork on the walls, with faded rectangles where his posters and other memorabilia had once hung. Several large cardboard boxes littered the floor, all taped shut with his name written in Yulia's messy handwriting and his walk-in wardrobe was cleared empty. He sighed. Not for the clothes, but for the only thing that he would have taken from this room.

Sitting on the edge of the bed, he pulled the first box toward him, opened the flaps and peered in. It was odd seeing all the knickknacks of his old life stacked away. He'd forgotten he even had most of the crap inside, having not really cared all that much about anything he owned back then. His guitar had been his only prized possession, and he'd sold that to get home to Jay. Sniffing back his tears, he rummaged through the contents of his miserable existence.

Not finding anything of importance, he kicked the box away and ransacked the next, then moved onto the final one. Opening the lid, he recoiled at the envelope dropped haphazardly on top. With trembling hands, he plucked it out and stared. Inside he knew were the photographs, the letters, the inner ramblings of a lover betrayed and a scornful son—all the evidence that his father had seen and used to send Stephen out of his life for good. Within those photos, those words, was a different Seb. Someone who hadn't known where life could really take him. One who had an almighty chip on his shoulder and a vendetta that he was never brave enough to do anything about. He'd ignore that too. He'd ignored what Stephen had put him through, all because he had thought it pointless. Why fight? Why retaliate? *If you can't change things, why bother?*

Shit.

Tapping his pockets, he cursed under his breath and threw the envelope to the floor. He pulled the first box back to him and sank his hand into the bottom, fishing out an old Zippo lighter. He sparked it, his already calloused thumb tip cracking on the rusty strike wheel. The fire nearly singed his eyebrows — it wouldn't have been the first time — so he turned the dial down, picked up the envelope and hovered one corner over the flame. The paper charred, and his fingertips were dangerously close to burning. After an intense moment of being transfixed on the orange glow, he stomped over to the ensuite bathroom and threw it down the toilet, flushing the singed ash to the sewers. *Where Stephen Coles belongs.*

The draught from the open bathroom window caused the outside bedroom door to slam. Flinching, Seb turned, then sucked in a startled breath. On the hook and gently fraying in the breeze hung a jacket Seb had all but forgotten about. Blue, with the printed white lettering distorted by the folds and made of a mesh material that staves off a fierce wind chill and torrential rainfall. Seb almost floated toward it, took it down and held it open in front of him to read the inscription. SPORTS SCHOLAR – RUTTMAN.

Falling to his knees, Seb hugged the jacket to his chest and sniffed for any hint of Jay's scent. He'd forgotten about that jacket, forgotten how warm he'd felt having it wrapped around him and forgotten he'd chosen to leave it behind when he'd left for New York. *How could I have ever considered leaving him?*

He stood, yanked open the bedroom door and slipped Jay's jacket over his own, then hurried to the end of the landing and leaned over the banister. "Yules!"

281

Yulia tapped out to the bottom of the hallway, her squeaky pumps echoing off the acoustic walls. She peered up, widening her eyes in concern.

"Is the landline still working?" Seb asked in desperation.

"Yes. But I disconnected the phone in your room. You have to use the one in your father's office."

Seb bundled down the stairs, kissed Yulia's cheek and hurtled into his father's office the other side of the atrium. *Funny how that hasn't yet been gutted of all valuables.* He leapt over the desk and into the leather armchair, picking up the dual office phone. Why hadn't he remembered any bloody numbers? *Damn mobile phones for fucking up the ability to memorise important connections.* The only one he knew by heart, he dialled.

"Mr. Saunders?" Martin's voice sounded confused as fuck. Seb didn't blame him. It had probably been a fair few years since he'd been called from this number.

"It's Seb."

"Oh. Right. You went *home*?"

"No. I went back to Kensington. Dad's selling the house. I needed to get stuff."

"Right. Seb, listen—"

"I thought I was meeting my dad today at the Royal about the house. Stephen was just there, and I had no idea he would be. My dad found out all about what happened, fired him. That's it in a nutshell. I did *not* go there to meet the wanker. You know that right?"

"Yeah. Course. But you need to say that to Jay. He showed me the photo that was leaked in the press, and believe me, it looks dodge as fuck. You seen it?"

"No. I don't want to. Whoever took it and sent it in was out to screw us, me maybe? I wouldn't even put it past Stephen himself. So I need Jay's number, I left my phone at home. You got it?"

"No, mate. No, I don't think I have. Noah's with Ann, ask him."

Seb sighed, the unexpected guilt kicking in. "No, I'll leave them alone. Listen, Martin, I'm sorry."

"For what?"

"For storming out. Not talking to you guys first. For being me."

"Hey, you're Seb. I've come to accept that you walk first, regret later. Does this mean you're not going solo?"

Seb laughed, shaking his head at the absurdity. "When has that ever worked out for me? I need you guys to ground me, or fuck knows where I'd float off too, right?"

"True facts. Listen, we're not opposed to a tour. Or a re-sign, but I just think we need time to think about it. We've all got so much going on, you included. Let's concentrate on making great music. Then America will come to us. Just like Sony did."

Seb nodded, mainly to himself. "You're right. We never did want mainstream appeal. We wanted just enough success to not have to get a real job, and I'm sorry I pressured you both into doing so much. I just saw the stars, y'know? I guess, I still want to prove something to all those who said I couldn't do it. And to those that said Jay and I couldn't work. I wanted to shove us so far down their throats they'd be shitting my lyrics."

"I know you did. You're Sebastian."

"Thanks, Martin."

"For what?"

"For always being right. For always being the one to talk sense into me. For always being there."

"No problem. But I did think I'd passed the baton to Jay."

"Yeah, but I haven't learned to listen to him yet."

"You should. The man's in a state. Heartbroken. And we all know what that does to a bloke, right?"

The poignancy of Martin's statement hit Seb where it hurt and he slammed the phone down, leapt out of his seat and across the atrium to fiddle with the locks on the front door.

"Are you leaving, Sebastian?" Yulia stood at the archway entrance to the main drawing room, her rain coat buttoned up and hands clasped behind her back.

"Yes. I've got all I need. Thank you."

"Are you sure?"

Seb furrowed his brow. Yulia brought her hands around and held out a shoe box—All-Stars, Limited Edition, with stickers laden all over the crumpled cardboard.

Seb tilted his neck. "How did you know I'd want that?"

Yulia smiled. "What else do you have here that you can't replace?" She cupped a hand to Seb's cheek and stroked a thumb over his stubble. "There's something else, too, I put in. And my new address is on a card." She tapped the box lid. "Send me a note every now and then. Don't let me know how you are by reading you in the papers."

Seb smiled, then kissed her cheek. "Thank you."

Taking the box, Seb stepped out into the grounds. The house didn't need a second look as he strode across the gravel driveway. That part of his life was over.

Can I salvage any of the new one?

* * * *

"Riley." Jay wriggled his shoulder, freeing himself from Riley's hold.

"Come on, Jay." Riley's smile didn't falter, nor did his lecherous gaze. "I know you and Seb have this thing, whatever. But what do you really have in common? Is there anything keeping you together?"

Jay narrowed his eyes. "What?"

"I can understand the lust, sure. But the love? Really? Yeah, he's got that dark, moody vibe and a real, nice, tight arse. I'd've given him a go, for sure. But you," Riley pointed a finger, "you have the edge. I like blokes that keep you guessing. I think we'd be great together. A nice fuck, followed by watching the football. Fucking perfect, you ask me. And I wouldn't be forcing you to tell people about me. I'd be happy being locked in your closet. You should give this a chance. Like you would have done all those years ago."

Jay's mouth parted, making way for words that didn't follow. This was doing his nut in. *Would I?* If Jay had known back then that Riley had feelings for him, would he have given him a chance? Jay had often wondered if the only reason he'd stolen a few kisses with Tom back at school was because Tom had been the first openly gay man he'd even met, so Jay had leapt at him when the chance arose to find out what his own feelings were all about. Would it have been different if Riley had made a pass at him — and not in the football sense? Would Jay have remained in the closet, catching a few chance liaisons with another footballer going through all the same stuff he was? Would he have even dumped Ann, or would he have done it all behind her back and lead the life of a closet player?

Would I even be injured, right now? If that brawl on the pitch hadn't happened all those years ago, Jay would have signed pro at eighteen as predicted by his Academy coach. University wouldn't have ever been an option. *I wouldn't have crashed into Seb.*

And that was what really mattered. Wasn't it?

"And, hey, if your fella's been playing away, then what's the greatest revenge? As you know, I've got a camera." Riley winked.

Jay met his gaze, searching for something in those eyes that would tell him what to do right then, the same way Seb's deep brown doe eyes had always managed to give him direction. But had those eyes been telling him the truth all this time? Or did they hide a multitude of sins? Jay didn't want to believe that Seb could have wanted to risk ruining their relationship, but do people really know anyone at all? Take him and Ann for example. She hadn't guessed about his sexuality even whilst they had dated, and now Jay had just found out she had been sleeping with Noah, often behind her boyfriend's back, for at least two years.

Jay hung his head, his fists forming tight balls. Was that what bands did when they toured? All those times Seb had stayed in hotels during gigs, when Seb had regaled stories of both Noah and Martin's conquests, and yet claimed he had remained in his hotel room. Jay couldn't believe that it might not be true. Not Seb. Not *his* Seb. But he had, hadn't he? Seb could separate the two things. Love and sex? They weren't combined in Seb's mind. He had managed to be in love with Jay and yet sleep with a man in New York. Why would it be any different now that they were together? And was it all because Jay couldn't give him what he needed?

286

Jay stood, a little too quickly that his knee gave in and he grabbed the counter, sucking in through gritted teeth.

Riley held his elbow and chuckled. "Bit keen, are we? I'll call a cab."

Jay clung onto the counter, waiting for the shooting pain to subside. He could not let this injury get the better of him. Not this time. He had to find the strength. Maybe Ewa was right—progress was all in the mind. Maybe that was what his whole problem was—his lack of courage. Riley had been right about one thing in his big speech— Jay and Seb barely had anything in common. They'd been brought up at different ends of the District Line, West to East, rich to poor. They roamed in different circles. Even their interests were polar opposites. *Did it matter?* The fact that the one thing they did share was their complete stubbornness and deep passion for their career goals often pulled them in conflicting directions. Would one of them always have to make a sacrifice to please the other?

Would it always be Seb? Because Jay hadn't been doing much sacrificing lately. Had he ever? Jay hung his head with the realisation. *Shit.*

"I'm going to head to the little boys' room." Riley rubbed Jay's back. "Then I'm game to get out of here too."

Jay called over the barmaid. "JD. Double." He needed courage, and it seemed to work for Seb.

Once handed to him, Jay downed the lot in one swift gulp. At least the alcohol would be good for something—dull the pain he was about to go and put himself through. But he had to. He had to prove it to himself. He had to prove it to Seb.

His phone buzzed on the counter, lurching Jay's pounding heart into his throat. Pressing his finger to the button and illuminating the screen, he cursed. It wasn't a

287

new message. Just a reminder of Ann's old one. Blinking to focus on the words, Jay could hardly see straight. Not being a big drinker, the small amount of alcohol he'd consumed had fuzzed his vision along with his rationale. He slid the phone to him and composed a reply.

Head fucked. Bit drunk. Riley wants to blow me.

Confident in his plan, Jay straightened. It was about time he tried something new and let himself go, become more like Seb. He took a deep breath when Riley returned with a brazen smirk.

Jay didn't even care that he'd be the one to wipe that smile from his face. Again. *Hope it won't have to be with my fists this time.*

* * * *

Seb jumped off the DLR, the shoebox tucked under his arm, and rushed up the mountain of steps, cursing himself for not taking those runs with Jay when he could have. Reaching the top, he had to stop for breath. *You'd think I'd be fit by now!* Slapping a hand on the exit wall, he used it to accelerate himself out of the station and into Greenwich High Street. Most of the late-night haunts were closing — Seb had no clue what time it was, having no watch or phone to check but he guessed it had to be hitting eleven if it was shoving-out time.

Passing the Court Yard pub on the corner, he had to dodge a bloke slamming out of the double doors and stumbling onto the street, phone to his ear asking for a cab number. He hurtled over the cross roads by the church, then sprinted up the residential street. *His* residential street. Reaching his detached house, he stopped at the gates and heaved in a deep breath. The lights were off. *Where's the welcome home this time?*

Fighting off the dejection, he scrunched his All Stars on the gravel driveway. Jay's car sat wedged next to his VW, so Jay couldn't have gone anywhere. Reaching the porch, Seb tapped his pockets. *Shit.* In such a hurry to storm out earlier, he hadn't taken his phone or his keys. For the second time that day, Seb had to knock on the door of a house he called home.

Clearing his throat, he rapped his knuckles on the wood. This was not one of his finer moments, but he refused to be humiliated by it. He waited, on the doorstep, listening for any movement behind the walls. He knocked again. "Jay?"

Nothing.

Scrubbing his brow, he shuffled his feet on their welcome matt and knocked again. Harder this time, then crouched and opened the letter box. "Jay?" No reply. "Please, baby, open the door." He wobbled unsteadily, and his thighs stretched the rips on his skin-tight jeans. What he'd give for a bit of give right then. "Don't make me sing through this letterbox. The neighbours hate my music as it is."

No answer. Seb hit his forehead to the wood, striking harder each time that he might knock some sense into himself.

"Right, I'm just going to have to do this here, aren't I?" *Oh the mortification! What would the Joneses think? Do I really care at this point?* "I would never, have never, *will* never cheat on you. Ever. Period. I love you, goddamn it! Even if you are a stubborn *fucking* arsehole!" He huffed. *Better calm it down, I'm meant to be apologising here.* He softened his voice to grovelling levels. "Even if you never open this door. Even if you've signed your image rights

289

over to the fucking BNP. Even if you *never* get yourself out of the damn hole you've been in since your injury, I'll fuck off everything, and everyone else, to tumble in there with you."

Seb's legs finally gave way and he stumbled, clutching the letterbox. "Bollocks. *Shit*! Baby, come on, please? I think this would be much better delivered to your face. Your beautiful, fucking, face!" He hung his head, sinking with the desperation. *Don't you dare give up, Saunders.* "I love you, Champ. I fucking love you. And I'd never leave you." He winced. "Not again...before you throw that one in my face. Which you can't, because you won't open the goddamn, fucking door! Jay!"

He thumped the wood, his irritation resurfacing. "It's still technically my house, so this has to be against the law and I have a lawyer. A good one...I'll call a locksmith." Seb screwed up his face. "Shit, I don't have a phone. But that won't stop me, Jay. I'll get in somehow. I'll get to you, I fucking will."

He rested his forehead on the door and lowered his voice to a resigned whisper. "Baby, I've come back. To you. I'll always come back to you."

Rocking in his crouched position, soft music played in his mind and he hummed a wistful melody. "Shit, Jay, I've just come up with a great idea for a song. I need my guitar! Open the fucking door!" He punched it.

A deep chuckle from behind made Seb swivel on his feet.

"Dude, I think you literally went through all the emotions in that speech."

"Fuck off, Noah." Seb stood. "You only know two. Hungry and horny."

Noah stuck his middle finger up, then quickly wrapped his arm back around Ann beside him.

"What are you two doing here?" Seb picked at the fraying lid of his shoe box, which could be the only contents he now owned. *What a fall from grace!*

"Jay sent me a strange message." Ann blinked a few times, concern written in her eyes. "I tried calling him back but no answer. Shit, Seb, what did you do?"

"Nothing!" Seb was close to stamping his foot. "I didn't do anything. I swear it, Ann. I swear it on that unborn child of yours."

"Oi!" Noah pointed a finger from around Ann's neck. "No bringing my kid into this!"

Seb rushed forward and grabbed Ann's hand. "I will explain all if you get me into that house. I need Jay to listen to me."

"You should have done it earlier."

"I know. I know. That's me, flight before fight. Not anymore. Get me in there, Ann, please."

"You're lucky I have a spare key." She stepped around Seb and unlocked the door, wedging her petite frame in the gap. "I don't know what he's doing in there, and I'm scared for you."

"Why?" Seb narrowed his eyes.

"He tell you about Riley?"

"The bloke he modelled for?"

"Yeah." Ann swallowed. "Jay sent me a text. I don't know what to make of it." She fished her phone out of her handbag and held it for Seb to read.

Seb could have thrown up all over it. Jay wouldn't. *Would he?* Would he really have sunk that low to get a revenge blow job? Was this all because of what Seb had done in New York—falling into bed with someone else because of all the hurt and anguish and every other fucking thing? Not Jay. Not his perfect, beautiful, blue-eyed Cockney boy. And who the fuck was Riley to come

291

onto his boyfriend? Hadn't he been the bloke Jay had pummelled on the pitch for saying a gay-boy couldn't play football? Seb's head hurt and his temple pounded like Noah's kick-drum.

Swallowing down the bile in his throat, he held out a hand to Noah. "You got your sticks?"

"What? You think I carry them around with me everywhere? And what you gonna do with them anyway? Drum lick the bloke to death?"

Nettled, Seb turned back to address Ann still blocking his entrance. "Let me by, Ann!"

"Oi!" Noah pointed a warning finger. "Yell at my pregnant girlfriend again and I'll slam your head against the wall. Then you'll find it difficult to go fucking solo."

The incredulous look that Ann gave Noah signified she didn't believe in his impulsive valour, but Noah nodded, with gumption, reconfirming in one scowl that he was a new man. Snubbing them both, Seb smashed his palm above Ann's head, rammed the door open wider and bounded into the house, his whole body in a state of tremble.

"Jay!" He ran to each room downstairs, clutching the box to his chest—kitchen, conservatory, main reception room, spare reception room, music room. Nothing.

Ann and Noah stood awkwardly in the hallway, but Seb didn't give them a second glance and leapt past, up the staircase two at a time. He checked every room on the first floor, leaving their bedroom until last. Because if Jay was in there with someone, he wanted to give him a chance to stop whatever it was he was doing as Seb wouldn't be able to hold down his non-existent dinner if he walked in mid-action.

Revealing the bedroom to be empty, Seb didn't know whether to be relieved or concerned that Jay clearly wasn't home. He could be anywhere. With anyone. Slumping back down the stairs to the hallway, he faced Ann with a sullen frown.

"Remember, this is Jay." She squeezed his arm. "He wouldn't ever."

"Really?" Seb hung his head. "Not even if he thought I had? Or that I might be leaving him?"

"Any of those true?"

"No." Seb met with Noah's dubious look. "No, the American tour was never an excuse to leave people behind. I'd planned on asking him to come with me, if his leg wasn't fixed. If it was, well, then we'd work it out. Trips home, he could fly out on the off season. But I get the baby thing. I do. I'm sorry I was an arsehole about it."

Noah nodded. "Yeah, you were a bit."

"Don't lay it on. I already spoke to Martin. We'll talk all this over. All three of us."

"So you're not walking out on the band?"

"No. Although, if Jay really is sat on the casting couch with his dick in the mouth of some homophobic, image-obsessed closet Queen, I may consider touring outer Mongolia. Indefinitely." Seb staggered back, the very thought squishing in his empty stomach. Grabbing the stair rail, he slid down to the first step, dropped the box at his feet and buried his face in his hands. "Shit. This is all my fucking fault. I deserve this. For leaving him in the first place. For that one nighter in New York. For being a mouthy gobshite and not listening to Jay. I've lost him."

Seb heard the kafuffle above him but ignored it to scratch his fingers through his hair.

"I am not qualified for this!" Noah's voice waded through the darkness. "Martin does this shit."

After a moment, Ann perched on the step beside Seb and slid a hand on his knee. "Do you want us to wait with you? Until he gets home?"

Seb shook his head. "No. It's fine. Let's face it, he might not even come back." He attempted a smile but didn't feel it.

Flinging an arm around him, Ann rested her head on his shoulder and Seb kissed her hair, accepting the comfort for what it was. He knew she belonged to Jay, but he wasn't too low to admit he needed her affection right then.

Seb nodded to Noah. "Take care of her. She's a diamond."

"I will. Call you in the morning."

After kissing Seb's temple, Ann stood and took Noah's outstretched hand. The door slamming shut behind their departure shunted the house in to a reproachful silence Seb couldn't accept. Nor could he muster any strength to lift himself up off the step. He stared at the door, willing it to open. For Jay to materialise and fall back into his arms. But this wasn't a fucking love song, or the music video to accompany it.

Hitting the shoe box with his trainer reminded him that he'd brought it along. *Rather pointless now.* He picked it up, placed it on his lap and lifted the lid. A bunch of envelopes sat on the top, wrapped together in an elastic band with his name and address scribed on the front in elegant blue fountain pen. He held the bundle and flicked through. Eleven in total. One for every year of his life that Sylvia had been missing. These were the birthday cards that his father had hidden, returning a cheque to her each year to keep her away. Seb shook his head. His father had

294

ruined so many relationships in his life, and it had all started with mother and son.

He dropped the envelopes back into the box and plucked out Yulia's picture postcard of a farm in Poland—the one she had visited since her daughter had married and returned to their motherland. Seb flipped it over and smiled. At least Yulia now had a home to retire to. *Good for her.* Rummaging deeper, he found an old rolled-up excise book. He chuckled as it unfurled and revealed his messy handwriting defacing the front. He hadn't given Yulia the credit she deserved. He flicked through the pages, sending a welcome breeze over his flushed skin. Lyrics, songs, guitar chords: none were lost to the back of a wardrobe anymore. He dumped it back in and his fingertips brushed a loose circular piece of metal at the bottom. He closed his eyes and sniffed. *Can I break down and cry now?*

The scratching of a key in the lock of the front door prevented that next fall from grace. Seb dropped the box to the floor, spilling much of the contents and his heart hammered so hard against his rib cage he thought he'd pass out before whoever it was made their entrance.

Jay walked in, closed the door, then stopped in alarm.

Grabbing the banister, Seb grappled to yank himself up. "Jay." He breathed the name off his tongue like a pleading call.

"Seb."

Seb swallowed, his throat so dry the task became difficult. "We should talk."

"Yeah." Jay nodded. "Yeah, we should."

CHAPTER EIGHTEEN
Own Goal

Seb hung his head and Jay had no idea where to start. Or even *who* should. But it didn't matter as instinct took over. He lunged forward, slipped a hand around Seb's neck and pulled him off the step to kiss him. It didn't taste the same, not now it was he who had the whisky remnants and Seb lacked anything at all. But Jay delved deeper anyway, entwining his tongue with Seb's in reunion. The rush of it all sent shock waves to his fuzzy mind, releasing his leftover dull ache to an explosion of desperation. He dug his fingertips into Seb's skin, clinging onto the man as if his life depended on it. Maybe it did? Maybe life as he knew it.

Seb ran his hands up Jay's back, returning the kiss with as much enthusiasm. Surely that was a good sign? When he reached Jay's shoulders, he gripped them tight. "Baby." Seb planted kisses along Jay's jaw, to his neck, nipping as though Jay was his meal.

Jay needed to touch Seb's flesh, but there was too much material. Seb never wore so many clothes. Not even in the height of winter. He fumbled with the zip, but searing pain hindered any ability to figure out where the coat started and Seb began. He grimaced, sucking in through gritted teeth.

Seb pulled away. "Shit, baby, you okay?"

"Yeah, fine." Jay tried to get his lips back on Seb's, he didn't want to stop. Not now he'd got the blood flowing to where it should. *Finally*.

Seb slapped a hand to Jay's chest and pushed him back, arching an unconvinced eyebrow. "The knee?"

"No."

"Jay, you just yelped in pain."

"It wasn't a yelp."

Seb clamped his hands on his hips. "What would you refer to it as?"

Jay cocked his head. "An unexpected jolt?"

Seb shook his head. "It's okay. If you're not feeling it, we shouldn't push it. We need to talk anyway, right."

"I'm fine." Jay clenched his jaw, he didn't want to talk. He didn't want another fight. What he wanted, what he needed, was Seb. He'd always need Seb. *And if the man just let me at him…*

As Seb brushed his fingertips over Jay's cheek, his eyes filled with a deep sympathy Jay couldn't abide. He grabbed Seb's wrist and slapped his hand down onto his groin.

"That answer your question?" Jay arched his own fucking eyebrow.

Seb cupped the bulge. "I'm not sure." He travelled his gaze downwards, a smirk dancing on his lips, until he stopped and gasped. "What the fuck is that!"

297

Dropping Seb's arm, Jay rubbed a thumb over the plastic wrapped around his left-hand ring finger. "This?" He held it up.

Seb snatched his hand and inspected the black ink smudge beneath the clear film. "Is that a — "

"It's a guitar." Jay shrugged. "Pretty small, and it's meant to have an S going through the strings, but to be honest with ya, babe, I was in so much fucking pain I had my mince pies closed through most of it." He winced. Seb's delicate finger running along the burn stung more than the needle had.

"You got a *tattoo*?"

"Yeah." Jay tried with a smile. "I wanted to prove something to myself."

"What?"

"How much I love you. How much I want people to know. That I ain't scared of this." Jay waved his hand. "Not so much the needle, but, yeah, that was a fucking eye opener. Or not. How do you do this all the fucking time?"

Seb's laughter bounced off the walls and warmed Jay's heart. "Who did it?"

"Sirus. Down the road. Next to the pub. I ain't sure they should have a place like that next to a boozer. Still, the guy did it despite my 'inebriation', so he put it. Guess there are perks to being recognised."

"You've been *drinking*?"

"Yeah. Look, it's been a strange day all round. But I learned something today that I should have learned a long time ago."

"What was that?"

"Not to let people dictate who I am, who I should be and how I should be running my life. *Our* life. If we still have a joint one?"

Seb bowed his head, mumbling his reply to the hardwood floor. "I saw your earlier message to Ann, so you tell me."

Jay's stomach lurched and he desperately tried to recall what he'd written. *Shit.* Had he told her about Riley? He fished out his phone, scrolling to the sent messages and his eyes fluttered closed. That did not come across like he'd expected. *Thanks to JD.* Shoving the phone back into his pocket, he dragged his hand through Seb's hair, to his neck and yanked him forward for a languid kiss.

"Never." Jay slid his forehead along Seb's. "It's only ever been you. It will only ever be you. I had no idea about him or how he'd felt about me. He asked if I would go back and change it all, what happened on the pitch that day and with Tom. And you know what I said?"

Seb shook his head, biting his lip with his eyes so wide the brown swirls were like an endless cavern that Jay had lost himself in. Or found his true self.

"I told him not a chance. 'Cause if that fight hadn't happened, if he'd not been so scared to admit what he wanted, I wouldn't have met you."

"How did he take that?"

"Not great. But I left him behind after telling him I wouldn't sign the endorsement deal."

"You already signed it?"

"Nah. I didn't. He threatened it, yeah, But I signed the test shots only to be seen by the company. I read the contract, Seb. I knew what to look for. He can't use those images for shit. If he does, the club'll come down on him so fucking hard he won't get up."

"But—"

"You should listen me every now and then. Try it. You might like it."

Seb smiled. "Maybe. So…we're good?"

"Depends on what you had to say?"

"Well, I gave you the best speech of my life earlier, but you missed it because you'd decided to deface your finger with ink. Guess you'll have to wait for the record to come out."

Jay breathed through a laugh. "Then maybe I'll give you mine? For *my* record, I'm sorry. I've been a prick. I know it. Even before the injury. I fell in love with you because of your confidence, because you stuck two fingers up at everyone, because you were everything I ain't. Then when I got you, I told you to not be you. I don't want you to be anyone else. I don't wanna have to live in the shadows anymore. I love that your mouth runs away with you, I love that you stand up for what you believe, I love everything about you. All this, was my issue. I let football rule us. Then after the injury, I pushed you away 'cause, I guess, part of me, blamed you for it." Jay hated that he had to admit that, but he had to. It was only fair to explain why he'd acted the way he had and get everything out in the open.

"I'm so fucking sorry, Jay." Seb's eyes glazed over. "I'm sorry I didn't think what would happen to you by me being so…vocal. I hate that you were injured, and that I could have been the cause."

"You weren't." Jay gripped Seb's neck. "You, me, our relationship, it ain't the cause. It's pricks who think we should hide, or not exist at all. And I'm gonna do something about it."

"What?"

"I'm gonna talk about it. I'm gonna start opening my mouth. Like I said I would. I'm gonna be the one to stand up and get people to accept. And I'm gonna do it all by getting back on that pitch and being counted. And

300

now I got you with me when I'm there." Jay ran his thumb over the tattoo on his finger, and sucked in through gritted teeth at the sting. "'Cause if I don't do it, no one else will. All I've done this past year is show others that it'd be easier to stay in the closet. I ain't doing that anymore. When I saw that fucking picture, I knew it was me that had pushed you back to Stephen." Jay hung his head, muttering the hardest part to the floor. "I'm now so fucking scared that if I don't stand up and be the man *you* need, then I'll lose you in the end."

"Baby." Seb leaned forward to rest his forehead on Jay's. "You couldn't ever lose me. Well, unless you say you bought Attax last album." He breathed through a nervous laugh, then gripped Jay's neck with an unaccustomed seriousness. "And you did *not* push me back to Stephen, or to anyone. You are all the man I'll ever need. Football, no football. Whatever happens, I'm yours and you're mine. *We're* the first team. The band, the club? They're the B-side."

"I love you." Jay almost choked on the words, like it was the first real time he'd ever said them. Perhaps it was. Perhaps the past year he'd only thought he had been in love. Now, though, now he knew it for sure. And the thought of losing it, of losing Seb, trampled him like a stud to the knee. "I love you so fucking much it hurts. You've made me a better me. I don't know how to do all this without you."

"I'm not going anywhere." Seb took his hand and kissed the tattoo. "I love you, too. I should never have left the first time, I'm not making that mistake again. The tour, that was *never* me leaving you. Everything I've become is because of you. Everything I was before you doesn't exist. The tour's on hold. Maybe we'll go when we're a bit more established. Us, and the band. Right now, I'm here for you. Like I should have been from the beginning."

Jay fought for the words to ask the next question, but he had to know. "Why *were* you with him?"

"My father. He called a meeting, selling the house and offering me my stuff back. Stephen was there and it all came to a head. Will pretty much chucked him out destitute. I didn't tell you because, honestly, baby, there was nothing to tell. The whole thing was so insignificant to me. I should have mentioned it, and I probably would have done eventually, but I was just so psyched about the tour, about you going back to West Ham, about the possibility of a fucking great future together. I'm sorry that I stormed out, or that my actions could have made you think that I'd go back to him, or to anyone. I'd live a life of abstinence if I couldn't have you." Seb smiled. "There really is no point dropping a league when you've had a taste of the premiership."

"That's a football reference."

"It is. I'm like a pro boyfriend now."

"What's the offside rule?"

"It's when you kiss me."

Jay laughed, but did it anyway. Because he couldn't not. He'd heard enough, and it was about time that they made up in the proper sense. So he kissed him, took his hand and led him up the stairs.

"You sure you're up to this?" Seb asked, voice tight.

"The knee is fine. Full range of movement and the advice is to keep active." Jay bashed open the door to their bedroom.

"And the finger? I'm surprised you're not bleeding everywhere. Alcohol thins the blood."

"That why it hurts so fucking much?"

"It's your finger, Champ, there's nothing there to cushion the needle. You've opted for the most painful location. Dumb arse." Seb slapped his chest. "Next time, I'm coming with you."

"Ain't no next time. I've had one of the biggest back fours in the Premier League ram his studs into my knee, two surgeries to fix it, physio, but this," Jay held up his hand, "stings like a bitch." He met Seb's gaze. "A passive-aggressive one."

Seb bit his lip. "Jay, about that—"

"I was. And I'm sorry. But right now, I need you."

That seemed to be all the encouragement Seb needed as he kissed Jay, soft and sweet, slow and seductive. Jay tingled with the excitement and drew Seb in closer, ruffling Seb out of two jackets. *Two jackets?*

Jay checked the blue coat crumpled in a heap on the floor. "That's my old—"

"Mesh is making a comeback."

Jay pressed his lips to Seb's ear. "So am I."

"So I see." Seb trailed his hand down to Jay's groin, the bulge through Jay's tracksuit trousers thickening and sparking his revival.

Gripping Seb's wrist, Jay encouraged the over-the-clothes massage for a while, working himself up. When it wasn't enough, he delved Seb's hand underneath his waistband and into his boxers. Seb hummed, wrapping dry fingers around Jay's erection and tentatively stroking. Jay let him take over from there, let him control what was going to happen. Jay was his, after all.

Jay grabbed the neck of his T-shirt and yanked it over his head, his hair flopping into his eyes. He blew it away so he could settle his gaze on Seb and dragged his trousers and boxers to the floor. Kicking them away, he stood naked in front of the man he loved, open and inviting.

"Personally." Jay nipped Seb's earlobe. "I think you have too many clothes on."

Seb smiled. Then with one last stroke of Jay's hardened cock, he stepped back and stripped. Jay watched, a thrill tap-dancing down his spine. Seb squirmed out of his too-tight clothes, exposing his tight skin and body of ink. Thousands of people wanted that view, but it was Jay who got it and he planned to be grateful for that fact for as long as he could.

Stepping forward, Jay kissed him, swiping in with his tongue to taste. There was no fear this time. There was no holding back. And Jay had to prove it, as Seb wasn't going full force. Grabbing a handful of Seb's arse, Jay tugged him closer and Seb slapped against his chest. Jay ground their cocks together and shivered at the jolt of desire that trickled down to his balls and his demanding dick. With pre-cum seeping from the tip already, it was like his cock had been missing his mate as much as Jay had and it painted Seb's cockhead with a glistening sheen.

Jay buried his face into Seb's neck, raging his tongue all over the supple skin and drank in the delicious scent. He grunted, and impatiently grabbed both cocks in one gluttonous hand. He jerked hard, willing them both to a point of no return, and groaned with every heated pump.

"Feels so good, baby. Keep it coming." Seb trailed his fingers through Jay's hair, gripping the strands and forced him up for a hungry kiss.

Jay pumped harder, squeezing his cock against Seb's and slapped his other hand behind Seb's head to lock him in a dirty mouth-fuck. It was glorious, combined together in Jay's hand the way they were, but Jay needed more. He had to get more.

Ripping Seb's head away, Jay stared into the blackened eyes that gazed back at him. He inhaled sharply, feverish with what he wanted to do. It could hurt, but the pleasure-pain threshold had already been scaled and jumped, and there was no stopping him now.

"Jay—"

Seb didn't get to finish whatever it was he wanted to say as Jay dropped down and sank his knees into the carpet. Fondling Seb's balls, Jay opened his mouth and sucked Seb's cock to the back of his throat. He had to keep one hand on the floor, just in case the knee ruined the moment, but he gave it as good a job as he could. Swirling his tongue over every inch of flesh, swiping the head, lapping the salty residue squirming from the tip, Jay purred all through it and Seb grunted, plunging deeper into Jay's throat. And Jay took it, took all of it, with fucking pleasure.

"Jay, fuck, get on the fucking bed!" Seb scraped his guitar-playing fingernails along Jay's scalp. "I really want to ravish you, right now."

Slurping off, Jay smiled at the plummy delivery in Seb's voice. The mockney act Seb put on for everyone else all but forgotten, and the public-school-educated swine was restored. And Jay fucking loved it. Seb grabbed Jay's hand and yanked him up, slapped his mouth to his and kissed him all the way to the bed with an urgency Jay shared.

"On your back," Seb demanded. "I don't want to hurt you."

Jay slid onto the mattress, slinking into the unmade sheets. "You ain't gonna. I'm good."

"You will be when I'm finished with you." Seb smirked, humming deep in his throat and crawled on top of Jay.

And ravish he did. For what felt like hours. Every kiss Seb planted tinged Jay's skin. Every lick, every scratch of his nails, and the vibrations of Seb's groans thundered through Jay's eager body. Jay lay there, allowing Seb to work his cure all over him and let go of all inhibitions. He now understood what Ann had been banging on about. Gripping the spongy pillows, Jay thrust his body up in impatience.

"Down, boy." Crouching on his knees between Jay's legs, Seb tapped Jay's stomach. "I'm taking this nice and slow. No room for mistakes." He stroked his hands up the inside of Jay's thighs and over to his hips. "Not this time." Shuffling Jay down, Seb kissed Jay's abs, teasing Jay's legs apart and kept his eyes focused on Jay above, possibly waiting for his wince, his suck-in of breath, or any indication of painful spasms.

Jay didn't give any. So Seb travelled up his body, reaching for the lube in the bedside drawer, kissing Jay's lips as he went. "You stop me if you need to." His gentle hushed voice tickled against Jay's cheek and he erupted in goose pimples.

Jay sucked on Seb's bottom lip. "You're the only thing I wanna feel tomorra."

Seb chuckled, his chest vibrating against Jay's. "I really must to start listening to you more."

Seb sloped off Jay to coat a generous amount of liquid over his dick and slid the flesh in and out of his balled fist. He took his time, taunting Jay with his masturbatory hand-job and licked his top lip, fluttering his eyes shut.

Jay leaned up on his elbows. "You want your hand, or me?" It was an honest question.

Answering with actions, Seb grabbed Jay's bad leg and lifted it up to drape over his shoulder. Jay lay flat and Seb shoved Jay's other leg away with less care or attention, then squeezed more lube onto his palm. He worked his fingers through the crevice of Jay's arse and teased for a while before inserting two.

Jay writhed, lifting his backside off the bed. There wasn't any pain, not really, not in comparison to the last few months. And the pleasure of Seb fondling his spot overrode anything else, especially when he tugged Jay's cock in sync. Jay thought he was going to spill all then. But Seb knew, he always knew how far to take it. *To the edge.*

"Get in me." Jay gritted his teeth, urging himself not to end this before they'd both got what they so desperately needed.

"Bossy." Seb tutted but obeyed the order by lining his cock up at the ready, then held his breath as he eased his way through the ring of muscle. "Fuck, yeah. God, so fucking good."

Tightening his legs around Seb's back, Jay dug his heels in, encouraging Seb to go deeper, harder. He could take it. He needed it. More than even *he'd* realised. And every inch that vanished inside him stretched him to the max and it was fucking glorious.

Lowering his head, Seb kissed him. "I love you, baby." He drew out, then slipped back in. "I love you. So. Fucking. Much."

Jay should probably have returned those three words, but he was so engulfed in the moment he could do nothing except kiss. It was as if his brain had switched off and his instincts had finally taken over. Clutching onto

307

the crunchy spikes of Seb's hair, Jay crushed Seb onto him with the power that he remembered his trained legs could have. Nothing else mattered anymore. Not football, not the injury, not the media. It was just the two of them, together, merging as one to Seb's rhythmic beats. *Nothing can top this.*

With no skin untouched, Seb's moistened body slid with Jay's and he pounded harder into him, grunting with each magnificent thrust. Jay threw his arms back, scrabbling to find something to hold on to as he trembled with the anticipation of what was to come. Seb raged his hands along Jay's sides, over his arm pits and pinned Jay's wrists to the bed. *Grounded.*

It's time. "I love you, too, baby."

Probably not expecting the heartfelt sentiment, and with a deep and wanton moan that vibrated in Jay's thickened balls, Seb came inside him. He slid his hands up to entwine his fingers with Jay's, gripping on to ride out the orgasm to a rampant end. It was delicious to watch, to feel it, and be a part of it.

Jay didn't know how he managed it, but Seb regained his composure at lightning speed to pull out of him and lower Jay's leg to the bed, before shuffling down and gobbling Jay's raging cock to the root. It only took a couple of sucks and Jay shot his pent-up load down Seb's glorious throat. Seb swallowed it, suckling Jay dry and held Jay's gaze as he did so. Quivering, Jay's whole body convulsed with its delirious release. Seb slurped off, and crawled up to reach Jay's lips, finishing the session off with a mouth-watering kiss.

"What a comeback." Seb collapsed on Jay's chest, his heaving breath scattering the hairs on each nipple.

Jay chuckled. He threw his arms around Seb and was content to stay that way until morning. Or until next week. Next month. Whenever he thought he might be able to move again.

CHAPTER NINETEEN
Back on my Feet

"Morning, handsome."

"Morning yourself." Jay smiled, sliding his leg across the bed and stroking his toes down Seb's leg.

It wasn't the first morning after, nor the second. They'd been pretty much rolled up in the duvet for a few days straight, only venturing out to eat, shower and bathe Jay's finger in Seb's healing cream. The R and R part of Jay's recovery now seemed to be going to plan. The next stage was imminent.

"How long have you been awake?" Seb returned the foot fondling beneath the sheets.

"A while."

"Uh-huh." Seb yawned and stretched. "Could've made a start on coffee."

"And miss out on you waking? No ta." Jay rubbed his nose to Seb's and kissed the tip.

"You're especially jovial. How's the tatt doing?" Seb reached for Jay's hand, entwined their fingers and pulled it up to his lips. He kissed first, then checked the ink work. "It's pretty good. Once that soreness goes down, it'll be blinding."

"Yeah?" Jay pulled his hand away, still not used to having the guitar outline drawn on the back of his finger. But he liked it. "I still scrub my hands, thinking it's a stain."

Seb chuckled and swept back Jay's fluffy hair from dangling in his eyes. "You've made me want a new one. A football, perhaps? On the same hand? Matching pair."

Jay knew he was joking, but shrugged with nonchalance. He honestly wouldn't care. The last few days Jay had made a lot of promises to himself, and one was that he would no longer rein Seb in for his stupid decisions and runaway mouth. He wouldn't. He really wouldn't. *Honest.* He bit his lip.

"Maybe 'Rutters' stamped on my forehead?"

He's trying to rile you. Don't rise to it. "Why stop there? Put it on your arse."

"Then no-one will see it." Seb pouted.

"I will." Jay grabbed a handful of Seb's backside and squeezed.

"I could, of course, go naked on stage. I think that might sway anyone away from thinking I've gone mainstream."

Jay snorted. "Do what ya like, babe." He kissed him. "I mean it." And he did. Although, deep down, he had his fingers crossed in the hope that Seb neither got the tattoo nor bared all in front of a crowd. But he enjoyed the look of surprise spreading across Seb's face. Chuckling, Jay rolled away from him and sat, dangling his legs over the bed. He pressed his foot to the carpet, testing it. His knee hadn't hurt on first waking for the last couple of days, so he leaned more weight onto it and

311

smiled. "I'm gonna go for a run. You need to come with me."

Seb slammed back against the headboard. "Champ, you know I—"

Jay threw a stern glower over his shoulder. "I need you to. I have to go and I need a pacemaker."

"I'll never keep up."

Shoving Seb's shoulder, Jay urged him out of bed. "I ain't believing any of that bullshit about you not able to manage a light jog. I've seen you dance and I've seen you fling yourself about on stage for two-hour sets. Get the fuck up."

"We going now? Not even breakfast first?"

"We'll get something on the way back. We're outta grub and there're plenty of cafes down Southbank." Jay stood and made his way to the ensuite bathroom.

"Southbank? Why are we going there?"

Jay poked his head out, doing his best to keep anything from showing on his face. "Less hills."

"But it's busy." Seb frowned. "With people."

"You forgotten that you like people? We'll do the river run. Means I can take it easy. Get up." Jay flung a towel at him.

Catching it, Seb pouted. "I'd forgotten how utterly aggravating your self-motivated arse could be."

Jay stuck his middle finger up, but his lips curved into a smile and he continued his morning ritual with a squishy stomach. One last look in the mirror and he took a deep breath, telling himself this was right. This was what he had to do. He just hoped it went according to the plan he'd hacked up overnight. *As long as the blasted thing stays in my sky rocket.*

Padding back into the bedroom, Jay stopped short. Seb held out his arms in display. The full West Ham kit,

312

number nine Ruttman stamped on the back, hung off Seb's slender frame and his shit-eating grin pushed every one of Jay's buttons. His *old* ones. The ones he'd torn off one by one over the last few nights.

Passing, Jay kissed him. "Looking good, babe." He pulled out the drawers for his own running gear, rifling through with a breezy whistle and chuckled at Seb's returning huff.

Once dressed, trainers on, and swigs of water taken, Jay led Seb out the house. Apprehension drained off his shoulders and he smiled. God he'd missed the early morning runs. *Crack of dawn just ain't the same unless you're pounding the pavement.*

"Why don't we just run here?" Seb waved a hand up the street. "There are flatter parts of the park."

"Remember when you said you'd start listening to me?"

"No."

Jay slapped the back of Seb's head, but didn't say anything else and trundled off through their residential street. Seb huffed, following along beside him. The High Street was fairly quiet, only a few dog walkers and newspaper scramblers were sharing the crisp blue sky and empty path with them. Jay concentrated on getting his legs to where they needed to go, and as they came up towards Cutty Sark, Jay chucked a left and joined the riverside walkway.

He was probably attempting too much too soon, but he was desperate to prove himself. He could do this. He had to do this. And now he had a *reason* to do this. And as the stretch burned through his legs, he smiled against the breeze. He'd missed this — missed the air in his lungs, his trainers pounding London pavement, and the endorphin rush to his brain. It was blissful.

Half an hour in, and the unusual-for-Seb silence broke. "You all right?" He didn't sound out of breath, which was either a good sign or one that Jay was taking this far too easy.

"I'm good."

In the distance, the peaks of Tower Bridge seared into the low clouds. Jay upped his pace, every long stride ridding him of the fear of pain. Peace and tranquillity, everything a run had provided for him before, came back to him. Just like Seb had.

Seb ambled off ahead, Jay's name and jersey number plastered on his back, and Jay breathed through a fond chuckle.

"We crossing north?" Seb called, jogging backwards to face him.

"Nah, head toward City Hall."

"You got it, Champ." Seb twisted, chucking a left to avoid heading onto the bridge, but ran to his own tune. Out of time, no pacing, and all over the shop, dodging those who walked the riverside path toward him. The way Seb should.

This, this was everything. Until—

"'Climbing high, pounding the street...'" Seb's effortless singing voice carried through the breeze toward Jay. "'Shed my tears, broke through myself...'"

Bollocks, he's performing a new fuckin' song! "Seb?"

"'Following through, now I'm up on my way...'" With a hop, skip, and criss-crossing his feet, Seb ignored Jay's pleading call. "'I'm a man who'll take you all on!'"

"Seb!" Jay gritted his teeth through the yell.

Seb punched the air out in front of him. "'Too many times, I fell to the ground...'" He twisted and winked. "'But I won't stay down for long...'"

Jay made cutting motions with his hand across his neck as another couple of runners passed Seb, then him, and chuckled.

"'I won't lose the dreams that I have...'" Seb's singing increased in volume that it could be heard over the foghorns of the passing Thames clipper boats.

Jay regretted ever asking the man to come with him.

"Tell me how to shut you up," he called.

"You know how, baby," Seb replied whilst twisting a three-sixty. "'I'll fight to the death 'til I'm free!'"

He couldn't very well stick his dick in Seb's mouth out here—the only foolproof method that ever got him to shut up. Apart from that one time that Seb had used it as a microphone. *What do I see in this man, again?* He got his answer as Seb stopped, spun and met Jay's gaze with a salacious grin.

Jay shook his head. "Don't. Please, just don't."

"Oh, come on, Champ. I'm on a roll here!" Seb threw his arms in the air and raised his voice to pelt out what Jay assumed was the starting line of his new made-up chorus. "'I got iron in my blood, love in my heart, I'm the—'"

Fuck my knee. Jay sprinted, full-pelt, like he had a chance at goal, and slapped his mouth onto Seb's. He sliced through with his tongue to drive home to the back of the net. *Score, one-nil.* Seb attempted to continue his performance through the violation, but soon gave up and wrapped his arms around Jay's neck, humming into the kiss.

"Fucking gross." A bunch of hooded clad youths cycled past on BMXs and spat on the ground by their feet.

315

In a complete disregard for life and or limb, that he'd just got back full use of, Jay stuck his middle finger up behind him, refusing to end the PDA. Not just because it had achieved the task of shutting Seb up, but also because, well, he quite liked it. And should do more of it. *To hell with every bastard who says otherwise.*

Tyres scrunched on gravel halting the bikes to a stop. Jay's heart pounded. He twisted, shoving Seb firmly behind him, and faced out the groups of lads. It'd been a while since he'd been in a street scrap, and he wasn't quite match-fit yet, but there was no way he could walk away from this. Seb trailed his hand down Jay's arm, clutching onto his fingers. Jay didn't think he was scared—Seb rarely thought that far ahead—but more he just wanted to keep up the public display, reaffirming their team status.

"'Ave a butchers, Trev." Black Hoody nudged his mate. "That's Rutters."

"Rutters? West Ham?" Matey squinted, raking his disbelieving gaze up and down the full length of Jay. "Shit, yeah, it is." The bloke raised his chin, then nodded in approval. "All right, mate? How's the knee."

Jay narrowed his eyes. "Better."

"Good to hear. Got a season ticket, me. Cannot wait for you to get back on that pitch."

Jay snorted. "Cheers. Won't be long."

"Better not be. I put a score on a twelve to one that you'd be back before the end of the season and get a hat trick."

"That's some bet." Jay squeezed Seb's fingers behind him, in a bid to reassure and also to prove that he wouldn't let go. Not like he would have probably done before. New him.

"Yeah." The kid angled his neck to peer behind Jay. "That your fella?"

"Yeah." Jay nodded. He bit down on his need to inhale a deep breath. That would show he was scared, ashamed, worried. He wasn't any of those. Not anymore.

"Tell him his last album was pony. I want a refund."

Jay bit through a smile and hung his head, choosing the moment to check on Seb behind him. Seb's eyes narrowed, brow furrowing.

"Laters, mate." The lad spun his bike around and nodded for the others to follow. They did. Some gave a glower, some a grimace, others a wave.

"What the fuck does pony mean?" Seb asked as Jay spun to face him.

Jay kissed him.

"Pony does not rhyme with anything good." Seb stuck his hand on his hips.

"Pony and trap." Jay bumped his shoulder to Seb's and started up with the run.

Seb stayed where he was for a while, and Jay could practically hear the cogs turning in his brain. Eventually, he caught up to Jay with a yell of, "*Motherfucker!*"

Jay chuckled and rubbed a soothing circle over the small of Seb's back. They settled to an easier side-by-side pace with the River Thames swashing in gentle waves beside them. They dodged through the milling tourists and morning commuters rambling around the Mayor of London's wonky glass house, and onward to pass HMS Belfast floating guard on the river, then around the heritage site of Southwark Cathedral. It was almost like Jay was seeing his city for the first time, now with open eyes. He'd run so many east London streets, often tracing the path from memory, that he'd all but forgotten he lived

317

amongst such steep history and romantic architecture. *Does Seb feel the same?* He glanced to his right, where Seb jogged beside him with a smile. Seb caught his eye, and winked. *Yeah, perhaps he does.* They'd never done this — never been out, together, as tourists in their own city. They'd left that to when they'd been away, when Jay hadn't feared being seen, or snapped by the paparazzi. This time, however, he couldn't have wanted that more.

A few passersby did recognise them, mainly due to Seb wearing Jay's kit, and they scrambled to get their phones out in time to take a snap. Perhaps they even managed it. Jay smiled, wondering where those images would end up by the close of play.

"Ever been on the London Eye?" Seb nudged Jay's shoulder with his own, nodding up to the huge Ferris wheel tipping over the heads of the buildings.

"Nah."

Seb laughed. "What type of Londoners are we, eh?"

"Proper ones. We'll go on it one day."

"I'd want it to go fast. Like it's on speed. Be sucked onto the glass through G force. Fuck all the sights."

Jay chuckled, then pointed ahead. "Take the steps. Millennium Bridge."

"The *bridge*?" Seb shook his head. "Can't we stop for a coffee yet?"

"And mess with my cortisol levels?" Jay pulled a face he hoped came off as serious.

"I swear that is absolute bollocks."

"Tell that to the nutritionist at West Ham."

"I will, because he's seriously stunting my ability to remain amiable."

Jay arched one eyebrow. Seb snickered and scaled the steps onto the bridge two at a time, almost tripping on the last one and having to be held up by an elderly gent with a walking stick. Jay cracked out a laugh and Seb held his middle finger up to Jay once the gent was out of view.

Couples, families, mums with buggies and teenagers either bunking school or late for it were all crossing the bridge both ways. It meant Seb had to dip in behind Jay to let them pass and they ambled along in almost slow motion. Jay glanced out to the river, taking in the view that was currently being stencilled and charcoaled onto paper from the dozens of street artists stacked along the railing. Tower Bridge gleamed to his right, with Big Ben and the Houses of Parliament peeping through the gaps on his left. East and West. *This'll do.*

Jay stopped.

Seb had jogged on ahead before he'd obviously noticed Jay was no longer with him, so he stopped and twisted around. "You okay?"

Jay bit his lip and nodded, gazing out to the distance. A tiny slither of apprehension rippled in his gut, but he shrugged it off to produce a wide-toothy smile at Seb.

Seb cocked his head. "Champ?"

"Shut up." Jay walked forward and placed his hands on Seb's shoulders, steering him backwards to stand against the railing.

Seb opened his mouth.

"I said, shut it." Jay gripped Seb's lips between his finger and thumb and squeezed. Not enough to hurt the fella, but enough to drum home that he meant it. He smiled, nodded in approval, then sank to his knees.

"Ja—"

Jay peered up with a stern glower and Seb slammed his mouth shut.

"Sebastian Michael Saunders…"

"Whoa!" Seb held up both palms. "Shit. Fuck! *What*?" He darting his gaze at the sudden approaching onlookers.

Jay tutted. "Keep your trap shut! I love you. Sometimes, I ain't sure why."

Seb breathed through a laugh, his body trembling. There were a few more chuckles from behind and the odd click of a camera or two, so Jay assumed they were surrounded by onlookers already. But Jay focused solely on Seb and how his dazzling dark eyes never left his.

"But I do. And I'm ready for the whole damn world to know about it. So let's start here. Let's be us. Me and you. Together. Against the world. Our team, our band, dancing to our tune. If no-one sings with us, or passes us the ball, then fuck 'em." Jay stuck his hand in his pocket and when he pulled it out, he produced the solid silver ring he'd found online and had express delivered to the house when Seb hadn't been looking. Thick metal, chunky, simple and understated. "I want you to wear this." He held it up. "Until the day we can get proper hitched. 'Cause we'll be campaigning for it, yeah? Loud and proud. 'Cause, Seb, I ain't mucking about. I'm in this for the long haul. I ain't letting you go again. I want you, I *need* you and I love you."

It seemed as though everyone sucked in a breath, and Jay had to grit his teeth to stand the pain of being down on bended bad-knee after a five-mile run. When the silence dragged, Jay slapped his hand down to rest on his knee. "All right, you can say somethin' now."

"Fuck me," Seb breathed out, then shook his head. "Sorry. Sorry. That just fell out my mouth." He crouched to Jay's level and slapped the back of his hand to Jay's chest. "You bastard."

That wasn't what Jay had expected and he baulked. He kinda wished he now wasn't on full display. But this had been his plan—to finally rip the last part of his bandage off and to prove to Seb he could be the man he wanted.

"I was going to do it!" Seb slid his hands around Jay's neck, clamping his fingers together and tugging Jay forward to rest their foreheads together. "I went all the way back to fucking Kensington to get the ring. Family heirloom, priceless piece of gold! My granddaddy's. Jesus, Jay!"

"Okay…"

"But *I* was going to do it *in private.*" Seb gritted his teeth. "And then you come out here like this, bended knee on the effing Millennium Bridge. What the fuck, Jay! What the actual fuck?"

"I thought it was time. Perfect place. Show the world." Jay's confidence in his plan was now wavering and his legs were in danger of buckling. A simple 'yes' had been what he'd been after. And expected. Hoped. He licked his dry lips, tasting the congealed moisture from the run.

"It *is* perfect." Seb kissed him. "Anywhere you chose would be perfect. You're fucking perfect. And I fucking love you." He planted soft kisses all over Jay's face. "Yes, I'll wear your bloody ring. Yes, I'll marry you when the time comes. Yes, I'll make a life with you. I'll have kids with you—"

"Hold up." Jay held up a hand, staving off repeated kisses. "I ain't said nothin' about kids."

"But you will." Seb smiled, and kissed Jay's lips. "Until then we can get a dog. No, two dogs. One dark, handsome and morose. The other blond and scrappy."

"You sayin' I'm scrappy?"

321

Seb shrugged, then kissed him. "I love you scrappy. You're my bit of East End rough."

Jay laughed.

Seb tugged him closer, swiping his forehead to Jay's and his features drew serious. "I'll say yes to anything you'll ever ask me."

Jay smiled. "Will you come to my next game?"

"With fucking bells on."

"No bells."

"Whistles? Trumpet? That crackling thing you wave in the air."

Jay balled the front of Seb's shirt, *his* shirt, into his clenched fist and yanked him forward for a languid kiss. He drowned out the cheers and claps, and snaps of photographic evidence that would find its way to the morning papers and online before that, and indulged Seb in a public kiss that they hadn't shared since university. Things had been so different back then. Easier. He'd forgotten how to be that carefree. He'd been institutionalised by the club, by the fans, by the media, by football, and had forgotten what really mattered. Seb. Love. *Family.*

"And I'm gonna come to every one of your gigs," Jay declared on separating from the kiss. "When I can. I will. I want front row tickets to Glasto."

Seb grinned. "Deal."

"I'm sorry I shied away from it before. But that ends now. Both ways, Seb. You and me. Together. A unit. We come as one, right?"

"You bet." Seb kissed Jay's temple. "You want a hand getting up?"

"Yeah. Better had." Jay gripped Seb's hand and pushed up, Seb guiding him to his feet. The dull ache in his knee was back, but it wasn't going to ruin the moment. He'd just made a giant leap into the unknown. This would be news, splashed over every media channel there was. It would make it into the football press, make it back to his club, to the players, the fans...

But he was back on his feet. And he was ready to face this, head screwed firmly on. No more 'blocking it out'. No more 'switching it off'. *Healed.* Double proper.

The crowd parted and drifted off to wherever it was they were heading and Jay took Seb's hand, slid on the ring, and interlaced their fingers to lead him toward the north side of the bridge. Seb held their hands up, kissing Jay's knuckles and used the opportunity to check out the ring.

"Nice." He nodded in approval.

"Looked like it'd suit ya. No bling. Understated."

"Wait til you see yours, diamond-encrusted crown jewels all around it."

Jay must have displayed a look of pure horror as Seb hacked out a laugh. At least now they could find a decent cafe. Jay needed the rest. Taxi home and all. Indulge Seb in the luxury lifestyle he was born for.

"Why this bridge?" Seb suddenly asked through the breeze.

"You'll call me a soppy git."

"Probably." Seb shrugged. "Tell me anyway."

"It's halfway." Jay held onto the railing at the steps and stopped to take in the view.

"Halfway to what?" Seb furrowed his brow.

"Halfway, east to west. Blackfriars, over there —" Jay pointed to the tube station north of the river — "is the half way point between High Street Ken and West Ham on the District Line. It's kinda halfway between you and me. Our middle ground."

Seb smiled, then leaned in and placed a soft kiss to Jay's lips. "Soppy git."

CHAPTER TWENTY
Comeback

"Shove over, fella." Bryan scaled Seb's legs and crashed down onto the plastic seat beside him, the waft of hot meat pie sickening Seb's stomach.

Grimacing, Seb tugged the ends of his denim jacket to wrap around himself. "It's fucking freezing."

"Mate, you came to a football match. In that." Bryan ripped open the plastic packet and bit into the sloppy pastry, meat juices trailing down his chin. He waved the pie over Seb's choice of clothing—the usual ensemble of tight ripped jeans, thin T-shirt and black denim jacket. "Ain't you never been to a match before?"

"Yes." Seb rubbed his hands together and blew on them to get the feeling back in his fingertips. "Once. And I was in the VIP seats. Which is where I thought we would be today. I'll bet they have Champers on ice up there." Seb nodded in the general direction of the West Dr Marten's stand that housed the WAGs in the VIP suites and beyond to the board rooms, the offices, and the dressing rooms where Jay was no doubt going through his match-day ritual.

"To experience real football atmos, you gotta be in the terraces. Bobby Moore stand is where it's at. We're behind goal line for a start. You wanna be here when Jay slams that ball to the back of that net, dunt'ya?"

Seb shrugged. He would, but he'd also like a glass of Champers and to be warm when he saw it. Sighing, he nodded. No, this was right. To be here amongst the —

Seb jolted at the sudden roar of 'Irons, Irons, Irons' coming from the nine thousand spectators surrounding him. And his eardrums split when Bryan joined in, spitting crumbs all over those in the seats below. The noise was more deafening than a Drops festival gig. At least Seb could be assured that the years playing rock at full decibels hadn't destroyed his hearing.

Seb sat back and tried to enjoy his first ever stint of being a football spectator. The fans the opposite end of the stadium attempted to drown out the home crowd with their own chanting renditions, but failed miserably when West Ham belted theirs out harder. Seb winced. Not an in-tune voice among the lot of them. Zoning into the lyrics, he did chuckle at the creative use of words to describe each team.

"Can feel that in your gut, right?" Bryan nudged Seb's knee with his own. "We been doin' this for fucking years. It don't get old. Right, Dad?" He turned to a zoned out John Ruttman beside him.

John nodded, steely blue eyes focussed out front and jiggled his knees. Ever the stance of a man who was either cold, or bricking it. Seb couldn't blame him. At least Seb's unsuitable attire for a freezing eight p.m. kick-off mid-March in London could mask the reason behind his own quivering.

327

"'E's nervous." Bryan leaned in to whisper in Seb's ear. "'E's always nervous before one of Jay's games, but, well, this one's different, ain't it?"

Seb nodded, understanding all too well. Jay's first match back after injury had come a full seven months after injury. Which had felt like a lifetime. For Jay, for Seb, and evidently for the club who had relied on Jay's goal scoring to keep them afloat in the Premier League. But, apparently, six months was standard recovery period. If only Seb had known that a few months back. Still, he was here now. And since the whole almost-proposal on the packed-out bridge back in November at prime commuter time, Jay had faced the whole injury, and their relationship, head on. No holds barred. He'd been a machine.

"He's on form." Seb rubbed his hands together, staving off the cold but also the sudden judders. "He's been working out daily, runs morning and night, extra physio sessions. The club wouldn't have given him the all-clear if they didn't think he was ready for a starting line-up. Right?" He checked for anything in John or Bryan's face to suggest the contrary. They knew more about all this stuff than Seb did. Seb only relied on what Jay had told him over the past few months.

"Sure." Bryan nodded.

"It ain't just his fitness I'm worried about." John stared ahead to the pitch laid out in front of them in its perfectly luscious green rectangle.

Seb wringed his twitching hands in his lap. "Honestly, John, I've never seen Jay more ready to face it. Head on. He's got this."

John slowly met his gaze and, after a brief pause, he smiled. "Yeah. I seen it. Couldn't be more proud of him. Both of ya. The way you've handled the obsession around the both of ya, 'specially since bridgegate—"

Seb bellowed out a laugh, cutting John off. "Bridgegate?"

"Bab's aint over it, y'know." John peered back out to the pitch, chest rising. "Tellin' the world first before her. It's a no-no."

"Right." Seb winced. "Not even us buying you a house down the road got her over it, no? Using the equity from the sale of my father's house to bring you closer to us, and still your son's most romantic gesture is considered a scandal?"

"It's a bleedin' scandal it's in the media." John tutted.

"That I agree with. But, it does help drum up free promotion for Ruttman Records." Seb grinned. The Drops were now completely independent, having turned down the deal with Sony. Seb could never have walked away from his band mates for a contract, regardless of how much money the label threw at him. And, by fuck, had Kenneth tried—even claiming he'd find Seb session musicians with awards galore behind them. Instead, with the money left over from the Kensington house sale, Seb set up his own record label. Saunders already had its own name in a business venture and Seb had high hopes that he'd, one day, become a Ruttman himself. Not just an honorary one.

"And cheers for Lily's trust fund, by the way." Bryan nudged Seb's knee. "Was generous."

Seb smiled, and nodded, accepting the thank you. After Will had sold the Kensington mansion, Seb had been offered half the equity. Seb hadn't wanted to take it, claiming it felt wrong somehow. He didn't need, nor want, the money. But Will Saunders hadn't ever lost a deal, and so a Christmas present had been received in the form a seven-figure cheque stuck inside a card with the simple message, *you earned this*. Between the house for Jay's parents, a trust fund for Lily, a little spread between Martin and Noah, and another lot to Ann to spend on the baby, the rest had gone into the record label. It had also inadvertently got them a cleaner, to Jay's utter dismay. Seb was just glad that Barbara, claiming she was no charity case, often brought a lasagne along with their ironing.

Seb had also set a little aside for a potential wedding, should one ever happen.

Things were rather rosy. Grand. *Beautiful*. No loose ends. Except this one. Jay's return to the premier league, to football, and, as fate would have it, to the man who had caused Jay's injury. All of that filled Seb with apprehensive tension. Regardless of how much Jay had convinced him he was ready, he was a different man to the one who'd been knocked down, and that he wasn't going to let it get to him, the team, and the two of them.

Seb now fully understood the things Jay faced being out and open. Not all the media response to 'bridgegate' had been positive. But Jay had come to accept that whatever he did, he couldn't please everyone. So he'd been pleasing himself, and Seb, by actually answering to media interviews and allowing Seb to respond in his true fashion.

It had done wonders for him. For his public persona, for his self-esteem and, not to mention to anyone else, but for their bedroom antics.

Seb smiled into his lap as he remembered the latest Ruttman reply to the press's ask of whether he feared there would be a backlash on the pitch at tonight's game.

Jay had smiled to the camera and said, "I'm counting on it." The cheeky glint in Jay's eye had been unmistakable.

Seb was snapped from his mental musings when Bryan and John launched from their seats and threw up their arms, both belting out the words to West Ham's official song. Out of tune.

"Get up, fella. Sing!" Bryan tugged Seb up by his jacket.

After a shake of his head, Seb held his arms high and joined in with the last line, "Pretty bubbles in the air..." The stadium thrummed with fierce claps. "West Ham!"

Bryan twisted his neck and curled his lips in a snarl at Seb.

"What?" Seb clapped along with the rhythmic chanting.

"I said sing. Not fucking harmonise."

* * * *

Jay blew out a lungful of air into the hostile dressing room. He'd completed his match-day ritual and now awaited the team talk from Sergio among all the other players kitted out and ready for the game ahead. The hostility had come from his return, he knew that much at least. And from his press conference earlier where Jay had no longer stuck to the standard media-trained responses he once would have. New him. No longer gagged, or suffocated by the need to be what everyone expected — quiet, reserved, unretaliating.

The team were clearly on edge. Except this time, Jay didn't let that affect him. He shook his shoulders out for the arrival of their manager and squad coaches. Sergio was met with a lumbering silence and not the raucous banter that he would have normally stopped dead by his brusque entrance. The men all clambered to their bench seats and sat with professional obedience. They listened through the tactics, the game-play, the wheres, hows and whens that Coach Alonso rattled through, and nodded with accustomed compliance. Sergio eyed each player with suspicion. Settling his gaze on Jay, he snapped the lid on his marker pen and the tap echoed through the room.

"We are a team." Sergio gave a curt nod. "Each and every one of you is here because I chose you to be. Because you are my team, my choice." He slapped his chest, hard. "My belief in you all should be what brings you together. Whether you like your fellow man, whether you agree with his choices, whether you cannot stand the smell of his cologne, you are his teammate and will treat him as such. Any wavering to that will be preyed on by those out there." He pointed the tip of his pen at the closed dressing room door. "And that has been evidenced recently. You will not allow that to happen again. Or pay the price. Is that clear?"

The team nodded, some mumbling their agreements to their studs. Jay drifted his gaze to the team, many refusing to make eye contact, then back to his manager.

"If a man is targeted, you stop it," Sergio continued, obviously not feeling like his team weren't cottoning on to his motivating methods. "We stand united. We are *West Ham* United. We do not let anyone off lightly. Not this time. Not on my watch. Ruttman!"

Jay snapped to, eyes wide. "Gaffer?"

"Welcome back. The pitch is yours. The team is yours. We are *all* behind you. Know that."

"Yes, Gaffer." Pride bubbled in his chest.

"Make us proud. Make your family proud. Make the nation fall to their knees for you."

A few player sniggers were stopped by Sergio's glare. Including Jay's own one. Slip of the foreign tongue, Jay hoped.

"Gaffer?" Jay found his voice.

"Yes?"

Jay stood and cleared his throat. "I've had iron in my blood since birth. My whole family are West Ham supporters. I'm an east Londoner. I'm a footballer. I'm a goal scorer. I ain't here to make a mockery out of anyone, least of all West Ham. I'm here 'cause I deserve to be. Like all of us do." He shrugged, but stood firm, tall. *Proud.* "That's all. Ain't no-one gonna make me think I don't deserve to be on that pitch. Knock me down, I'll get up. Break my leg, it'll heal. I'm tough. And I'm back. To show that I mean business. The moment Sergio put me in this team I became a role model and I take that fucking seriously. I think you lot should too."

He breathed in deeply and held Sergio's gaze. Sergio nodded. Once. And a smile crept up on his lips. The first clap came from Davies and he jumped to his feet for a standing ovation that was promptly followed by the entire back eight. Bruno stood and stalked toward Jay from his bench the opposite side of the horseshoe. Slapping a hand on Jay's shoulder, he nodded and ruffled Jay's hair.

"We're all with you. Let's prove that to the fucking nation!" He tapped Jay's cheek and heckled out a wailing yell.

Muscles flexed as the tribal roar bounded through the walls and the team clamped studs onto the linoleum floor out to the tunnel. Sergio squeezed Jay's arm.

"I think you might have changed the West Ham motto. *You* are the academy of football. The future. Remember that when you're out there."

"Cheers, Gaffer."

At this point, whether they won or lost, Jay felt like he was on top. He'd made a small triumph at least. He'd faced it. He'd spoken up. He wasn't burying anything anymore. And if Chelsea came at him, so be it. He had a team behind him. And a fiancé in the stands. That was enough to put the fire back in his gut.

Standing in line, Jay peered over to the blues. Three men back, the man stood. Alejandro Romero. Jay caught his eye. Perhaps it was the camaraderie from his team, the euphoria at being back, or the voices that still swam around in his head that made him do what he did next.

He scooted out of line, headed to the opposition team and held out his hand to Alejandro.

"All water under Stamford Bridge." Jay urged Alejandro to take his hand. Not because a camera had zoomed into their personal space, but because he wanted this over.

Alejandro glanced down, his lips unfurling. He darted his gaze to the camera, then back to Jay. He had no choice, so when he took Jay's hand with one firm shake, Jay knew it wasn't heartfelt.

"If ever you wanna talk." Jay winked. "I been there." Why he felt the need to say that, he'd never know. The look on Alejandro's face made it worth the while and Jay stifled a chuckle before returning to his position in the line and meeting with Bruno's furrowed brow.

"You just put a target on your knee." Bruno shook his head.

"Bring it the fuck on."

Bruno snorted, then rolled his shoulders as he followed the officials out onto the pitch.

The boom from the crowd rumbled in Jay's gut and he sucked it in like a drug. The singing rang in his ears along with the drone from the boisterous chants, the piercing cheers and rhythmic roars. He was back. Where he fucking belonged.

The line-up, the set positions and the kick-off whistle happened in a daze and Jay was off. He chased the ball, he collided with the brutish back four, he slide tackled, and enjoyed every counting-down second of it. He threw himself into the game — the real him, the true him. The one who knew the man he loved was in those stands watching his every move. This game was for Seb.

When the tackle came, and Jay knew that it would, Jay was ready for it. Alejandro had waited long enough, trailing it out until the seventy-fifth minute and a nil-nil score sheet. Perhaps it was desperation, perhaps it was pure hatred. Perhaps it was something deeper-rooted, like Riley's attack had been. There had been snarls of disapproval, yells of slurs unreached by official ears, a few trips along the way, but none of that had put Jay off his game. Because he had accepted it. Nothing could get to him if he knew it was coming and he had his team's backing. Both teams. His West Ham brothers, and his family. His *and* Seb's family. A unit. *United.*

Jay bounced at the halfway point as Davies slammed his shoulder into the Chelsea defender, expertly winning the ball. He passed almost immediately to Carlton, who set off at pace and sailed the ball across to Bruno. Captain used his bulk to guard off the oncoming blues and sprinted pitch left, rounding the ball toward Jay. A brief look up, and Jay set off for his middle position ready to receive the overhead pass.

Alejandro came at him, but this time Jay saw him. He expected it. And as he leapt up to receive the ball, Jay dropped his shoulder, flicking his forearm out to prevent the man getting any closer. But Alejandro didn't jump with him. He wasn't going for the ball, nor for Jay's weakened knee, or any part of Jay's anatomy. Instead, he grabbed the bottom of Jay's shirt that had drifted out from his elastic shorts and yanked. *Hard.* So much so that the impact not only had Jay flopping to the ground on his back, it also ripped the entire side stitching of his jersey, revealing his re-honed and perfected abs to all those in the Bobby Moore stand.

Jay leapt up, eyes narrowed and spat on the grass, the glob missing Alejandro's bright yellow studs by mere millimetres. Jay wasn't staying down this time. He was facing it out. Whatever came. The referee's whistle shrilled around the roaring stadium as the entire West Ham team pelted up to the penalty spot. Bruno and Davies took turns in yelling obscenities at Alejandro's face whilst shoving him in the chest. Alejandro, hands in the air, shook his head and said his excuses in his mother tongue. A couple of the other players started in on the ref, wailing their disgruntled messages until they were as red in the face as their claret kit. A few others sidled away, getting into their own scraps with Chelsea players.

It was like a mass brawl on the pitch. One that Jay zoned out of and instead focused on the linesman. He smiled when he noted the official held his arm out wide, his flag pointing to the left. Home side. Jay's point. Penalty. *Thank you, Alejandro.*

Sorting out the players on the pitch took a fair few minutes and Jay waited anxiously, ball tucked under his arm ready for the instruction. The referee, whistle tucked between his lips, made mad hand gestures to each of the players to settle down. Many did, moving away. Chelsea surrounded the middle-man for a while, before they realised they had no case. Alejandro had let them down with that blatant attack. Again.

Sergio called Jay off the pitch to the sideline, replacing Jay's shirt with a new one. The only words the gaffer said was, "Follow it though." Jay nodded, then jogged back to the goal line.

The referee had called Alejandro over. Jay couldn't hear what was being said as the deafening roars from the stands drowned it all out. He took the moment to peer up behind the goal to the terraces. The Bobby Moore stand. Ten rows up, left of the steps. The Ruttman seats—the three spaces that had belonged to his dad, Bryan and him for as long as Jay could remember, handed down from his grandfather. He hadn't been lying about iron being in the blood. His great-great-grandfather had worked at the original Thames Ironworks that had formed the team back in 1900. Now someone else occupied that third seat. Or, more accurately, was standing, biting his thumbnail with a brow so furrowed his forehead looked dehydrated. Jay winked.

Another whistle shriek and Jay whipped around to witness the red card struck in the air and Alejandro trailing off the pitch to boos and cheers. The referee indicated for Jay to step forward and take the penalty shot. Jay inhaled deeply, clutching the ball, then walked, slowly, to penalty point. He dropped the ball. All his team stood behind him, blues dotted between the claret, and the anticipation was felt in every sharp palpable breath.

Jay took five steps back. He locked eyes with the goalkeeper. The all-in green keeper jumped on the spot, punching each glove and making himself big, intimidating. Jay didn't even take a breath. He lurched

337

forward, full speed, full throttle. The keeper leapt, wrong side, and the ball shunted to the back of the goal, shaking the net that barely contained his three-point win.

The spectator stands erupted in roars. Jay ran forward, hands clenched, biceps bulging, pounding his fists in the air. He stopped at the sideline where the spectator stands jumped in waves of excited cheers that rattled the plastic seats. Jay grabbed the badge on his shirt and screamed to the crowd, searching for Seb. Locking onto his gaze, he smiled. There he was. Watching. Cheering. *Supporting*. Like all good fiancés should.

Keeping his head high, he laughed as he was leapt on from behind by his entire team, each one cheering into his ear. The roaming camera zoomed in on his face, and Jay took that as his moment. His comeback. Struggling to free himself from his team horde, he kissed the guitar on his ring finger, then held it up to the stands for each and every spectator.

The other lads stepped back, allowing Jay his moment. He blew another kiss to the stands. This time to Seb. To show himself.

To finally *be* himself.

EPILOGUE
Bells & Whistles

June 2008

Jay stood in front of the full-length mirror, fixing his hair into some sweeping, textured style using some of Seb's better quality gel whilst reciting lines in his head. Nerves didn't cut this one. He took a deep breath, his lips drying and focused on trying to tie the cravat into the knot he'd been shown at the store.

He stopped short when Seb entered their room.

"Fuck." He slapped his hand down, catching Seb's gaze through the reflection. "You don't half look good in that."

Smiling, Seb held out his arms in display. The tailored light-grey morning suit with fitted ivory waistcoat clung to his slender frame and silken sky-blue cravat tied in a perfect ruffled knot brought out the sparkle in his dark eyes. His hair, void of the usual

339

mussed-up spikes, had been brushed to the side with a hint of blue at the tips, just to give him that edge he demanded.

"Not so bad yourself, Cockney boy." Seb stepped up behind him, dropping his chin onto Jay's shoulder. "You okay?"

"Nervous."

Seb chuckled, then stepped back to eye Jay in the mirror. "You need help with that?"

"Better had."

Draping his arms over Jay's shoulders, Seb tugged one silk end and wrapped it across the shorter side.

"You learn to do this somewhere?"

"All posh boys have to know how to tie a Windsor knot and wear an Ascot from birth. The ones who don't get thrown on the scrap heap. AKA, state school." Seb shuddered.

Jay snorted. Seb's brash wink through the reflection made him smile and he watched as Seb expertly whipped the silk end across. "What's an Ascot? I take it you weren't talkin' the races?"

Seb focused on threading and looping Jay's cravat up and over. "A casual cravat. Day wear. Less formal. One you *would* wear to the races."

"You ever been?"

Seb tucked the ends into Jay's buttoned waistcoat and brushed his hands down the front. "Yes. Best way to do business. My father owned a horse for a while too. Stupid thing never won."

"Yeah?" Jay noted the sudden flicker of melancholy crossing Seb's features. "You should invite him round."

Seb peered up, locking onto Jay's gaze through the reflection. "Are we ready for that?"

"I am if you are."

"Maybe. But let's get this done first." Tapping Jay's shoulders, Seb kissed his cheek. "Perfect."

Smiling, Jay twisted in Seb's arms and went in for a deeper kiss.

"Oi!" Bryan stuck his head in the door, cravat flapping around his neck and huffed. "I'm shitting myself here and you're getting in a quickie?"

Sliding his hands down the small of Seb's back, Jay glanced over Seb's shoulder and noted his brother's unknotted cravat, undone waistcoat and uncufflinked shirt.

He drifted his lips to Seb's ear. "You better work your fingers on him, an' all."

"I don't do ménage." Seb twisted, quirking an eyebrow. "Especially not brothers."

Bryan grimaced. Chuckling, Seb meandered over to him and worked his upper-middle-class dressing habits on the older Ruttman. He didn't linger over it, though, not like he had with Jay. All business. With a deep breath, Jay rummaged in his suit trouser pocket and fished out a jewellery box. He handed it to his brother. Bryan widened his eyes as he snapped open the red velvet box to reveal solid gold crossed hammers cufflinks, the West Ham emblem. He smiled. Then held out his arms to Seb, allowing him to fix them on for him.

"I also left the real Tiffany for mum and Cheryl in their hotel rooms." Jay slipped into his tails.

"Cheers, bro." Bryan scrubbed a hand through his trimmed stubble and did one last check of himself in the mirror. "Pub?" He slapped Jay's chest and bolted out of the bedroom.

Stopping at the door, Seb eyed Jay. "You okay?"

"Just realised I ain't been to a wedding before. Nor am I good at making speeches. Can't you do it instead?"

341

Seb laughed. "You'll be fine. It'll be much better coming from you."

Jay tapped the blazer pocket holding the speech he'd scribbled. "You ever been to a wedding before?"

Seb's dashing smile faded and he scraped his polished dress shoes along the fibres of the carpet. "Yes."

Jay nodded. "Stephen."

"It was awfully tedius." Seb shook his head. Not so much in denial but more to rid it of the thoughts, Jay suspected. "I got drunk on the free Champagne, made a scene by telling Lisbeth there was an exact replica of her dress for sale in Debenhams window and then threw up on my father's date's lap before entrees were served." He gave a twisted smile. "Good times."

"I'm surprised you went."

Seb shrugged. "Did you not hear? Free bar." He angled his head toward the exit. "Speaking of which..."

Whilst not technically free, considering Jay and Seb had contributed a hefty amount to the behind-the-bar tab, Bryan's wedding to Cheryl was still going to be a pretty decent affair. The ceremony and the reception were all in one place—a remote manor house-slash-hotel just off the A13 and into the leafier county of Essex where Cheryl was from. Bryan, Jay and Seb arrived in style, parked up Jay's BMW on the gravel front and headed into the venue that was awash with milling guests.

Everyone took their seats in the smaller function room that was decorated in pink and light blue sashes. Seb had to squeeze onto the second row behind the groom's family, and managed to mask any uncomfortable feeling he might have had at not really knowing anyone. Jay had to leave him to it, as he was needed up front to stand beside his twitching brother.

As the tinkling music started, Bryan faced the incoming and heaved in a deep breath. Cheryl looked radiant, as of course she would, in a beautiful, sparkling diamante-ridden strapless dress and her platinum blonde hair twirled into plaits and curls, topped off with a tiara. Bryan choked, holding a fist to his mouth to no doubt prevent anyone thinking he might be crying. Jay knew better though. That view of the bride elegantly walking down the aisle, one hand looped into her father's and the other clutching the hand of her daughter, who was in an exact replica of Cheryl's dress, was enough to make the lump in Jay's throat difficult to hide.

Jay roamed his gaze over the sea of guests and landed on the second row. Seb smiled, winked, and Jay's stomach fluttered as he zoned out the goings on beside him. Would it ever be like this for them? Would they be able to do the traditional set-up amongst family and friends? And what would that even look like? He couldn't imagine the Saunders settling in alongside the Ruttmans. Would Seb even want them there? He might be talking to both Sylvia and Will now, but it wasn't happy families. Not yet. Jay hung his head. It wasn't like they had a choice anyway.

Bryan nudged his arm, jolting him to the present. "Rings, mate."

Shit. *First job failure.* Handing over the two solid platinum bands from his trouser pocket, Jay mouthed his apology.

The rest of the service went off in tradition and Bryan and Cheryl emerged from the hall husband and wife. The formal stuff ensued, with posed photos in the grounds and the marquee swarmed with guests getting their fill of the free Champagne and beer. Off-season meant Jay grabbed for a bubbly which made the

343

pleasantries of meeting Cheryl's horde of bridesmaids that much more bearable.

Through the crowd, Jay caught Seb's eye. He clutched a glass of Champagne, appearing as awkward as hell as Barbara introduced him to a load of extended family that Jay didn't even recognise. She stroked down his hair, and Jay chuckled into his glass as Seb ran his fingers through it to sort it out.

With their gazes finding each other across a crowded room, Jay was thrust back into those memories of three years ago when their eyes had met across a busy Underground bar, then again, a year later over the heads in a VIP lounge of the Red Bull arena. But this time, Jay read something else in those dark eyes that focused in on him. Something struck him. A realisation, perhaps? Seb had that very same look that Bryan had worn when Cheryl had walked down that aisle, their daughter clopping behind.

Sucking in a breath that curdled with the fluttering in his chest, Jay, mid-conversation with the Matron of honour, held up a finger from around his glass.

"Sorry. I gotta chip."

He snaked through the throng of bodies, stopping a couple of times to shake hands or kiss the cheeks of people he didn't know if they were bride or groom side, and made his way to Seb. It was as if he was being pulled there by some invisible thread and Seb's eyes watched him all the while, urging him ever closer, like they always had. *They probably always will.*

Seb smiled as Jay approached. "Hello, there, handsome."

Pressing his lips to Seb's ear, Jay planted a soft kiss. He then opened his mouth to make way for words this time, not actions.

"Oh, Jay, love, there you are!" Barbara grabbed his arm and yanked him away. "You must remember the Barratts, don't ya? Used to live down our way til they moved out to Essex. They only bloody well know Cheryl!"

The couple looked to be in their sixties. Older than Jay's folks, anyhow. Floral dress for the lady and a dark-brown pinstriped suit for the balding guy. Jay did the polite thing and shook their hands, although he had no recollection of what his mother had said he should have.

"This is the younger one," Barbara prattled on, taking a sip of the Prosecco and winking. "The footballer."

"So this one'll be next, will he, Babs?" Mrs. Barratt asked the inevitable question that always falls from the lips of those already hitched at a wedding to those who, obviously, aren't.

"Oh, you never know, Vera." Barbara smiled. "They may well make it legal yet."

"Legal?" Mr. Bartlett's brow wrinkled.

"Gay marriage." Barbara pointed to Seb. "Seb, I introduced you earlier, is his partner. Other half." She flicked her gaze to each gaping-open mouth. "Boyfriend?"

"Oh, yes, I see, of course!" Clearly, Mr. Barratt didn't see.

Barbara opened her mouth, but whatever she was planning to say was cut off by the boom from the master of ceremonies. "You may now all take your seats for the wedding breakfast."

Sighing, Jay leaned back to Seb's ear. "I—"

"Come on, love!" Barbara yanked him away yet again. "Plenty of time for that later." Someone was obviously excited about this part of the day, as Barbara dragged Jay toward the head table and Jay had to watch Seb bundle off to one of the far round tables.

Tucked in his seat, Seb flicked out the swan-shaped napkin and draped it over his lap. He rested his elbows on the table surface, fingers tapping against his lips, and peered over to the front-facing rectangle table decorated with white lilies and green foliage. Jay sat at the end, chatting to the bride's parents, laughing, blue eyes shining, and looking every bit as gorgeous as he ever did. Seb didn't think his heart could swell any more for the blond Cockney lad, but something about being here, at a wedding, made his heart leap from his chest for him to wear it on his sleeve, nestled alongside the number nine tattooed on his wrist. *Soppy fucking git.*

"If the wind changes, you'll stay like that."

The chair beside him scraped out and Ann, light blue wraparound dress hugging her fuller frame and the developing baby bump, plonked herself down and nudged her shoulder against his.

"Stay like what?" Seb asked.

"With that sappy grin on your face. It's nauseating."

Seb breathed out a laugh. "How's things with you?"

"Good. Giving up drink when you're with a bloke in a band is pretty hard going, though. But he's quit the fags, so I gotta show willing, right?"

"Absolutely." Seb held up his glass and tapped it to Ann's water, keeping his lips tight not to mention that, on occasion, Noah sneaked outside during rehearsals and came back reeking of nicotine. Which was a good thing as Noah pulled out the chair beside her, sat, and gave Seb a glare of warning.

Ann shifted in the seat. "Bloody hell."

"What's up, babe?" Noah plonked his pint on the table and shifted to run a hand up Ann's back.

"Kicking again."

"He's not kicking. He's playing the drums." Noah smiled and held a hand over Ann's protruding belly. "Rocking out in there, little guy?"

"You know it's a boy?" Seb asked, eyes focused on the movement bubbling along Ann's tight chiffon.

"No." Ann tutted. "He just thinks it is."

Seb smiled, but couldn't shift his gaze from the bump.

"You want to feel?"

Shaking his head, Seb sipped from his glass. "No. No, it's okay." He'd had many a conversation with Cheryl about how her body became everyone else's property when she was pregnant and so Seb had avoided putting his hands on Ann since the bump had emerged. Even if he wanted nothing more than to feel the growing baby. What the hell had happened to him? And Noah, if the look on his sappy face was anything to go by.

Ann grabbed his hand and settled it on her stomach when a tiny kick tickled his palm. He couldn't stop his eyes from welling. "Kid's got rhythm."

"Like it couldn't, right?" Ann tsked. "You want kids, Seb?"

Rubbing along her bump, Seb wanted to feel every kick. Now she'd given him permission, he wanted to lap up as much of it as he could. "Sure." That fell from his mouth before he'd even allowed the concept to develop in his mind. "I'd have a ton of little Jay's chasing their footballs if I could."

Noah snorted into his beer.

Ann nudged his leg. "Well, this is all yours after, if you want it."

Seb snatched his hand away. "I'm not taking your baby!"

"Damn right! That's mine." Noah picked up his pint and took a gulp, narrowing his eyes at Seb.

"No, idiots." Ann reshuffled in the seat. "I mean the womb. I was reading up on surrogacy."

Seb flinched. "You what now?"

"Hang on." Noah plonked the pint back down. "I'm not sure what I think about you banging either of those two, regardless of what sexuality they claim to be."

"Christ, Noah, sometimes I wonder about you. Let's hope this baby gets my looks and brain and your..."

"Musical ability?" Noah suggested.

"Erm." Seb screwed up his face, then placed a hand on Ann's knee. "I'll give it lessons."

Ann smiled. "FYI, they *artificially* inseminate their mushed-up semen into me."

A bowl of noodle soup was placed elegantly down in front of them all by the roaming waitress. Noah grimaced, staring into the contents.

Shaking out her napkin, Ann leaned over to whisper in Seb's ear. "Think about it."

Well, he certainly wouldn't be thinking about anything else for a good long while.

The dinner was simple, elegantly so. Food to please the masses. And after the plates were scraped clean, the speeches ensued. From the gushing father-of-the-bride, to the rolling around on the floor laughing unofficial best man, Mitchell's speech, to Bryan's simple, "ain't she stunning? Now she's proper mine, let's get pissed." Then it was Jay's turn.

Seb settled back in his chair, watching his boyfriend flush with nerves, unfolding the paper in his shaking hands. Amazing how that guy could fight off a bunch of men tackling him at goal, but ask him to stand and say a few words to a crowd and his confidence all but diminished. Licking his lips, Jay peered up to the crowd. Seb willed some of his own brash self-assurance to seep over to Jay, but osmosis didn't work when it came to personality traits.

Jay wasn't going for the laughs. He'd known there'd be no point. Bryan did enough of that himself. And Mitchell had had that covered. Jay had wanted the opportunity to show the room, mainly Cheryl, who she had really married. And Seb couldn't wait for the reaction.

"I was about seventeen when Bryan came home one night to brag he'd met the bird of his dreams. Middle of the night, we shared a room and he woke me up to tell me this Cheryl he'd just met was a stunner. The most beautiful girl in the world, he'd said, which, back then, meant the Moon and Stars boozer down Ford Lane."

A ripple of laughter followed, and Seb's smile magnified with pride.

"He'd said she was the one. When I asked how he could know that, they'd only just met, that he didn't exactly have a track record for keeping girlfriends, his reply was one I'll never forget. As a seventeen-year-old lad who'd recently become single" — Jay's gaze flickered over his sheet of paper and found Ann's — "and struggling to come to terms with who I was, I couldn't really see how one person could make you feel like that. But Bryan replied with, 'When you know, you know, dun't ya? When you don't know, you muck about.'"

Jay folded the paper and let it rain onto the table. "Now, I know we ain't no Shakespeare in our family, but that's a pretty accurate statement of what love is. Bryan didn't muck about. Six years later, he has a gorgeous daughter, and now a beautiful wife and I've never known him to be so happy. So, thank you, Cheryl. For taking him out of my bedroom, and into yours. I needed the space for a start."

Seb drifted his champagne glass to his twitching lips, glancing around the room at the muffled chuckles.

"And thank you, Bryan. For always being there for me. For being a big brother I could look up to and learn from. Kinda. 'Cause I ain't mucking about, either."

Seb's heart pummelled against his rib cage, bursting to be set free. That bit had been an impromptu add that Seb hadn't been aware of. And he realised right then, for all the buffoonery of Bryan Ruttman, that he'd been the consistency in Jay's life. The one to help him admit to who he really was. And Seb was now ever grateful to the man.

"I ain't one for big speeches," Jay continued, snapping Seb from his thoughts. "So I'll just leave that there. And end with asking everyone to raise their glasses for the happy couple, Mr and Mrs Ruttman. I couldn't be more proud of you, bruv."

Everyone stood, repeated the line and drank. Sniffing, Bryan wrapped his arms around Jay and held him, his shoulders shaking. Seb watched, being the last to sit back down and waited to hold his glass up to Jay's across the room, that sappy grin no doubt now a permanent fixture on his face.

The day then merged into the evening affair. Seb and Noah made their apologies to the table and scurried out to the main hall where Martin awaited them, single-handedly managing set-up. Like old times. Settling into their accustomed three-piece set-up, the band started the instrumental intro as the guests milled through from the dining area and the new evening-only invites headed in via the main entrance. Seb had decided on a few covers to ease in the unfamiliar-with-their-music crowd gently.

Jay meandered to the bar and perched on the stool. The dance floor cleared out with the guests creating a circle around the black tiles. Ending the interlude, Seb wrapped a hand around the microphone.

"Can we have the newlyweds to the centre for their first dance, please?"

Taking Cheryl's hand, Bryan led her to the centre of the dance floor. He looked nervous, blowing out a puff of air, but as he settled his hands on Cheryl's hips and she rested her forehead against his, he seemed to ease off any care that he was on display for all to watch. Seb drifted his fingertips along the A chord, strumming the sweet melody that he had composed for this moment and softened the impact of his voice for the words that followed.

As Seb sang the lyrics he'd written for Bryan and Cheryl, he couldn't help seeking out Jay through the crowd. He found himself singing to him instead, phasing out all the others in the room until they became a blur and all he could see was Jay. The song was a pretty decent fit for him too, their relationship, and he wanted Jay to know it. To *feel* it. The way Seb did. Gradually, other couples joined the newlyweds on the dance floor—parents, grandparents, and friends of friends. Jay remained seated at the back, those piercing baby-blues shimmering and not faltering from gazing up at Seb on stage. *Adoringly.* Like he always would.

351

Suddenly, for what could possibly be the first time in his life, Seb didn't want to be on the stage. He didn't want to be on full show. He wanted to be among the crowd, fused with the other couples, and to serenade Jay across the floor. Martin nudged Seb, and pressed on the backing track. Smiling, eyes focused ahead, Seb slipped off his guitar and allowed the pre-recorded track to continue into the next song, with Martin and Noah offering the live version over the top. Martin could sing, not as well as Seb, but he could hold a tune enough for Seb to have allowed the moment.

He waded through the crowd toward Jay. After seizing the glass clutched in Jay's hand, he settled it on the bar and entwined Jay's fingers with his. "Dance with me." It wasn't a question. It was a demand. And Jay reacted the way Seb knew that he would. He allowed himself to be led, by Seb, to the dancefloor. This time not to somewhere private, not away in the shadows, but among the other couples. Where they belonged.

Slipping his arms around Jay's neck, Seb rested his forehead to Jay's. Jay curled his arms around Seb's back and swayed gently. Seb wasn't going full out tango on this one. This one, he just wanted them to flow as one. And he smiled all the way through it.

"I love you, Jay. Forever and always."

"Back at ya, babe."

The End

ABOUT THE AUTHOR

Brought up in a relatively small town in Hertfordshire, C F White managed to do what most other residents try to do and fail—leave.

Studying at a West London university, she realised there was a whole city out there waiting to be discovered, so, much like Dick Whittington before her, she never made it back home and still endlessly search for the streets paved with gold, slowly coming to the realisation they're mostly paved with chewing gum. And the odd bit of graffiti. And those little circles of yellow spray paint where the council point out the pot holes to someone who is supposedly meant to fix them instead of staring at them vacantly whilst holding a polystyrene cup of watered-down coffee.

Eventually she moved West to East along that vast District Line and settled for pie and mash, cockles and winkles and a bit of Knees Up Mother Brown to live in the East End of London; securing a job and creating a life, a home and a family.

After her second son was born with a rare disability, C F White's life changed and it brought pen back to and paper after having written stories as a child but never had the confidence to show them to the world. Now, having embarked on this writing journey, C F White can't stop. So strap in, it's going to be a bumpy ride.

Other books by C F White

Responsible Adult Series
Misdemeanor
Hard Time
Reformed

St. Cross Series
Won't Feel a Thing

The District Line Series
Kick Off
Break Through
Come Back

Misdemeanor (Responsible Adult #1)

Excerpt

Chapter One

The Sun Keeps Rising

"Shit!"

Micky cursed loudly and squinted through the morning glare to read the alarm clock that was obviously having trouble performing its one and only basic function. He threw off his duvet and jumped out of bed, his foot landing on a plastic wind-up toy penguin discarded on the floor. The penguin openly mocked him by tossing itself into a noisy backflip.

"Fuck!"

Micky cursed again, bending down to pick up the toy and throw it savagely against the wall. It shattered into a million pieces and Micky felt instantly guilty.

"Flynn!" he yelled, hopping over to his bedroom door and yanking it open. Treading more carefully to the bathroom opposite, he rubbed his eyes before coming face-to-face with himself in the mirror above the sink.

He looked like shit. No change there. The three hours of almost sleep he'd gotten obviously hadn't done anything to improve on his disheveled appearance. He ran a hand over the stubble on his chin. He needed to shave but now didn't have the time. Micky turned on the tap, dunked his head under the cold stream and squeezed paste onto his toothbrush.

"Flynn!" he shouted again, louder this time, before shoving the toothbrush into his gob and brushing vigorously. The minty taste did nothing for his dry mouth.

"Yes, Micky," came a quiet little voice from the bathroom doorway.

Still holding the toothbrush between his lips, foam dripping out from the side of his mouth, Micky turned.

"We're late," he said, trying to suck the minty drool back up and stop it escaping from the corners.

"I'm dressed," Flynn replied with a huge proud smile.

Flynn stood in the doorway, clutching another wind-up plastic toy. He kept spinning the thing around, setting off an ear-piercing buzz as it unwound at double speed. He appeared so small and fragile. More like a five-year-old than his actual eight years. He'd gotten dressed. Sort of. He'd managed to pull on his gray school trousers over his pajama bottoms and his army-green jumper clung inside out. No socks, and his mousy-brown curls stuck out from his head in all directions.

Micky's heart melted a little at the sight.

"Well done, Flynn." Micky finished brushing his teeth, spat down the plughole and cupped a handful of water into his mouth to rinse. Turning back to his brother, Micky then crouched in front of him. "But how about we try taking the pajamas off?"

Flynn looked down, waggling his toes, and back up at his big brother. "Why?" he asked, confused. "I put them back on later."

Micky laughed. The kid had a point.

"Come on." Micky took hold of Flynn's hand to walk him back into the small box room. It had twin beds, pushed up against opposite sides. One had used to belong to Micky before he'd moved into the master bedroom.

"What time did you get up today?" Micky asked, dragging Flynn's jumper over his head.

"Five five two," Flynn replied.

He wound up the blasted plastic toy again and Micky breathed in deeply, preventing his immediate instinctive reaction to take the thing and smash it against the wall in comradeship with its penguin mate.

"That's early," Micky said, pulling off Flynn's pajama top then rooting around in the drawer for his brother's school polo shirt. He found it scrunched at the bottom and helped Flynn squirm into it while trying to smooth out the creases.

"For what?" Flynn asked, holding on to Micky's shoulder as he knelt and stepped out of his trousers.

"Everything," Micky replied with a yawn.

"Daddy didn't say it was."

Micky looked into Flynn's blue eyes. The white starburst pattern within them gave him the feeling of being hypnotized. Micky blinked.

"Dad's not here, Flynn," Micky said slowly, standing to inspect his now school-uniform-clad little brother.

"Yes, he is." Flynn smiled widely, his plastic toy buzzing in his hands.

Micky stared down at for a brief moment, then spun around and ran full pelt down the stairs and into the living room. The place was dark and dank, stinking of booze and fags with beer cans littering the floor.

Micky yanked open the curtains to witness the disgusting figure sprawled on the sofa. Tatty stonewashed denim jeans bagged around his knees and the T-shirt he wore, once white in color, was stained yellow with patches of Micky didn't want to know what. His greasy, graying hair hung around his face like rats' tails. He was snoring and every breath out from his wide-open mouth filled the room with a putrid stench.

Micky kicked at the arm dangling off the sofa. The man grumbled but didn't move. Micky kicked him again, more fiercely. Opening one eye, the brute belched as he squinted through the glaring sunlight.

"Get the fuck out," Micky demanded.

The laughter that followed made Micky's skin crawl, along with the irritating scratching of fingernails across the man's chest. The shirt rubbed against the curly dark hairs scattering his fat body and made the unbearable scraping of nails down a chalk board.

"*Now*," Micky growled.

The grunted response wasn't something Micky could decipher, nor did he care to. Micky watched with contempt as he rolled off the sofa and landed on the floor with a thump. Several beer cans crunched under his heavy frame and he rolled again to push up on to all fours. Grunting once more, he heaved himself to stand. He tripped on his own feet and clutched at the wall. Micky clenched his fists at the ready as the second loud belch blasted out and Micky had to turn away from the oncoming stink.

"Money," he demanded, holding out a hand.

"Get fucked," Micky spat back.

"Then I take his."

He staggered over to the fireplace mantelpiece and made a grab for the handmade clay moneybox shaped like a car. Micky wrapped firm fingers around his wrist and squeezed tightly.

"Over my dead body." Micky gritted his teeth. Clutching the wrist harder, he used his other hand to root around in the dirty jeans pocket and yanked out a key. Shaking his head, Micky shoved him away. "Now leave, before I fucking kill you."

"Micky?" Flynn's delicate little voice squeaked from the living room door. He clung to the plastic toy still in his hand, his eyes tightly shut.

Micky ran over, picked him up and settled him on his hip. For an eight-year-old, Flynn weighed no more than a couple of stone, his body skin and bones. It wasn't his fault. It was the condition. Flynn rested his head on Micky's shoulder, wrapping his arms around his big brother's neck, still clamping his eyes shut.

"It's okay, Flynn. Dad's leaving now."

BUY LINK

Printed in Great Britain
by Amazon